GATHERING STORM

The Sequel to

THROUGH A GLASS

So well done was this book that Y I Lee has again left me wanting more, and as an author of fiction, I do not say this lightly, for I seldom read other fiction authors work, unless I know it will take me where this author's work does.

Paula Rose Michelson, author of Christian fiction, nonfiction and self-help books.

GATHERING STORM

The sequel to

THROUGH A GLASS

This is a work of fiction. Any resemblance to actual people or places is coincidental.

Cover design by http://loveyourcovers.com/

Prologue

Sandra could feel her cheeks flushing, as she struggled to get the key in the door.

"Is Irene there?" John asked.

"I don't think so; I've been knocking and ringing the bell for ages."

"Your voice sounds muffled, I can hardly hear you."

"Sorry, I'm trying to support the phone on my shoulder and open the door at the same time. There are so many blasted keys!"

John could hear the frustration in Sandra's voice. "Do you want me to come?"

"Please, if you can spare the time. I'm worried about her. I've not seen or heard from her since the last time we spoke, and that was a little heated to say the least."

"Okay, stay put, I'm on my way." Grabbing a coat off the hook, John slammed the front door and hurried down the lane to Irene's house. As he drew near he could see Sandra waiting by the open door. "I'm glad you waited," he said. "It's best we go in together."

Sandra felt the small hairs rise on the nape of her neck. She stared at John. "You're scaring me now! What are you expecting to find?"

John forced a smile. "Nothing I hope; she may have gone away."

Frowning, Sandra pushed the front door open. "I hope you're right."

"Stop fretting, Irene's not the type to do anything stupid."

You don't know how drunk she used to get. Sandra thought as she led the way into the lounge. "Everything looks normal in here," she said softly.

"Why are you whispering?"

"I don't know I just feel tense. Let's try the kitchen." Sandra's stomach churned uncomfortably as she led the way along the passage. The house felt cold...abandoned. Sandra shivered and rubbed her arms.

"Are you alright?" John asked.

Sandra nodded. "It's a bit chilly that's all." Reaching the kitchen she stood in the doorway...once a room alive with chatter and the warm aroma of coffee, it now felt cold and unwelcoming. *Where are you, Irene?* She felt John's warm breath on her neck as he leaned over her shoulder.

"Tell you what. I'll go upstairs and have a hunt round, you see if there's anything in here to indicate where she may have gone."

Sandra nodded. Her heart sank as she gazed around the large kitchen. *Where do I start?* Rubbing her hands together she rested them prayer like against her chin. *If it was me, where would I leave a note?* Her eyes settled on the kitchen dresser. Holding her breath she hurried over to it and picked up a bundle of papers and letters. Chewing her lip she sifted through them...her heart sank. She looked up as John entered the room.

"Anything?" he asked.

Sandra shook her head. "Did you find anything upstairs?"

"Nothing, it all looks very neat and tidy."

Sandra couldn't help noting the sadness in his eyes. "I'm sorry to drag you into this, John. I know it can't be easy for you."

He shrugged his shoulders. "I'm okay. Irene made it plain she wasn't interested, so what could I do?" Sighing softly he gazed around the kitchen. "Nevertheless, I would hate to think she's in some kind of trouble."

"Me too," Sandra said.

John followed her towards the kitchen door. "Is that it; are we just going to leave?"

Sandra shrugged. "What else can we do?" She paused with her hand on the banister. "Are you sure you didn't miss anything upstairs?"

"I don't know, I have no idea about women's stuff!"

Sandra couldn't help smiling. "Let's take one last look. I might notice something, being as I'm a woman!"

"Okay, no need to be sarcastic."

2

Sandra led the way upstairs. The first two bedrooms were of no interest. As she made her way to Irene's room she told John to look in the bathroom.

"I already did."

"Look again. See if her toothbrush is there, and check the wall cabinet."

Grumbling under his breath John did as he was told. "There's no toothbrush or paste," he shouted.

Joining him in the bathroom Sandra checked the cabinet. "Her cleansing wipes and some make-up is missing as well."

"You can't expect me to know about things like that. I'm a man."

Sandra chuckled but made no comment. "I think we can relax," she said. "Irene had a dark blue rucksack which is missing. She also had a small box containing something that was very precious to her, that's disappeared, plus other bits and pieces. So I guess we must assume she's gone away."

They could see the relief in each other's eyes.

John took Sandra's hand and smiled. "Now if you'd come up here in the first place instead of me, we would have found this out sooner."

"True, sorry about that. Never mind, at least now we know Irene's away, so we don't need to worry about her." Sandra pulled him towards the stairs. "Come on let's go to yours and have a drink. All this stress and worry has made me thirsty."

John followed her to the front door and waited while she locked up. "What spurred you to come for the weekend and check on Irene?" he asked. As Sandra turned, he noticed the sadness in her eyes.

"I'm fond of her, and I hated the fact that our last conversation was bitter and angry." She frowned as she touched John's arm. "I was upset with her for hurting you. I felt she played with your emotions and led you on."

"I'm okay Sandra; I've lost out on love a few times in my life. So don't worry, I'll survive." He paused and gazed at her. "I'm still curious though. Why did you choose this weekend to come?"

"I received a letter from Irene's gardener, and what I read worried me. He was tidying up and cutting the grass for the last time before winter sets in, and when he went to the bottom of the garden to the compost heap, he found broken glass everywhere, and a painting so wet and damaged, he said it was unrecognizable."

"Goodness! Shouldn't we go and take a look?"

Sandra gave him a reassuring pat. "No, it will be dark soon, and anyway the gardener said there was no sign of blood or any indication that something bad had happened."

John raised an eyebrow. "Why would Irene leave a painting in the garden? It's not the sort of thing she would do."

Sandra shrugged as she glanced over the garden fence. "You're right, but I have no idea why. Maybe she was painting down there and forgot about it. She'll have to sort it out when she gets back."

"That's if she comes back."

Sandra looked up at him, her eyes wide with surprise. "Why do you say that?"

John's lips puckered as he slowly shook his head. "I don't know, I just have a feeling we won't see her again."

Seeing his resigned expression, Sandra was at a loss for words. *I hope he's wrong*, she thought as she linked arms with him.

They walked back to John's cottage in silence, the only sound the crunch of their shoes on the gravel road. Lamps came on in the houses they passed. The soft light created deep shadows in the twilight, adding to their feeling of melancholy.

Chapter 1

A crescent moon hung in the starless sky, its fragile light impotent against the darkness cloaking the land of Feritas. A small settlement clustered at the base of the rocky hillside; soft lamplight glinted in cottage windows, as though blinking in the darkness.

Perched on the summit of the hill; Feritas castle towered over the small village like a huge bird of prey. Deep in the bowels of the castle, King Murkier strode along a dimly lit passage. His frustration increased as he hurried down the stairs towards the basement. "This better not be a waste of my time," he grumbled.

The moment he opened the cellar door the dank musty smell assailed his nostrils. Narrow stone steps descended into darkness. An occasional torch attached to the stone walls afforded a flicker of light. The King's nose wrinkled in disgust as he carefully negotiated the slippery steps. Resting a hand on the damp wall he gripped any protruding stone for added security, and tried to place his feet where the steps were widest and less worn down. He reached the basement and sighed with relief.

As he wiped his hands on his cloak; a large rat scurried past. The rodent's sudden appearance gave the King a fright and he lashed out with his foot. The rat squeaked in protest as it narrowly escaped a kicking from the Royal boot. The creature scooted down the dark passage and disappeared. "Clear off!" King Murkier snarled, his face twisting in a grimace of disgust.

With his lips pressed tightly together, Murkier strode towards a wooden door and lifted the heavy metal latch. Pushing the door open, he stepped into a large dimly lit space; numerous stone pillars supported the low roof. A few torches attached to the wall and a small fire in the far corner, were the only source of light.

Closing the door, King Murkier glanced around. On the far side of the room he spotted a small grey haired man leaning over a small table.

The man was so engrossed; he was unaware of the King's presence.

"What have you called me down here for?" King Murkier bellowed. Pulling a corner of his cloak over his nose to minimize the stench, he strode across the room.

Taken by surprise the small man started. "My Liege, forgive me! I had no idea you were here." He fell to his knees and crawled towards the King.

"Get up man. What is so important you wished to see me at this hour?" Grimacing, he pulled his cloak tighter over his nose and mouth. "This place stinks. Hurry up; what is it you want to tell me? And for your sake it'd better be good."

The small man scrambled to his feet, his strange grey eyes clouded with anxiety as he gestured towards the table and urged the King to follow him. "Please, come and see My Liege. What I have to show you is of paramount importance and most disturbing!"

King Murkier grunted with impatience as he followed him to the table and watched him stare intently into a large round mirror.

"An hour ago I studied my mirror and saw a vision. Normally, as you know, My Liege the visions I see are clear, but this time it was shrouded in a mist." He ran a shaky hand across his mouth and glanced at the King.

The King straightened and frowned at him. "So why am I here?" He growled. "You just said you had something of importance to show me. So show me!"

"Yes My Liege. If you look into the mirror the vision will appear." The seer's hands trembled as he positioned the mirror so they could both see into it…silently they watched and waited. Gradually the surface of the mirror clouded and the vague shape of a figure could be seen stepping into view.

"You see, My Liege, the vision is indistinct…impossible to tell if what we are seeing is male or female, although I would say female. Can you see how bright it is behind the person? It's as though they are stepping through a reflective surface." He paused and squinted at the King. "Like a mirror!" His thick grey brows knit in a troubled frown as he studied the vision.

"Who is it?" The King asked.

The seer's eyes darkened with concern as he looked at the King. "This person is someone of great importance to your enemy,

Prince Zatao. The vision is unclear; nevertheless I've seen enough to know it is a warning. Their arrival is imminent and the subsequent union between this person and the Prince will bring about a dynasty of unstoppable power."

Pushing the mirror aside, he faced the King and bowed his head. His voice faltered as he said, "My Liege, I would advise you to find out all you can about this person. You need to know when they are likely to arrive, and intercept them." He clasped trembling hands and stared at the floor. "This is the person who will help Prince Zatao defeat you."

King Murkier scowled and paced the floor. In the torchlight his tall frame cast long dark shadows across the walls.

The seer trembled as he watched him. He knew giving the King bad news was a possible death sentence. The man's trembling increased as he recalled the demise of his predecessor. He wrung his sweating hands as the King whirled round to face him. His master's voluminous cloak billowed…dust rose into the air. The seer coughed and covered his mouth with a shaky hand.

King Murkier leaned down, his face so close to the seer's he could smell the terrified man's breath. In a voice low and menacing, he asked, "How do you suggest I find the information I need to apprehend this person?" His black eyes bored into the seer's as he raised his head and moved away.

Like a frightened rabbit the seer stood frozen to the spot. His heart raced, his body swayed; he clutched the rim of the table for support and lowered his head.

The King rolled his eyes and gestured impatiently with his hands. "So, do you have a suggestion?" His eyes narrowed. "For your sake I hope so."

The seer raised his eyes to the king's face. "I believe I do, My Liege. There is an influential man residing in Prince Zatao's castle who with a little coercion could be persuaded to spy for you. This man is greedy and has ambition…it is his weakness."

The King's mouth twisted in a cruel smile. "And does this man have a name?"

The seer smiled. Success calmed his racing heart. Gazing boldly at the King he rose to his full height and squared his shoulders. On the wall behind him his tall dark shadow belied his diminutive stature. "His name My Liege is Traditor."

With a delighted grin, the King turned and strode to the door. As his hand grasped the latch he turned. "You have done well, seer. Keep me informed of events as they unfold, I need to stay ahead of the game. If we succeed in destroying Prince Zatao, your reward will be great. If we fail—" he didn't finish the sentence, but stared long and hard at the small seer.

The frightened man bowed his head and held his breath. The expression on the King's face was enough to freeze running water. As the door slammed shut and the King's footsteps receded, the seer exhaled and collapsed onto a wooden stool. Resting his arms on the table he pulled the mirror closer. "Show me what I need to know." As he peered into its dark depths his chest tightened, beads of sweat glistened on his brow. He knew if he failed to guide the King correctly, the consequences would be too horrific to contemplate.

⇜⇜⇜

King Murkier paced the vast throne room, his features contorted with rage. In the flickering light of a candle his tall dark shadow danced macabrely on the walls. He swung round and faced the two men cowering before him. "I want the land of Luminaire, and its ruler Prince Zatao! His kingdom...his throne belong to me." Snarling, he balled his fists...long nails dug into the palms of his hands. "We failed at the last attempt; I will not fail again." He glared at the two men. "My seer informs me, someone is coming...someone who will strengthen and unite the land of Luminaire. I want you to find out who it is, and when they arrive capture them and bring them here to me. I intend to use them to set a trap that will destroy Prince Zatao."

Grouchen, the king's chief adviser raised his head; his eyes flickered nervously as he watched the king. "May I speak My Lord?"

King Murkier swung round and faced him. His black eyes narrowed with impatience.

Grouchen visibly shrank under the king's gaze.

His companion, Ergon wiped his sweating hands on his robe. He flinched as King Murkier snapped.

"Speak man!"

With his heart in his mouth Grouchen bravely took a step forward.

Ergon kept his eyes lowered, hoping to appear invisible.

Wiping beads of sweat from his top lip, Grouchen met the king's gaze. "I confess My Lord with regard to the stallion, August, we advised you incorrectly. The animal should have been killed rather than imprisoned. Without the horse Prince Zatao would have been defeated, and his land and people would be yours." Grouchen glanced at Ergon hoping for support, but none was forthcoming.

Ergon stood with bowed head, his eyes fixed on the ground.

King Murkier rose to his full height. "Exactly!" he bellowed. "I insisted the horse should die, but you convinced me otherwise, and like a fool I listened. Due to your erroneous advice, Prince Zatao and his wretched female companion found the horse and released it." He glared at the two men. "You both showed treasonous contempt for my wishes, and for that you should have died. I've allowed you to live because you are useful to me. But mark my words, one more mistake and I will not be so merciful."

He glanced towards the raised dais. His wife Ballista lounged on her throne sipping wine from an ornate goblet. Pointing at her, he glared at the two men. "Even my wife, Queen Ballista gives wiser counsel than you overfed buffoons."

The queen tittered and swept her long black hair over her shoulder. "Come My Lord," she coaxed. "Relax, come and sit here beside me; take a glass of this delicious wine." She played with a strand of hair and smiled at him. She relished the power she had over him…basked in the knowledge he couldn't resist her.

With a flourish of his long purple cloak, King Murkier strode along the red carpet to his sumptuous gold throne. "Bring me wine," he ordered a trembling servant. He reclined and took the proffered goblet. Draining the contents in one long gulp, he licked his lips. Rubbing a hand over his mouth, he gazed at his wife.

Her flushed cheeks and slightly parted lips excited him. "More wine my dear?" he asked.

She nodded and smiled at the huskiness in his voice.

The King snapped his fingers at the servant hovering nervously behind the throne. "Bring more wine," he bellowed.

The queen leaned closer to him and stroked his hand. "Would you like me to impress upon these dullards how important it is that Prince Zatao is destroyed, My Lord?" She turned to face them. "Maybe I can make them understand, and if not we can enjoy the spectacle of their deaths." She giggled with delight at the thought of it.

The King nodded and gestured with a hand.

Grouchen and Ergon huddled together. They feared the Queen, for she had the king's ear and his heart, and was known for her ruthlessness and cruelty.

"Come closer," she demanded. "I would advise you to listen well to what I am going to say, for this is your last chance."

Trembling, the two advisors inched closer to the dais, and fell to their knees.

King Murkier and Ballista stared at them, their faces hard and stony.

The king swirled the wine around in his goblet, before taking a long swig of the blood red liquid.

Ballista leaned back on her throne and stuffed a plump date in her mouth. "These are delicious My Lord where did we acquire them?" She licked her fingers enjoying the sweet stickiness.

King Murkier grinned, he was always happy to please her. "Don't you remember my love? A few months ago I sent our army to conquer a small, insignificant land many miles to the east of here. They were a strange people, and the land was overly green and lush. Not a place we would wish to live…far too bright! However, they grew the delicious fruit you are eating. If you remember we destroyed most of the land, and its people, but we brought their king and his family back here."

The queen sat for a moment deep in thought. "Ah, yes, I remember. We killed the king and his family, except the youngest daughter? What a public spectacle it was! I'm sure the people of our land enjoyed the day of celebration. " She stared at the two advisors as they knelt before her trembling. Her lips twisted in an evil grin. She turned to the King. "What happened to the daughter?"

"Don't you remember dearest? We gave her to our youngest son as his wife. It's always good to inject some fresh blood into the family."

The queen took a sip of her wine and nodded in agreement. "And what about the land, what became of it?"

The king laughed and thumped the arms of his throne with delight.

Startled, Grouchen and Ergon jumped, but kept their eyes fixed on the ground.

"It is conquered beloved, and the people who remain are my slaves. They pay taxes and spend their days growing and tending the food that you so enjoy eating."

Delighted, the queen clapped her hands, and gave the king a beaming smile. "So how big is our kingdom now, My Lord?"

"Vast my love, it is vast!"

As Ballista gazed proudly at him, she saw his expression change. His eyes darkened, his features contorted with anger. Rising to his feet he glared at the men cowering before him.

"Nevertheless, I want the land of Luminaire and I will have it!" His voice rose in frustration. "Prince Zatao's kingdom will become part of my empire, making me the undefeated conqueror of the entire world."

Grouchen raised a trembling hand. "May I speak My Lord?"

King Murkier stared disdainfully at him; his hand went to the hilt of his sword. "You dare to open your mouth without my permission?"

Queen Ballista leaned forward. "Allow him to speak, My Lord. Let us hear what he has to say, and then you can kill him."

With his hand still clutching the hilt of his sword, King Murkier glared at Grouchen. "Speak," he growled.

Grouchen's body shook, he could hardly breathe. Opening his mouth to speak, his voice was no more than a whisper.

"Speak up man!" The king bellowed.

Grouchen sat back on his heels. His leg's ached from kneeling for so long. Clearing his throat, he mustered every ounce of courage. "My Lord, if I may advise you. Prince Zatao's land is many miles from here on the other side of the mountain. Furthermore, he is a mighty man of valour and faith, commanding loyalty and respect from his vast army and subjects. We all remember the defeat we suffered at his hand. And as you have said My Lord, he achieved this victory with the help of a girl from another kingdom, plus his ability to take on the form of a huge stag. His name Stagman, still stirs reverent fear among his people."

Grouchen averted his eyes and bowed his head. "I know we failed you, My Lord. If his horse August had died as you wisely instructed, Prince Zatao's land of Luminaire would be yours." He cowered as he heard the King growl and approach him. Grouchen's voice faltered as he continued. "We do not have the power or the resources to wage war against him. If we do, we will lose everything My Lord the king has achieved with such bravery and wisdom."

Those last words saved his life. The king was a vain and arrogant man. Even so his face flushed purple with rage. He gritted his teeth as he towered over the trembling advisor.

Grouchen crouched in humble obeisance. He hoped his words though true would not cost him his life.

"Be calm My Lord," Queen Ballista purred. "Let me explain your plan to these inept men." She rose to her feet and made her way along the red carpet. Her black gown rustled and swayed as she moved close to the advisors.

Breathing heavily King Murkier returned to his throne, and snatched a goblet of wine from his servant. His eyes narrowed into cruel slits as he watched his wife approach the trembling men.

The two men dare not raise their eyes but stared at the hem of her gown.

"Look at me!" she snapped. "And take note of what I am about to tell you. Your lives depend on it."

The terrified men raised their heads and stared up at her. The sweat on their faces glistened in the candlelight.

Ballista could smell their fear. She leaned forward and stared into their frightened eyes. "My Lord the King must have this person. Whoever they are, they must not be allowed to escape. Do you understand?"

The two men nodded, their bodies visibly shook at the menacing tone in her voice.

"The King has chosen two of his finest warriors for the assignment." She straightened and lowered her voice. "Your task is to make sure they have the best horses from our stables, and enough supplies for the journey. You will instruct them to ride to the land of Luminaire. Once there, they must make their way under cover of darkness to the village of Wedon, where they will meet a man...a spy who resides in Prince Zatao's castle."

She paused and cackled with delight at the thought. "This spy will supply the information we need pertaining to the arrival of this person, along with Prince Zatao's daily schedule. Instruct our warriors to keep a low profile, and when they have the information…make haste to return, stopping for nothing and no one. It is imperative we receive the information as soon as possible." Her lips twisted in an evil smile. "Soon Prince Zatao will be destroyed, and then My Lord the King will be the greatest and richest monarch in the world." She turned and gazed adoringly at him.

The king left his throne and walked towards them. "Well said my love you have explained my plan perfectly." He fixed the two men with a steely glare. "Do you understand?" he demanded.

The two advisors looked at each other and nodded.

The king continued through gritted teeth. "Once we have this person in our clutches…Prince Zatao will be defeated." With his hands on his hips he burst out laughing. The heinous sound bounced off the walls.

With a shudder of fear Ergon raised his head. "Now we understand My Lord, and indeed your plan is good. However, may I humbly beg your indulgence?"

Grouchen stared at his companion…shocked to hear him speak.

Ergon bravely continued. "Is there no way of knowing who this person is?"

The king rolled his eyes. "Who they are is unimportant. It's enough that they are coming. My seer has warned me, if I wish to destroy Zatao, I must capture them, and do it before they reach his castle." Murkier scowled at the two men. "Do not fail me," he growled.

Ergon raised a trembling hand. "May I be allowed one more question My Lord? Who are the warriors chosen for this task?"

Surprised by Ergon's boldness, the King nodded. "Their names are Muglwort and Zworn. You will find them in the garrison, awaiting your instructions. Do not delay for time is short."

The king walked back to his throne and sat down. He stared at the two men. "Go!" He said with a dismissive wave of his hand.

Scrambling to their feet, Grouchen and Ergon backed reverently along the red carpet. With bowed heads they waited as a guard opened the massive wooden door. Once outside in the dimly lit corridor, they breathed audible sighs of relief.

"I'm concerned," Ergon whispered, as he wiped beads of sweat from his top lip.

Grouchen's bushy eyebrows arched as he studied his friend. He could see the anxiety in Ergon's eyes. "Why?" He asked.

Ergon took hold of Grouchen's sleeve. "Let's go somewhere more private. This castle has ears."

They hurried along the dingy corridor to Ergon's private room. Safely inside he bolted the heavy door and faced his friend.

Grouchen seated himself by the fire. "So, tell me what troubles you?"

"I believe the King should have gone to the Lord of the underworld and sought his help in this matter."

Grouchen leaned back in the chair and stroked his thick beard. For a moment he closed his eyes as though deep in thought. When he spoke his voice was hushed. "No, Ergon, we sought their help last time we attacked Prince Zatao, and we were defeated!"

Ergon drummed his fingers on the arm of his chair. "Yes, I know, but at that time he was able to use the power of the stag. This time with the help of the underworld we could take him by surprise."

"It wouldn't work, and you know how much the king detested those useless ersatz and goblin creatures. The only weapon from the underworld...remotely effective, were the trees; and even they failed! So, I advise you not to suggest it...not if you wish to live!" He frowned at the younger man. "If you remember, it was your idea to imprison Prince Zatao's stallion instead of killing it. We are fortunate the King has not killed us."

Ergon scowled, he knew Grouchen was right.

Grouchen rose and stretched his hands towards the fire. "Understand this; I have been with the king many years. And I know that even if we sought help from the Lord of the underworld, and were successful in defeating Prince Zatao, there is no way the King would share the victory; in which case we would find ourselves at constant war with them...not a prospect I wish to dwell on."

Stroking his long grey beard, he returned to his seat and stared long and hard at Ergon. "Do not mention the underworld to the King," he said firmly.

Ergon squirmed under his gaze. Grouchen's voice held a warning...matched by the fear in his watery blue eyes. "Very well, I understand," Ergon said, averting his eyes.

Grouchen relaxed in his chair. "Good, because if this person is as influential as the King's seer believes, and if by holding them to ransom we bring down Zatao's dynasty, then as far as I can see, as long as the spy in Zatao's castle is reliable, this plan could work. I pray the gods it does! To be on the losing side against Prince Zatao alias Stagman, is not a thought worth contemplating." Rising to his feet, Grouchen waved a hand at Ergon. "Come, we must find the warriors and send them on their way. Time is short."

Chapter 2

The setting sun cast long shadows as Irene and Sandra walked arm in arm through the village towards The White Horse pub. The day had been pleasant...warm and sunny. However, the approach of evening brought a distinct nip to the air, heralding a frosty night. In the soft twilight the old pub looked cosy and welcoming. Grey smoke curled out of the tall chimney...soft lamplight filtered through the lattice windows.

"I love this old pub," Sandra said, as she pushed the door open.

They were greeted by noisy chatter and the clink of glasses.

"I'll get the drinks, you find a table," Sandra said making her way to the bar.

Frank the landlord greeted them. "Good evening ladies, what can I get you?"

Irene smiled at him. "I'll have a fruit juice please."

"Me too," Sandra said.

Frank waved them away from the bar. "Go, sit yourselves down; I'll bring the drinks over."

They settled at their favourite table close to the inglenook fireplace.

Irene draped her coat over the back of the chair and stretched her hands towards the roaring fire.

Sandra watched her. "You've seemed a little pensive today, Irene. Are you alright?"

Irene fiddled with the crystal pendant around her neck.

Concerned, Sandra reached across and touched her arm. "Come on, you can tell me."

Irene leaned back in her chair. "I'll tell you in a minute." She could see Frank approaching with their drinks.

"Here we are ladies," Frank said with a cheerful grin.

Sandra hoped he wouldn't hang around and chat, as she wanted to hear what Irene had to say. Fortunately the pub was busy so Frank wandered back to the bar.

Sandra rested her arms on the table and leaned closer to Irene. She could see confusion in her friend's eyes. "Okay, what's bothering you?"

Without hesitation Irene blurted out. "Last night John asked me to marry him."

Sandra nearly fell off her chair. "Wow! That's great." Her delighted smile waned as she studied Irene's face.

Irene frowned and picked at the edge of her beer mat. Sandra's reaction was what she'd expected. But she couldn't share her friend's joy. There would be no celebratory drinks…no happy announcement to the patrons in the pub.

Sandra stared at Irene, troubled by the emotionless expression on her face. "You've refused his proposal, haven't you?"

Irene nodded and lowered her eyes. She felt awful and yet strangely relieved.

Sandra slumped in her chair. "Why, Irene? John is mad about you, and I thought you really liked him. You've seemed close this past year."

"I like him a lot, Sandra, but I'm not ready to get married, not yet anyway. There's something I need to do first. I haven't actually refused him." She noticed the spark of hope in Sandra's eyes, and couldn't help smiling. "I've asked him to wait…to give me a little more time and he has agreed."

Sandra's brow creased as she studied her. "Ever since you first met John at your exhibition, you've seemed a little melancholy. What is it, Irene. Can I help?"

Irene cleared her throat and took a sip of her drink. "I'm not sure you can," she said softly. Averting her eyes, she stared at the fire. Ever since leaving Stagman, and returning to her own world, his presence filled her waking moments…her dreams. She had hoped selling the painting would set her free; but her need to return and be with him grew more intense with each passing day.

Her close relationship with John did little to assuage her growing need for Stagman, rather it intensified it! His amazing likeness to Stagman didn't help; it increased her pain, to the point

17

where she was forced to do something about it, or continue to die a little more each day.

Sandra's firm touch on her arm made her jump.

"Sorry, Irene, I didn't mean to startle you, but you were miles away."

Irene sighed. "I know, sorry. What were you saying?"

"Does this have anything to do with that painting? What was it called?" She massaged her temple in an effort to jog her memory. "It was something like Through a—"

Swivelling in her chair, Irene faced her. "It was called Through a Glass."

"That's it; you seemed to have a bit of a thing about it."

Irene lowered her eyes and fiddled with her necklace. *How can I explain, there's no way I can tell her about Stagman and Mira. She wouldn't understand. But I need to find that painting, I won't rest until I do.*

Sandra took her hand. "Irene what is it? You look so pale. Please tell me, there must be something I can do to help."

"I don't see how. Unless you know who bought the painting. I need to find it, Sandra. I want to buy it back! Please don't ask me why…I can't tell you."

Sandra could feel Irene's hand trembling. "Don't upset yourself; if this painting is all that stands between you and John, I might be able to help." She saw a glimmer of hope in Irene's eyes, and gently squeezed her hand.

"Could you, really?" Irene's stomach fluttered with excitement as she stared at Sandra.

"I'll get in touch with Peter Myer's the gallery owner. He has a record of every sale." She gave Irene a serious look. "Now, I don't want you to get your hopes up. He may refuse to tell me anything, he has the right. Nevertheless, I will ring him tomorrow and see what I can find out."

Irene threw her arms around Sandra's neck. "Oh, thank you. I can't tell you how grateful I am."

Chuckling, Sandra disentangled herself from Irene's arms. "Don't strangle me, or I won't be in a position to help you."

Irene laughed as she stood and collected their empty glasses. "I'll tell Frank we need more drinks. Do you want the same? "

"No, I'll have a glass of red this time."

"Okay, I won't be a minute."

Sandra was pleased to see the sparkle return to Irene's eyes. Nevertheless, something about the situation perturbed her. *I wish I knew what it was about that painting.* She frowned and rubbed the back of her neck. *What if I can't find it? There's no guarantee Peter Myer's will help me; and even if he does—what then?* Her brow furrowed as a deep sense of foreboding settled on her. She looked across at the bar; Irene was chatting with a few patrons as she waited for their drinks. Sandra sighed. "Oh, Irene, why is this painting so important? What are you getting yourself into?"

⊰⊰⊰

John stared out of the kitchen window. The night was as dark as his mood. Each time he thought about his proposal to Irene and her refusal, his melancholy increased. The small velvet box containing the ring sat on the kitchen table. Frowning, he slumped in a chair and toyed with it. *I wish I understood why she wants to wait.*

He went to the kitchen cabinet, grabbed a glass and a bottle of whisky and returned to the small sitting room. Settling in the armchair by the fire he poured himself a good measure. Sipping the amber liquid he gazed around the room. A couple of Irene's paintings adorned the walls; he couldn't help smiling as he looked at them. He turned his attention to the conservatory; he hadn't attempted to do much in there, it still looked like Irene's studio. A couple of old paintings she didn't want were propped against the wall.

John sniffed the air; the faint smell of oil paints still permeated the small cottage. He sighed as he swirled the whisky around in his glass. Embarrassment and the pain of rejection stabbed like a knife, and for a moment his eyes blurred with emotion. Raking a hand through his hair, he muttered. "Once she sorts herself out she'll accept my proposal." He took a swig of the whisky, enjoying the warmth as it trickled down his throat. He gazed at Irene's painting hanging above the mantelpiece. *I can wait, Irene. I love you, and I know you love me; you just don't know it yet.*

A loud knock on the front door interrupted his thoughts. "It's open," he called. He listened to the light footsteps on the tiled kitchen floor, and looked up as Sandra poked her head round the door.

"Are you okay?" she asked.

John could see the concern in her eyes, and it stung his pride. "Come in if you're coming," he snapped. "I gather Irene's told you she refused my proposal."

Sandra moved to the chair on the other side of the fire and sat down. "Yes, she has. Sorry if I'm disturbing you."

John made no comment; he stared at the fire, watching the smoke drift up the chimney.

Feeling the tension in the room, Sandra played nervously with her fingers. She gazed at the bottle of whisky. "Any chance I could have one of those?"

"You know where the glasses are." John continued to stare into the fire as she went to the kitchen.

"Do you have any ice?" Sandra asked, taking a glass out of the kitchen cabinet.

"Of course, it's in the freezer."

Sandra could tell by his gruff tone, that he found her presence irritating. Nevertheless, she was determined to stay and talk to him.

The ice clinked in her glass as she carried it back to the sitting room and poured herself a small measure of whisky.

John's eyebrows arched as he watched her. "How can you adulterate good malt with ice?"

Grinning, Sandra raised her glass to him...pleased to see a faint smile lessen the pain in his dark eyes. "I won't stay long so don't worry. I just wanted to have a quick chat."

"Does Irene know you're here?" John asked. Taking a gulp of whisky, he rolled the glass between his hands and studied her.

Sandra chewed her bottom lip and nodded. She hated being caught in the middle...hated the anguish she could see in her cousin's face. "We had a couple of drinks in the pub before I came here. She's expecting me back for supper." Sandra sipped her drink and looked at John over the rim of her glass.

"You'd better not hang around then," he said dismissively.

Sandra flinched at the bitterness in his voice. She wanted to encourage him, but still felt a sense of foreboding, so dare not give him false hope. Placing her glass on the table, she stared at him.

John returned her gaze; the genuine sympathy in her eyes thawed his irritation.

Sandra reached across and touched his arm. "Look John, if I understand correctly, Irene has asked you to wait...not actually refused you." She sat back in her chair and gave him a questioning look. "When you first met Irene at the exhibition, do you remember the painting she was looking at?"

John nodded. "Yes, it was fascinating. I remember commenting on it. I liked her technique, her loose almost abstract style of painting, and yet the picture looked so real I felt drawn into it." A bemused look came into his eyes as he recalled the experience.

Sandra smiled, she could almost see his tension melt away and felt encouraged to continue. "The painting was called Through a Glass, and Irene wants to buy it back. I've promised I will ring the gallery owner tomorrow. However there's no guarantee he will be willing or even able to help; also the person who bought the painting may not wish to part with it. Legally, Irene doesn't have a leg to stand on, but she's determined to try, and I've offered to help her." Sandra stared at John and shrugged. "I can only do my best, and if finding the painting brings you both together then it will be worth it."

John's grateful smile was all the thanks Sandra needed. She downed the remainder of her drink and got to her feet. "I'll give you a ring and let you know how it goes."

John stood and put an arm round her shoulder. As he walked with her to the front door, he could feel the heaviness lift. "Thanks cousin," he said placing a kiss on her cheek.

"There's no guarantee," she replied.

"I know, but thanks for being willing to try. I'll speak to you soon."

As John bolted the cottage door, his heart clutched at a seed of hope. He needed to hold onto the belief that Irene would return to him. But deep down uncertainty chipped away at his fragile hope. *Will she come back? Have I lost her?* A sudden pain as sharp as a knife pierced him...beads of sweat glistened on his brow. He leaned against the door and groaned with frustration. "I won't let her go, I can't." His words were breathy with emotion. His dark eyes glinted with resolve as he vowed to fight for Irene.

Chapter 3

The next day dawned bright and sunny. Irene sat on her swing seat and gently rocked. This was her favourite place in the garden…a secluded spot hidden from the house by thick shrubs and a couple of gnarled old apple trees. She leaned back on the cushions and closed her eyes enjoying the warmth of the autumn sun on her face. A soft breeze rustled through the leaves; Irene opened her eyes and gazed at the branches above her head, she smiled. *I love this time of year, the leaves look so pretty.*

As she continued to gently swing she heard a familiar sound and instinctively looked towards the Buddleia. The bushes lovely conical flower heads had long since turned a grubby brown. Underneath the bush a blackbird's bright eyes watched her, his black feathers gleamed like ebony in the sunlight. He came out from beneath the bush and softly chirped.

This had been the routine since he first tamed her a few months ago. Most days after lunch she would sit on the swing seat with a book and a few raisins to nibble on. She found it relaxing before going to work in her studio. It was on one of these days the bird first appeared. Neither her movements nor her voice appeared to disturb him.

"Hello little boy," Irene said quietly. "I know what you want." She put a hand in the pocket of her jacket and threw some raisins onto the grass. "Come on then," she encouraged. The little black bird scrutinised her for a moment before leaving the safety of his bush and gobbling down the juicy fruit. Then, with a loud cry, he flew into his favourite tree.

Irene chuckled, all summer he had visited this part of the garden, seeming to choose the moment she came to sit on the swing seat. His friendliness had increased as the summer progressed. Irene knew he was a wild creature; nevertheless as the months passed she'd grown increasingly fond of him.

Turning her attention to the magazine on the seat beside her, she picked it up and thumbed through its pages, hoping it would distract her while she waited for Sandra to finish her call to Peter Myer's at the gallery. Her heart fluttered with expectation, her hands felt clammy...the pages of the magazine stuck to her moist fingers. Dropping it onto the seat, she wiped her hands on her jeans and peered through the trees at the house...still no sign of Sandra.

This phone call's taking an awful long time. I hope it doesn't mean there's a problem. She pushed into the grass with her foot, easing the seat into a gentle swing. She tried to relax, but her body twitched with agitation as she stared with hope filled eyes towards the back of the house.

⊰⊱⊰⊱

Sandra sighed as she replaced the phone in its cradle. Her chat with the gallery owner, Peter Myer's had proved fruitless. She stared at her reflection in the hall mirror; she looked pale...the strain on her face was plain to see. "How am I going to tell Irene?" She could feel a headache coming on and rubbed the back of her neck. "I need this like a hole in the head," she grumbled.

Deciding a cup of tea might ease her tension she went to the kitchen. As the kettle boiled she grabbed a couple of mugs and stared out of the window. It was the sort of bright frosty day she loved, cold, but in a sheltered spot the sun's warmth could still be felt.

Through the trees she could see flashes of movement as Irene rocked the swing seat. Sandra's heart sank. "I'm going to have to tell her, but she won't like it." Sandra continued talking to herself as she made the tea and put the mugs on a tray. *I have a feeling a stiff whisky would be more beneficial than tea.* The thought brought a fleeting smile to her face.

Balancing the tray on one hand she opened the back door with the other. "Oh well, here goes," she muttered, as she followed the path to the bottom of the garden.

⊰⊱⊰⊱

Irene halted her swing and moved the magazine and cushions, making room for Sandra and the tray. She lifted a mug and smiled.

23

"Great, thanks; I was just thinking I could do with a cup of tea." She took a sip of the hot brew and stared at Sandra. "Did you make the call? What did Peter say?" Sandra's troubled expression banished Irene's confidence, her shoulders slumped. "I gather the news is not good."

Sandra nodded, "I'm afraid not." She cupped the warm mug between her hands and averted her eyes. She needed a moment...needed to gather her thoughts.

Irene put her mug on the tray and waited for Sandra to speak. Her friend's tense posture made her uneasy. She leaned forward and fiddled with the long sleeves of her jumper. "Tell me," she eventually said. "It's not your fault if he can't help. I'm grateful you tried."

Sandra put her mug on the tray; she swallowed to relieve the ache in her throat. "I did try," she said, raising her hands in a gesture of defeat.

Irene touched her arm and smiled. She could see the concern in Sandra's blue eyes. "Look, stop worrying and tell me what he said."

Sandra relaxed as the swing seat gently rocked. "Okay," she said softly. "From what Peter told me, it seems the person who bought your painting has gone bankrupt. They've sold pretty much everything in an auction...furniture, paintings, antiques, the lot. Peter says they've moved abroad and the house is on the market."

Irene's voice faltered as she asked. "How does Peter know all this, and does he know where the painting is?"

Sandra met her gaze but quickly looked away.

"What?" Irene exclaimed. "For goodness sake, Sandra, tell me!"

Sandra breathed a sigh. "To answer your first question, this person's financial problem was well known among the art fraternity. And as to your second question, Peter has no idea what happened to the painting. He was due to attend the auction, but unfortunately a family member became sick and so he couldn't attend. He sent a member of his staff but they arrived late, and your painting along with a few others was already auctioned, and no one has any idea what happened to them."

Irene groaned, she stared unseeing into the distance and clenched her fists. Her emotions were a mixture of anger and sadness. She closed her eyes to quench the tears.

Moved with concern, Sandra put an arm around her shoulders. "I'm so sorry, Irene. I really had no idea how much this painting means to you. I wish I could do more to help."

Irene brushed away a tear and faced her. "I'm okay, don't worry. I will find the painting. I don't care how long it takes, I'll find it!"

The determination in her voice took Sandra by surprise. *Gosh this painting must mean everything to her. I wonder why? Its good work, but—*

Irene's sudden movement interrupted her thoughts. "It's getting cold let's go indoors." She grabbed her magazine and picked up the tray.

Sandra followed her into the house. "Are you sure you're okay?" she asked.

Irene stood at the sink and washed the mugs. "I'm fine. However, when you leave tomorrow to go back to London, I'd like to go with you. I know what you've told me, but I need to see Peter myself."

"He won't be able to tell you anything, Irene."

"Maybe not, but he might have some idea how I can trace the painting. I need to see him; I have to try and find it. I won't rest until I do."

Sandra could see the flush of colour on her cheeks…the determined set of her jaw. She knew there was no point in arguing. "Okay, come back with me it's no problem, you're more than welcome to stay at my place."

Irene smiled and gave her a hug. "Thanks, I know you don't understand why it's so important to me, and I'm sorry I can't explain; but I do appreciate your help and support."

Sandra smiled; relieved to see Irene's mood had lifted. "You're welcome, but I must warn you I'm making an early start in the morning, so I need you to sort out those paintings for me. The gallery would like at least three more."

Irene nodded. "I'm on it, and don't worry I'll be ready to leave tomorrow when you are."

Sandra took a seat at the kitchen table and watched Irene prepare a salad for their evening meal. Irene's discordant humming brought a smile to Sandra's face.

Irene glanced at her and arched a brow. "What?"

Sandra chuckled. "Name that tune in one."

Irene laughed as she handed her a glass of wine. "Are you trying to say I hum out of tune?"

Sandra raised her glass. "Here's to the sound of discordant humming."

Irene pretended to scowl as their wine glasses met in a toast.

Sipping her wine, Sandra pondered the transformation in Irene's mood. *I'm glad she seems more relaxed and happy, but I wish I could shake off this sense of foreboding.* The feeling nagged at her, undermining her hope that this perplexing situation might have a positive outcome—especially for John.

❧❧❧

Sandra yawned as she leaned against the marble work-top, and waited for the bread to pop out of the toaster. The highly polished surface gleamed in the early light filtering through the kitchen window. She smiled as she gazed around; spacious and well equipped, the kitchen was her favourite room in the apartment. It was the main reason she'd bought the place. She enjoyed staying with Irene…loved the village of Zeal and the surrounding countryside, but this apartment was her home, and she thrived on the buzz of city life.

A frown creased her forehead as she thought about yesterday, and the journey home from Zeal. She'd wanted to make an early start, so they hit the road after breakfast. Unfortunately, the minute they reached the motorway they found themselves in a never ending traffic jam. It was late afternoon by the time they crawled into the city and eventually parked outside the apartment.

Sandra bemoaned the wasted day as she placed slices of hot toast in the rack and poured boiling water into a pot of freshly ground coffee. The enticing smell of coffee and toast brought a smile to her face. *Never mind, I'm home now and it won't take me long to catch up on work.* She looked up as Irene entered the kitchen. "Ah there you are. How did you sleep?"

"I slept well, thanks." Irene stood at the kitchen window and rubbed the sleep from her eyes. She gazed at the dark clouds scudding across the sky. "It looks as though it's going to be a wet day." Turning she sat at the table and buttered a piece of toast.

Sandra nodded and poured her a cup of coffee. "Do you want me to drop you somewhere?" I have to take your paintings to the gallery in Bond Street."

"Bond Street will be fine; I can browse a few of the gallery's and antique shops around there, before I go and see Peter."

Sandra studied her, trying to read her expression. "I've told you what Peter said, Irene. After the auction the painting could be anywhere; it could even have gone abroad."

"I'm aware of what he said, and if I can't find it, well, that's that; but I need to try. Somehow I know it's here in London, don't ask me how, I just do."

Sandra could see the determination in her eyes; she shrugged and sipped her coffee. "No problem, but before you go on your hunt maybe you could help me deliver the paintings. Later I'll be free for lunch if you want to meet up?"

Irene nodded. "That sounds good; I'll go and get ready."

The taxi ride to the gallery was pleasant. As they turned into Oxford Street, Irene gazed wistfully at the shop windows. She sighed as she watched eager shoppers throng the busy street.

Sandra smiled at her. "Once we've delivered the paintings, do you fancy a coffee and a look round Selfridges? You said you needed new shoes."

Irene fought the desire to say yes, she loved Selfridges. She shook her head. "I can't, Sandra. I need to find the painting." She averted her eyes from the tantalising shop windows, and stared straight ahead.

Before Sandra could say any more they arrived at the gallery. The taxi driver helped them unload the paintings.

Maggie Forsyth the gallery owner rushed to greet them. "You made it just in time. It's beginning to rain." She gave Irene a hug. "It's so good to see you."

Maggie was a large woman and her embrace was akin to a bear hug. Irene grinned at Sandra as she extricated herself. "It's good to see you too, Maggie." She gazed around the small gallery and smiled. "This exhibition looks good."

Maggie gushed with delight. "I'm glad you like it. Let me show you where your work is hanging. A number of your paintings have sold which is why I need these." She called a member of her staff, and gave instructions for the new work to be hung later in the day.

She turned to Sandra and Irene. "Come to my office, we'll have a coffee."

"We can't stay long," Sandra said. "I have an appointment and Irene is on a mission."

Maggie arched a quizzical brow. "Really, how intriguing."

Irene felt her cheeks flush; she wished Sandra hadn't said anything as she was loath to discuss the situation with Maggie.

However, Maggie's interest was piqued, and Irene found herself talking about her search for the missing painting.

Maggie listened intently as she handed them each a coffee. "It's strange, but—"

"What's strange?" Irene searched Maggie's face noting the thoughtful expression in her eyes.

"You say Peter Myer's had intended to go to the auction, but didn't make it."

Irene nodded, her eyes glued to Maggie.

Intrigued, Sandra put her cup down. "Do you know something about the painting, Maggie?" she asked.

Maggie sat down and nursed her coffee cup. "Not really; I was due to attend the same auction. But I got held up in traffic and was late. I was after Irene's painting and a couple by another artist. I managed to purchase one by the other artist, but sadly Irene's painting had already been auctioned."

Irene groaned with disappointment. Nevertheless, she felt sure Maggie knew something. Pushing her chair back, she paced the room. Pausing a moment she rested her palms on the desk. "Do you have any idea who bought the painting?" She stared at the gallery owner willing her to remember something, anything that might be of help. "Please, Maggie, think!"

Maggie could see the desperation in Irene's eyes. Leaning back in her chair, she closed her eyes and tried to recall the events of that day. After a moment she raised a finger and gazed at Irene. "I do remember something." Her voice faltered.

Both Sandra and Irene sat forward and gazed intently at her.

Maggie smiled nervously and held up a hand. "Whoa, I can't guarantee it will be of much help to you."

"Tell me!" Irene said.

"Well, like I said, I was late arriving and most of the paintings I wanted were already auctioned, including yours Irene. I was disappointed, but I managed to bid successfully for other work." She paused and took a sip of her coffee.

Irene drummed her fingers on her knee, silently willing her to continue.

Maggie could see the tension on Irene's face, she put her cup down. "I'm not sure how this is going to help, but while waiting to pay I saw a batch of artwork being carried out to a van, and your painting was among them."

Irene's gasp was a mixture of excitement and despair. "Who purchased it? I need to know, tell me."

"Goodness!" Maggie said. "Why so desperate?"

Sandra frowned. "Just tell us, Maggie, please."

Maggie tilted her head and gazed from one to the other; the desperate pleading in Irene's eyes unnerved her. She raised her hands palms out. "Okay, it's not much, but I have a friend who works in the auction house. I was curious myself as to who bought the work, so I asked him. He couldn't give me a name; however he did say that the paintings were going to a local dealer somewhere in this vicinity. Does that help?" The look on Irene's face made her smile.

"Maggie, you're a treasure, thank you."

"Glad to be of assistance."

Sandra took Irene's hand and squeezed it. "There you are that narrows down your search a bit."

Irene's hands tingled with excitement; she could hardly wait to get going.

Maggie's brow wrinkled in a frown. Resting her arms on the desk, she leaned towards Irene. "I don't wish to burst your bubble, but you do realise there are an awful lot of Galleries and antique shops in this area?"

"I know and that's why I'm leaving now."

Sandra and Maggie followed her into the gallery.

"Do you have your phone?" Sandra asked.

"I do. I'll ring you as soon as I've found the painting."

"Don't forget lunch," Sandra called.

"I won't. Thanks again, Maggie."

"My pleasure, glad I could help."

Irene waved and without a backward glance stepped onto the pavement.

✎✎✎

Irene stood for a moment trying to get her bearings. It was rush hour and people shoved her aside as they hurried to work. Staring through the milling crowd she noticed a small gallery across the road. Water colours and modern sculpture were artistically displayed in the window.

Her body tingled with excitement as she pushed through the crowd. Going against the flow earned her a few scowls of irritation. Irene ignored them and forced her way through to the other side of the road. She stood expectantly in front of the gallery and gazed at the artwork in the window, there appeared to be little in the way of oil paintings.

A bell above the door jingled softly as she entered. From a room at the back of the gallery a tall thin man hurried to greet her. He smiled and twirled the elaborate moustache adorning his lip. "May I be of assistance?" he asked.

Irene gazed at the artwork on the walls and breathed a heavy sigh.

The tall man cocked his head on one side. "What is it you are looking for? Maybe I can help."

Irene stared round the gallery. "I'm looking for a particular oil painting."

"Oh dear, I'm sorry, but as you see, we deal in water colours and limited edition prints."

Irene thanked him and turned to go.

The man followed her to the door. "Sorry I couldn't help. But if you walk further down the road there's a large gallery that specialises in oil paintings."

Irene's eyes brightened. "Thank you I'll have a look."

"I hope you find what you're looking for," the man said closing the door.

Irene pulled her coat close and shivered; there was a distinct nip in the air. She looked up at the sky. Dark rain clouds scurried across the heavens. *That's all I need…rain!*

Glancing at her watch, she scowled, it was already nine thirty. *At least it's quieter, now rush hour is over.* Hurrying down the road, she made her way towards an exclusive looking gallery. The large building occupied a corner site. In each section of the window a large oil painting rested on an easel, with smaller works of art displayed around them. Everything about the gallery exuded quality and style.

Irene pulled her hands out of her pockets and smoothed her coat. With a deep breath she raised her chin and entered the premises. She perused the hanging artwork and her heart sank...there were no landscapes. The works on display were huge abstracts and still life.

"May I help?" asked a small attractive woman. Her short red curls bounced as she walked towards Irene.

"I hope so," Irene said as confidently as she could. "I'm looking for a particular painting, a landscape."

The woman shook her head. "We will be having an exhibition of landscape paintings in a day or two. But at the moment they are in the store room." The woman noticed the look of desperation in Irene's eyes. "Allow me to give you a brochure, if you can come back I'm sure you will enjoy the exhibition, and maybe find what you are looking for."

Irene stood tall and stared at the woman. She was determined not to leave until she had exhausted every avenue. "May I ask if you've received an auction delivery in the past week?"

The woman's eyebrows shot up as she studied Irene. "We received two landscape paintings a couple of days ago. Why do you ask?"

Irene's heart leapt into her mouth. "Please, is there any chance I could see them?"

Surprised, the woman straightened her blouse and stepped back. "Certainly not!" her voice rose with indignation. "The paintings cannot be viewed until they are in the exhibition." Frowning, she nodded pointedly towards the door.

Irene moved towards her...hands out, pleading. "Would you be willing to describe the paintings for me? Please, that's all I ask."

The woman rolled her eyes and tutted. The desperation in Irene's voice disturbed her. She backed away and glanced towards the telephone. "Both paintings are by the same artist. He paints Cornish landscapes." Shifting behind the counter, she watched Irene, her hand poised near the phone.

"Thank you," Irene said softly. With a heavy sigh she opened the door and stepped onto the pavement. A blast of cold air hit her in the face like a hard slap. She shivered, her shoulders drooped; pulling her collar up against the cold, she wandered along the narrow street in search of the next gallery. Hoping, praying Through a Glass would be there.

Chapter 4

Irene turned off her mobile and dropped it in her handbag. Leaning back in her chair, she sipped her latte. From her secluded spot in the corner of the small café she watched people hurry in for their lunch. The over-worked coffee machine spluttered and hissed as it heated the milk to a white froth. In the small kitchen, the larger than life chef piled grilled bacon into freshly made baguettes. The tantalising smell made Irene's mouth water. Outside the rain fell and strong gusts of wind attacked the open umbrellas.

Shivering, Irene wrapped her hands around the steaming mug, and rotated her shoulders to ease the tension. Sandra's phone call had taken her by surprise. She'd forgotten all about joining her for lunch. Irene felt awful for standing her up, but there was no way she would halt her search, not with the old antique shop staring at her from across the road. Sipping her coffee, she studied the old place. *It doesn't look very promising but it's the only building I haven't investigated.*

Irene leaned down and loosened the laces on her shoes, her feet ached. For hours it seemed she had wandered up and down the street enquiring in every gallery and antique shop, even those in the side streets but no luck. This shop was her last hope. Out of sight in a narrow street, she would have missed it, had she not been desperate for a rest and a cup of coffee. She peered at the rather tatty sign above the door, painted in peeling white paint were the words, 'Second Time Around.'

Irene finished her coffee, and retied her shoe laces. Her stomach lurched as she stood and took a deep breath. Could her racing heart and sweating palms indicate she'd found it at last? Grabbing a paper napkin, she wiped her hands.

A waitress came and cleared the table. She glanced at Irene. "You alright love? You look a bit pale."

Irene retrieved her handbag and smiled at the girl. "I'm fine, thanks."

"Well I wouldn't hang around if I was you, looks like it's going to bucket down with rain soon."

Irene nodded and made for the door. Without knowing quite how, she found herself outside the old shop. She clutched the strap of her bag and peered in the dirty window. *This is crazy, how can my painting be in here? It's a dump.* Her hopeful anticipation turned to doubt. Nevertheless, she felt impelled to enter the shop and take a look round.

A dank musty smell greeted her as she pushed the door open; she wrinkled her nose in protest. The shop was larger than she imagined, it stretched to the back of the property. She gazed around and groaned, *this is a nightmare, where do I start?*

Every available shelf and display cabinet…every inch of floor space was covered with antiques and bric-a-brac. Artwork of dubious quality adorned the grubby walls. Long since abandoned cobwebs clung to the ceiling. Irene shuddered and pulled her coat close against the chill. She frowned. *This is gross! But I can't give up, this is my last hope.* Irene knew she needed a strategy; an aimless search would be useless and add to her frustration. "Right," she muttered. "I'll start with the artwork on the walls." Squaring her shoulders, she walked around the room before making her way down the long passage to the rear of the building.

One grubby bulb hung from the ceiling; in the dim light Irene found it hard to see. Hearing a sound she flinched and swung round. It suddenly occurred to her she was alone. She wondered where the owner could be. Clearing her throat, she called. "Hello, is anyone there?" Her voice faltered and sounded breathy; clenching a fist she called again, this time louder.

A man's sudden appearance startled her. She jumped back and clutched at her heart. "Goodness, you scared me half to death!"

"I'm sorry my dear, I was unaware I had a customer." His face creased in thought. "I must fix the bell over the shop door. Can I be of help?"

Irene relaxed, the old man seemed nice enough and she liked his twinkly blue eyes. "No thank you, I'm just browsing."

He smiled. "Well browse away my dear. If you need help call me." He turned and disappeared into a small dark room. Irene shuddered…*spooky! This whole place is spooky.* Pulling her coat collar up to her chin, she continued the search. "This is ridiculous!" She

34

muttered. "How could my painting be in a place like this? I need to go."

Turning she made for the door, but came to an abrupt halt. With a groan she stared into the street; rain was falling like stair-rods. The few people caught in the storm huddled under umbrellas and hurried to find shelter. Against her better judgment, Irene decided it would be best to wait awhile. If she left the shop to hail a taxi she would get soaked.

"You'd best wait till it stops."

Irene's heart leapt into her mouth; she whirled round.

The old man stood behind the counter staring at her. He could see the fear in her eyes. Raising his hands he quickly apologised. "Sorry my dear, I didn't mean to startle you…again."

Irene glared at him, but his warm smile quickly thawed her annoyance. She turned her back and stared through the glass door at the lashing rain. The intensity of the storm caused a river of water to rush down the street. She sensed the man watching her and turned her head to look at him.

The old man could see the tiredness…the despair in her hazel eyes, and his heart went out to her. He had observed her from the side room, earlier, and noticed she was only interested in the oil paintings, particularly the large landscapes. "Are you looking for a specific painting?" he asked.

The question surprised Irene. She nodded and walked to the counter.

He noticed the spark of interest in her eyes.

Irene's heart shouted 'ask him'…her mind told her 'it's not here.' Resting her hands on the counter top, she stared at him. "I'm looking for an oil painting…a landscape."

"Umm," the old man thoughtfully stroked his chin. "I have some artwork in a back room; you're welcome to take a look. If you follow me I'll show you." He left the counter and shuffled towards the dimly lit passage.

Irene frowned. *Rain or no rain, there's no way I'm following you into a back room!* Her heart pounded as she backed towards the door. Through the rain she could see the comforting lights of the little café across the road. Her hand closed around the door handle, she would have to make a dash for it. Better to get soaked than be attacked by a strange shop keeper.

The old man turned, surprised to see her standing in the same spot. He saw the fear in her eyes and the realisation dawned on him. "Oh my dear, there is no need to be afraid. I mean you no harm." His face creased in a friendly smile.

The warmth in his pale blue eyes gave Irene a little reassurance. *Maybe I'm being silly; he seems nice enough.* She let go of the door handle and faced him.

He moved towards her and held out a reassuring hand. "I have a few paintings in my back room. You may not find what you are looking for, but you are welcome to have a look." He gestured towards the passage with his hand.

Irene stayed by the door, her eyes narrowed as she stared at him. *He has honest eyes, but can I trust him?* She glanced across at the café, her instinct was to leave, but what if her painting was in that room. If she left she would never know. Her heart raced…her stomach churned.

In a dark corner of the shop the sombre tick of an old clock seem to echo in the tense silence. Irene's hand trembled slightly as she brushed a strand of hair away from her face. Her cheek felt cold.

The old man returned her gaze; he could see she was anxious. "How can I reassure you my dear? You must believe me, I mean you no harm." He looked around the room and gestured with his hand. "Such as it is, this shop is my livelihood, and I don't go around attacking my customers, it's not good for business." His eyes twinkled with amusement.

An involuntary smile softened the concern etched on Irene's face. "I'm sorry, but these days you—"

"Don't explain my dear I quite understand. The room is just down on the right. I will remain here and leave you to browse in peace." He glanced at the clock in the corner. "I will be closing the shop in half an hour."

"No problem," Irene replied. "I know what I'm looking for so it won't take me long." She hurried down the passage and entered the small dimly lit room. She stood for a moment allowing her eyes to adjust. A shaft of light shone through a small window high up in the wall. In the corner of the room illuminated by the light from the window, she noticed a number of large canvases stacked against the wall.

Moving closer, Irene could see most of the frames were old fashioned…ornate and heavily gilded. Her heart sank. She gazed around the room; apart from the stack in the corner there were no more paintings. Irene clenched a fist with frustration. *I doubt for one moment it will be among this lot.* Disappointment constricted her throat. She groaned and pulled back the first picture. *I guess as I'm here I may as well take a look.*

As she pulled each canvas from the stack her doubts were confirmed, but she gritted her teeth and carried on. Particles of dust rose in the air. She sneezed and stopped for a moment to blow her nose. As she stuffed the tissue in her pocket she noticed the last few canvases were unframed. Irene's heart leapt with hope, she took a few deep breaths. "Stay calm," she whispered.

She had exhibited Through a Glass unframed, so unless its owner had framed it…it could be here. Irene stared at the canvases, almost too afraid to look. She brushed the dust off her hands and reached for one. The first few were the wrong size; she had to move them to reach the larger paintings resting against the wall. Eventually, she was left with two, her heart rate increased as she stared at them. With a trembling hand she reached for one and turned it around, it was a modern landscape. With a deep sigh she stacked it with the others.

Irene could hardly breathe. Swallowing the lump in her throat, she faced the final canvas; the rush of blood to her head was deafening. Something about the back of the canvas was familiar. "Oh God, please let it be mine." She clasped her hands to her chest they felt clammy. "This is ridiculous, I must pull myself together." Wiping her sticky hands on her jacket she reached for the canvas and turned it around. Her hands trembled as she stared at the familiar painting. Her squeal of delight brought the old man. He poked his head round the door.

"What is it, are you alright?"

"I'm more than alright!" Irene beamed with delight and showed him the painting. "This is what I've been looking for. I can't believe I found it in your shop!"

The old man grinned. "I'm delighted, it obviously means a lot to you."

"More than you know," Irene said softly. "I'm curious though. It was auctioned so how did it end up here?"

The old man raised an eyebrow and tapped the side of his nose. "My son helps me out sometimes; he went to the auction and bought them for me. Along with this shop I own a small auction house and they would have been sold on in a week or two."

Irene could hardly believe her good fortune, she'd found the painting just in time. She was so thrilled she could hardly contain herself.

The old man chuckled, her shining eyes and flushed cheeks were such a contrast to earlier. "Shall we go through to the shop and wrap it? It's still raining outside."

Grinning like a Cheshire cat, Irene nodded. She walked towards the door but then remembered the paintings she'd moved. "Before we go, let me help you put the other paintings back."

"No, it's alright my dear, they can stay where they are; I have to catalogue them anyway. Come along, let's get you sorted and on your way home."

Irene clutched the painting and followed him. She gripped it so tightly her knuckles whitened.

The old man tore off a large sheet of bubble wrap from a roll behind the counter. Carefully, he placed the painting on it and for a moment studied it. "This is extremely good; I'm not surprised you wanted it."

Irene smiled but made no reply.

The old man secured the bubble wrap with sticky tape and handed the painting to her.

"How much do I owe you?" She asked. Her heart slumped as she remembered what the painting had originally sold for. She studied the old man's face.

He returned her gaze his face expressionless. He could see the concern in her eyes...the silent pleading. "Take it my dear, it obviously means a lot to you." Irene's startled gasp brought a smile to his face. "Take it as a gift from one art lover to another."

"But I can't!" Irene's face flushed with embarrassment. "I was so rude earlier, mistrusting you. I'm—"

He reached across the counter and patted her arm. "No harm done. Take the painting and enjoy it." He smiled. "It looks like a beautiful place."

Irene nearly replied, but clamped her lips shut in time. Gazing at him, she couldn't help noticing his wistful expression...a strange faraway look in his eyes. She held the painting close. "Thank you for your kindness," she said. "I do appreciate it."

"You're most welcome." He looked out of the window. "It seems to have stopped raining for the moment. I suggest you leave before it starts again."

Irene reached out a hand. The old man took it and gave it a gentle squeeze. The strength of his grip surprised her.

"Enjoy the painting," he said softly. For a moment his eyes bored into Irene's. "I hope the choice you make will bring you much happiness."

Irene returned his gaze, her brow furrowed in surprise. *What a strange thing to say.* She followed him to the door and stepped onto the street. A stiff breeze whistled around her legs; the large canvas responded like a sail, she gripped it tighter.

As she gazed up and down the narrow street, the metallic sound of a bolt being pushed home caused her to swing round. Briefly, she saw a tall figure back away from the door and vanish into the shadowy interior of the shop. Irene gasped; the hair rose on the back of her neck. Moving closer to the window, she squinted through the glass, but could see nothing. A cold tremor ran up her spine; clutching the painting, she moved away from the shop. A deep voice startled her and she spun round.

"Is everything okay?"

It was the chef from the café. "Yes, thank you." She could hear the nervous tremor in her voice.

He nodded towards the antique shop. "I saw you peering through the window. The old place is seldom open these days. The owner turns up occasionally and then disappears for weeks on end." He stared at the bubble wrapped picture in Irene's hand. "Looks like you chose the right afternoon."

Irene could only nod, her thoughts focused on the shadowy figure she'd seen—or thought she'd seen. Her heart beat so fast she could feel the colour drain from her face.

The chef studied her. "Are you sure you're alright, you look as though you've seen a ghost."

Irene took a few deep breaths. *I must calm down.* She glanced towards the main road. *I need to get away from here.* Looking at the chef, she forced a smile. "I'm fine, but it's been a long day." Irene squared her shoulders and secured the strap of her bag. Gripping the painting with both hands she hurried towards the main road. The street lights cast a friendly glow, and the sight of scurrying commuters eased her tension.

The chef followed her to the corner of the street. "Wait here," he said. "I'll find you a taxi; you still look a bit shook up." His piercing whistle and waving arm caught the attention of a black cab, the vehicle pulled up at the curb and the chef helped her in.

"Thank you," Irene said with a warm smile.

"You're welcome." He turned away and was soon caught up in the throng of people hurrying along the street.

"Where to love?" The taxi driver asked.

Irene gave him Sandra's address and settled back in the seat. With a relieved sigh she rested the painting against her leg, she could hardly believe she'd found it. She couldn't stop touching it...holding it close, as though to convince herself it was real.

Exhausted, her head flopped against the head rest; she rubbed her tired eyes, the motion of the taxi lulled her. For a moment she closed her eyes...in an instant her mind returned to the old shop and the tall figure she'd spotted in the shadows. A shudder went through her, and she sat up. *Who was he?* Her racing heart answered her silent question. "Oh Stagman," she whispered. "I've found the painting. I pray God I find you."

Chapter 5

The taxi driver cursed as they turned into Oxford Street and joined the crawling rush hour traffic.

Irene sighed and prepared herself for a slow journey home. She gazed into the shop windows as the taxi crawled by.

The driver knew the city well, and by using the back streets he managed to avoid the worst of the hold-ups. In no time he was parked outside the entrance to Sandra's apartment. "Okay love this is it," he said.

Irene clambered out of the vehicle and eased the large painting through the cab door. She paid the driver and made her way to the apartment. Once inside she closed the door and leaned against it. Her heart pounded with a mixture of relief and excitement. Her fingers gripped the bubble-wrap covering the painting. *I can't believe I found it.*

Her thoughts returned to the shop and the tall figure. *Did I really see someone, or was it my imagination playing tricks on me?* Irene frowned as a feeling of de- ja- vu made her stomach lurch. *It feels like the first time I looked in the mirror and saw Stagman hiding in the trees.* At the thought of him her heart beat so fast she could hardly breathe. Placing a hand over her chest, she took a few deep breaths, grabbed the painting and hurried into her bedroom.

Carefully, she removed the bubble-wrap and propped the canvas against the wall. Sitting cross legged on the bed she gazed at it, her emotions in turmoil. Tears trickled down her cheeks. It was like finding a long lost friend. Irene raised a hand and brushed away her tears. "Not just a friend," she whispered softly. "But my passport to the man I love." The word love struck her heart like an arrow, and brought fresh tears. "Oh Stagman," she sobbed. "Why has it taken me so long to realise?" She buried her face in her hands and rocked.

The sound of a key in the front door, and Sandra's voice brought her up with a start. She shot to her feet and wiped her face.

Straightening her hair, she went to the bedroom door. "You're back," she said with a smile.

Sandra went into the kitchen and heaved a carrier bag onto the counter. "The traffic is horrendous!" She glanced at Irene as she grabbed the kettle and filled it with water. "How was your day?" She noticed Irene's red rimmed eyes. "Did you find the painting?"

Rather than make eye contact, Irene busied herself putting away the contents of the carrier bag. It gave her a moment to compose herself and figure out a way of telling Sandra about the painting.

Sandra watched her, aware she was stalling. "Well, did you find it? I've been thinking about you all day."

"I'm sorry I forgot about joining you for lunch."

Sandra frowned and placed her hands on her hips. "Apology accepted! Did you find the painting?"

"Yes, I did." Irene smiled as Sandra visibly relaxed. She could see the relief in her eyes.

"Awesome! Where was it?"

Aware of Sandra's inquisitive nature, Irene hesitated a moment. No way did she want to go into detail about the shop, the old man and the shadowy figure. "I found it in an old antique shop off Bond Street." She glanced at Sandra as she put a bag of pasta in the cupboard.

Sandra smiled and raised her hands. "Brilliant! Maggie was right, then."

"Absolutely, come and see it." Relieved there were no more questions, Irene led the way into the bedroom.

Sandra stood beside her and studied the painting. "It certainly is a good piece of work; but I'm still not sure why you were so desperate to get it back?" She faced Irene. "Now you've found it, does this mean you'll accept John's proposal?"

Cringing, Irene kept her eyes on the painting. She could feel the colour rise on her cheeks. "Actually, I would like to return to Zeal as soon as possible, if that's okay?"

Sandra took it as a yes, and clapped an arm round her shoulder. "That's great news, I am pleased." She was so delighted she didn't notice the anxiety in Irene's eyes. "I can take you home tomorrow if you like?"

"That would be good, Sandra, thanks. I do need to talk to John."

"Oh, Irene, he's going to be so happy. We'll leave first thing after breakfast."

Irene gave her a weak smile; she could feel a sinking in her stomach. She dreaded speaking to John, what could she say to him? 'I'm really fond of you, but I'm leaving to be with the man I truly love and I won't be coming back.' Irene's heart sank. Her only consolation was Sandra's willingness to drive her home, and not having to answer too many questions about the painting. Irene sighed softly as she lifted her case off the chair and put it on the bed. "It's sorted then. I'm going to have a shower before dinner, and then I'll pack."

Oblivious to Irene's dilemma, Sandra beamed and left the room.

≈≈≈

The journey home to Zeal was uneventful, if a little tedious, due to Sandra's constant desire to talk about Irene's relationship with John. By the time they reached Irene's house, Sandra had them married off and producing children.

Close to pulling her hair out, Irene breathed a sigh of relief when Sandra told her she'd arranged to go and have a coffee with John. It gave her time alone…time to think. She knew Sandra would tell him that his marriage proposal was about to be accepted, but she didn't mind. *He'll know the truth soon enough, I just have to figure out what to tell him, without hurting him too much.*

She dropped her case in the hall and ran upstairs to her bedroom. Sitting on the side of the bed she pulled open the drawer of her bedside cabinet and lifted out a small wooden box. Turning the silver key she slowly raised the lid. A small glass horse rested among rich folds of red satin. Carefully, she lifted it out and rested it in the palm of her hand. Leaving the bed she walked across to the window and held the small horse up to the light. The crystal body flashed and sparkled. "We're going home," she whispered. As the words left her mouth her eyes moistened with emotion. She knew she was making the right decision. She belonged with Stagman. Her heart leapt with joy as she put the glass horse away and ran downstairs to make lunch.

Sandra could hardly contain her excitement as she drove to John's cottage. She could see him waiting for her by the front door.

Hope sparkled in John's eyes as he watched her get out of the car and saw her wide grin. He took her hand. "Come on," he said ushering her into the kitchen.

The rich aroma of coffee filled the small room. Sandra sat at the kitchen table and sighed with contentment.

John handed her a mug of steaming coffee. "So, tell me, why are you so excited?" He sat across from her his dark eyes glued to her face.

Sandra's cheeks flushed with excitement. "You must have some idea."

John leaned back in his chair. "I have, but I need to hear you say it. I'm almost too afraid to hope."

"Well, feel free to hope cousin, because Irene is going to accept your proposal of marriage."

John's eyes widened…his eyebrows arched. "She found the painting."

Sandra nodded. Sipping her coffee, she peered at him over the rim of the mug. "I don't know when she'll come and talk to you, but don't push it, give her time. She doesn't seem quite herself at the moment, probably due to the fact she's had a lot to think about of late, and finding the painting wasn't easy."

John smiled. "Oh believe me, I can do patience. I've waited this long, I can wait a bit longer, especially now I know she loves me and wants to be my wife."

Sandra reached across the table and patted his hand. "I'm really happy for you, John. I never believed this would happen. After all these years the right woman has come along at last."

John nodded and stirred the coffee round in his cup; he could feel the colour rising on his cheeks.

Sandra rose from the table. "I'll leave you in peace. I'm having lunch with Irene and then driving back to London." She walked round the table and hugged him. "Be happy," she whispered."

John stood and held her close. "Thanks, and don't worry there will be an invitation in the post."

Sandra dug him in the ribs. "There'd better be." She pulled away and looked up into his face. "You take care of yourself and I'll see you soon."

⤌⤍⤌

Irene heard the crunch of tyres as Sandra's car pulled onto the gravel drive. She knew what to expect and her heart fell. *She's going to be hyper, and talk about John and weddings all through lunch.* Hearing the front door slam, she groaned in resignation.

"Irene, I'm back." Sandra shouted.

"I'm in the kitchen." Irene looked up from laying the table and attempted a smile. She didn't need to ask how John was; Sandra's elated expression said it all.

"Oh, Irene, John is over the moon and so am I."

"That's good," Irene said hoping her voice didn't sound too flat. She turned away and busied herself emptying new potatoes into a serving bowl.

Sandra sat at the table and fiddled with the fringed place-mat. "Are you okay, Irene? You seem a bit low."

Irene handed her a plate. "I'm fine; I just have a lot on my mind at the moment." She covered the lie with a broad smile.

"I can imagine," Sandra said with a chuckle.

Irene blushed but made no comment. As expected over lunch their conversation revolved around John and marriage. The torture didn't let up until Sandra drove away a few hours later.

Irene stood in the sitting room listening to the silence. Sighing with relief, she ran a weary hand through her auburn curls, and collapsed into an armchair. "I love Sandra, but enough is enough." Resting her head on the back of the chair she closed her eyes. *I must talk to John soon.* The thought weighed heavy on her. *I hate to lie, but I can't tell him the truth. I'll have to say I'm going away for a while. I just won't say when or where.* She groaned and brushed a hand across her forehead. *He's going to be so hurt, but what can I do?* She opened her eyes and stared into the fire. "I love Stagman," she whispered. "And I need to go to him as soon as possible." As she thought about him, her stomach fluttered…her heart raced.

I'll speak to John tomorrow morning and get it over with. The decision made, Irene felt the burden lift. *Once I've arranged everything, I should be able to leave in a couple of days.* She rose from the chair and threw a log

45

on the fire. As she watched it burn, memories of Mira's cottage filled her thoughts. "Oh, Stagman, I can't wait to see you!"

A sudden concern brought her out in a cold sweat. He *promised to wait for me, I hope he is.* Her mouth twitched in a nervous smile. "Of course he is," she muttered firmly; however a nagging doubt negated her confidence. Her breathing accelerated as she squared her shoulders and tried to banish the thought from her mind.

Chapter 6

A fierce gust of wind swirled along the main street of Wedon, increasing in violence as it blew around the Stag pub. The old pub sign creaked in protest as the howling wind rocked it back and forth. Tethered at the side of the building, two black horses snorted and stamped their feet.

Inside the pub, Koren the landlord frowned as he wiped a damp rag over the wooden bar. "It's blacker than Moondor's cave out there," he grumbled.

Rafus leaned against the bar and nodded in agreement. "You're right there, and it looks like there's heavy rain in the offing."

Koren moved towards Rafus, wiping the bar as he went, his eyes glued to the two men huddled in the corner. He nodded discreetly in their direction. "Apart from them strangers it's a quiet night."

"Not surprising," Rafus said. "That stiff wind and darkness is enough to keep most sensible folks at home."

Koren raised an eyebrow. "What you doing here then?"

Rafus grinned. "Ah well, it weren't like this when I left home."

Koren leaned in close to him. "You're right, this wind and strange darkness only arrived when they turned up." He lowered his voice as the two hooded men turned and stared at them. He shivered under their gaze and lowered his eyes. "They make me nervous," he whispered.

Rafus nodded and went to turn round.

Koren grabbed his sleeve. "Don't look at them," he hissed. He shivered again, and rubbed his arms. "It feels cold in here tonight." He looked across at the fire; the logs were blazing merrily in the deep grate. He gazed around the small room; the warm glow from the fire and the soft light of oil lamps, gave the room a cosy feel. Nevertheless, as Koren's eyes settled on the two strangers the hair

47

stiffened on the nape of his neck, and he couldn't shake off a feeling of doom.

Rafus leaned over the bar his voice hushed. "It's not cold in here, Koren, it's them. It was alright till they arrived." He ran a hand through his hair; a deep sense of unease made him restless. Grimacing, he glanced towards the door. "I'll be on my way in a minute."

"Don't go, Rafus, not yet. Here, have another drink, on the house."

Rafus watched him grab the handle of the pump and pull a beer.

Koren's hand trembled as he put the pint in front of him. "Stay a bit longer," he pleaded.

Rafus nodded and took the pint. He could see the fear in Koren's eyes. "Don't worry mate, I'll stay a bit longer." He glanced into the dark corner; the two strangers appeared deep in conversation...leaning in close and whispering.

Koren's wife Safi appeared from a back room with a tray of clean glasses. She put the tray down and stood beside him. "Look at them," she grumbled. "They've been nursing those drinks for the past half hour."

"Shush!" Koren said.

Safi frowned. "They can't hear me and I don't care if they do. There's something about them I don't like."

Koren took her by the arm. "I agree with you, but keep your voice down."

As he spoke the two men looked across at them. Black hoods obscured their features. Nevertheless, their hidden stare was enough to paralyze the three at the bar.

Safi trembled and moved closer to Koren. He put a protective arm round her.

"Who are they?" Safi asked. "They're not from round here."

Koren frowned. "I don't know."

"It looks to me like they're waiting for someone." Rafus whispered. He picked up his beer and took a long gulp.

Just then the door burst open; an icy blast swirled around the room rattling the windows and causing the curtains to billow. Logs on the fire hissed and crackled as frenetic flames devoured them.

All eyes in the room watched the tall stranger slam the door shut and hurry over to the two men in the corner. Pulling his black cloak around him, he sat on a stool with his back to the bar

Rafus downed his beer, and moved away from the bar. "I must get home," As he buttoned his coat he could see the anxiety in Koren and Safi's eyes. "Sorry, but I can't stay any longer; with this awful weather, Imigin and Rolo will be worrying about me."

Koren gave him a reassuring smile. "It's okay, mate, we'll see you soon."

Rafus nodded. "Keep me informed about those men," he whispered. Raising a hand in farewell, he hurried for the door. He could feel the eyes of the three men in the corner of the pub watching him. He was never so relieved to get outside.

Lowering his head, he pulled the collar of his coat up against the cold wind. It swirled around stinging his face and blowing his hair into his eyes. Leaning into the wind, he struggled down the road to his cottage. In the darkness, he was grateful a few of the homes he passed still had lights on. Nevertheless, it seemed to take forever to reach his front door.

He stood outside for a moment to catch his breath. Glancing back towards the village; one or two cottage lights flickered in the inky blackness. Rafus frowned and ran a hand through his hair. *Something is wrong!* His face darkened with concern as he lifted the latch on the door and went inside.

◈◈◈

Back in the pub the three strangers hunched over their table. In the shadowed corner of the bar they were barely visible; and since the arrival of the third man their voices dropped to a whisper. The two warriors leaned towards the new arrival, their eyes mere slits as they studied him.

Traditor sat rigid on his stool, his left hand resting discreetly on the hilt of a small dagger. In the centre of the table a candle flickered. He could see the flame reflected in the soulless eyes of the men watching him. "I've told you why I'm late," he hissed. "It's not easy for me to leave the castle. But if you want my help and information, then I suggest you give me more time. I can't just leave; I have to have a valid reason."

Muglwort, leader of the two warriors rested an elbow on the table...pushed his hood off his face and peered at Traditor through cold black eyes.

Traditor's shoulders and back stiffened as he locked eyes with him. Muglwort's gaze pierced him like a laser. Traditor instinctively tightened his grip on the dagger.

Muglwort's bushy red eyebrows arched and his mouth twisted in a grin...a grin that didn't reach his eyes! "We understand," he said in a voice as rough as sandpaper. He prodded Zworn's arm. "Our friend needs a drink; he's come a long way." He glanced sideways at Traditor. "I'm guessing that's not your real name?"

"You guess correctly."

Muglwort winked at Zworn as the big warrior banged his tankard on the table.

Traditor frowned and raised a hand. "It's alright, I don't want a drink."

Zworn thumped him on the shoulder. "Course you do. We must toast this new alliance. Our King is pleased to have you on board." His raucous laughter swelled as he raised his tankard and bellowed. "More drinks landlord, and be quick about it."

Koren looked over at the table and nodded. His heart pounded with supressed anger as he filled fresh tankards and put them on a tray.

"I'll take them." Safi said.

Koren took her arm. "No! Go in the back room out of the way."

She pulled out of his grasp. "Let me go, Koren. I sense there could be trouble and my presence might defuse it."

"Okay, give them the drinks and get back here."

Safi nodded and picked up the tray. She held it so tight her knuckles whitened, she could hardly swallow her mouth was so dry. She reached the table and with a trembling hand placed a tankard in front of each man. With her eyes averted she gathered the empties. Fear at their closeness brought her out in a cold sweat.

Zworn chuckled; the low eerie sound startled her. Consumed with fear and the desire to get away, she didn't notice his raised hand, until she felt the sting on her backside. She yelped and leapt backwards.

Raucous laughter echoed round the room as they watched her pick up the fallen tankards and rush back to the bar.

Koren grabbed the tray from her and glared at the men. "I told you to let me go." His body shook with anger.

Safi placed a gentle hand on his arm. "Leave it husband there's no harm done. Look they are relaxed and laughing."

Koren had to agree, she was right. The tension had eased and the three men were talking and drinking.

Muglwort slapped Zworn on the back. "You and women my friend; no buxom woman is safe around you!" He chuckled with delight and banged his tankard on the table, spilling the amber liquid over the sides.

❧❧❧

Koren's breathing accelerated as he watched the three men huddle round the table. They were gulping beer and talking in hushed voices. Wiping the sweat off his top lip, he tried to keep a low profile. He turned as Safi appeared from the back room. "Stay out of sight," he whispered. "I'm hoping they'll be gone soon."

Pursing her lips, Safi handed him some clean glasses. "They are evil," she hissed through clenched teeth.

Koren nodded and hunkered down behind the bar. He grabbed some bottles from a crate and stacked them on the shelf.

Safi joined him. "Where do you think they've come from?" She could see the fear in Koren's eyes as he glanced at her.

"I don't know," he whispered.

Safi shuddered. "I feel uneasy, like something really bad is going to happen. We should tell the village elders."

"Don't worry, I will." Koren said.

The sound of chairs scraping on the wooden floor...the thud of booted feet and tinkling spurs brought Koren out in a cold sweat.

He gripped Safi's shoulder and pushed her to the floor. "Stay there and don't make a sound."

Safi crouched behind the bar. Underneath the shelf there was a large gap, her husband used it to store the wooden crates, it was empty as he had already stacked the shelf. Backing into it, she ducked down and listened. She could hear heavy footsteps...saw the trembling in her husband's legs. She put her hand out to touch and reassure him, but decided against it. *I don't know what's happening, I*

51

mustn't distract him. Crouching low, she tried to calm her breathing. Strands of mousy hair escaped her bonnet and stuck to her sweating brow, she brushed it aside.

Koren watched the three hooded men walk towards the door. His heart sank when one of the men turned and strode towards him. Koren stood rigid; his racing heart thudded painfully in his ears. Gripping the edge of the bar, he stood like a rabbit caught in the light of a hunter's torch.

Zworn reached over the bar and grabbed the front of Koren's shirt. Lifting the hood away from his face he glared at the terrified man.

Koren struggled to get his breath as he stared into dark soulless eyes. Half over the bar, his feet dangling, Koren tried to raise his upper body and pull back.

Sneering, Zworn yanked him closer, forcing him to make eye contact. Koren's strangled cry of fear and pain amused Zworn, his sneer evolved into guttural laughter. Twisting the shirt tighter, he pulled Koren closer to his face. "Where's the woman?"

Koren's eyes bulged as he tried to breathe, sweat glistened on his face. He stared into Zworn's cruel face, and saw death. Black spots danced before his eyes as his heart slowed...dizzy and nauseous his body sagged. He managed to raise a hand and clutch at Zworn's cloak. Opening his mouth he tried to speak, the strangled sound caught in his throat.

Zworn sneered. "Have we lost our voice?" With his free hand he reached into his cloak. "You have seen my face, landlord."

Koren's eyes widened in fear as the flashing blade thudded into his back, piercing his heart.

◦§◦§◦§

Seeing her husband's legs rise off the floor...hearing his laboured breathing, Safi cringed and stifled a gasp. She could hear a man's voice...harsh and mocking; her hand shot to her mouth, tears trickled down her cheeks.

Crouched under the shelf, Safi waited, but hearing no further sounds, decided to take a look. She was about to move, when the thud of boots and clink of spurs drove her further under the shelf. Seeing the tall shadow come round the bar, she froze. The desire to

52

scream overwhelmed her. She shoved a fist in her mouth and closed her eyes.

A loud impatient voice bellowed from the front door. "Come on Zworn, she's not there, so leave it."

Safi's right leg cramped, she gritted her teeth with the pain, but stayed still and held her breath. She could feel sweat trickle down her back, her clothes stuck to her.

Zworn wrinkled his nose and sniffed the air. "I can smell her," He growled.

Muglwort scowled with impatience. "It's the landlord you smell, come on; the spy's waiting with the horses."

Safi heard a grunt of annoyance, followed by footsteps moving away towards the door. She stayed still, afraid to move, until she heard the clatter of horse's hooves. In the ensuing silence she listened, and waited for Koren to lower himself to the floor. "Why isn't he moving?" Rubbing her cramped leg, she eased out of her hiding place. Using her hands she pulled herself out.

Something red dripped onto the back of her hand. Safi stared and touched it with her finger. Another drop fell and she looked up. Her husband's feet hung over the edge of the bar…blood dripped onto the floor.

Safi scrambled to her feet; at the sight of her husband her eyes widened with shock. Wrapping her arms around her waist she doubled over. Her body shook, her screams reverberated around the room.

⋙⋙⋙

Darkness embraced the three men as they galloped away from the village and melted into the surrounding forest. Muglwort led the way urging his horse on…raking the stallion's flanks with his spurs. In single file the other two followed, galloping hard along a path that took them deeper into the forest.

Bringing up the rear, Traditor flicked the reigns over his horse's neck urging the smaller animal to keep up.

They galloped into a small clearing and Muglwort held up his hand. The other horses skidded to a halt around him…nostrils flared, bodies flecked with sweat.

Muglwort turned in the saddle and spoke to Traditor; his voice low on the edge of a threat. "We will not meet again in the village.

53

Choose a more secluded place next time." He scowled and pointed a finger at him. "When next we meet, be on time and make sure you bring positive news. Our Lord, King Murkier is not known for his patience." He pushed his horse closer to Traditor's and glared at him. "Neither am I!" He growled.

Traditor could feel the colour drain from his face. He nodded and took a tighter grip of his reigns as his horse shied away from Muglwort's aggressive stallion.

With an evil laugh, Muglwort swung his horse round and cantered across the clearing. "Don't leave until we're out of sight," he yelled.

⋞⋞⋞

Traditor glowered and clenched a fist as he watched the horses vanish from sight…listened to the thud of their fading hoof beats. Fear clung to him as he sat on his horse alone in the darkness. Raising an arm he wiped the sweat from his brow. *How the heck am I supposed to find out who this person is? Or when they are coming?*

A deep sigh escaped through his clenched teeth, his forehead wrinkled in a worried frown. Lifting the hood of his cloak off his head, he ran a shaky hand through his blond hair. "What have I got myself into?" His brown eyes darkened with anxiety.

Urging the horse forward, he loosened the reigns and rested his hands on the pommel of the saddle. He sighed, the journey home to Castle Eternus would be long, but his horse knew the way. He patted the animal's neck and settled in for the duration.

⋞⋞⋞

Deep in the forest thundering hooves raced towards the distant mountain. In the ensuing silence the mournful howl of a lone wolf drifted on the air. The sound reached the ears of Grey Cloud standing on a high plateau. He stood with his ears pricked. The light of understanding flashed in his golden eyes.

Thor stood beside him. "What is it, father?"

Grey Cloud raised his lip in a silent snarl.

"Was it thunder?" Thor asked.

"No my son, I wish it was. Your sister is returning she will tell us." Lowering his head, he sighed. *Her news will not be good.* With a low

54

growl he moved to the edge of the plateau. Over the years his golden eyes had grown dim, but they brightened as he spotted a lone wolf, swift and surefooted racing along the narrow track.

Jet ran towards them, breathing hard she fawned at Grey Cloud's feet. The tip of her tail flicked in greeting as her tongue caressed her father's face. "Men have come, father," she whimpered. "Two of them, riding black horses with feet like thunder." She lay beside her father panting with exhaustion.

Grey Cloud nuzzled her shoulder. "It begins again," he said softly.

Thor's blue eyes clouded as he studied his father.

Grey Cloud stared into the distance, a thoughtful expression on his face. He was old now, his grey coat had grown white over the years, and his bones ached in the cold of winter. He glanced at Thor. "We must journey to Castle Eternus." His lips rose in a snarl. "Our Prince must be informed."

Jet rose to her feet. "When will we leave father?"

"Tomorrow night." Grey Cloud's gaze drifted over the treetops, and away into the distance. *The journey will be long. I hope I can make it.* He turned and walked into a large cave. Thor and Jet followed him. The remainder of the pack rested in the shadows at the rear of the cave.

A battle scarred brindle wolf approached Grey Cloud. "Has it begun?" He asked.

Grey Cloud nodded. "It has, Remas. The four of us will leave for the castle tomorrow night at sunset. The rest of the pack will remain here."

Remas lowered his head. "Another war…this is not good," he growled. "Not good at all."

Chapter 7

Pounding hooves shattered the tranquillity of early morning. Nervous sheep scattered…pheasants took to the air with cries of protest.

Prince Zatao cantered to the top of a small knoll and pulled August to a stop.

The big stallion's sides heaved as he stood and caught his breath.

Zatao leaned forward and patted his shoulder. "You need more exercise, boy."

August threw his head up and down as though in agreement.

Zatao chuckled as he rested his arms on the pommel of the saddle. His eyes drifted towards his home in the distance.

Castle Eternus, with its tall turrets and gothic windows, was the jewel in the crown of Luminaire. Built of local yellow stone, the majestic building shimmered like gold in the morning light. A wide moat teeming with fish encircled the castle.

Tenant farmers grazed their flocks on the lush parkland. In the dense forest, deer and other wild game roamed freely. Prince Zatao's hunting parties were famed across the kingdom. The Prince delighted in the self-sufficiency of his estate.

He closed his eyes for a moment as a rush of gratitude filled his heart. He gazed heavenwards and mouthed a silent, thank you. His peaceful moment was broken by the sound of approaching hooves. Twisting in the saddle, he looked round as Mira reined her horse beside him. She leaned forward over the horse's neck to catch her breath. When she looked up at Zatao her green eyes flashed with annoyance. "You didn't wait for me," she grumbled. "I wasn't ready!"

Zatao chuckled. "My dear sister, if I gave you a half mile start, you would still lose."

Mira brushed a hand through her long golden hair, and glared at him. "Merry's a thorough-bred, I'm sure if you didn't cheat we could beat August."

Zatao reached over and put a hand on her shoulder. "You might for the first hundred yards."

Mira frowned, she knew he was right. Merry was a good sixteen hands, but August dwarfed her. She smiled and patted the filly's neck. "Never mind, girl," she said softly. "You're fast enough for me." Straightening in the saddle, Mira surveyed the tranquil scene. "What a beautiful morning."

Zatao nodded. "It is."

Mira heard a tinge of sadness in his voice and peered up at him. "What troubles you?" she asked. "You've seemed quiet this morning."

Zatao gripped his reigns, his leather gloves squeaked with the pressure. "Last night I had a dream." He looked down at Mira. "I dreamt about, Irene."

Mira stared into his troubled eyes. "You dream of her often. Why is this time different?" She reached up and touched his arm. "It is so long since we last saw her." She gazed into the distance and sighed. "How wonderful it would be if she returned, but I can't believe we will see her again, not after all this time."

A brief smile flashed in Zatao's dark eyes…quickly replaced with concern. "This dream was different Mira. This time I was so close to her. We were in some sort of shop, a dark and musty place. I watched as she searched and found the painting." He placed a hand over his racing heart and closed his eyes for a moment. Gaining some composure he continued. "She is coming to me, and the joy I felt was inexpressible. It was wonderful to see her. However, as I reached out to her something huge and dark came between us, and she vanished."

Mira shifted uneasily in her saddle. "It was only a dream, my Prince."

Zatao gazed at her and shook his head.

Mira's heart felt like lead in her chest. "But you've dreamed about Irene before."

Zatao nodded. "I know, but this time it was different, this time I was with her." He balled a fist and raised his eyes heavenwards. "I feel such heaviness in my spirit. I'm convinced she is in danger!"

"Very well," Mira said a determined tone to her voice. "I will spend a time of quiet and seek God's guidance. You must ride to Gormrun and speak to the prophet; for we must have this dream confirmed."

Zatao looked at her and smiled. "Your words have reinforced a decision I made earlier this morning. I shall ride to Gormrun after breakfast. Come, let's go home."

࿇ ࿇ ࿇

Prince Zatao's manservant followed him down the wide staircase to the great hall. "Your jerkin, My Lord," he said.

Zatao took the leather coat. "Thank you Merton. Fetch my sword." Zatao tightened the belt around his waist; took the proffered sword and placed it in the scabbard. "Have you seen my brother this morning?" He asked.

Merton shook his head. "No My Lord, I believe Prince Aldrin is still in his room."

Zatao frowned. "Well when he deigns to surface, ask him to keep a watch over Princess Mira. I could be gone most of the day."

Merton bowed low. "I will My Lord."

Prince Zatao stood for a moment in front of the huge door. The thought of finding the prophet was daunting enough; speaking to him was something else entirely. He squared his shoulders. *Oh well, here goes.* Taking a deep breath, he stepped forward. The armed guard twisted the iron handle, and swung the castle door wide. Zatao strode through and paused on the top step.

For a brief moment the tension melted from his face. Below in the courtyard his majestic white stallion, August, stood placidly beside the stable lad, Taris. The huge stallion dwarfed the diminutive boy. As the Prince donned his gloves, he made a mental note. *I must keep an eye on this lad; he has a way with horses.*

Taris bowed his head as the Prince approached. Swallowing hard he handed Zatao the reins.

The Prince smiled. "Thank you, Taris. How is your mother? Has her health improved?"

The boy raised his head, his eyes wide with surprise. "She is well My Lord, thank you."

"That is pleasing to hear." Taking the reins Prince Zatao put a foot in the stirrup and swung into the saddle. "You may go," he said

58

kindly to the lad. Turning August he cantered across the wide courtyard. The horse's hooves clattered on the cobblestones. As they drew close a burly soldier raised the portcullis and Zatao urged August over the wooden bridge straddling the moat, and away towards the forest.

⋘⋘⋘

Draped in a bathrobe, Mira stood at her bedroom window. She swallowed nervously as she watched her brother gallop towards the forest. "Stay safe," she whispered.

"My Lady, will this be to your liking?"

Startled, Mira turned from the window to see her maid, Anya, holding up a dark blue gown.

Mira nodded and took it from her. Removing the bath robe she allowed Anya to help her dress.

"Will you need me this morning, My Lady?" Anya asked as she brushed Mira's long golden hair.

Mira studied her maid in the dressing table mirror. The girl's green dress complemented her red hair. But as Mira gazed at her, she noticed the strain on the girl's face...the anxiety in her hazel eyes. "Are you unwell?" Mira asked.

Anya placed the brush on the dressing table and stepped away, her cheeks flushed under her mistress's gaze. Clasping nervous hands, she shook her head. "No My Lady, but I have somewhere I need to go this morning."

Mira's green eyes narrowed as she studied her. *Something about this feels wrong.* She shrugged. "I won't need you until later," she said rising from the chair and smoothing her skirt. "However, I expect you to bring my lunch at noon. Cold meat and side salad is all I desire. I shall take it in the breakfast room."

"Very well My Lady, and thank you."

Mira waved a hand towards the door. "You may go."

Bobbing a curtsy, Anya hurried from the room.

Tilting her head, Mira watched her close the door. She waited a moment before leaving the room. Standing in the doorway she looked up and down the corridor; Anya had vanished.

Mira made her way to the main staircase, her thoughts centred on the maid. *She seems concerned about something. I wish I knew what it was; but unless she tells me I can't help her.* With a shrug of her shoulders, she

59

hurried down the stairs and across the huge foyer towards a small door. Lifting the latch she pushed the heavy door open. In an instant she was cloaked in an atmosphere of peace.

Mira closed the door and leaned against it. Her eyes roamed around the small space. Sunlight filtered through two large stained glass windows on either side of the small altar. The reflected colours danced on the surrounding walls. A lush red carpet covered the centre aisle between the wooden pews. There were four pews on one side of the carpet and four on the other.

Closing her eyes, Mira allowed the peace to sooth her troubled spirit. She loved this room; it was her favourite place in the whole castle. As a young girl, whenever the family couldn't find her; they knew this was where she would be. The memory brought a smile to her face.

Checking the door was closed; she walked down the centre aisle of the little chapel, and fell to her knees at the altar. For the next few hours, Mira prayed and meditated in the peaceful silence. By the time she left, she knew Zatao was right. However, not only did the darkness and danger threaten Irene. It also threatened Mira's entire family, and the land of Luminaire.

Chapter 8

Anya's pulse raced as she left her mistress and hurried along the corridor. She reached Prince Aldrin's private chamber and stood trembling at the door. *I wonder why he wants to see me.* Fear made her sweat. Clasping her hands at her breast, she tried to steady her rapid breathing. Taking a deep breath she stepped forward and tapped on the door.

"Come."

Anya's hand shook as she clutched the door handle and entered the room.

"Don't be afraid my dear, close the door and come here."

With her head low, Anya walked towards him. Peering under her lashes, she noted the austere decor of the room. The plain drapes at the windows...walls devoid of decoration or artwork.

Sitting at a large mahogany desk in the corner of the room, Prince Aldrin grinned as he watched her approach.

Anya reached the desk and stood with her hands clasped...the only way to stop them shaking.

"Look at me," Aldrin said.

Anya raised her head. She had seen the Prince on numerous occasions as she went about her daily work, but never this close. His resemblance to Prince Zatao was uncanny and took her by surprise. They could have been twins. Anya stared into his eyes. The coldness she saw in their depths unnerved her. Lowering her head she stared down at her hands. They felt clammy, but she knew if she wiped them on her dress, he would see her anxiety.

The Prince watched her and smiled. "There is no need to be afraid."

Anya raised her head. *He is handsome when he smiles.* The thought brought a flush to her cheeks, and she cringed with embarrassment.

The Prince chuckled, left his seat and moved to where she stood. Perching on the edge of his desk, he studied her.

Anya felt like a small bird trapped in a net. Her legs trembled so violently she feared she would collapse to the floor.

Aldrin smiled and took her hand. "I have an assignment for you," he said, in a hushed voice.

Anya looked into his face, her hazel eyes wide with surprise. In a faltering voice she asked. "What is your command, My Lord?"

Aldrin's smile broadened, but it didn't reach his eyes.

Anya's breath caught in her throat, she wanted to pull her hand away and run from the room.

Aldrin stared at her through narrowed eyes. Most women found him irresistible. But this maid's nerviness annoyed him. However, on reflection it occurred to him it was something he could exploit. *After all*, he thought, *her demure and timid disposition is one of the reasons I chose her.* Tightening his grip on her hand he pulled her closer, with his other hand he reached out and clasped her chin. Raising her head he forced her to look at him. He could see the fear in her eyes. Controlling his impatience, he spoke softly to her. "Anya, that is your name, I believe?" He cocked his head to one side as he released her.

Anya nodded, surprised he knew her name.

He smiled. "I've watched the way you serve Princess Mira. Your loyalty and discretion have been noted." He leaned closer. "Now listen to me. There is a spy in this castle, and I need to know what it is they are looking for."

Anya gasped, her hand shot to her mouth.

"Exactly," Aldrin said, pleased at the effect of his words. He knew he had her undivided attention. His facial expression softened. "Your task my dear, is to be my eyes and ears. I need you to inform me if you see or hear anything that seems strange or new, whatever it may be. Do you understand?"

Anya nodded, but her brows knit with confusion. "How will I know what to tell you?"

"Tell me anything and everything; I will decide what's important. Your job is to relay the information. My job is to keep my brother Prince Zatao and my sister Princess Mira safe." Aldrin gazed long and hard at Anya. "Do you think you can do this?" He asked. "It is a commission of great importance."

"Oh yes My Lord. It will be my privilege and honour to assist you." She bowed her head.

Aldrin smiled with satisfaction. "You may go now, but before you do, take this." He handed her a tiny book. "Look inside," he instructed.

Anya took the book and opened it. She leafed through the pages until she reached the centre of the book, and there to her surprise the remaining pages had been cut out, leaving a space large enough to hold a folded piece of paper. "It's like a little box," she said.

Aldrin nodded. "Yes it is and it's small enough to fit under my door. If you hear anything remotely interesting, write it on a piece of paper…put it in here and push it under my door. Have you got that?"

She nodded. "Yes My Lord."

"However, I must warn you. Should you fail me, or tell anyone of our secret agreement, you will be putting my family in danger, which is treason! You know the penalty for such a crime. Do we understand each other?" He rose to his feet towering over her.

Anya gazed up at him, seeing his grim expression, the colour drained from her face. Wiping a trembling hand across her mouth, she swallowed hard.

Aldrin studied her with raised eyebrows.

Anya nodded. "I understand My Lord," she said in a voice no more than a whisper.

"Good, now you may go."

Without hesitating, Anya fled the room. She hurried along the corridor and dashed up the stairs leading to the servant's quarters. Once inside her room she locked the door and collapsed onto her bed. Her heart pounded, she massaged her temples to ease the tension.

Swinging her feet to the floor she sat on the side of the bed and reached into the pocket of her dress. Holding the small book in her hand the realisation struck her, what happened was real! She had been summoned by the Prince and given an important job to do. Wrapping both hands round the little book, she held it against her chest. "I must not fail. My Lord, Prince Zatao and his family are depending on me." Her stomach lurched. Rising to her feet, she pocketed the book and made her way to the kitchen. It was time to fetch her mistress's lunch.

Hurrying down the back stairs into the basement, Anya followed the gloomy passage towards the kitchen. A strange, but not unpleasant sensation coursed through her. Instinctively her shoulders went back and her pace increased. She smiled. *I have an important job to do. I am needed!* She pushed open the kitchen door and waited by the counter. "Princess Mira's lunch, cold meat and a side salad to be sent to the breakfast room," she called.

A deep voice from the bowels of the kitchen shouted back. "It will be sent up in five minutes."

Anya made her way upstairs and knocked gently on the door of the breakfast room. Entering, she found her mistress seated by the window reading a book. "Excuse me My Lady, your lunch is ready." She went to the dumb waiter in the corner of the room, picked up the tray of food and carried it across to the dining table.

Mira took her seat and unfolded her napkin. As she picked up her cutlery she glanced at Anya. "You seem a little on edge. Is everything alright?"

Anya lowered her eyes and self-consciously smoothed the skirt of her dress. "Everything is fine, My Lady." She felt heat rise up her neck and travel to her cheeks.

"You look a little flushed. Perhaps you should go and rest for a while. I won't need you until this evening."

"Thank you, My Lady." Bobbing a curtsy, Anya hurried from the room. Closing the door she leaned against it and took a deep breath. *That was close, I must pull myself together.* Raising a shaky hand, she patted her hair into place.

Warm sunshine filtered through a narrow window at the side of a small door. Lifting her skirt, Anya walked towards it. *I need some fresh air. A walk in the garden would be good.* Strolling across the lawn to a small copse of trees, she saw a bench and sat down. A soft breeze stirred the branches above her head. She looked up and sighed. *What Prince Aldrin has asked of me is a hard thing. I hope I can do it.*

Her shoulders drooped with the weight of the burden. Concern for her mistress and the royal family weighed heavy upon her. She was not one for scheming and spying, she considered herself an open and honest person. Nevertheless, Prince Aldrin's threat to her personal safety drove her to fulfil his wishes, whatever the outcome.

Chapter 9

Prince Zatao pushed August hard. He needed to reach Gormrun, find the prophet and get home before dark. The stallion galloped flat out, his hooves pounding the forest track. Up ahead, Zatao spotted a sign post and smiled; they'd reached the crossroads.

Pulling on the reins he eased the stallion to a steady canter, and patted the animal's neck. "Easy boy, we've covered a lot of ground." They reached the crossroads and pulled up in a cloud of dust. Zatao studied the sign post. To the left and thirty miles away was the village of Wedon. The wider path to Gormrun was to the right. Zatao sighed with relief when he saw they only had five more miles to travel.

Pulling August round he urged the stallion into a gentle walk. They had galloped nonstop for the first fifteen miles, and he could feel the horse blowing from the exertion. Zatao sat back in the saddle and let the reins hang lose. August snorted and dropped his head, grateful for a chance to catch his breath.

The forest path widened the further they went. On either side he could see an occasional cottage tucked in among the trees. The sound of children's voices drifted on the air, accompanied by the barking of a dog. As they drew closer to the village, Zatao raised the hood of his cloak and tucked his sword into the folds of the garment. Concealed by his cloak, Zatao hoped to be unrecognisable. But it occurred to him that riding August into the village nullified his attempt at concealment. The big white stallion stood out like a sore thumb.

Tightening his reins, Zatao guided August off the path and in among the trees. He dismounted and looped the reins over a branch. Patting the horse's neck, he whispered. "I won't be long."

August snorted and nudged him, pushing him back a pace

Zatao smiled and stroked the horses head. "Stay quiet now." As he left the trees and stepped onto the road, an old farm cart laden with straw bales lumbered towards him. Zatao hurried towards it and held up a hand.

The driver pulled the old horse to a stop and peered at him. "Yes," he said in a voice like gravel. "What do you want?" Spitting on the ground, he rubbed a grubby sleeve across his mouth.

Zatao moved closer and lifted the front of his hood. "I'm looking for the Prophet. I hear he lives in these parts."

The man rested his arms on his knees and stared at him. "Who wants to know?"

Zatao's eyes darkened as he lowered his hood and stepped closer.

The man's horse shied and threw his head up. The driver tightened his hold on the reins and pulled back. "Whoa, steady there you old brute!" Raising a fist he glared at Zatao. "What are you doing to my horse?" He shouted.

Zatao grabbed a rein and leaned closer. "I'll ask you again. Where can I find the prophet?" The edge in Zatao's voice unnerved the man.

Swallowing nervously, he twisted the reins around his hands. "He lives in the forest, the narrow path's back there," he said indicating with a nod of his head. "Follow it for about two miles and you'll find his cave."

Zatao stepped away and gave the horse a slap on the rump.

The animal snorted and shot forward. "Hey!" The driver yelled as he grappled with the horse. Getting the animal under control, he stared back down the road. His bushy eyebrows met in a frown. "Where'd he go?" Scratching his head, he stared into the trees on either side of the road. *Who was he, and why did he want to see the prophet?* Shrugging his shoulders, he turned and flicked the reins. "Get up there," he growled. Resting his back against a straw bale, he let the horse plod towards the village.

Anyone who wants to traipse through the forest to see an old prophet must be mad, or desperate! "Not my problem," he muttered. Pulling a piece of straw from a bale, he chewed on it.

❧❧❧

Zatao held August's bridle. "Quiet boy," he whispered. Pushing branches aside, he looked down the road. He could hear the distant rumble of the straw cart, but it had vanished round a bend.

"Okay, time to go." He led August onto the road and swung into the saddle. Urging the horse into a trot he scanned the side of the road, searching for the forest path. The tension in his shoulders increased as he gripped the reins. *It must be here somewhere.* He slowed August to a walk. *I hope I haven't missed it.* Spotting a break in the trees, a relieved smile replaced his worried frown.

Reining August, he leapt to the ground. His heart sank as he stared at the narrow path. "I hope we can get through here." August could sense his master's anxiety and nudged him. Zatao patted the stallion's muscled neck. "Okay, come on, but we're going to have to force our way through."

The path led them deep into the forest. Overhead the dense branches formed a shield against the noonday sun. Nevertheless, the muggy heat combined with anxiety brought Zatao out in a sweat. "This path seems never ending," he muttered. "I hope that wagon driver's not sent us on a wild goose chase." Stopping for a moment, he brushed an arm across his brow; his hair was dark with sweat.

August whickered softly as Zatao looped the reins over a branch. "I'm going on, August, but you'll have to stay here." Reaching in his saddlebag, he pulled out a water bottle and took a long swig. Pouring some water into his cupped hand, he splashed it over his face and wiped away the residue with his sleeve. Unhooking his cloak he tossed it over the saddle.

"You must be quiet," Zatao said patting the stallion. "I'll be as quick as I can." He had a feeling, finding the prophet would take longer than he hoped. His lips twitched in a smile as he watched August nibble grass growing at the base of the tree. *You'll be okay here*; he thought as he straightened his shoulders and strode along the narrow path.

Apart from the snap of twigs and crunch of leaves under his feet, the forest was quiet. *I wish I'd thought to bring the water.* Dismissing the thought, he pushed through a thick shrub blocking his path. Up ahead he noticed the trees appeared to thin out, allowing shafts of sunlight to pierce the gloom. Increasing his pace he hurried towards the light and found himself at the edge of a small glade. Shielding his eyes against the brightness, he saw a cave on the far side of the glade.

The slight figure of a man dressed in grey apparel sat at the entrance tending a fire. With his head down, his long beard and equally long hair concealed his face. Stepping forward, Zatao asked. "Are you the prophet?"

The man raised his head and stared at him.

Zatao stopped in his tracks, stunned by the eyes that pierced his own; they were as blue as a cobalt sky. Their radiance accentuated by the surrounding greyness of the elderly man's appearance and apparel.

The man studied the young Prince before indicating to a large stone. "Come, sit beside me."

Rolling his eyes, Zatao lowered his tall frame onto the boulder. "I ask again, are you the prophet?"

Concealed by his hair the old man's smile went unnoticed.

With a shrug of impatience, Zatao rested his arms on his thighs and watched the flames consume the logs on the fire. An old kettle rested on two flat stones in the centre of the fire. He could see it contained some kind of liquid and wondered what it was.

As if to appease his curiosity the old man took two tin cups and filled them from the steaming kettle. He handed one to Zatao.

Zatao's nose wrinkled as he sniffed the strange liquid. "What is it?"

"Nettle tea," the old man replied. "Drink, it will refresh you for your journey home."

Zatao took a sip of the hot brew, it didn't taste too bad. He cupped the mug between his hands and looked at the old man. "So, are you—?"

The old man raised a hand dismissing the question. "You know who I am; just as I know who you are, and why you are here." He paused and sipped his tea. "In your dreams you see a young woman, a woman who is dear to your heart."

Zatao's eyes widened in surprise…his heart skipped a beat as he gave the old prophet his undivided attention.

"She is returning to you. However, her presence will instigate darkness and war." He turned and looked long and hard at Zatao. "Be ready young Prince, the gathering storm approaches; for beyond the mountains a king is rising fuelled by the fires of hatred and greed. His flame is fanned from a coal on your own fire."

Zatao's jaw clenched, his hands balled into fists. "Are you saying there is a traitor within my castle?" He could hardly breathe as fear and anger consumed him.

The old man reached out and placed a hand on his arm. "Isolate the coal and it grows cold and ineffective."

"How can I? I have no idea who it is."

"Stand firm, let wisdom and love be the ground upon which you stand. For this is the armour you must wear. As such, your war is not against flesh and blood, but against the rulers of darkness, who wish to destroy this land and your dynasty."

Zatao's arms rested on his thighs, his hands hung limp over his knees...his head drooped. "I can't let her return to the scenario of war again." Tears filled his eyes; angrily he brushed them away and raised his head. "Somehow I must stop her, at least until I find the traitor in our midst."

The prophet's grip tightened on his arm. "You cannot stop her; she will arrive within a few days."

Swallowing hard, the Prince trembled as he stared into the old man's eyes.

"Stagman," the prophet whispered. "Stir up the power within you. The fire of war must blaze, but if you trust the one who is above all, you will come through unharmed."

The Prince stood and gripped the hilt of his sword. Hearing the prophet call him Stagman, brought a flush of fiery heat through his body and the warrior within raged! He planted his feet, towering over the prophet. "When will the attack come?"

The old man stared up at him, gazing into eyes ablaze with power and fury.

"You have a few weeks, in which to find and isolate the coal within your midst. Hold fast and assuage every decision with mercy." Clutching a walking stick, he staggered to his feet and reached for the Prince's hand. "May God protect and guide you, giving you peace with the one you love." He turned and shuffled into the cave.

As Prince Zatao watched him go, his heart burned with invigorating strength, and a confidence grounded in the one he trusted above all others. Retracing his steps, he hurried along the track to where he'd left August.

❧❧❧

Prince Zatao heeled August urging him on. The stallion pricked his ears and increased his pace. Zatao leaned forward in the saddle pushing the stallion to the limit of his endurance. A cold sweat clung to Zatao's body as the prophet's words rattled round in his head. *A traitor within my own walls! How can it be?* He gritted his teeth as faces… names flashed before his eyes. His stomach knotted as he contemplated the seriousness of the situation…the near impossibility of finding the traitor before it was too late.

Sitting back in the saddle he eased August into a canter. The realization that someone within his own household meant him harm was like a knife piercing his heart. Reaching with his right arm, he gripped the hilt of the sword hanging from his side. "When I find them, they will die!" He clenched the sword so tightly, a cramping pain shot up his arm. He let go of the sword and pulled August to a stop. Resting his hands on the pommel of the saddle, he took a few deep breaths to calm his racing heart and stem the rage rising within him.

Thoughts of Irene being harmed flooded his mind. "Oh God, I must keep her safe." His hand shook as he fumbled with the collar of his shirt. The intensity of his feelings for her…panic at the thought of losing her, suffocated him. Swinging a leg over the stallion's neck he leapt to the ground. Undoing the top buttons of his shirt, he breathed in the cool evening air and allowed his racing heart to slow. "I must trust God; with His help this situation will be resolved." His positive words filled him with peace, dispelling the fear and rage. He stood erect and squared his shoulders. His eyes flashed with confidence as he said firmly. "Victory will be mine."

Grabbing the reins he pulled August away from the grass verge and leapt into the saddle. The clink of metal bit against teeth made Zatao smile. "Enjoy your grass," he said patting the stallion's neck. August threw his head in the air and snorted. Still smiling Zatao kicked him into a trot. "Come on, we're nearly home."

Up ahead the forest of trees thinned out, allowing a partial view of the castle and surrounding parkland. Closing his eyes, Zatao rotated his stiff neck. The thought of a hot bath and a change of clothes spurred him on. He was about to push August into a canter when he heard the mournful howl of a lone wolf.

August shook his head; a low squeal of fright accompanied his fierce tug on the reins.

Zatao pulled him up. "Steady boy, it's only a wolf." Raking a hand through his hair, Zatao squinted through the trees. Leaping from the saddle he grabbed hold of August's bridle. "Easy now, I think I know who it is, but he's a long way from home." He rubbed a soothing hand down the stallions head, as another long howl pierced the silence.

Zatao stood close to August his eyes scanning the surrounding forest. The setting sun cast long shadows over the ground. Through the trees his castle and parkland shimmered in the dying rays of the sun. He was about to remount, but paused when he heard a rustling close at hand.

August threw his head up, and pulled back.

Zatao grabbed the reins. "Whoa, steady boy." As he calmed August, a large white shape emerged from the undergrowth and slunk towards them.

"Apologies My Lord, I did not wish to startle you. I hoped you would recognise my howl."

Zatao dropped to one knee, and held his hands out in welcome as Grey Cloud approached him. "I knew it was you, Grey Cloud, but it seems August has a short memory." He looked up at the stallion. "See, I told you it was a friend." He chuckled as he stroked the big wolf. "How are you old friend? It's so good to see you." Rising to his feet, he gazed into the wolf's golden eyes.

Unable to hold eye contact, Grey Cloud sat on his haunches and lowered his head.

Prince Zatao could feel the hair rise on the back of his neck; his heart sank. "You bring news…bad news."

Grey Cloud nodded and looked into the bushes; at his silent signal three wolves appeared and sat beside him. Grey Cloud rose to his feet and stood beside Zatao. He looked up at the Prince. "My Lord, may I introduce my son, Thor, my daughter, Jet and my second in command, Remas." Grey Clouds eyes darkened as he urged Jet forward. "Tell Prince Zatao what you saw."

Overcome by Zatao's presence, the young wolf trembled and lowered her head.

Zatao knelt and stroked her. "Don't be afraid, tell me," he said softly.

Raising her head, Jet fixed him with her amber eyes. "I saw two men dressed in black, they rode huge horses. As they galloped away their feet sounded like thunder."

"Which way did they go?"

"They went towards the land of Feritas." Jet's voice faltered. "This means war, doesn't it."

The Prince nodded and stood erect, sweat glistened on his forehead. He stared down at Jet. "You say there were two of them?"

"I glimpsed a third rider, but he remained as the others galloped away. I didn't see where he went because I was afraid and ran to tell father." The tip of her tail flicked nervously, she bowed her head. "I am sorry, My Lord. I should have stayed and perhaps followed him."

Zatao frowned. "Hindsight is not a good friend, Jet. Never mind you have confirmed what I already know. There is a spy in our midst!" He balled a fist and thumped it into the palm of his other hand. "I will find out who it is, and mark my words they will pay for their treachery."

Grey Cloud stepped forward. "Is there anything we can do to help, My Lord?"

Zatao stared at the wolves and smiled. "Yes my friends keep your eyes and ears open. Be ready and alert for I may need you."

The wolves bowed and backed away. "We are here to serve you," Grey Cloud said. The others nodded in agreement.

Zatao watched them melt into the undergrowth. "Thank you old friend," he said softly. Grabbing the reins he vaulted into the saddle and urged August forward.

❧❧❧

Mira heard August's hooves clatter over the cobbles as he galloped into the courtyard. Running out of her room, she hurried downstairs, waiting impatiently as Zatao climbed the steps towards her. Clasping his outstretched hands, she asked. "Did you find the prophet? What did he tell you?" Her eyes searched his face, he looked tired.

Zatao put an arm round her shoulders and led her into the castle. "I found the prophet. He confirmed Irene is on her way here, but he also said war is imminent. Not only that, as I drew close to home, I met Grey Cloud and he confirmed spies have trespassed on our land, and it seems one of them resides in our midst."

Mira's hand flew to her mouth. "There's a spy! Here in the castle?"

Zatao said no more as his servant Merton arrived. Removing his gloves and jerkin he handed them to him. "Run me a bath, Merton and leave out a change of fresh clothes."

"Yes My Lord; and what time should I tell cook to serve the evening meal?"

"Eight o'clock sharp. We will eat in the main dining room."

"Very well My Lord," Merton said and hurried away.

Zatao turned to Mira. "Have you seen Aldrin today?"

"No I haven't. What do you mean there's a spy here?"

"I can't say anything at the moment; we will discuss it over dinner. Do me a favour, find Aldrin and tell him his presence is required this evening. As a family we have serious issues to discuss." As he gazed at Mira's upturned face, his expression softened. Cupping her chin he kissed her on the forehead. "Did you discover anything in your time of quiet?"

Mira nodded. "You were right when you said, Irene is in danger." She frowned and twisted her fingers. "However, not only Irene; so are we." She looked up at him, her eyes wide with fear.

Zatao pulled her into his arms. As he embraced her he could hear the prophet's words ringing in his head. *If you trust the one who is above all, you will come through unharmed.* Holding her by the shoulders he eased her away and stared into her eyes. He could feel her hands trembling as she clutched his wrists. "Don't be afraid, Mira. If we stick together as a family we will come through this. Now go and find Aldrin. I will see you both later."

"Don't say too much over dinner," Mira advised. "Remember the servants!"

"Don't worry; from now on caution must be the watch word." With a troubled sigh he watched Mira hurry away. "I hate intrigue," he growled. Squaring his shoulders he took a few deep breaths and gazed around the opulent hall. Ornate hangings adorned the panelled walls. In the middle of the room stood a large table, the dark wood enhanced by the thick red carpet covering the floor and the winding staircase. In the centre of the table a sweet smelling floral arrangement perfumed the air.

Zatao studied the large oil painting hanging above the fireplace. His father's image stood in regal pose, his gloved hand resting on the ornate hilt of his sword. In the trees behind him could be seen the faint image of a stag. Zatao moved closer and stared up at the painting. His father's strong, but kindly face peered down at him.

Zatao sighed and rested a hand on the mantle. "I don't know what to do father. How do I resolve this situation?" He lowered his voice. "It seems we have a spy in our midst." His dark eyes narrowed…his blond eyebrows met in an angry frown. Staring up at his father's face, he felt a strange nudge to turn and look at the family crest hanging above the main door.

Resting against the mantle he studied the crest. Engraved above the image of a white stallion and a stag were the words, 'When power and strength are divided; when wisdom stands alone, then falls the mighty kingdom and the stag will rule the throne.'

Unity, he thought. *We must remain united as a family.* As he thought of the stag, power surged within him…his heart raced…adrenalin coursed through his veins. With a low growl he clutched at his chest and stood tall, fighting the ascendency of the stag. Gradually his pulse slowed and he regained control. He swung round as footsteps approached.

✥✥✥

Merton bowed low. "Excuse me, My Lord, I have run your bath." He could see beads of sweat glistening on Zatao's top lip and forehead. Not wishing to draw attention to his master's obvious distress, Merton lowered his eyes and indicated towards the stairs. His voice faltered as he advised the Prince to take his bath while the water was still hot.

Merton wrung his hands as the Prince swept past him, and hurried towards the stairs. It had been a number of years since he'd seen his master in this state. And then it was due to the kidnap of August, his master's stallion.

Looking up at the portrait of King Asa, he put his hands together as though in prayer and rested them against his lips. Over the past few hours heaviness hung over the castle like a cloud and it bothered him. His worried sigh echoed around the vast space. "Something is wrong…very wrong!" he muttered to himself.

Chapter 10

Irene woke and peered at her alarm clock. It was seven thirty and she'd hardly slept a wink all night. She felt nauseous…butterflies fluttered in her stomach; she groaned, and for a moment lay with her eyes closed. "Today's the day; how am I going to tell him? I need to choose my words carefully. He's such a dear man and doesn't deserve to be hurt like this, but what can I do? I love him, but not enough to marry him." She sighed and rolled her eyes.

She'd phoned John the night before and arranged to meet in the pub the next morning for coffee. Remembering his reaction to her voice, she cringed with guilt. His delight was unmistakable…the breathless huskiness as he spoke her name; and then the hint of disappointment in his voice when she suggested meeting at the pub, rather than the cottage. *I'm such a coward; but if I'm alone with him I may lose my nerve.*

Sitting up, Irene ran a hand through her tousled hair. Her stomach rolled with anxiety; no way could she tolerate food this morning, so breakfast was out. Weary, she scrambled out of bed and went for a shower. As the hot water washed over her she felt her body begin to relax. Refreshed, she wrapped a towel round her head, snuggled into a cosy dressing gown and went downstairs to make coffee.

A few hours later she was dressed in casual attire and making her way to the pub. Pulling her jacket close against the cold wind, she glanced at the sky; it was grey and overcast…indicative of her mood. Irene's heart pounded as she reached the door of the pub, and saw John's Mercedes in the car park. "Oh God; I need your help." She whispered.

Standing outside for a moment, she took a few deep breaths before pushing the door open. A few locals hovered at the bar, but it was too early for the lunch trade. John sat in their favourite place close to the inglenook fireplace. Logs crackled and hissed in the heat of the flames. Pine scented smoke drifted up the chimney.

Frank, the landlord looked up from pulling a pint and grinned at her. "Morning, Irene." He nodded in John's direction. "He's waiting for you."

Irene acknowledged Frank with a muted smile…inside her heart hammered! Gripping the strap of her bag she manoeuvred through the tables towards John.

⪻⪻⪻

John's eyebrows arched in appreciation as Irene approached. Dressed casually in jeans and a dark green sweater…auburn curls bouncing round her shoulders; she looked stunning. John smiled and stood to his feet. "Irene, sweetheart, I've missed you so much." He felt her body stiffen as he pulled her into his arms and kissed her. Holding her away he gazed into her eyes. "Are you okay? You seem a little tense."

Irene could feel her face flush as she returned his gaze. Lowering her head, she pulled away and sat on the sofa. "I'm okay, John, but I do need to talk to you." She patted the seat beside her.

With his eyes glued to her face, John lowered his tall frame onto the sofa. "Sandra tells me you found the painting. I'm really pleased. You'll have to show it to me. I confess I've forgotten what it looks like."

Before Irene could reply, Frank arrived with coffee. "Here we are," he said. "I'll bring the lunch menus over later." He put the steaming cups on a small side table and returned to the bar.

John handed a cup to Irene. "I ordered these while waiting for you."

"Thanks." Irene took the cup and gratefully sipped the strong brew. She watched John drink his coffee and stare thoughtfully into the fire. She could almost hear the confusion rattling round in his head, as he tried to understand the vibes emanating from her. *Oh, God this is awful. How do I tell him?* She put her cup down and took his hand. As he turned to look at her, the uncertainty and sorrow she saw in his dark eyes tore at her heart.

"Tell me, what's on your mind, Irene. I had assumed perhaps wrongly that once you found the painting we could begin our lives together. But I feel you drawing away from me. Why? Please be honest with me."

Irene sighed. In one way his question made things easier for her, but no way would she lie. *But how do I tell him the truth without giving too much away?* Picking at her nails, she tried to ignore the cold sweat creeping up her spine.

John watched her. His heart pumped painfully in his chest as he waited.

Irene clasped her hands in her lap, they felt clammy. Raising her head, she glanced at him...unable to make eye contact she lowered her head.

John gently raised her chin, forcing her to look at him. His eyes narrowed...his voice faltered as he asked. "Is there someone else?"

Irene's heart lurched, heat rose up her neck, colouring her cheeks.

John took his hand away, and leaned forward resting his arms on his thighs. Glancing at her, he clenched his fists. "Who is it?"

Irene's mind whirled as she watched him and attempted to collect her thoughts. She tried to speak but her throat constricted.

"Tell me," John growled.

Chewing her bottom lip, Irene ran a shaky hand through her hair. Her voice faltered as she tried to explain. "It's someone involved with the painting. I need to go away for a while and sort out my feelings." It wasn't the whole truth and Irene cringed. Reaching out she touched his arm, but he pulled away.

"Don't play with me, Irene. I'm not stupid! You've been distant for months now."

"So why did you ask me to marry you?"

"Because I love you, and I thought it was what you wanted. It's what I want." He frowned. "Obviously I was wrong!"

Irene looked down and wiped her clammy hands on her jeans. "I'm so sorry, John. I can't marry you, I need to go away."

"You mean you want to go to this other man." John's voice rang with bitterness. "Who is he? You owe me that much at least."

Irene turned her head away. "No, I'm sorry John, I can't tell you." Rising to her feet, she grabbed her jacket and bag. "I must go." For a moment, she gazed at him. He sat hunched on the couch his handsome features twisted in anger and pain. Tears of guilt pooled in her eyes. "John, I'm so sorry, I—"

His head snapped up. "Go!" He gestured impatiently with his hand. "I hope you'll both be very happy." He sneered and turned away from her.

৯৩৯৩৯৩

John watched Irene go; as the pub door slammed shut behind her, it felt like a slap in the face. His heart hammered in his chest. The anger and loss took his breath away. He banged a fist into the couch. Aware people were watching him, his face reddened with embarrassment. Sitting back against the cushions, he tried to slow his breathing. *I must calm down.*

Frank the landlord had seen the heated discourse and tentatively approached John on the pretext of putting fresh logs on the fire.

John tried to assume an air of normality as he watched him.

"Can I get you another coffee?" Frank asked him.

"No, but I'll have a whiskey, a double!"

"Right you are." Frank returned a minute later with the drink. Clearing his throat, he handed John the glass and asked if Irene would be back for lunch? John's dark scowl was all the answer he got. Rubbing the back of his neck, he beat a hasty retreat.

John downed his whiskey in a couple of gulps and left the pub. Climbing into his car he drove towards home. Passing Irene's house he stopped for a moment, wondering if he should go and knock on the door. He could feel the nervous tick in his cheek as he stared longingly at the house. "What's the point?" He groaned. "She's made it quite plain there's someone else." Thumping the steering wheel with his fist, he revved the engine and drove away.

৯৩৯৩৯৩

Irene hovered behind the curtains in her bedroom. She hoped John couldn't see her and prayed he would drive away. Her grip on the curtain relaxed as her prayer was answered and the car disappeared down the lane. Irene felt awful, but whatever the consequences the decision was made—she was leaving this world and returning to Stagman.

Taking a deep breath, she placed a hand over her racing heart. *Calm down girl, there are things to do before you can leave.* Placing her hands on her hips she stared around the room. *First things first, I need a full length mirror.* Smiling, she raised a finger in the air. *There's my old one down in the basement, I just hope I can find it.* Irene tutted and shook her head. "Now I wish I'd kept it in my studio, instead of having the one wall covered in mirror glass."

Grumbling to herself, she rushed downstairs and hurried to the basement door. Pausing at the top of the stairs, her nose wrinkled in protest at the damp smell. She switched on the light...the effect was minimal, but enough to enable her to see. Irene scowled as she descended into the dimly lit space. *I hate basements!* She waved an arm in front of her face in case there were any cobwebs. The thought of walking into one made her skin crawl.

Reaching the bottom she looked round, and her heart sank. The substantial space was cluttered with old furniture...boxes she'd never found the time to unpack and numerous discarded items. Feeling a headache coming on, she massaged the back of her neck.

Out of the corner of her eye she noticed a mirror in the far corner and moved eagerly towards it, but it turned out to be oval and made to hang on a wall. She needed the full length one. Wiping her hands on her jeans, she sighed with frustration. "It's here somewhere, but where?" Grumbling to herself she pushed and pulled at smaller items of furniture...squealing in disgust each time a spider scurried away.

"This is hopeless; where the heck have I put it? I guess I'll have to use the one in my bedroom." Groaning, she rotated her stiff shoulders. *Trouble is, with its wooden frame it's so heavy, and someone might get suspicious, and wonder what a free standing dress mirror is doing in the garden.*

Irene shrugged and turned to leave, and that's when she saw reflected light in the corner. "There you are!" The mirror lay on its side covered in dust and cobwebs. Grinning with relief, Irene raised a triumphant fist. Adrenaline coursed through her, cancelling all fear of spiders as she pushed an old armchair aside.

Carefully, she dragged the mirror out, it was damaged and spattered with paint; nevertheless it was like finding an old friend. Breathless with joy, she leaned it against the wall. "I have the painting, and now I have the original mirror...my doorway into

Stagman's world." Her whispered words echoed in the quiet of the basement.

Clasping her hands under her chin, Irene gazed lovingly at the old mirror. "Everything has fallen into place so quickly. It's as though I've been guided towards this moment." Her voice faltered. "God knows how I feel about, Stagman...how much I need to be with him. It's taken me awhile to realise it!" Dropping her head, she stared into the mirror. "Still, I hope what I'm doing is right; not just for me, but also for Stagman."

As Irene gazed at her image in the mirror, she felt her muscles relax and her breathing slowed as the tension melted away. With a happy smile, she grabbed the mirror and hauled it up the basement stairs, and into the hall.

Chapter 11

Merton stood in the housekeeper's private sitting room…a cosy space, made all the more pleasant by the occasional female touch. Two small armchairs sat in front of the blazing fire, logs crackled and hissed in the heat. Outside rain pattered against the small window.

Bella, the housekeeper, a plump grey haired woman with warm brown eyes, gestured to the other chair. "Sit down Merton, you look hot and harassed."

Merton ran a hand over his balding head, it was slick with sweat.

"Open the door if you're hot." Bella said with a chuckle.

Merton was quick to comply. Sighing with relief, he sat in the armchair and mopped his brow with a large handkerchief. "Why is it women always feel the cold?"

Bella smiled and patted his hand. "Now, tell me. Why are you so flustered this morning?" As he leaned towards her, she stared into his face noting his worried frown and accelerated breathing.

Merton placed a hand over his heart and took a few calming breaths. In a low conspiratorial voice, he tried to explain the reason for his obvious distress. "My master's told me that tomorrow I am to ride with a small escort to the other side of Wedon. In a cottage on the edge of the great forest, someone will be waiting for me."

Bella gasped and placed a hand over her mouth. "Gosh! I would be concerned if I had to ride through the great forest."

Scrunching the handkerchief in his hand, Merton scowled at her.

Bella could see the nervous tick in his cheek. "I'm sorry; I didn't mean to add to your anxiety. I'm sure you'll be fine, and at least you will have an escort."

"Humph!" was Merton's only response.

"So, who is this person?" She asked. "It must be someone close to the Prince."

Tapping the side of his nose, Merton stared around before answering. "I can't be certain, but I think I know who it is." Leaning close to Bella, he whispered. "I know it's a female."

Bella leaned back in the chair, fanning her face with a hand. "Oh my! Prince Zatao has entrusted you with a huge responsibility."

Merton nodded. "Tell no one, Bella. What I've told you is strictly between us."

"Don't worry, Merton. Your secret is safe with me." With a sigh she eased her ample frame out of the chair. "Let's have a cup of tea, before I organise the staff to get lunch prepared." She peered through the door into the staff dining room. No one was there.

�< ⋖ ⋖

Sitting at the kitchen table, Anya overheard much of their conversation. When she heard Bella rise from her chair to make tea, she tiptoed away. Her heart raced as she hurried along the corridor to her room. Once inside she pulled open a drawer in her bedside cabinet and retrieved the small box.

Hunting round she found some paper and a pencil and quickly wrote down what she could remember. Anya's hand shook as shame suffused her neck, blushing pink on her cheeks. She heard heavy footfalls coming along the passage and froze. Nervously, she chewed her bottom lip as she concealed the box and note in the folds of her skirt. The footsteps receded and she breathed a sigh of relief. Opening the box, she folded the paper and carefully pushed it into the small cavity.

Leaving her room, Anya all but ran down the long corridor to Prince Aldrin's suite. Her insides quivered...she could hardly breathe as she pushed the box under his door. On the other side of the door footsteps approached, Anya turned and fled along the corridor.

Rounding a corner and out of sight, Anya paused and leaned against the wall to catch her breath. Her heart beat so wildly she felt sure she would collapse and die. A tear trickled down her cheek, angrily she brushed it aside. *After what I've just done, I should die.*

Guilt felt like a lead weight as she moved away from the wall, smoothed the skirt of her dress and followed the long passage to the back stairs. She was about to descend when Bella the housekeeper appeared with an armful of bedding.

Seeing Anya, Bella frowned. "What are you doing here? The guest quarters are being decorated, and are out of bounds."

Anya's throat closed, she could hardly speak. She decided a half truth was better than lying. "I had a message to deliver, mam." She coughed and tried to swallow, but her throat was dry.

Bella studied her through narrowed eyes. When she spoke her voice was sharp as a knife. "Very well, but do not trespass here again." Shifting the heavy bedding in her arms, she scowled at Anya. "I believe your mistress is looking for you, you will find her in the library. I suggest you go to her."

"Yes, thank you, mam," Anya said bobbing a curtsy. She hurried to the stairs. As she descended, her slow smile of relief turned to a full grin. Reaching the bottom, she stood by the kitchen door and placed a shaky hand over her heart. "Phew! That was close."

The loud tinkle of a bell on the wall startled her. She looked up, it was her mistress. Smoothing her skirts and straightening her hair she hurried to the library. Her eyes sparkled as she tapped lightly on the door. *Maybe spying for Prince Aldrin was not so bad after all.*

✄✄✄

Prince Aldrin paced his room; his head lowered…fists clenched. The conspiratorial atmosphere pervading the castle made him nervous. Two days had passed since his brother, Zatao had requested a family dinner, and blathered on about the importance of family unity in times of crisis. However, nothing concrete had been said and Aldrin growled in frustration.

He guessed his brother's caution was due to the presence of the servant's in the dining room. He frowned. "So why didn't we meet in his office?" He banged a fist into the palm of his hand.

Thoughts of Anya came to mind. "She may know something; I need to have a little chat with her." As the words left his mouth, he heard a scraping sound outside his door, and the small box was pushed under. Aldrin strode across the room and swung the door open in time to see Anya disappear round the corner. Chuckling, he stooped to pick up the box. "Okay my sweet, what do you have for me?" Sitting at his desk he opened the box and pulled out a folded scrap of paper. Flattening it out on the desk, he screwed up his eyes to read Anya's tiny writing.

'My Lord, I am not sure if this important. But while in the servant's quarters I overheard Merton, telling the housekeeper that he'd received instruction from Prince Zatao. He is to meet someone and escort them here to the castle. From what I could hear, he is going to a small cottage on the edge of the great forest about ten miles from the village of Wedon. That is all I know My Lord, I hope it is useful.'

Prince Aldrin smirked. "Oh yes, my timid little red head, this information is more than useful." Leaning back in his chair he linked his hands behind his head and gazed upwards. "I wonder who it is. But at least now I know why the guest quarters are being decorated!" A sudden thought occurred to him; lowering his arms he picked up the paper and studied it. *There's no mention when Merton is going.* He frowned and rubbed his chin. "I need to find a pretext to speak with him."

Later that day, Prince Aldrin cornered Merton in the small passageway leading to the stables. "Ah, there you are Merton."

Merton bowed and stared blankly at Aldrin. "How can I be of help, My Lord?" Merton lowered his eyes and fiddled nervously with his ear. His role was to serve, Prince Zatao. He had little contact with his brother…a man who instilled a measure of fear in most of the castle staff.

Aldrin could see the beads of sweat on Merton's top lip. It pleased him, but for the moment he needed to gain the man's trust. Lowering his shoulders, he assumed a relaxed posture. "I'm looking for my servant," he said in a voice uncharacteristically gentle. "Have you seen him?"

Merton's inaudible sigh of relief did not escape, Aldrin. His eyes glinted with satisfaction.

Merton put his trembling hands in his pockets and nodded. "I saw him in the kitchen just a moment ago, My Lord."

"Good, when you next see him, send him to my quarters."

"Yes, My Lord, right away." As he turned to go, Aldrin stopped him.

"My brother tells me you are going on an errand for him."

Merton's eyes widened as he stared at the Prince. He swallowed nervously. *How does he know? My master said apart from Princess Mira and myself, the trip was to be a secret.* His face reddened as he realised he'd disobeyed his master by telling Bella about it. *Surely she would not have told anyone*. He could feel the Prince's eyes boring into him. He shuddered and lowered his head.

Aldrin grinned. *This is easier than I could have hoped...like playing with a pathetic little mouse.* "So, when do you leave?"

"Tomorrow morning." Merton mumbled his eyes fixed on the ground.

"I'm sorry, I didn't catch that." Aldrin could hardly quell the laughter bubbling inside him.

Raising his head, Merton stared at the Prince; he felt the colour drain from his face. His breath caught in his throat as he drew back. "I leave early tomorrow morning, My Lord." He bowed and backed away. "If you will excuse me I must attend to my master."

Prince Aldrin smirked. "By all means, go. I hope you enjoy your trip." He chuckled as he watched Merton's hasty retreat. *This is turning out better than I could have hoped.* His grin of satisfaction widened as he turned on his heels and climbed the narrow stone steps to the roof of the castle.

Chapter 12

The soft fluttering of wings alerted Grouchen to the pigeon's arrival. He smiled as he retrieved the bird from the windowsill, and saw the tiny tube attached to its leg. "Hold still now my beauty." Gently, he untied the tube and released the pigeon out of the window.

Ergon, hurried across to him. "Is it a message from the spy?"

"I believe it is. I do hope so; for the King's mood grows darker each day."

Ergon shuddered. "Indeed it does. Quick see what it says."

"Patience my friend," Grouchen carefully opened the tube and pulled out a small slip of paper. His bushy eyebrows arched as he read the message. Slowly the tension on his face melted away and a satisfied smile flickered at the corners of his mouth.

Ergon frowned and grabbed him by the sleeve. "Tell me, what does it say?"

"It is good news my friend. Come we must seek an audience with the King."

Ergon swallowed nervously. "But it's late and he has not asked to see us. You said yourself his mood is not good!"

"Oh, believe me his mood will change when he sees this."

Ergon shuddered. "I hope you're right. I do not wish to lose my head this night."

Grouchen waved a hand at him. "Stop worrying!" Clutching the precious message, he hurried along the dimly lit corridor towards the throne room.

Ergon's hands trembled as he clutched the collar of his cloak and followed him.

Outside the door to the throne room the guards brought their long pikes together. The metallic clunk echoed in the corridor. "Stop right there," one of them snarled.

Grouchen stood his ground and demanded to see the King. "We have an urgent message; he will wish to see us." Seeing their unyielding stance, he held his head high, and said firmly. "Be it on your own heads, if you refuse us."

With a grunt of disdain, one of the guards swung the mighty door open and disappeared inside.

Grouchen's courage slowly ebbed as they waited; wiping the sweat from his lip, he moved closer to Ergon.

"I hope you're right about this," Ergon whispered.

Before Grouchen could reply, the guard returned and ushered them inside. "His Majesty will see you," he growled.

The two men stood shoulder to shoulder, trembling...frightened eyes gazing down the long red carpet. Apart from two wall torches behind the throne, the vast room was in darkness. The Kings voice boomed. "Come forward! I hope you have a good reason for disturbing me at this hour."

The menace in his voice terrified the two men. Their limbs shook as they glanced nervously at each other and slowly walked forward. Reaching the steps to the dais they fell to their knees.

King Murkier leaned forward and gestured impatiently with his hand. "So, what news do you have for me?" His piercing eyes studied the frightened men.

Grouchen held out a trembling hand. "My King, a short while ago a carrier pigeon brought this note from the spy in Prince Zatao's castle."

The King's eyes widened and the corners of his mouth flickered in a smile. Snapping his fingers, he gestured for Grouchen to approach.

With lowered head, Grouchen drew near and fell to his knees. His hand shook as he handed the note to the King.

Reclined on his throne Murkier studied it. As he digested each word, he could feel the small hairs on the back of his neck prickle with excitement. "This is indeed good news. However we have no time to spare." Rising to his feet, he clapped his hands.

A servant ran forward. "Yes, My Lord?"

"Fetch Muglwort and Zworn and be quick about it." He turned to Grouchen and Ergon. "You may leave. Should you be needed I will summon you."

The two advisors bowed and retreated from the throne room. Their relieved sighs echoed through the long corridor as they hurried away to their quarters.

Muglwort and Zworn followed the servant into the throne room. Still half asleep, nervous fingers fumbled as they attempted to put the finishing touches to their attire.

Muglwort swiftly buckled his belt and stepped forward; with clenched fist he thumped his chest in salute. "How can we serve you, my King?"

"Come closer," the King demanded.

Muglwort could smell Zworn's fear as he stood beside him. His own heart pounded painfully in his chest. He could feel cold sweat trickle down his back. With head lowered he glanced at the King, noting the crumpled paper in his hand and the flush of excitement on his face. Muglwort's racing heart slowed a little with relief.

The King leaned towards them. His voice rose with excitement, as he said. "At last, I have received word from the spy in Prince Zatao's castle." His hand trembled as he waved the small scrap of paper in the air. "My seer's warning has come to pass. There is someone coming who will empower my enemy, Zatao. You will snatch this person before they can reach his castle, and bring them here to me."

Muglwort raised his head. "May I speak my King?"

Murkier waved a hand impatiently.

"How will we know who this person is?"

The King leaned back on his throne and licked his lips. His eyes narrowed as he caressed the fur collar of his cloak. "My seer assures me, the person you are looking for is female." His eyebrows arched...his low chuckle spiralled into hysterical laughter.

Muglwort and Zworn glanced at each other as they watched him, unsure how to respond.

Slapping his thigh, the King bellowed. "This task will cause you no problems. A welcome distraction from your normal duties, I would say." He gasped for breath as his laughter increased.

Muglwort chuckled. "Indeed, my King." He thumped Zworn on the back and both men burst into laughter.

Abruptly, the King's mood changed. His brow furrowed...his chin jutted. Rising from the throne he squared his shoulders and focused on Muglwort and Zworn. Both men dropped to one knee with heads bowed.

"You are to leave at first light. As you enter the land of Luminaire, keep a low profile. Make your way to a small clearing a few miles from the village of Wedon. Conceal yourselves there and wait. This woman and her escort will have to pass through the clearing in order to reach Zatao's castle. Grab her and get back here, fast! Do you understand?"

Both men nodded.

Zworn raised his head. "Will we be alone, my King?"

"No, you will have a small company of soldiers. When you grab the woman, leave no one else alive." He swung round and headed towards a door behind the throne. "Go now, and do not fail me!"

Muglwort and Zworn swaggered from the throne room.

"Fail!" Zworn said with an evil grin. "This will be the easiest and most pleasant task we've had in a long while."

Muglwort rested an arm on his shoulder. "It certainly beats trying to keep the peace in the Border lands." Laughing heartily, they made their way to the barracks.

Chapter 13

Merton paused outside Bella's sitting room. *How am I going to ask her?* Frowning, he rubbed his chin. *I can't believe she would have told anyone.* His heart thumped as he raised a hand to knock on the door; but before his knuckles touched the wood the door swung open.

"Merton, what are you doing there? Come on in." Bella smiled and motioned to a chair. "I was about to go upstairs and check on the guest suite, but I can spare you a moment."

Merton cringed as she fixed him with her warm brown eyes...honest eyes. Unable to meet her gaze, he stared at his hands. He swallowed but his throat was so dry the saliva stuck.

Bella patted his hand and stared into his face. "Merton, what on earth is the matter? Has something happened in regard to your trip?"

He shook his head. *It's no good, I'll have to ask her straight out.* Raising his head he returned her gaze, his voice faltered slightly as he asked. "Bella, did you tell anyone about the trip I'm making tomorrow?"

Bella stared at him, her eyes wide with surprise. "How could you think I would betray your confidence?!" Her chin trembled. "What kind of friend do you think I am?"

Merton couldn't look at her; burying his face in his hands, he mumbled. "I'm so sorry, but I had to ask."

Bella sat back in her chair and folded her arms across her chest. "You are accusing me of betraying our Prince. I would never do such a thing!"

Unable to hold eye contact, Merton glanced at her. Her hurt look pierced his heart.

Bella threw her head back and glared at him. "Why would you think I betrayed you?"

Merton shook his head...in a hesitant voice he explained how Prince Aldrin had cornered him and made it known, he knew about the trip. "I don't think he knew when I was leaving," he explained. "But I was so nervous, I told him." Tears welled in his eyes.

Seeing his distress, Bella's heart softened. "It's obvious someone overheard us talking about it." She scratched her head. "I can't imagine who, as there was no one around at that time."

Merton rose from his chair and paced the small room. "What should I do, Bella? I've let Prince Zatao down. He distinctly told me that only Princess Mira and I knew about it, he didn't mention Prince Aldrin." Merton trembled so hard his teeth chattered.

Bella gestured to the chair. "Come Merton, sit down. Getting yourself upset will achieve nothing, and anyway you're wearing my carpet out." Her attempt at humour fell on deaf ears. "This situation may not be as bad as you think," she said softly. "Have you considered talking to Prince Zatao about it?" She could tell by Merton's rigid stance and the beads of sweat on his pallid skin...the suggestion was too fearful to contemplate.

Bella rose from her chair and took him by the sleeve. "Sit!" She said pushing him into the chair. "I'm going to make a cup of tea, and you need to calm down." She watched him as she put the kettle on, and took cups and saucers from the dresser. He sat hunched in the chair his head in his hands. Bella placed a hand over her heart and softly sighed. *How can I help him?* She handed him a cup of tea and stared into his troubled face.

Merton raised his eyes. "Thank you, Bella" he said softly. "I am sorry for mistrusting you; please forgive me."

"It hurts you think I'm incapable of keeping a confidence. But I forgive you. Nevertheless, I still think you should talk to Prince Zatao. You have served him for many years...he knows you are trustworthy." She saw the panic return to Merton's eyes. "Look, you know him perhaps better than anyone. Has he ever treated you cruelly or unjustly?"

Merton shook his head. "He has always been kind and patient."

"There you go, then." Bella smiled.

Merton's cup rattled in its saucer, his hand trembled as he steadied it. "I have seen him angry though, Bella. He is a good ruler, but he does not suffer fools gladly! And I have been a fool." He lowered his head.

Bella reached over and touched his hand. "You are not a fool my friend. You trusted me and your trust was not misplaced." She stared at him…reassured to see the light of belief in his eyes. "Somehow we were overheard. But I will find out who it is, and believe me they will be the one to fear Prince Zatao's wrath. Now finish your tea and go and talk to your master. God will be with you, so do not fear."

❧ ❧ ❧

Prince Zatao rested his arm on the leather patch of his mahogany desk, his brow creased in a frown of concentration. The nib of his pen scratched over the surface of the paper as he wrote. Hearing a tap on the door he looked up as Merton entered the room. "Ah, there you are. I would like some…" his voice trailed off, as he noticed his servant's hunched demeanour and trembling hands. Resting his pen in the inkwell he pushed his leather chair back and rose to his feet. "You look unwell, Merton, is something wrong? Are there problems regarding your journey tomorrow?"

Merton's mouth felt dry as sandpaper, his heart all but stopped! Bathed in light from the window, his master's towering form and shimmering corn coloured hair reminded Merton of an angel. *An avenging angel*, he thought. His trembling legs became as rubber. Falling at the Prince's feet, he prostrated himself in obeisance. "I have failed you, My Lord," he sobbed.

Zatao's eyes narrowed, moving closer he loomed over him. "What do you mean, you've failed me? Explain man, and get up off the floor!"

Merton scrambled to his knees, his head bowed. He flinched as Prince Zatao grabbed him by the arm and hauled him to his feet.

"I said, stand up!"

Unable to make eye contact, Merton stood trembling.

Folding his arms across his chest, Zatao snapped. "Merton, I grow tired of your strange behaviour. Tell me what is wrong, or face my wrath."

Merton swallowed. *O God, that's what I'm afraid of.* Raising his head, he stared into the Prince's eyes. His racing heart slowed as he saw concern in their dark depths.

Zatao seeing he had the man's attention moved behind the desk and sat in his chair. Leaning his elbows on the polished surface,

92

he steepled his long fingers, rested them against his lips, and studied Merton. "Right, now let's get to the bottom of this. Why have you failed me?"

Taking a huge breath, Merton blurted it all out before fear could immobilise him again. As the words tumbled from his mouth he watched his master's lips curl with anger...his hands ball into fists. Hardly daring to breathe, Merton wiped the sweat off his forehead. "I am so sorry, My Lord. I only told Bella because I was nervous about the trip...conscious of the huge responsibility. I needed someone to talk to, and I knew I could trust her. But someone must have overheard us and told Prince Aldrin." Merton gasped and stepped back as Prince Zatao rose to his feet.

Seeing Merton's fear, Zatao snapped. "For goodness sake man; settle down. You would have known before now if I was going to punish you." His eyes darkened as he glared at Merton. "Believe me, your own words and foolish indiscretion, are enough to deserve punishment. I should have you flogged."

Zatao rose to his full height; placing his hands on his hips, he stared into his servant's pleading eyes. "I'm sorry you feel I have burdened you with too much," he said coldly. "I felt I could trust you to bring someone precious safely here to me. Perhaps I was wrong."

Merton flinched at the Prince's icy tone, and the disappointment he saw in his eyes. Tears of remorse trickled down his cheeks. "I do apologise, My Lord." His master's tight lips and dismissive wave of a hand cut Merton like a knife. "Please master," he begged. "Give me another chance. I promise I won't let you down."

Ignoring him, Zatao walked across the room and eased a large map off the wall. Flattening it out on the top of his desk he studied it, all the while muttering softly to himself.

Standing stiffly with lowered head, Merton watched him.

Prince Zatao looked up and beckoned to him. "Come here and look at this."

Merton leaned over the desk, his eyes following the Princes finger as he traced a line across the map.

"When you meet up with my friend and return home with her, ride through the village of Wedon as arranged, but do not stay on the main road."

Merton's head tilted to one side as he asked. "May I know why, My Lord?"

Prince Zatao looked up from the map and studied him. He could see genuine alarm on Merton's face. "There is a spy among us," he growled. "I believe if you return on the main road, you will ride into danger."

Merton gasped. "My Lord, I hope you don't think I am a spy!" Seeing Prince Zatao's fleeting smile, he breathed a sigh of relief.

"No, Merton," Zatao said. "I am disappointed in you. However, I do not believe you are a spy." He pressed his lips together hardening his expression. His eyes darkened as he stared into Merton's face. "If I did, you would not be standing here."

Reassured, Merton relaxed; nevertheless the threatening tone in the Prince's voice unnerved him.

Prince Zatao turned to the map and using his finger prodded the area he wanted Merton to look at. "I need you to concentrate," he said firmly. "When you leave the village of Wedon, you will see a narrow track to your left." He pointed it out on the map and traced it all the way to the castle. "This forest path is not well known, so it should be safe. Unfortunately, it's rough and narrow and will add extra miles to your journey, but whatever you do, stay on it."

He straightened and stared down at Merton. "Your casual disregard of my orders for secrecy has lengthened the journey for my friend, and your foolish prattle has put her in danger. Bring her safely here to me, or suffer the consequences. Do you understand me?"

Lowering his head, Merton stared at his clenched hands. "Yes, My Lord," he said softly.

"Very well, now go. I will see you before you leave in the morning."

Merton bowed and hurried from the room...relieved to have escaped a beating, or worse.

⤙⤙⤙

Prince Zatao toyed with the plate of food on his desk. After his meeting with Merton, he needed to be alone...needed to think. *Was I too hard on him? In all the years he's served me, he's never let me down.* Frowning, he forked a piece of chicken. *I'll have a word with him tomorrow.* He heard a soft creak as the library door opened. His lip curled with annoyance. "I said I do not wish to be—"

"I'm sorry Zatao, I don't wish to intrude."

Zatao relaxed and smiled. "You are always welcome, Mira." In a fluid motion he stood to his feet indicating the armchairs by the fire. "Come, sit down. What can I do for you?"

"I believe it's what I can do for you." Mira said as they relaxed in the chairs.

Prince Zatao stretched his long legs, resting one over the other as he studied her. Raising his hands, he said. "You have my undivided attention."

Mira smiled, amused by his arched brow and quizzical expression. "You spoke with Merton this afternoon," she said studying his face.

"Is that a question, or a statement of fact?"

Mira chewed her bottom lip; she knew she was treading on dangerous ground. Her brother would brook no interference when dealing with the servants. "Don't be cross, Zatao," she said gently. He looked calm, but the tick in his cheek revealed his irritation.

Zatao sat up; resting his arms on his knees he stared into the fire.

"You're wondering how I know?" Mira said.

He glanced at her and frowned. "Lately, it seems there are no secrets in my castle."

Mira smiled as she discreetly watched him. Even though he was her brother, and having one of his crabby moments…in the soft light of the fire he was beautiful!

"What?" He said without looking at her.

She chuckled. "Nothing, it's just your expression."

Grinning, he sat back in his chair. "I don't think you came to discuss my expression. So, how can I help?"

Mira folded her hands in her lap and tried to relax. Taking a deep breath she told him how she'd met Merton on the stairs. "He seemed really upset."

Zatao raised a hand as though about to speak.

Mira jumped in. "Please, My Lord, let me finish. Merton's distress had nothing to do with you. Although, he's saddened that he's let you down, and convinced you will never forgive him."

Zatao sighed and rolled his eyes. "Of course I will."

"You know that, and so do I," Mira said. "But Merton doesn't. He loves you and knows he has betrayed your confidence."

Zatao rested his hands on the arms of the chair. "I've already decided to speak with him tomorrow before he leaves." Leaning back against the cushion, he closed his eyes and asked wearily. "So what else is worrying him?"

Mira pursed her lips. "He can't understand how Aldrin knew about the trip, and why he's behaving so strangely." She paused and gazed at Zatao. "I must admit I'm finding it a little disconcerting myself."

Zatao straightened, and ran a hand through his hair. "I too, would like to know how he knew. However, as to his behaviour, that's partially my fault. I've not been as open with him as I should've been. As you know, he was away during the time of August's kidnap, and so he knows nothing about Irene, or how close we came to disaster. I've never mentioned her in his presence. But it's obvious he knows someone is coming, and feels left out because I've said nothing."

"You could be right," Mira said. "He's aware the guest quarters are being refurbished. I guess that would be enough to make him curious."

"Well I would be. Wouldn't you?" Zatao said with a smile.

Mira put a hand to her neck and cleared her throat. "I suppose so."

Zatao could hear the hesitancy in her voice. "Don't worry about Aldrin. He's peeved because I haven't told him what's going on, and he likes to be in the know."

Mira's lips curled in a faint smile. She loved the way Zatao always defended their younger brother. Nevertheless, she agreed with Merton…something didn't feel right. Rising from her chair she straightened her skirt. "I'm going to the chapel for a time of quiet, are you coming?"

Zatao nodded. "I will join you in a moment." Left alone he returned to his desk. Taking the piece of paper he'd written on earlier, he folded it. Pressing his signet ring into the hot wax, he sealed it and locked it away in his desk drawer.

Leaning back in his chair, he entwined his fingers behind his head and stared up at the ceiling. The delicate crystal drops on the chandelier reflected the soft light of the setting sun. Numerous sparkling hues danced across the ceiling and walls.

Closing his eyes, Zatao whispered. "Irene." His heart raced at the sound of her name. Easing out of his chair, he leaned against the desk. "Stay safe my darling." He smiled as thoughts of her brought a pleasant fluttering in his stomach…a desperate yearning to hold her. "I will see you soon," he murmured.

Chapter 14

Irene sat at the kitchen table and sipped her coffee. The toast lay on her plate untouched. Her hand trembled with emotion as she thought about Sandra's phone call the night before. Putting her mug down, she sighed and rested her chin in her hands. She could still hear the anger in Sandra's voice as she berated her for the way she'd treated John.

Chewing her lip, Irene felt her cheeks flush with guilt. She had tried so hard to explain, but there was a limit to how much she could share, and Sandra didn't want to listen; her concern was naturally for John. *I can understand that,* Irene thought. She moaned softly as the heated conversation rolled around in her head.

A tear trickled down her cheek; raising a hand she brushed it aside. *It was not my intention to hurt either of them.* Rummaging in the pocket of her jeans she found a tissue and blew her nose. *I've burned my bridges now, so I will have to go.* The thought cleared any doubt and confusion from her mind.

Rising from her chair she stood for a moment and closed her eyes. "It's now or never...no point in delaying the inevitable." Irene felt her pulse rate increase as Stagman filled her thoughts. With a breathless gasp she clutched the back of the chair, as the sweet scent of bluebells and pine needles permeated the kitchen. Dizzy with hope her eyes shot open...she was alone. Placing a hand over her heart, she waited for the light-headedness to pass.

Feeling stronger and buoyed with expectancy, she tidied up the kitchen, before hurrying into the lounge and grabbing her jacket. In her rucksack she'd packed a few clothes, toiletries, food and water; the bag felt heavy on her shoulder.

Opening the small pocket at the front she checked the box containing the glass horse was safe. With a sigh of satisfaction, she placed her arms through the straps of the bag, lifted the painting off the couch and walked with determined strides to the back door and out into the garden.

A cold blustery wind greeted her. Securing the painting between her legs, she pulled her scarf tighter, zipped her jacket, and then hurried along the gravel path to a secluded part of the garden, where the mirror waited...resting precariously against the delicate branches of a tree. Trembling with nervous excitement, Irene eased the painting into the branches of a bush, opposite, checking it reflected fully in the mirror; after a few adjustments she was happy.

A sharp gust of wind whistled through the trees, causing the painting to rock in its fragile cradle. The mirror moved forward...Irene thrust out a hand and eased it back. "Oh God, please let the mirror open soon." Irene's breathing accelerated as she watched between the painting and the mirror.

She had purposely chosen to place both items in such a way, that once she crossed into Stagman's world both the mirror and painting would fall to the ground and remain hidden. No way did she want anyone to follow her! With regard to the mirror she'd placed bricks on the ground so that when the mirror fell it would hopefully shatter. As for the painting, Irene hoped the wind would dislodge it and the winter weather would ruin it.

Ringing her hands, Irene huddled against the wind. She glanced at the mirror. *Please, hurry up!* Her heart pounded, her stomach tightened with tension. Pacing, she glimpsed her house through the trees. Chewing the inside of her cheek, she tried to smother the sadness and uncertainty threatening to overwhelm her. "I've been happy here; I've loved this old house," she murmured. Tears moistened her eyes, as she thought of Sandra and John. *I'll miss them so much; they were good friends, especially Sandra.*

She glanced at the mirror...it was flat and unmoving. *Oh goodness, I hope it's going to work, before I change my mind.* The sound of fluttering wings and a loud squawk interrupted her panicked thoughts. Swinging round she saw her friendly Blackbird perched on a low branch, his bright beady eyes studying her.

"I'm sorry little one, no raisins today." Irene turned to the mirror; waves of motion were rippling across its surface. "At last!" She exclaimed. For a moment she hesitated, the tension in her stomach increased. Holding the straps of her rucksack, she took a

deep breath, and in a determined voice said. "It's now or never."
Without a backward glance, Irene stepped through the mirror.

Beaming with delight, she cried. "Hello Birch tree." Thrusting
her arms out, she twirled laughing hysterically. Dizziness brought her
to a halt and she slumped to the grass. Gasping for breath she sat
quietly, allowing her racing heart to slow. Above her head, tree
branches rustled as a gentle breeze agitated the leaves. In the distance
she could see the small bridge straddling the rushing waters of the
stream. Stretching her arms behind her, she leaned back and listened
to the sound of the water as it bubbled over rocks and
boulders...*reminiscent of laughter*. The thought made her smile.

Gazing at the familiar landscape, Irene noticed a movement to
her right. Staring at her was the Blackbird. With a gasp of surprise,
she shot up. "Oh, no! He must have followed me." Irene's heart
sank as she peered into his bright eyes. "I'm sorry little boy, but I'm
afraid you're stuck here now. Her brow creased with worry. *He can't
understand me, so how am I going to help him?*

Looking across the river at the forest, she indicated with a
hand. "I suggest you fly over there and make a new home. There
must be loads of Blackbirds in there." Scrambling to her feet, she
stared down at him. "Look, little boy. I know you don't understand
me, but there's no going back. Like me, you'll have to stay here
now."

"I do understand you, and my name is not little boy! It is
Blackwing." Fluffing his feathers he fixed her with bright enquiring
eyes. "What is this place? And how did I get here?"

Irene stood open mouthed...speechless! Lowering herself to
the ground she stared long and hard at the bird. "Did I imagine it, or
did you speak?"

"I spoke," he said stretching a wing. "I always have, but it
seems in this place you can understand me." He hopped closer. "So,
what is this place?"

Irene sighed and ran a hand through her hair. "It's hard to
explain. I can't tell you where we are because I don't know what it's
called. All I can tell you is, I painted it from my imagination and it
turned out to be a real place." She smiled as pleasant warmth flushed
her neck and cheeks.

Blackwing saw the faraway look in her eye. "So you've come
back to be with someone."

Irene nodded. "Yes, if he will have me."

"Tck" Blackwing grumbled. "I wish I hadn't followed you now, and I don't suppose you have any raisins?"

"I didn't ask you to follow me." Rummaging in the pocket of her jacket, Irene found a couple of dried raisins. "Here," she said dropping them on the grass. She couldn't help smiling as she watched him gobble them down. "I have to go," she said rising to her feet.

"Can I come with you? Please, I don't know this place."

Irene could see the panic in his eyes. She sighed and shrugged her shoulders. "Okay, but if you see a place you like, I suggest you make it your home, because I'm not sure what's in store for me." The sudden realisation she was alone, and had no idea where to go, felt like a punch in the stomach. Gripping the straps of her rucksack she took some deep breaths. Gradually, her racing heart slowed and the uncomfortable tightness in her stomach eased.

Blackwing watched her...his body tense, his wings poised. "Are you alright? You look scared."

Irene dropped her hands to her side and raised her head. "For a moment I was scared, but a friend of mine lives in a cottage close by." Securing her rucksack she hurried towards the bridge. "Hurry up if you're coming," she shouted.

Blackwing took to the air and followed her.

Irene's stomach fluttered with anticipation as she strode over the bridge and followed the path towards the cottage. She could see it in the distance and her pace increased. However, her eyes narrowed as she drew closer. *Why is there no smoke coming from the chimney?*

Blackwing flew above her head. "Is that the cottage?"

"Yes."

"Are you sure your friend lives here? It looks empty to me."

"Of course it's not empty."

"Looks like it from up here." Blackwing said.

As Irene reached the gate her heart sank with dread. The cottage did indeed look empty, and in desperate need of restoration. The paint on the door and around the window frames was cracked and peeling. Dirt and cobwebs clung to the glass. Creeping ivy climbed the walls, probing for entrance into the roof. Broken tiles lay smashed on the ground.

Weeds and brambles choked the once pretty garden. In one of the windows, Irene could just make out a glass vase, containing a few dead bluebells. Clutching at her throat she sobbed. *O God, what's happened here? Where's Mira?* Brushing away her tears, she battled against the frightening scenarios seeking to fill her thoughts.

Blackwing flew onto the gate, his bright eyes studied her. "Are you alright?"

Irene pulled a tissue from her pocket and blew her nose. "What do you think? No I'm not! It's obvious this cottage has not been lived in for quite some time. My friend isn't here, and I don't know where to go or what to do." Raising her head, she groaned.

"So what are we going to do?" Blackwing asked.

Irene flashed him an irritated glance. "You can do whatever you want. All of this—" she made a wide sweep with her arm. "It's all yours." She sighed. "As for me, I have no idea."

Blackwing hopped along the top of the gate towards her. "I'm staying with you."

Irene gave him a sardonic smile. "Why? Could it be the raisins?"

"Hardly, it seems you don't have any."

"True, not at the moment anyway."

"So, can I stay with you?" He could see Irene's expression soften.

She nodded. "Of course you can, I would be grateful for the company."

"Good, that's settled then. What are your plans?" Blackwing asked as he fluttered to the ground and searched hungrily for something to eat.

"What plans?" Irene chuckled at the irony. "For the moment my only plan is to get inside the cottage." She clutched the gate and took some deep breaths. Her hands trembled as she lifted the rusty latch…opened the gate, and with a bravado she didn't feel walked towards the front door.

"I'll stay here if you don't mind," Blackwing mumbled through a mouthful of worm.

"Whatever," Irene said with a shrug. Wiping her clammy hands on her jacket, she reached for the handle; the cottage door was already slightly ajar, she pushed, but it resisted her efforts. She tried again, and this time her forceful shove opened it enough to squeeze through. Her breathing accelerated as she walked in and gazed around the familiar room.

A pale shaft of light filtered through one of the windows. Specks of dust danced in its rays. Joining her palms, she rested them against her lips as though praying. *Mira, where are you?* Sighing, she raised her eyes to the ceiling. "Oh God," she whispered softly. "I hope she's alright."

Rubbing her tear-filled eyes she stared at the familiar room. Apart from the dust and cobwebs, nothing had changed. In front of her, the large inglenook fireplace with the bread oven at its side, reminded her of happier…warmer times. Her chin quivered as she placed a hand on the back of one of the small armchairs in front of the fire. The room was cold; she shivered as the chill crept into her bones. The dank musty smell irritated her nose. Sneezing, she rummaged in her pocket for a tissue and burst into tears. "Oh, Stagman, Mira, where are you?"

Irene rested her arms on the back of the chair and forced herself to calm down; her body trembled with tiredness and emotion. Her eyes felt hot and gritty. *I'm so glad they can't see me looking like this.* The thought stirred more emotion, but she quenched it. Deciding she'd seen enough, she walked out of the cottage. The afternoon sun greeted her; she raised her head to its warmth.

⋦⋦⋦

Perched on a branch, Blackwing rubbed his beak against the rough bark, removing the residue of his worm lunch. Overhead, a flock of birds soared across the sky. Blackwing's heart ached with homesickness as he watched them. How he longed to be back in Irene's garden. *I wonder if they were blackbirds.* He flew to a higher branch in the tree, but the flock had already disappeared.

A noise from the cottage caught his attention, his head tilted to one side as Irene squeezed through the cottage door. Her presence cheered him. Flapping his wings, he chirruped a greeting. "Is there any way I can help?" He could see the tiredness and tension on her face, the puffiness around her eyes.

Irene shook her head. "Not really, but thank you."

"You should sit down and rest. I've seen a bench around the back under an old apple tree." He flew down by her feet. "Come on

I'll show you." He flew low guiding her around the side of the property.

Irene's head drooped…her hands hung limp as she followed him.

The rear of the property looked as derelict as the front. A thick carpet of weeds covered the ground. Mira's small hen house had all but disappeared under a blanket of bind weed.

"When were you last here?" Blackwing asked.

Irene grimaced as she stared around. "It must be about three and a half years ago."

"Well it sure is a mess," Blackwing said with a shake of his head.

Removing her rucksack, Irene rotated her aching shoulders. "It doesn't take long for nature to take over," she said, flopping down on the bench. With a heavy sigh she rested her arms on her knees. A loud rumbling in her stomach nudged her to open the rucksack and retrieve the sandwiches and water she'd packed. *I'm glad I thought to bring some food; I must have known Mira wouldn't be here.* She sniffed and wiped her nose.

"Do you want some, Blackwing?" She asked throwing him a bit of crust.

Blackwing's eyes brightened as he grabbed it and rubbed it vigorously over the ground.

Irene watched him and chuckled. "I think you'll find it's already dead."

"Tck," Blackwing responded through a mouthful of bread.

Irene smiled at him; grateful she was not alone. Finishing her sandwich she took a sip of water and looked around. The setting sun cast long shadows over the ground. Irene frowned as she packed the sandwich box and bottled water in the rucksack. "It will be dark soon," she groaned.

"Where will you spend the night?" Blackwing asked.

"I hate the thought of staying in the cottage, but I may have to." She pulled her jacket close. "If I stay out here I'll freeze." She clenched her fists. "I wish I could remember how to get to Wedon village, but even if I could, it's too late now." She looked at her watch, it was already five thirty. The thought of getting lost in the forest at night brought her out in a cold sweat.

"Maybe we could try and find it tomorrow," Blackwing suggested.

Irene's lips quivered in a smile as she nodded. "Looks like I'll have to stay in the cottage." Rising to her feet she rubbed the back of her neck to ease the tension. Dumping her rucksack on the bench she scoured the ground around the apple tree. "I'm going to collect some fire wood. Do me a favour Blackwing, go and check the chimney for me, it could be blocked."

Blackwing flew up and perched on the edge of the chimney. He peered in. "It looks clear, but I can't be sure if it's blocked further down." He flew to a low branch on the apple tree and watched her.

"I guess I'll soon find out," Irene said adding more twigs to the bundle in her arms. For the next half hour she busied herself collecting twigs and logs.

Blackwing flitted from branch to branch. "That's a lot of wood," he said.

"Well, once I'm in that cottage, I'm not coming out again." Her voice rang with determination. Loading her arms with a large bundle she carried it into the cottage. It was already dark when she returned for her rucksack and the remainder of the wood. She looked up at Blackwing perched in the apple tree. "Where will you sleep?"

"I will stay here for the night."

"Okay, stay safe."

"I will, and you," he said, tucking his head under his wing.

☙❧☙

Irene entered the cottage and busied herself arranging wood in the grate. Sighing, she placed the palms of her hands on her aching back. *I need matches*, she thought. *And paper would help to get it started.* Mustering her courage she went into the kitchen. Gazing around the abandoned room, her throat thickened, tears welled in her eyes. Gripping the back of one of the chairs, she swallowed hard. In her mind's eye she saw Mira working at the sink, and Stagman reclined at the table his long legs stretched out in front of him, one leg resting over the other as was his habit.

Irene clutched her throat as a sob escaped. "Oh, Mira, where are you?" Her heart raced so hard, she felt it would explode.

105

Collapsing onto a kitchen chair, she rested her head on her arms, and took a few deep breaths; gradually, her racing heart slowed. Rising from the chair, she went to the large dresser against the far wall. In the third drawer she found a box of matches and a bundle of papers.

Irene studied a couple of sheets, they were hand written recipes. "I'm sure Mira won't mind if I use these to start the fire." Grabbing the matches and a fistful of the paper she hurried into the sitting room. Dropping to her knees she screwed the paper tight and pushed it under the wood and lit a match. Raising her eyes heavenwards she prayed the fire would light…it did. Sitting back on her heels she mouthed a silent thank you.

Okay, now I need some light. Taking the matches she went across to the oil lamp, and gave it a shake; the resultant whooshing sound filled her with relief. Raising the top she lit the wick…turned a small dial and watched as the lamp blazed into life. Resting a hand on the table she gazed around the room. With the soft lamp light and roaring fire, Irene's thoughts turned to Mira and Stagman. *How am I going to find them? What if something awful has happened?* The unpleasant tingling in her stomach drove her to sit in one of the armchairs. Huddled over, she hugged her stomach and leaned towards the fire, allowing its warmth to sooth her.

Smoke wafted down the chimney forcing her to sit back. Frowning, she waved the smoke away with her hand. "To be expected I suppose," she muttered. "I guess the chimney needs sweeping." She pushed the chair away from the fire. "If I'm going to sit here all night, I certainly don't wish to suffocate."

In the distance Irene heard the mournful hoot of an owl; it made her think of Blackwing. *I hope he's okay.* Holding her breath she stared at the half open door…aware if she closed it, it might not be possible to open it in the morning.

Irene rubbed her eyes; combined with tiredness and smoke from the fire, they felt heavy and gritty. Resting her head against the back of the armchair, she prayed softly. The warm glow of the oil lamp, and the soft crackle of burning wood, reassured her. Closing her eyes Irene relaxed in the silence. "I'll just have a short rest," she murmured. But in no time she was fast asleep.

Chapter 15

Prince Zatao paced the great hall, his booted feet echoing in the vast space. Muttering under his breath, he clutched the folded paper bearing his seal. "Hurry up Merton," he grumbled impatiently. He stood for a moment by the window. Outside it was still dark, but in a few hours the sun would rise above the distant hills. Rubbing the back of his neck, he resumed his restless pacing.

The sound of the chapel door opening and Mira's voice startled him. "Good morning My Lord," she said softly.

Zatao swung round. "I didn't realise anyone was in there."

Mira detected the irritation in his voice and smiled at him. "Sorry, I didn't mean to disturb you." She lowered her voice. "Is Merton ready to—" Her question trailed off as Prince Aldrin bounded down the stairs.

"Just as well you did disturb him," Aldrin said with a chuckle. "His pacing is wearing out the floorboards." He strode over to Zatao. "Good morning brother," he said giving him a friendly punch on the shoulder.

Zatao's clenched jaw and narrowed eyes warned him off.

Prince Aldrin put his hands in the air and backed away. "You look agitated brother, what's the problem?"

This is all I need! Zatao thought trying to hide the irritation on his face. "I'm waiting for Merton."

Prince Aldrin stared into his brother's face. "You really should keep your servants on a tighter leash."

Seeing the amused twinkle in his eyes, Zatao scowled at him. "If you must know, I'm sending Merton to fetch a friend of mine."

Prince Aldrin winked at him. "Your agitation, brother, tells me this person is more than a friend."

Mira saw the colour rise on Zatao's face…the throbbing vein in his forehead. With a discreet flick of her head she caught Aldrin's attention and warned him to cease.

Aldrin got the message. "If you will excuse me My Lord; I'm going to walk the dogs."

Without making eye contact, Prince Zatao dismissed him with a wave of his hand. His dark eyes narrowed as he watched Aldrin hurry away. "Sometimes he can be so annoying," he said through clenched teeth. Seeing Mira's pursed lips, he asked. "What is it?"

Mira's voice faltered. "It's not something I can put my finger on, but I don't trust him." She paused and stared up at Zatao. "He seems strange lately, not himself," she said softly.

"You could say that. Mind you he's always been a little strange." Prince Zatao couldn't help smiling. However, his amusement evaporated as he noticed the worried frown on Mira's upturned face...saw the cloud of concern in her emerald eyes. Stooping, he took her by the shoulders. "Look at me," he said firmly. "Stop worrying about our brother. I know we have a spy in our midst." He shook her gently. "I'm not stupid, Mira, I'm aware it could be Aldrin, and in the likelihood of that being true, I have planned accordingly, so trust me."

"Oh, Zatao, I do trust you." She placed a trembling hand over her heart. "I feel so burdened. I love Aldrin, and can't believe..." her words trailed off as Zatao's finger covered her lips.

"Don't you think I love him too," Zatao pulled her close and wrapped his arms around her. "You are not to worry about this. It's my problem and I will deal with it."

Mira pulled away and stared into his face. "You will make sure—"

Zatao knew what she was going to say, he smiled. "Yes little sister, I promise I will make no accusations, until I am sure." He cupped her chin. "Now trust me and stop worrying." Taking her hand he pulled her towards the door. "Come, Merton and my men will be gathering in the courtyard, soon."

⁂

Merton stood in the stable yard, hugging his saddlebag and shivering in the cold; there were a few hours to go before sunrise. Oil lamps flickered in the darkness, casting long shadows over the cobbled yard. Around him stable boys ran to and fro...whickering horses were led from their stalls, saddles and bridles made ready for each mount.

A guardsman holding a lamp stood at attention barking orders. The stable yard rang with the shouts of men…clattering hooves, and the snorts of excited horses.

Merton cringed; it was too early for such an assault on his ears. Half asleep and unsure what to do in the noisy chaos, Merton stood in the relative shelter of an empty stall. Pulling at his beard, he stared wide eyed at the horses. His anxiety reached danger level as he wondered which mount would be his. His pulse raced as he contemplated his lack of riding skill. He was deep in thought, when he felt someone touch his arm; a young stable lad stared at him.

"Excuse me sir, my name is Taris. I've just come to tell you, your horse is ready. I've saddled a spare horse for Prince Zatao's, guest." The lad reached for Merton's bag, "May I take it sir, and fix it on the saddle for you?"

"Hmm, oh yes, of course." Merton hadn't realised how tightly he was clutching the bag. He relinquished it and followed the young lad across the yard to a relatively quiet corner where two smaller horses were tethered. The quietness of the two horses in the midst of the chaos filled Merton with a degree of confidence.

"This is your horse," Taris said as he secured the saddlebag, he could see the panic in Merton's eyes. "He's a good horse, sir, his name is Sage." He gave Merton an encouraging smile as he patted the dark bay's neck. "You'll be okay on him."

Unconvinced, Merton could feel his chest tightening, squaring his shoulders he breathed deeply. Gradually, the discomfort passed.

"Are you alright, sir?" The lad asked, concerned at the pallor of Merton's face.

Merton nodded. "I'm fine." He looked at the chestnut horse tethered beside Sage. "Is this the spare horse?" he asked.

Taris nodded. "Her name is Flame. She's excitable but safe." He stroked the mare's head. "We were told the visitor is comfortable around horses, so Flame should be perfect."

"Let's hope so," Merton said with a shrug of his shoulders.

Taris grinned as he untied Sage and handed Merton the reins. "Follow me," he said.

Merton recoiled as the horse's velvety lips brushed over his hand. He tried to put distance between himself and the horse without letting go of the reins.

The lad chuckled. "He won't hurt you, walk ahead and he'll follow."

Merton's legs trembled, as he walked behind Flame. Sage followed, giving him an occasional nudge.

Behind them, half a dozen guardsmen mounted their horses, clattered into the castle courtyard and formed a line. Taris led Flame to the other end of the line, and handed the reins to a guardsman, before discreetly vanishing from view.

Merton's heart sank when he saw Prince Zatoe waiting on the castle steps. His stomach rolled unpleasantly as his mind focused on the task at hand. *It's such a responsibility, I dare not fail him.*

Lost in thought; Sage's nudge in the small of his back nearly sent Merton flying. He righted himself and yanked on the reins. Out of the corner of his eye he saw a couple of guardsmen smirk…his angry glare dissolved their amusement.

With a resigned sigh, Merton positioned himself at the end of line. His shoulders drooped as he peered to his right at the mounted guardsmen towering over him.

Restless, Sage fidgeted and nibbled the sleeve of Merton's shirt. Merton found the horse's closeness, its warm breath strangely soothing. Releasing his tight grip on the reins he flexed his cramped fingers, and allowed himself to relax. He watched his master, and Princess Mira walk down the castle steps and approach a guardsman.

The solder dismounted and stood beside his horse with his head bowed.

Merton's curiosity was piqued as he watched them talk. When both men glanced in his direction he shifted uncomfortably and lowered his head, only raising it when he heard footsteps approach.

Merton's heart raced. "My Lord," he mumbled while wiping a sticky hand on his jacket. His eyes widened when he saw Prince Zatao's mouth soften in a smile. He glanced at Princess Mira, and bowed his head. "My Lady," he said, hesitantly.

Mira reached out a delicate hand and touched his arm. "It's alright, Merton." She looked up at Zatao.

The Prince nodded and patted her hand. He turned to Merton. "In truth you have let me down," he said. "However, I am giving you another chance, because I believe you are the man for this task."

Merton pressed a hand to his heart. "Thank you, My Lord. I promise I will not let you down again."

"I believe you, Merton." Prince Zatao smiled as he stepped closer, his tall frame dwarfing his trembling servant. "Now listen carefully," he said lowering his voice. "I have given my orders to the sergeant of the guard, and he knows you are to return using a different route." He glanced at the clock above the main door of the castle. "You have fifty miles to cover, and it's now four thirty; riding hard I estimate you should reach your destination in around five hours."

He gazed sympathetically at Merton. "I realise you're unused to riding, and I am sorry to inflict this upon you, but..." He lowered his head close to Merton's ear. "You are the only one in my employ I can fully trust."

Merton's head jerked back. He stared open mouthed at Zatao. "Oh My Lord, thank you! I promise your trust in me is not misplaced."

Prince Zatao nodded, and reaching inside his jerkin, he handed Merton the folded paper. "Take this, and show no one," he whispered. "Break the seal when you leave the village of Wedon, but only you are allowed to read it. Do you understand me?"

Merton's hand trembled as he clutched the folded paper and tucked it safely inside his shirt. "I understand My Lord," he said solemnly.

With a brisk nod of his head, Zatao took Mira's hand and walked to the castle steps, turning he studied the line of men. His voice echoed around the courtyard as he shouted. "Serve me well, and may God go with you."

Each man raised a fisted hand to his chest, before turning their horses and following the sergeant out of the courtyard.

Merton faced Sage and threw the reins over the horse's neck. *Oh well, here goes.* His heart pounded as he grabbed the stirrup and tried to put his foot in it.

"Here sir, let me help you."

Merton swung round as the stable lad, Taris, grabbed the bridle and held the horse steady.

"Thank you," Merton said with a relieved smile. The lad helped him scramble into the saddle and checked the girth. He handed the reins to Merton. "There you are sir." He smiled and patted the horse's neck. "Sage will follow the other horses, so I suggest you hold onto the pommel and let him go. You can trust him; he'll take care of you."

Taking the lad's advice, Merton gripped the pommel of the saddle and held on for dear life as Sage clattered out of the cobbled court yard in pursuit of the other horses.

❧❧❧

Prince Zatao and Mira stood on the steps and watched them go. The echo of hoof beats sounded hollow in the empty courtyard. Zatao stared into the heavens and closed his eyes.

Mira patted his arm. "They will find Irene and return safely, My Lord."

"I should be with them," Zatao replied, his voice gravelly with emotion. "Were it not for this spy situation and the threat of attack from King Murkier, I would be."

Mira moved close and stared into his eyes. "I could have gone My Lord. I wish I—"

"No, Mira! Don't even think about it." His eyes darkened as he stared down at her. "It was my desire to go...the fulfilment of my joy to welcome Irene personally into my home. Unfortunately, at this time I dare not separate the family. We must stay together."

Mira's shoulders slumped as she stared into his troubled face. "I do understand Zatao. Nevertheless, I'm sure my presence would have been a comfort to Irene. Not only that, I am proficient with a sword. I could have helped."

Zatao stooped and held her by the shoulders. "Listen to me, Mira, for my decision is final. You are not going, not now, not later." Rising to his full height, he said softly...ominously. "I advise you to obey me in this."

Mira could see the hard set of his jaw. A tear trickled down her cheek, but she resisted the urge to argue.

Putting his arm round her shoulders, Zatao brushed a strand of golden hair away from her face. "I appreciate your desire to help and there is something you can do."

Mira's eyes brightened as she stared at him. "What Zatao? Tell me, I will do anything."

Prince Zatao pulled her close and lowered his voice. "Contact the dove, Psalm. Ask her to shadow Merton and my men. Should they encounter any danger she can solicit help from Grey Cloud and his pack."

Mira smiled with delight. "What a wonderful idea. I will go and do it now."

Prince Zatao gripped her arm and held her back. "She must keep a low profile, Mira. No one must know she is there. Make sure she understands this."

Standing on tip toe, Mira kissed Zatao's cheek. "Trust me, my brother. And you know you can trust Psalm."

Prince Zatao smiled and hugged her. "I know I can. Now go!"

⋘⋘⋘

Mira needed no second bidding. Lifting her skirt she ran into the castle and along the narrow passage towards the stables. Pausing by a small door she lifted the latch and hurried up the stone steps to the roof of the building. Ignoring the pigeon loft she walked to the edge of the parapet and softly whistled.

Searching the sky she whistled again; in the distance a small shape flew towards her. Mira smiled and stepped away from the parapet as the small white dove fluttered to the ground.

"You called My Lady?"

"I need you to do something for me, Psalm," Mira paused and smiled. "Irene is returning to us, and—"

"Oh how wonderful!" Psalm said before Mira could finish. Flapping her wings she cooed with delight…realising she had interrupted Mira, she apologised. "What is it you would have me do?" she asked.

"I want you to follow Merton and the troop of guardsmen who have this minute left the castle. However, do not allow them to see you. Keep watch over them, especially when they return with Irene. But I must emphasise, Psalm, do not allow yourself to be seen. Prince Zatao does not wish his men to be undermined."

"I understand, My Lady. What about Irene, can I make myself known to her?"

"You can, but you must remain inconspicuous to everyone else."

Psalm's eyes sparkled with delight. "It will be so good to see her again."

113

Mira focused her attention on the troop of men galloping towards the forest, as the last horse vanished among the trees she turned to Psalm. "Shadow them well, Psalm. Should they find themselves in any danger, especially when returning with Irene, you must alert Grey Cloud!" Mira rubbed her hands together, her green eyes darkened with concern as she stared at the dove. "Do you understand me, Psalm? This is important."

"Don't worry My Lady. If I see or hear anything untoward, I will find Grey Cloud. Trust me, Irene will be delivered safely here to Prince Zatao." Stretching her white wings she rose into the air and flew toward the forest.

Placing her hands over her heart, Mira sighed as she watched her disappear among the trees.

∾∾∾

Prince Aldrin leaned against the trunk of the huge oak. A slow smile spread over his face as he watched the guardsmen gallop into the forest.

The two wolfhounds at his side yelped and fidgeted.

"Quiet!" Aldrin snarled. "They're not hunting." He yanked on the leads. "It seems a guest will be arriving soon." *It must be someone special to instigate all this trouble*, he thought. Taking a tight hold on the leads, he led the dogs back towards the castle. Reaching the stable yard he left the dogs with a kennel man and made his way through the kitchen garden to a secluded spot at the far side of the castle.

His feet crunched on the gravel as he followed the narrow path. Rounding the corner of the building he saw her. She was seated on a stone bench, her body hunched, her hands picking at the skirt of her dress. Hearing his approach, she looked up.

Her face blanched with dread... Aldrin smirked

∾∾∾

Anya hovered at the large window close to the castle door. In the torchlight the horses and riders looked huge...eerie. She peered discreetly around the curtain, watching her mistress and Prince Zatao talking with the guards. She caught sight of Merton and couldn't help smiling. His discomfort at being so close to horses was evident in his demeanour. Anya had never seen him look so unhappy and tense.

Her smile morphed into a giggle as she watched him struggle to get on the horse and then hang on for dear life as the animal raced after the other horses.

However, her enjoyment vanished when Prince Zatao and her mistress mounted the steps and made their way to the castle entrance. Swiftly she let go of the curtain and made a dash for a narrow passage with a small door at the far end, which opened onto the castle gardens.

Closing the door, she sighed and leaned against it. "I don't know why Prince Aldrin wants to meet me out here." Anya shivered in the cool morning air. *I hope he won't be too long. My mistress will wonder where I am.* Moving away from the door she followed the gravel path around the side of the building and spotted the stone bench where Prince Aldrin had told her to wait.

Agitated, she took a small handkerchief from her pocket and wiped beads of perspiration from her brow and top lip. *I wish I was not involved in this secrecy. But how does one refuse a Prince?* Closing her eyes she took a few deep breaths.

The sound of heavy footfalls on gravel alerted her; she raised her head as Prince Aldrin appeared round the corner. The unpleasant leer on his face made her cringe; nevertheless she rose to her feet and bobbed a curtsy. Smoothing her skirt she watched him approach.

"Sit," Aldrin said gesturing with a hand. He towered over her as she slumped onto the stone bench.

Anya peered up at him. Her voice faltered as she asked. "Why did you want to see me, My Lord?"

A devious smile crossed Aldrin's face as he rested his foot on the stone bench and leaned towards her, using his leg as an arm rest.

Flinching at his closeness, Anya lowered her head to avoid eye contact.

Leaning closer, Aldrin whispered in her ear. "Anya my dear, I called you here to inform you, that your service is no longer required."

Anya's head jerked back...wide eyed she stared at him. "Why? Have I done something wrong?"

Aldrin could see the panic in her eyes and his expression softened. He sat beside her and patted her hand. "No my little red head. You have fulfilled your assignment. There is nothing more for you to do."

Anya quietly exhaled. Her eyes searched his face as she asked. "So I don't have to put notes in the little box anymore?"

"No, your spying days are over."

Anya placed a trembling hand over her heart and lowered her eyes. His handsome face...bathed in unfamiliar kindness was mesmerizing.

Prince Aldrin's lips flickered in a secret smile as he caught the glimmer of relief in her eyes, and noticed the flush on her cheeks engendered by his closeness. *Don't worry little spy, I shall be keeping you close.* His eyes darkened as he rose to his feet and looked down at her.

Anya raised her eyes to his face, seeing the resumption of his hardened expression; she nervously twisted her fingers in her lap.

"There is one thing," he said, with a sinister edge to his voice. "Should it be known that you were briefly in my employ, then..." his hand moved to the hilt of his sword. "I will have no choice but to kill you. Do you understand me?" Bending down he grasped her chin and forced her to look at him.

Anya recoiled at the darkness in his eyes...his menacing glare. Nodding her head she tried to speak, but the dryness in her throat impeded sound. Swallowing hard she held his wrist and tried to pull her head away.

Releasing her, Aldrin growled. "I'm glad we understand each other." Patting the sword at his side he turned on his heels and strode away.

Anya's body shook as she nursed her sore chin and wept.

Chapter 16

Merton's body bounced and swayed in the saddle like a broken dummy, every muscle screamed with pain. Gripping the pommel of the saddle, he hung on for dear life, as Sage galloped behind the lead horses.

Behind him he heard a voice shout, "Keep your head down; watch out for low branches."

Merton's garbled reply was lost in the sound of pounding hooves.

Sage, urged on by the horses at the rear of the cavalcade, stretched his neck and raced to keep pace with those in the lead.

"I wish we could slow down," Merton moaned through clenched teeth. Up ahead he saw pale daylight through a break in the forest of trees, and his heart leapt. Catching a glimpse of a tall sign post, he clutched at the hope they might stop for a short breather.

At the head of the column, the sergeant slowed his horse and raised a hand.

Merton turned grateful eyes heavenwards, as Sage slowed to a walk and he was able to sit back in the saddle. Releasing his rigid hold on the pommel, his face creased in a wince of pain as he flexed his stiff fingers.

Reaching the signpost the horses were allowed to take a short rest. One or two guardsmen dismounted to stretch their legs.

Merton would have loved to join them, but decided against it. Instead he released his feet from the stirrups and let his body relax. He could feel Sage breathing heavily...see the flecks of sweat on his neck and shoulders. Stretching out a tentative hand, he patted the horse; the animal's skin felt wet and cold.

Looking at the signpost, Merton groaned. They still had some way to go. Reaching for his pocket watch he attempted to calculate the time they would arrive at Mira's cottage. Deep in thought, the sergeants booming voice startled him.

"Mount up! We'll be moving on in a minute," the sergeant shouted.

The loud command alarmed Sage, and he jumped forward, nearly unseating Merton.

A guardsman standing close by grabbed the reins. "Whoa, steady boy." He smiled and handed the reins to Merton. "Always remain alert when around horses," he said kindly.

Merton nodded and thanked him. With a dejected sigh he put his feet in the stirrups and waited.

৯৯৯

The sergeant sat on his large chestnut horse, and watched his men mount and re-form the column. "Right, now listen," he shouted. "We have thirty miles to go before reaching the village of Wedon." He pointed at the sign post. "From Wedon its ten miles further on to the old cottage." Turning in the saddle he looked down the long stretch of muddy road. "For the next four miles we'll keep the horses at a steady gallop and hopefully make up some ground. However, once we re-enter the forest we will be forced to slow down." Pulling his horse back onto the grass verge, he ordered the guardsmen in front to lead the column at walking pace.

The sergeant's eyes narrowed with concern as he glanced along the line at Merton. As Merton's horse passed by, the sergeant urged his mount forward and joined him. "How are you coping Mr Merton, sir?" he asked.

Merton glanced at him and tried to sit straight in the saddle. "I'm getting used to it." He lied through clenched teeth. "I'll either end up riding well, or be dead," he said with a wry smile.

The sergeant reached over and patted his shoulder. "You're doing well, sir. Nevertheless, I apologise for the speed you're forced to cope with; but you understand, I have my orders."

"I understand," Merton said. "Please don't worry about me."

The sergeant shook his head. *How can I not worry?* He thought as he looked at Merton's slight frame sitting hunched and tense in the saddle. "Once we get off this road and into the forest, our pace will decrease dramatically...more comfortable for you, I think," he said with an encouraging smile.

Closing his eyes, Merton nodded. "Thank you, sergeant."

118

The sergeant's mouth flickered in a smile. "Keep a tight grip on the reins and hang on," he advised. Urging his horse to the front of the column, he raised an arm and yelled, "Follow me."

Sage needed no bidding from Merton; as the lead horses broke into a gallop, he threw his head in the air and raced after them.

The ground reverberated to the deafening sound of thundering hooves. Clods of wet mud flew through the air, spattering horse and rider.

Merton struggled to keep his feet in the stirrups. With one hand he gripped the pommel of the saddle…with the other a handful of Sage's mane. Keeping low over the horse's neck, he groaned, closed his eyes and prayed.

When eventually the pace slowed, Merton slumped in the saddle, letting the reins dangle over Sage's neck, trusting the horse to safely traverse the rocky path. As they followed the lead horses he gazed wearily around; never was he so glad to be in a forest…grateful for the chance to travel at a slower pace. He imagined the guardsmen and their horses felt much the same. The horses in front looked hot and tired…their body's slick with sweat.

The four mile gallop to reach the forest had terrified and exhausted Merton. Sighing, he stretched his aching back; a breeze blowing through the branches cooled the perspiration clinging to his skin. Glancing up through the tree tops he caught a glimpse of the rising sun. *I'm hungry; I wish I'd eaten breakfast;* as if on cue his stomach rumbled. Reaching down he grabbed the water bottle hooked over the pommel of his saddle and took a long swig; hoping the cool water would dampen his hunger until they stopped to eat.

⤜⤜⤜

At the head of the column the sergeant remained alert. Up ahead he could see a break in the trees…hear the sound of trickling water. His horse snorted and raised its head; the sergeant patted the animal's neck. "Steady boy," he said quietly. Pulling the horse to a stop he turned in the saddle and addressed the guardsman behind him. "Follow me," he whispered to the man. "The rest of you remain here while we check this out."

Dismounting, the two men unsheathed their swords and cautiously entered the small glade. A rustling sound and a flash of white caught their attention; both men raised their swords and prepared to face a possible attack. But after a tense moment the young guardsman whispered. "I think it was a bird."

The sergeant nodded and gestured they should drop to one knee and continue to listen. In the ensuing silence all they could hear was the sound of running water.

Standing to his feet the sergeant sheathed his sword. "Fetch the rest of the men," he ordered. "We've made good time, so we'll take a short rest and eat."

৯৯৯

Psalm flew into a thick bush and perched on a high branch. "I'm too old for this," she tutted to herself. "They nearly saw me. I must be more careful."

She watched the small troop enter the glade and dismount. Her dark eyes filled with sympathy as she watched Merton struggle out of the saddle, and walk around for a moment to ease his stiff legs.

Psalms eyes brightened in a smile as she watched him collapse onto a fallen log next to a guardsman, and accept a welcome lump of bread and cheese.

Leaving the bush she flew to the top most branch of a tree and gazed around; her head cocked...alert for any sounds of danger; but apart from grazing horses and men's muted voices...silence reigned.

Chapter 17

Irene woke with a start, "Ouch," she groaned. Sitting forward she tried to massage the stiffness out of her neck. "I didn't mean to fall asleep in this stupid chair." Looking at her watch, her heart lurched. "Oh heck, it's nearly eight o'clock." Frowning, she gazed around the room, her thoughts consumed with finding the village of Wedon, without getting lost in the forest.

An unpleasant rolling in her stomach made her feel queasy. Wrapping her arms around her belly she rocked. *Why did I think after all this time, everything would be the same?* Struggling to her feet, she stretched her stiff limbs and squeezed through the open door. Bird song greeted her.

"There you are!" Blackwing chirruped. Fluttering to a lower branch he studied her. "How did you sleep?"

"What do think?" Irene said.

"You look awful, and your eyes are red."

"Thanks, you look good yourself," Irene said with a faint smile.

"I've been trying to wake you for ages," Blackwing said preening a tail feather.

"I wish you'd tried harder. I wanted to make an early start." Her throat constricted, but she fought back the tears. "I have no idea how to find the village, and I'm afraid I'll get lost."

"Hey, come on now! Don't forget you have me. I'll be your eyes in the sky. If there's a village around here, I'm the bird to find it." He cocked his head in a comical fashion, pleased to see a flicker of amusement in Irene's eyes. "Why don't you have something to eat before we make a start?"

Irene nodded. "I'm glad you're with me."

"It's not of my choosing," Blackwing replied. "But like you, I'll have to make the best of it. Go and eat. I'll be ready to leave when you are."

Returning to the cottage, Irene found her rucksack and sat in the chair. As she reached for the sandwiches her fingers closed round the small box containing the glass horse. Memories flooded back. Raising the lid, she gently touched the small horse. *Oh Stagman, how will I find you?*

Her shoulders drooped as she replaced the box in her rucksack and retrieved the sandwich container. The food looked unappetising, the bread was dry and curled at the edges, but most disturbing was the lack of water, the bottle was half empty. "I'm not going to get far on this, but it's better than nothing." Finishing her frugal breakfast, she put her arms through the straps of the rucksack and took a last look around the room.

Outside, she gazed at the sky; dark clouds billowed across the heavens, threatening rain.

"Are you ready to go?" Blackwing asked.

Zipping her jacket against the cool breeze, Irene nodded. With a heavy heart she trudged slowly to the garden gate. Her hand reached to open it...she froze! "What's that noise?"

"It sounds like horses," Blackwing whispered. Flapping his wings he fluttered from branch to branch. "Quick, you need to get out of sight."

Irene glanced down the lane, but all she could see was a cloud of dust rising into the air. Her eyes widened as she bolted to the rear of the cottage, and searched desperately for somewhere to hide. Her heart pounded in her ears as she hunkered down behind the apple tree, praying its wide girth would conceal her.

☙☙☙

Sitting straight in the saddle, a smile played at the corners of Merton's mouth. His body was paying the price; nevertheless he was getting to grips with this riding business. Holding the reins in one hand, the other resting on his thigh; he imagined he looked the part.

Sage snorted and shook his head as he plodded behind the lead horses. The atmosphere among the guardsmen was cautious but relaxed...their journey had proved uneventful.

For the sake of discretion and to save time, the sergeant decided they would bypass the village of Wedon and stick to the forest path.

Merton estimated they would soon arrive at the cottage. Remembering his master's note, he discreetly pulled it from inside his shirt and broke the seal. His mouth fell open as he read his master's words.

Hearing his gasp of surprise, the guardsman in front turned in the saddle. His eyes narrowed as he studied Merton. "Are you alright, sir? You look pale."

Remembering the note was for his eyes only; Merton took a calming breath and smiled. "I'm fine guardsman, thank you."

The guardsman nodded and urged his horse forward.

Merton re-read the note. My goodness, had I known this before we set out, I— he wiped a trembling hand across his forehead, he could hardly breathe. Slowly, he digested the words on the page. *The woman I am entrusting into your care is my future queen, Irene. No one but yourself must see this note; for her safety depends on total secrecy and your discretion. Protect her with your life, Merton.* His hand shook as he folded the note and tucked it away inside his shirt. *Oh My Lord, this responsibility is too great!* Placing a hand over his heart he slumped in the saddle.

Mulling over the enormity of his task, he was unaware they'd reached the perimeter of the forest. Deep in thought he was taken by surprise at the sergeant's command to gallop. Clutching the pommel of his saddle, he held on as Sage careered after the other horses towards a cottage a mile or so away.

⊰⊰⊰

Psalm left the guardsmen negotiating the forest path and flew ahead to the cottage. Her heart fluttered with excitement. She knew she had little time to warn Irene, that these guardsmen were here to escort her to Prince Zatao.

Reaching the cottage she fluttered onto the roof and gazed around. *Oh Irene, where are you?* Leaving the roof she flew across to the apple tree and perched on a low branch. A movement at the side of the tree caught her attention, she peered down. A figure crouched low against the trunk of the tree.

Raising her head, Psalm could hear the sound of thundering hooves. *I must hurry they'll be here in a moment.* Hopping from one leg to the other she cooed loudly. "Irene is that you?" Desperate to get

123

Irene's attention she flapped her wings. "Irene, it's me, Psalm. Look up."

Hearing a soft voice and flapping wings, Irene squinted into the branches of the tree. *I know that voice.* Recognising Psalm she squealed with delight. "Psalm is it really you?" She jumped to her feet. "Oh my God, it's wonderful to see you!"

"You too," Psalm said, flying to a lower branch. She stared into Irene's upturned face...wreathed in smiles. "I haven't much time, they'll be here soon."

"Who are they?" Irene clutched the straps of her rucksack and glanced around for a way of escape.

"It's alright Irene, they mean you no harm. Stagman—I mean Prince Zatao sent them to find you. They will escort you safely to his castle."

Irene sighed with relief. "How did he know I was coming?"

"I have no idea," Psalm said with a shake of her head. "Nevertheless, you have no need to fear; the Prince's servant, Merton, will take care of you." She glanced around before whispering. "Have you noticed a small blackbird following you? He could be a spy, although if he is, his attempts at keeping a low profile aren't working."

Seeing the twinkle in Psalm's eyes, Irene chuckled. "It's alright, Psalm, he's my friend; his name is Blackwing. Unfortunately for him he followed me through the mirror, so now he's stuck here."

"Oh dear; I thought he seemed a little lost and confused." Hearing the thud of approaching hooves, Psalm flew to a higher branch out of sight. "Don't let them know I'm here. My instructions are to watch over you, but to be inconspicuous." Her dark eyes narrowed as she watched the guard rein their horses and dismount. "Remember, I'm not here," she whispered and flew away towards the forest.

Irene smiled...grateful for Psalm's intervention and encouraging words. Moving away from the tree she watched the small dove fly towards the forest. "Oh Psalm, you don't know how wonderful it is to see you again." A deep sense of calm washed over her, as she approached the men waiting at the cottage gate. The thought of seeing Stagman took her breath away.

☙ ☙ ☙

Merton breathed a huge sigh of relief as he watched Irene approach. She was a welcome sight for his tired old eyes. Her long auburn curls bounced and shimmered in the sun…warm hazel eyes smiled at him.

Merton glanced heavenwards, thanking God she was safe. Seeing her, he understood his master's agitation and concern. This lovely young woman, his future queen, could be in grave danger!

Squaring his shoulders, Merton stepped forward. *Fear not My Lord. By God's grace we will bring her safely to you.* As Irene reached him, he discreetly bowed his head and smiled. "Greetings My Lady; I am Merton, Prince Zatao's servant. I have—" he paused and turned to the guardsmen. "We have come to escort you to our Lord, Prince Zatao."

Irene's heart leapt at the sound of his name. For a moment she felt light headed. Her voice faltered with emotion, as she asked. "How is he?"

"He is well, My Lady."

Irene's joyful smile waned as she looked back at the cottage. Clutching the collar of her jacket she faced Merton. "Do you know the lady who lived in this cottage? She was about my height with long blond hair and the most amazing green eyes. Her name was Mira." Running a jerky hand through her hair, she stared into his face.

"Princess Mira is well, and eager to see you."

Speechless, Irene stared at Merton. "Princess Mira?" she echoed.

Amused by Irene's incredulous expression, Merton smiled.

Irene grinned as the penny dropped. "Mira is Prince Zatao's sister."

Merton nodded.

Wrapping her arms around herself Irene shuddered with excitement. "I can't wait to see them. Do we have far to go?"

Merton rubbed the back of his neck and sighed. "I'm afraid we do, and I must be honest with you, the journey could be arduous. However, the guardsmen will keep us safe." He turned to the well-built man standing beside him. "This is Sergeant Azar, the commander of our troop."

The sergeant bowed. "It is an honour to serve you, My Lady."

Taken aback by the deference shown her, Irene smiled shyly at him. Her embarrassment increased as the rest of the troop, taking their lead from the sergeant, bowed their heads. Unsure how to respond, she could feel her cheeks flush pink.

Seeing her discomfort, Merton pointed to Flame. "We've brought a horse for you, My Lady. If it's acceptable to you, we would like to start back as soon as possible."

Irene's pulse raced. *Acceptable! You bet it's acceptable.* "I'm ready to leave when you are," she said eagerly.

"Good, My Lady," noting the sparkle in her eyes, Merton smiled.

"Do you have to keep calling me, My Lady?" Irene asked.

"Indeed I do, My Lady."

Irene rolled her eyes, but couldn't help chuckling. Looking round she spotted Blackwing. "Come on," she called. "We're leaving." Seeing Merton's quizzical expression she explained. "He's my friend and I want him to come with me."

"I understand, My Lady. Now, if you will follow me, I'll introduce you to Flame."

Flame whickered a soft greeting as Irene approached.

"She's lovely," Irene said, stroking the mare's neck.

"Do you ride, My Lady?" The guardsman asked, handing her the reins.

"I'm not particularly proficient, but I can ride."

The young guardsman smiled with relief. "May I be of assistance?" he asked cupping his hands.

Placing her foot in his hands, Irene giggled as he lifted her with ease onto the mare's back. Gathering the reins she thanked him.

Stepping back, he bowed, "My Lady," he said softly.

The corner of Irene's mouth flickered in a smile. *I'll never get used to this, My Lady business.* Settling in the saddle...breathless with excitement, she waited as Sergeant Azar called the men to order.

Positioning Irene and Merton in the middle of the troop, the Sergeant led the small party towards the forest at a brisk canter.

Merton cantered behind Irene, pushing Sage to keep up with the flighty mare. Seeing Irene's confidence and control over the horse brought a relieved smile to his face. However, as they drew close to the narrow forest path he could feel his chest tighten...aware of the possible danger lurking in the shadows. Raising his eyes heavenwards, Merton prayed for safe passage.

Reaching the edge of the forest, Sergeant Azar reined his horse and turned in the saddle. "Move as quietly as you can and stay alert." Resting a hand on the hilt of his sword he led them into the forest.

His body language and the tension in his voice did little to comfort Irene. Gripping the reins she hunched in the saddle as the mare followed the lead guardsmen deeper in among the trees.

Blackwing followed; flying low he skimmed the ground, his ebony feathers gleaming in the sunlight glinting through the forest canopy.

Chapter 18

Rolo and his friend Troy raced into Wedon village, their faces red…eyes wide with fear.

"Soldiers are coming!" They yelled.

Villagers rushed from their homes and crowded round the two boys. "Which direction are they coming from?" Grimes the shop keeper asked. "Were there many?"

The boys pointed behind them. "We counted six soldiers," Troy stammered.

Rolo nudged him. "Don't forget the two people who weren't soldiers."

Troy nodded; he could feel his face redden as agitation increased. "They'll be here soon, we'd better hide. I'm going to fetch my dad from the forge." Pushing through the crowd, he ran down the street as fast as he could.

Grimes clapped his hands together, the crowd hushed. "I'm closing my shop, I suggest we all go to our homes and stay hidden."

Without hesitation the crowd dispersed, leaving the street empty and eerily quiet.

Racing home, Rolo burst through the front door. Locking it, he leaned against the wood, panting…trying to catch his breath.

His parents appeared from the sitting room. His father Rafus stood in the doorway, staring at Rolo through narrowed eyes. Imigin peered at her son over her husband's shoulder, her face pale with worry.

"What on earth is going on?" Rafus demanded. "It sounded like the hounds of hell were after you."

Placing a hand on his chest Rolo took a few deep breaths. "Soldiers are coming, father," he stuttered. "Grimes told us to stay inside and lock the doors."

Imigin pushed past her husband and cradled Rolo. "Oh Rafus, what should we do?"

Her husband's jutting chin and firm stance gave her confidence. Feeling Rolo tremble, she stroked his hair.

"We stay put," Rafus said firmly. He went to the window above the sink and peered out.

"Can you see them, father?"

"No son, we're too far out of the village."

"Does that mean we'll be safe?" Imigin asked.

Hearing the nervous tremor in her voice, he smiled and took her hand. "If God wills," he said softly.

Imigin suddenly wailed and pulled her hand free. "Oh my, Rafus, we've forgotten about, Safi."

"Where is she?"

"I asked her to fetch more wood for the stove."

"Stay here, I'll fetch her." Rafus pulse raced as he unbolted the door. "Lock it," he instructed, closing it behind him.

"Be careful, husband." Imigin called softly.

❦❦❦

Irene shivered and pulled her jacket closer. Beneath the forest canopy it was chilly. She knew her discomfort was more to do with the memories of traveling this once dark and frightening path with Stagman, rather than it being excessively cold. This time however, the soft sunlight filtering through the branches endued the forest with a magical...benign quality.

In single file they plodded on and by mid-afternoon found themselves on the outskirts of Wedon. Remembering Imigin and Rafus, Irene smiled. *I wonder how they are; it would be so good to see them again.* She chuckled as Rolo filled her thoughts. *I bet he's all grown up, now.*

Turning in the saddle, she rested a hand on Flame's rump and asked Merton if they could stop in the village? "I have friends there," she explained. "It would be so good to see them again."

"We are stopping at Wedon, My Lady. We hope to find refreshment in the village pub. It's a long journey home so the horses will need rest and water."

The word home brought a warm flush to Irene's cheeks. With a happy smile she faced front and urged Flame to increase her pace.

After a while they left the forest path and followed the mud road into the village. It was strangely quiet for the time of day; not a

129

soul to be seen, not even a cat or dog. The small shop was closed and the pub looked abandoned.

Lifting his hand, Sergeant Azar brought them to a halt outside the pub, dismounting he tied his horse to a post.

His men followed suit. Merton and Irene remained in the saddle.

Sergeant Azar's face creased in a frown, as he stared at the deserted pub. "What's happened here?" Peering through the grubby window, he muttered. "Where is everyone?"

The small troop gathered round in defensive mode, their hands on the hilts of their swords.

Chewing her lip, Irene shifted in the saddle.

"I don't like this," Merton said glancing nervously around. "I think we should move on."

Sergeant Azar nodded. "I agree, but the horses need water and time to rest." He indicated to a trough at the side of the building. "As each man waters his horse; the rest of you stay alert."

Perched on the pub sign, Blackwing gazed around, his bright eyes missing nothing.

"Can you see anything?" Irene asked.

"No, the village looks deserted."

Irene tugged at the collar of her jacket. *This is crazy, where is everyone?* The hairs prickled on the back of her neck. "I'm going to find my friends," she declared urging Flame forward.

Sergeant Azar grabbed her reins. "No, My Lady, you must stay here. It's possible we are being watched."

"I don't care; I need to find my friends. I'm worried about them." Irene pulled on the reins. "Please sergeant let me go," she begged.

Unsettled by the tense atmosphere, Flame snorted; showing the whites of her eyes she shook her head and reared.

"Whoa there!" Sergeant Azar took a tighter grip on the reins and tried to calm the frightened horse.

"Let me go, sergeant." Irene cried. "Merton can come with me."

Merton kicked Sage forward bringing him alongside Flame. Sage's presence steadied the mare. "It's okay, sergeant, you can let her go." Merton noticed the flush of red on the sergeant's

130

cheeks…his furrowed brow. "Don't worry, I'll go with her," Merton said, hoping his voice sounded calm and reassuring.

"Alright, but one of my men will accompany you."

Irene could tell by his rigid stance…there was no point arguing. "Thank you sergeant," she said meekly.

The sergeant nodded and turned to a guardsman. "Go with Lady Irene and Merton," he ordered.

The guardsman swung into the saddle and drew alongside Irene.

With Irene sandwiched in the middle they walked their horse slowly down the road, each one watchful and tense.

Irene noticed a curtain move in one of the cottage windows. "The people are here," she whispered to Merton. "I saw a curtain twitch."

Merton nodded. "So did I."

"Me too," the guardsman hissed. "I wonder why they're all hiding. What are they afraid of?"

Irene shrugged. "Hopefully my friends will be able to tell us."

Flying ahead of them, Blackwing skimmed over the ground; alert for danger.

৵৵৵

Rafus hurried towards the wood shed and saw Safi approaching with an armful of logs. "Drop them Safi, come here quickly." She appeared not to hear, or see him. "Safi!"

She nodded acknowledgement, but continued to look over his shoulder.

Hearing the sound of hooves, Rafus swung round. His eyes widened and his mouth dropped open. "Irene!" Clasping his hands to his chest he beamed with delight as Irene pulled Flame to a halt and slid to the ground.

"Rafus, you're still here." Irene ran and hugged him. "I can't believe it! It's so good to see you."

"You also," he said. "Have you returned for good?"

Irene nodded. "Yes Rafus, I'm here for good." She turned to Merton and the guardsman. "This is Merton; he is Prince Zatao's manservant. Gesturing to the guardsman, she gave the man an inquiring look.

"Oh, sorry My Lady, my name is Amdor."

131

"Merton and Amdor are part of an escort sent by Prince Zatao." Irene explained.

Urging Sage forward, Merton bowed his head. "It is an honour to meet you sir."

Rafus's eyebrows rose in surprise as he returned the greeting.

Irene noticed Safi and acknowledged her with a smile.

"Where are Imigin and Rolo?" she asked looking towards the cottage.

Smiling at her puzzled look, Rafus took her hand. "Come," he said.

As they approached the cottage, the door slowly opened and Imigin peered out. Seeing Irene beside Rafus, she gasped and clutched the bodice of her dress. "Oh my, is it really you?" She opened her arms wide as Irene rushed towards her.

Rolo stood in the doorway watching as they hugged. "It's Irene!" he said gazing up at her.

Rafus laughed. "Indeed it is son."

Releasing Imigin, Irene stooped to embrace Rolo. "It's so good to see you again."

"Have you come to stay?" Rolo asked.

Irene nodded. "Merton and the guards are taking me to Stag...I mean Prince Zatao." The delighted twinkle in Rolo's blue eyes made Irene smile.

"Awesome!" he said raising a podgy fist. "Shall I go and fetch the other guards, father?"

"Are the rest of the villagers still hiding?" Imigin asked him.

"I think so."

"I tell you what," Rafus said patting his son's shoulder. "I'll fetch the remaining guards, you go to Grimes. Tell him friends have arrived and there's nothing to fear."

Imigin smiled and clasped her hands. "Excellent, the guards can put their horses in the paddock, I'm sure the donkey won't mind." Turning to Merton and Amdor she gestured towards the side of the house. "The paddock is around the back, when you've settled your horses, please come to the cottage."

Dismounting, Merton nodded his thanks; but his eyes were fixed on Irene.

Touching his arm, she smiled. "I'm quite safe Merton. Stop worrying."

"Very well, My Lady, if you're sure?"

"I am Merton. Please take Flame to the paddock for me." She handed him the reins.

Merton hurried the two horses towards the rear of the cottage. Guardsman Amdor followed him at a brisk trot.

Imigin chuckled. "It seems that dear man is concerned for your safety." She studied Irene. "They call you My Lady; is there something we should know?"

Seeing the anxiety in Imigin's warm hazel eyes, Irene gently squeezed her arm. "I have no idea why they call me that, and I'll be honest I'm not comfortable with it." She gazed pointedly at Imigin. "You are to call me Irene."

Imigin sighed with relief. "God forbid we should show you any disrespect!"

"Stop fretting, you haven't!" Irene chuckled at her troubled expression. "It is so good to see you all again."

"And you my child, and you." Turning to Safi, Imigin took her hand. "Irene, this is Safi, she is staying with us for a while. She and her husband Koren ran the pub; sadly he died in violent circumstances, which is why the pub is closed." Imigin put her arm round the girl's shoulders.

Safi lowered her head, chewing her bottom lip to quench the tears.

Irene hurried to her side and took her hand; it felt cold. "How awful for you; I'm so sorry."

"Thank you," Safi said in a hushed voice.

Irene gently squeezed her hand. "If there's anything I can do to help, please tell me."

Brushing a strand of mousy hair away from her face, Safi stared at Irene. "You are very kind, My Lady, but there is nothing you can do."

Gazing into grey eyes clouded with grief. Irene's heart filled with compassion.

Imigin gently stroked Safi's hair. "She has suffered a horrific trauma, and will stay with us for as long as necessary."

Safi's grateful smile didn't erase the pain in her eyes.

Imigin could see Irene and Safi were close to tears, to assuage their emotions, she grabbed their hands and led them indoors. "Come on now, we have food to prepare." Her brusque manner veiled her own compassion, while at the same time motivating them. In no time the small kitchen echoed to the clatter of pots, pans and food preparation.

Irene frowned as she watched Imigin, "I'm afraid we can't stay long," she said softly.

Imigin handed her a bowl of freshly picked peapods. "I know, but you have enough time to eat one of my chicken stews. They're legendary you know."

Irene chuckled. "There are enough peas here to feed an army."

Imigin looked up from dissecting a large chicken. "I am feeding an army," she said.

Irene laughed, and was delighted to see Safi's lips flicker in a smile. Sitting at the table they put the bowl between them, and shelled the peas.

⊰⊰⊰

Merton opened the gate to the paddock and led the horses through. On the far side of the paddock an old grey donkey sheltered under the boughs of a large oak tree. The animal's large ears twitched as he eyed them with half-hearted interest.

Merton held the gate open for guardsman Amdor. "Please hurry, I don't wish to leave Lady Irene alone for too long."

"Why are you so concerned?" Amdor asked as he tied his horse to the fence and undid the girth. "I'm sure she is safe with these people. She seems to know them well."

Merton rested Sage's saddle over the fence and undid his bridle. "My master instructed me to keep her safe."

Amdor watched him fumbling with Flame's girth and pushed him aside. "Here let me, you're all fingers and thumbs. Go and check on Lady Irene."

"Thanks," Merton said. Hurrying away from the paddock he rounded the side of the house as Sergeant Azar arrived with the rest of the guardsmen.

Rafus and Rolo followed them, with Grimes and a few villagers in tow. "Put your horses in the paddock round the back," Rafus shouted. "Show them Rolo," he said, pushing his son forward.

The arrival of the guardsmen calmed Merton. With a relieved sigh his tension evaporated. Peering through the kitchen window he

134

smiled at the sight of the women preparing food. The smell of frying onions drifted on the air; Merton's nose wrinkled in anticipation.

He jumped as Sergeant Azar's heavy hand gripped his shoulder. "Smells good, eh?"

Merton looked up at him and grinned. "It certainly does. I didn't realise how hungry I was!"

Imigin poked her head through the window and smiled. "The food won't be long. Find a place to sit, and when the food is ready Rafus will bring it out to you." She noticed Grimes the shop keeper and some of the villagers hovering on the periphery. "That goes for all of you," she said with a chuckle.

Chapter 19

Safi reached for a pea-pod and accidently brushed Irene's hand. "Excuse me," she said.

Irene gave her a warm smile. "Is Safi your real name?" she asked.

Safi looked up from shelling her peas. "My full name is Saffiera, but my husband always called me Safi." She sniffed and wiped her nose. "I can't believe he's gone."

Irene touched her arm. "I'm so sorry. Can I ask what happened?"

Safi finished shelling the final pod and handed the bowl of peas to Imigin. "He was stabbed to death," she said.

Irene's breath caught in her throat. "That's awful. Who would do such a thing?"

Imigin joined them at the table. "We have no idea. Safi and her husband Koren ran the village pub. On this particular evening three strangers arrived...no one knows who they were, or where they came from."

Irene felt Safi tremble beside her. She could see fear in the young woman's eyes as she recalled the horrifying events of that night.

"They were horrible." Safi said, burying her face in her hands. "You could feel the evil emanating from them." She burst into tears. "I've never been so scared."

Imigin patted Safi's hand and glanced at Irene. "Rafus went to the pub that night, but I confess, I didn't want him to go. The weather was awful...dark and stormy." She paused and lowered her eyes. "I was so relieved when he came home, but now I—"

Safi sobbed and clutched her hand. "Stop it, Imigin! If Rafus had stayed I'm sure they would have killed him too."

Tears trickled down Irene's cheeks as she watched the two women embrace. She didn't know what to say. There were no words.

Taking a hanky from her pocket she blew her nose. "I can't believe something so awful could happen in this small village."

Imigin released Safi and fetched the coffee pot. She sighed as she poured the strong black liquid into three small cups. "Drink this," she said, pushing a cup towards Safi.

Irene studied Safi as she sipped her coffee. The young woman's courage impressed her. "What will you do now?" she asked.

Lowering her head, Safi stared impassively into her cup. "I don't know," she murmured. "I can't stay here much longer." She raised her head as Imigin placed a gentle hand on her shoulder.

"You can stay with us for as long as you need."

Safi's lips flickered in a smile of gratitude. "Thank you, Imigin. But my cousin Verne and his family should arrive in a day or two."

Imigin glanced at Irene noting her puzzled expression. "Verne is taking over the pub from Safi," she explained.

Safi got to her feet and paced. "Never again will I go inside that pub," she said using her sleeve to wipe beads of perspiration off her face. "I couldn't bear it." Tears glistened in her eyes. "I need to get away from this village...try to forget what's happened." Slumping in her chair she fought to control her emotions.

"Where will you go?" Irene asked.

Safi sighed and ran a hand through her hair. "To be honest, I don't know," she said softly.

Safi's distress tugged at Irene's heart. Without thinking she blurted out. "You could come with us."

Stunned, Safi and Imigin stared at her.

Irene pouted and shrugged. "Well, you can't stay here for ever." She gestured with a hand. "Imigin's home is lovely, but small." Glancing at Imigin she quickly added. "I mean no offence."

"None taken," Imigin replied with a smile.

Safi patted Irene's hand. "Your offer is kind, but you are going to the Prince's castle. There is no way I would be allowed to accompany you."

"Oh yes there is! Leave it to me." Irene rose to her feet and squared her shoulders. Glancing back she smiled before hurrying outside.

Safi joined Imigin at the sink. "What do you think she's going to do?"

Through the window they watched Irene approach Merton.

Imigin chuckled. "Irene has changed since I last saw her. She is stronger and more determined...not only that, she has influence with the Prince. So I believe if she wishes you to join her in the castle... join her you will!" She turned to Safi. "If it is what you want?"

Safi nodded. "I have nowhere else to go, and I like Irene."

Imigin pulled her into a side hug. "Good, all I want is for you to heal and be happy."

Smiling, Safi rested her head on Imigin's shoulder.

⋘⋘⋘

Merton's stomach rumbled as he lounged on the grass with the guards. *I hope we eat soon, I'm starving.* Seeing Irene stride towards him he scrambled to his feet. He hoped she was coming to tell them the food was ready. However, her determined expression quickly dispelled that hope.

Irene's heart thumped as she reached Merton. *Right, how do I tell him I want Safi to come with us?* Clenching her fists she stared him in the eye.

Merton recoiled at the directness of Irene's gaze. "How can I be of help, My Lady?"

"I want Safi to come with us," she blurted out. Seeing the surprised look on Merton's face, she relaxed. "I think you'll agree it's awkward for a woman to be alone with all these..." she gestured with her hand at the reclining guardsmen. "The company of another woman would be beneficial for me, and I'm sure it would please, Prince Zatao." She gave him a persuasive smile.

Seeing the determined set of her jaw, Merton knew there was no point arguing. "Indeed, I see your point. However, I will need to speak with Sergeant Azar before making a decision."

"Great, ask him now, please." Irene noticed the amused twinkle in Merton's eyes as he bowed his head and went in search of the sergeant.

⋘⋘⋘

Grinning with success, Irene hurried to the cottage; the small kitchen was a hive of activity, with Safi, Rafus and Rolo putting plates heaped with chicken stew and thick slices of crusty bread onto trays.

"Can I help?" Irene asked.

"No!" was the unanimous response.

Imigin pointed at the table. "Sit down, Irene; I have your food here." She placed a bowl in front of her. "Rest and enjoy your meal."

"I admit I am hungry, and this is delicious," Irene murmured, between mouthfuls.

Rafus and Rolo took the food to the guardsmen, while Safi and Imigin joined Irene at the table.

Lowering her spoon, Safi stared at Irene. "What did you say to that man?"

"I told him you will be coming with us." Tearing off a chunk of bread, she mopped up the gravy in her bowl. Safi's wide eyes and open mouth made her smile. "He will inform the sergeant and get back to me."

"What if the sergeant says no?"

Imigin chuckled. "They can't say no to Irene."

"True," Irene said.

A tap on the door interrupted them. Merton popped his head round. "Excuse me, My Lady, may I have a word?"

Irene followed him out. "What are the arrangements?"

Merton glanced across at the sergeant and shuffled his feet. "He's not happy about it, but does agree, the company of another woman would be better for you. Nevertheless, if mistress Safi is to come he wants her to ride behind a guardsman…" he paused, his eyes searching the men reclined on the grass. "Ah, there he is Guardsman Romure." He pointed the man out to Irene.

Guardsman Romure saw them look his way and got to his feet. "I am pleased to be of assistance, My Lady." He bowed low. "Your friend will be safe with me."

"Thank you guardsman; I'm sure she will." Supressing a giggle, Irene gazed up at him. He was a giant of a man! Irene liked his twinkly blue eyes and wondered why she'd not noticed him before. Smiling with delight, Irene hurried to tell Safi the good news. She burst through the door and grabbed Safi's hand. "You are coming with us."

Safi put a hand to her face and stared at Irene. "Really, I can't believe it!"

Irene smiled at the relief on Safi's face. "It's all sorted. You need to pack your belongings, we will be leaving shortly."

"Oh, Irene, how can I thank you?" She burst into tears and threw her arms round Irene's neck.

Irene hugged her. "There's no need to thank me. I'm delighted to have your company." A sudden thought occurred to Irene. She gently eased Safi away. "Can you ride a horse?"

Safi shook her head.

Irene frowned and tapped her chin. *This could be a problem.*

Imigin drew alongside Safi and placed a supportive arm round her shoulder. "She's a quick learner, Irene; don't worry."

Safi smiled and squeezed Imigin's hand. "Imigin is right, Irene. I'll be fine, I promise."

Seeing the determined glint in Safi's eyes encouraged Irene. "Okay, as long as you're sure. You will be riding with guardsman Romure." She glanced out of the window. The guardsmen were leading their horses from the paddock. "It looks like they're ready to leave, hurry and get your things."

Safi dashed into the sitting room and returned with a small bundle.

"Is that all you have?" Irene asked.

Safi nodded. Dropping the bundle on the ground she embraced, Imigin. "Thank you for all your help and support. I will never forget you."

Imigin placed gentle hands on either side of Safi's face. "You take care of yourself. Keep in touch, if you can."

"I will write, I promise." Safi retrieved her bundle and stood aside as Imigin approached Irene.

"Thank you for everything," Irene said, as Imigin embraced her. "It's been so good to see you again."

Imigin placed a kiss on Irene's forehead. "Seeing you here fills my heart with hope. Stay safe child."

Outside, the chaotic sounds of horses and men drifted through the window. Sergeant Azar could be heard bellowing orders.

Irene kissed Imigin…grabbed Safi's hand and pulled her towards the door. "Come on we must go."

Safi halted in the doorway. She turned to Imigin. "Please, tell Verne where I've gone."

Imigin smiled and gestured with her hand. "I will child. Now go, and may God protect you both."

ᷮᷮᷮ

Perched on the roof of the cottage, Blackwing's bright eyes gleamed with amusement as he watched the chaotic activity below. Stretching his wings, he relaxed in the warmth of the sun.

He looked up as a gentle breeze rustled through the tree tops. As he stared at the sky, out of the corner of his eye he saw a flash of white. He turned his head in time to see a small white bird fly past and vanish in the trees.

His eyes narrowed with curiosity. *That's the first bird I've seen close up. I wonder who it was.* His thoughts were interrupted by loud voices and movement below. It was time to move on.

Chapter 20

A milky dawn rose over Feritas castle and the surrounding lowland, its fragile light impotent against the early morning fog.

Muglwort and Sworn marched into the stable yard and scrutinised the four mounted warriors waiting for them. Their dark attire and concealed faces merged with the black horses they rode.

Pulling the hood of his cloak over his head, Zworn asked. "Will four be enough?"

Muglwort's eyes glinted as he snarled. "More than enough, these are four of the best from my own legion. One of these warriors would be enough! But to be sure we succeed; the King commanded we take a small troop."

Sworn grunted approval and mounted his horse.

Muglwort eased enormous hands into black leather gloves.

A stable lad approached leading a huge black stallion. With trembling hands he handed the reins to Muglwort.

Thumping one gloved fist into the palm of his other hand, Muglwort grabbed the reins and shoved the frightened lad aside. The stallion's excited squeals and clattering hooves reverberated around the yard. Muglwort yanked on the reins. "Stand!" he growled. Having quieted his horse he faced the men.

"You know our orders," he said glowering at them.

The men nodded staring at him with soulless eyes.

Clamping a fist around the hilt of his sword, Muglwort rose to his full height. "We ride hard...we ride fast. But when we reach the land of Luminaire we move with stealth, keeping to the forest paths." Throwing the reins over his horse's neck, he leapt into the saddle. "Failure is not an option, do you understand me?"

Each man responded by thumping his chest with a gloved fist.

Returning their salute, Muglwort led the way out of the castle. In single file they descended. Following the steep track they passed the cluster of houses nestled at the base of the hillside.

Through the swirling fog, the villagers heard the thunder of approaching hooves...panicked and fled to their homes.

Amused by the peoples fear, Muglwort and Sworn chuckled.

Reaching the base of the hillside the six warriors melted into the fog. Shrouded in swirling obscurity, they galloped towards their goal, the distant mountain and the land of Luminaire.

The snow-capped peak of the great mountain rose above the fog as though beckoning them on.

Muglwort slowed his horse and raised an arm. "Slow down!" he yelled.

Zworn and the warriors reined their horses. The animals clustered around, agitated and flecked with sweat.

Muglwort stared around, waiting for his racing heart to slow. He revelled in the call to action...loved the adrenalin rush.

Zworn eased his horse alongside Muglworts, his eyes focused on the mountain. "We've made good time." He grinned at the glint of victory he saw in Muglwort's eyes.

Muglwort nodded in agreement. "It's close; soon we'll cross the border into Luminaire." Flicking the reins, he spurred his horse forward.

Zworn and the warriors followed him.

Riding at a steady canter they reached the base of the mountain. Easing to a walk they traversed the large clearing in single file. Scattered over the ground were the skeletal remains of ersatz and goblins. The bones were picked clean and bleached by the sun.

Muglwort sneered. "Useless!" he growled. He stared at the forest bathed in early morning sunshine and clenched a fist. "This land will be ours. We will have the victory."

Zworn heard him and chuckled.

The horses picked their way between rocks and bones as they followed Muglwort towards a break in the trees.

"There's the path," he said pointing. "Be as quiet as possible. I don't want our presence revealed."

Entering the forest, the warriors vanished unseen into its depths. It was noon when they reached the small clearing a few miles from the village of Wedon.

Muglwort dismounted and wiped the sweat from his brow. "Okay this is it. Now we wait."

Zworn leapt off his horse and joined him. "How long do you think they'll be?"

Muglwort frowned as he looped his horse's reins over a branch. "Your guess is as good as mine." He turned to the four warriors. "Get off your horses' and conceal them among the trees. We could have a long wait."

With the horses hidden in the shadows, the six men slumped to the grass their ears tuned to every sound, blood pumping with the anticipation of what was to come.

❖❖❖

Irene smiled as she watched Safi ride behind Guardsman Romure. The young woman's arms were wrapped so tightly around him, Irene wondered if the man could breathe. She stifled a chuckle as she recalled Safi's initial reaction to the sight of Romure's huge bay horse. However, the guardsman's charm soon calmed her, and she had giggled like a school girl when he lifted her with ease onto the stallion's broad back.

Irene clicked her tongue urging Flame to keep pace with Romure's horse. Behind her, Merton and three guardsmen followed. Irene's thoughts turned to Imigin and Rafus and for a moment a lump rose in her throat, she sniffed.

"Are you alright?" Merton asked.

Irene raised a hand. "I'm fine. I was just thinking about Imigin and the family. It was so good to see them again, even if only briefly."

"They are nice people."

Irene nodded. "Yes, they are. I hope I get to see them again."

"I'm sure you will." A sudden concern made the hair rise on the back of Merton's neck. *I need to tell Prince Zatao about the people of Wedon. They could have need of his protection.* He frowned and took a tighter grip of his reins. Raising his head he saw Sergeant Azar standing in his stirrups and pointing to the left.

Irene turned in the saddle. "Merton, what does he mean?"

"He wants us to leave this path and take a secondary. It will be a longer journey, but safer than the main path."

"Why? I don't understand."

Seeing the confusion in Irene's eyes, Merton sighed. He didn't want to tell her, but felt he should. "I don't want you to worry, but

144

Prince Zatao believes a trap has been set for us in a clearing a few miles from here."

Irene's eyes widened. "How does he know that? Why on earth would anyone want to trap us?"

Beads of perspiration peppered Merton's forehead as he tried to find the words to explain. He slumped in the saddle as Sergeant Azar trotted towards them.

"Come on, move along we don't have all day," Sergeant Azar shouted as he turned his horse and returned to the head of the column.

Merton exhaled with relief as he followed Irene onto the narrow path. *I shall have to tell her at some point, but at least now I have time to find the right words.* He frowned. *How do I tell her there's a traitor in her new home? And the country she has chosen to adopt is on the brink of war.* Merton clenched a fist. *There are no right words. Whatever I say, will scare her!*

Sergeant Azar's booming voice startled, Merton.

"Keep moving!" He bellowed. "Don't stray off the path."

⚘⚘⚘

Blackwing flew ahead of the small troop. Perching on a branch, he pecked at the bark in search of grubs. *I wonder why they've left the main path.* He chirruped a greeting as Irene passed under the tree.

Looking up, she smiled at him. "There you are! Don't lose sight of us."

Blackwing rolled his eyes. "As if," he muttered. Preening his feathers he watched them pass beneath the tree. A movement above his head alerted him; he flinched and shifted under a leafy branch.

"It's alright. I mean you no harm."

Blackwing stared around searching for the owner of the voice.

"I'm here, look to your left."

Blackwing's eyes flashed with impatience. "I don't see you!" he snapped.

Psalm chuckled and flapped her wings. "Goodness! You will have to be more alert if you're to survive here."

Blackwing scowled at her. "You sneaked up on me."

"Exactly, and if I could, so could those who mean you harm." She flew to his branch and perched beside him. "My name is Psalm; I'm a friend of Irene's."

"My name's Blackwing and I am also her friend."

Psalm cocked her head. "I know, Irene told me."

"She did, when?"

"I spoke to her when she was hiding at the cottage."

"I didn't see you."

"Exactly, need I say more?"

"Tck!" Blackwing responded.

Psalm's eyes twinkled as she asked. "So how do you know her?"

"In my world, Irene used to feed me raisins. When she vanished through strange moving water, I followed." He slumped on the branch. "Now I'm stuck here."

Seeing the anxiety and sadness in his eyes, Psalm hopped closer. "It's alright, don't be afraid."

Flicking his tail, Blackwing snapped. "I am not afraid!" Seeing her tilted head and quizzical expression, he insisted. "I'm not."

"I believe you. Like I said its okay, there are plenty of blackbirds here. I'm sure you will settle in well."

As she spoke, Blackwing's heart raced, he felt giddy with relief.

Seeing the hope in his eyes, Psalm smiled. "When we reach our destination, you will love it."

Blackwing lowered his head and studied her. "How do you know where we are going?"

"I know, because I live there." Psalm lowered her voice and stared him in the eye. "You know Irene has come here to be with Prince Zatao."

Blackwing nodded and moved closer to her. The conspiratorial atmosphere made him nervous. "Irene told me she'd come here to be with someone. I didn't know it was a Prince." Cocking his head to one side, he asked. "Why are we whispering?"

Psalm stared at the surrounding forest, her sharp eyes penetrating the shadows. "Danger is everywhere," she said softly. "Warriors from another land are waiting in a clearing a few miles from here. They don't know we've left the main path."

"What are they waiting for?"

Psalm frowned as she explained. "They are here to kidnap Irene."

"Tck" Blackwing said crossly. His voice faltered as he asked. "Why do they want Irene?" His eyes widened as he realised the seriousness of their situation. "What if they find out we've left the path and follow us?"

"Shush, stay calm," Psalm said. "They want Irene because they know her capture will weaken our Prince." Raising her head she peered around. "We are safe for the moment; this path is so narrow and restricted they won't risk a confrontation."

"What can we do?" Blackwing asked.

"There's not much we can do. I will return to the castle and inform my mistress of the situation. You continue to follow Irene and her guardsmen. If there is any sign of danger give your raucous warning call. I have friends in the forest who are aware of the situation and will respond, so don't worry." She hopped onto a branch above his head and prepared to fly off.

Flying up beside her, Blackwing asked. "Are you sure they won't follow us?"

"I'm sure; but they won't give up either, Irene couldn't have chosen a worse time to return."

Chapter 21

The seer trembled as King Murkier strode across the room towards him. The king's robes swirled...dust rose in his wake.

The seer fell to his knees. "My Liege, forgive me." His voice faltered. "I apologise..."

The King raised a hand dismissing his explanation. "For your sake, I hope the news is good."

The seer raised his head. The King's dark stare and tapping foot did little to dispel his anxiety. The news was bad and the small man could think of no way to sugar coat it. *Oh my, how do I tell him?* Wringing his hands he struggled to find the right words.

The Kings foot tapping increased in intensity. "I'm waiting." he growled.

Slumped on his haunches, the seer dropped his head. "We have failed, My Liege," he mumbled. His dry throat threatened to choke him; he swallowed hard and stared at the ground. Peering under his lashes he saw the King move closer. His heart pounded in his ears...he struggled to breath.

The King's voice was deceptively soft as he asked. "What did you say?"

The seer could feel the colour drain from his face; his voice faltered. "We have failed." Trembling, he raised his head and stared into the King's blazing eyes.

King Murkier towered over him, his fists clenched. "Explain failed!" he demanded.

"I saw the woman; she is with Prince Zatao's guards. They were on the forest path a few miles from the clearing where your warriors are waiting." He paused.

"Continue," the King growled.

The seer's voice stuttered as he tried to explain the small troop's sudden disappearance. "They simply vanished! One minute I could see them, the next they were gone. I can only assume, Prince

Zatao knowing the geography of his land, found a path so well hidden they might as well be invisible."

"No!" the King's booming voice bounced off the walls. The edge of his cloak caught the seer in the face as he swirled around and paced the floor. Striding across the room he glared at the man lying in a crumpled heap...stared into frightened eyes pleading for mercy. "You have let me down for the last time!" The King roared.

Blood oozed from a cut on the seer's cheek. Cowering on the floor he raised a shaky hand and covered the wound, blood seeped through his fingers. He tried to speak but his throat constricted.

Leaning over the seer, the King pointed a well-manicured finger at him. When he spoke his voice was low and menacing. "Instruct my men to return. I will deal with you later." He swung round and left the room, slamming the door behind him.

Struggling to his feet, the seer leaned heavily on the table. His hands trembled as he pulled the round mirror closer and stared into its dark depths; his own ashen face stared back at him. Closing his eyes he took a few deep breaths, gradually his racing heart slowed. Sitting on his wooden stool he clutched the mirror in both hands and waited. Grey swirling fog clouded the glass; allowing his mind to go blank he stared into it. After a moment the fog cleared and an indistinct image appeared. His knuckles showed white as he gripped the mirror and concentrated.

Staring into the glass he saw Muglwort and his men reclined on the grass...dozing. Closing his eyes the seer placed his bloodied hand over the image and mumbled incoherent words. After a moment the image faded. The seer slipped off his stool and slumped to the floor, unconscious.

⁂

Muglwort's eyes shot open. Brushing beads of sweat from his brow, he scowled and eased away from the tree he was using as a back rest.

Sprawled on the grass beside him, Zworn peered up out of one eye. "What's wrong? You look like you've seen a ghost."

Muglwort grunted and jumped to his feet. "Come on, get mounted we're leaving."

Zworn and the four warriors roused themselves and stared blankly at him.

Ignoring them he strode over to his horse. "It looks like the plan has changed." Leaping into the saddle, he waited for them to mount up.

Zworn nudged his horse closer. "What's going on? We should wait, they'll be here soon."

Muglwort shook his head. "No they won't. I had a weird dream…I heard a voice telling us to come back."

"What! You're kidding me." Zworn stared at him. "You're ordering us back because of a dream. What makes you think it was true? It will be our heads if you've got it wrong!"

Grumbling among themselves, the four warriors nodded in agreement with Zworn.

Muglwort sat tall in the saddle and squared his shoulders. Their stony expressions made him nervous…he sensed dissension. Even Zworn his long-time friend was glaring at him. "Look, I can't explain why I believe the dream. I just know it's true. In the dream I saw Zatao's men leave the main path. I tried to follow but heard a voice calling me back." He paused and raised a hand. "You're going to have to trust me. Whatever happens, it will be on my head."

"You're damn right it will!" Zworn said raising a fist. "Why can't we follow them?"

Muglwort stared into the distance; closing his eyes he tried to remember what he'd seen. "The path they travel is nothing more than a narrow track. Unless you know it's there, it's impossible to find." His leather glove squeaked as he balled a fist and glared at them. "Don't you think I want to go after them?" With a frustrated growl he spurred his horse forward. "I know the voice I heard in the dream; it's the King's seer. He speaks with the King's authority. We have to return."

⇜⇜⇜

Irene's head drooped; tiredness cloaked her like a heavy blanket. Shivering in the afternoon chill, she pulled her jacket closer. Peering through the forest canopy she could see dark clouds gathering.

Merton followed her gaze. "It looks like it's going to rain," he said.

Turning in the saddle, Irene nodded. "I hope it doesn't."

"Indeed My Lady." His brow furrowed. "You look cold and tired."

"I am." Facing front, Irene eased her feet from the stirrups. Her legs were stiff and aching.

Merton shook his head as he watched her. "I will see if we can stop and rest."

"That would be good, thanks Merton." Irene slumped in the saddle; holding onto the pommel she let her legs swing.

Sitting astride Guardsman Romure's horse, Safi heard their conversation. Releasing her tight grip on Romure's tunic, she turned and peered at Irene. "Are you alright?"

"I'm fine, just cold and tired. You seem to be getting the hang of riding," Irene said noting Safi's relaxed demeanour.

Safi placed a confident hand on the horse's rump. "It's not so hard, once you get used to it."

Guardsman Romure burst out laughing. "Perhaps I'll dismount and see how she does on her own."

The look of terror on Safi's face made Irene smile.

In a flash Safi turned and wrapped her arms round Romure's waist. "Don't get off," she pleaded.

Romure chuckled; his blue eyes twinkled as he patted her hands. "Fret not, little maid. You're safe with me." Romure heard her sigh, felt her head rest against his back. Her closeness awakened feelings long buried. Aware of his racing heart, Romure squared his shoulders and urged the horse forward.

They plodded on, the pace torturously slow. When they first took the path, it appeared reasonably wide and unobstructed. However, as they progressed Brambles and thick bushes obstructed their progress. Now, the path they traversed was barely wide enough for a man, never mind a horse. Occasional low branches forced them to duck their heads.

Irene's mount, Flame, became increasingly agitated...shaking her head and snorting. Irene wasn't overly concerned, with three horses in front and four behind there was nowhere for Flame to go. Nevertheless, Irene replaced her feet in the stirrups and took a firmer hold on the reins.

Merton could see the tension in her shoulders, but there was nothing he could say or do. Standing in his stirrups he tried to see what was going on up ahead. He could see Sergeant Azar and a guardsman had dismounted. They were using their swords to cut a swathe through the undergrowth. Raising a hand, he shouted.

"Sergeant, will we be stopping soon?" His voice resonated in the relative quiet of the forest...heads turned with surprised expressions.

A guardsman at the front shushed him.

Feeling colour rise up his neck, Merton slumped in the saddle. "We need to rest," he muttered.

Sergeant Azar paused in his attack on the foliage. "I heard you, Merton. Keep your voice down. It's possible there might a place to rest further on."

Irene looked round and smiled at Merton. "Thank you," she said softly.

"You're welcome, My Lady."

The small troop continued on. Pine needles carpeting the moist ground muffled the thud of the horse's hooves. The only sound to impinge on the silence...the thump of steel against shrub and branch as Azar and the guardsman battled to clear the overgrown path.

Irene sighed; fidgeting in the saddle she tried to find a comfortable position for her numb behind. Leaning forward she patted Flame's shoulder. The mare plodded behind Romure's horse, her head low her ears back. Irene could feel the animal's exhaustion.

Rubbing her tired, gritty eyes, Irene stared enviously at Safi. The young woman rested against Romure's back...obviously asleep. Irene wished she could do the same.

❧ ❧ ❧

Blackwing flew ahead his bright eyes alert for danger. So far he had seen nothing untoward. Apart from a few skittish deer and numerous rabbits, the forest appeared uninhabited...strangely quiet.

Rising higher, he perched on a pine branch and peered through the forest canopy. "Tck," he grumbled. "Looks like a storms brewing." Launching off the branch he flew lower, skimming the forest floor. *Now I know why it's so quiet.*

He flew on until he lost sight of the guardsmen and eventually found himself on the edge of small clearing. He chirruped with excitement. *Good place to take a break. I'll go back and tell Irene, she looks like she needs a rest.*

Skimming through the trees he flew past Azar and the guardsman still hacking through the undergrowth. Settling on a low

152

branch adjacent to Irene, he called out. "There's a small clearing up ahead." He could see a flicker of relief in Irene's eyes.

"Really! Are you sure?"

"Tck," Blackwing shook his head. "I'm the bearer of good news and you doubt me."

"I'm sorry, Blackwing. After riding on this path for so long it came as a surprise."

"A pleasant one I hope."

"Oh yes," Irene grinned and turned in the saddle. "Did you hear that, Merton? There's a clearing, and it's not far away."

Sighing with relief, Merton replied. "I did My Lady...good news indeed."

Irene turned to Blackwing. "Go and tell Sergeant Azar. They must be exhausted, this news will encourage them."

Blackwing nodded and flew to the front of the column, where Sergeant Azar and the young guardsman were still hard at work.

Hearing the news Azar smiled and lowered his sword; wiping the sweat from his brow, he slapped the younger man on the shoulder. "That's good news, eh Garth."

The young guardsman nodded, encouraged by the positive glint in Azar's eyes.

Azar raised his sword, and attacked a low branch with renewed vigour. "Come on son," he encouraged. "We've not far to go now." Pausing to catch his breath he stared ahead. *I pray God; this clearing is safe, and not a trap.*

Chapter 22

Psalm soared above the tree tops, wishing she could fly higher and faster. But fear of attack from predatory birds forced her to stay low. However, her anxiety for Irene and the guardsmen outweighed all other concerns. *I hope they're safe. If there is trouble, I hope Blackwing remembers what I told him to do.*

Her heart fluttered in her chest as she pushed herself to the limit of endurance. *I'm too old for this!* Her breathing accelerated as she searched the terrain below for a glimpse of Castle Eternus. *I must be close...surely.*

Flying above a copse of tall pines, she caught her first glimpse of the castle. "Oh thank the heavens." Drawing close to the castle, she flew to her mistress's window; dropping down, she settled gently on the deep window ledge and tapped the glass with her beak.

Panting, she slumped on her tummy and tried to catch her breath. Looking through the glass she could see the room was empty. *Oh dear, I hope she comes soon.*

Mira had heard the dove's arrival...heard the insistent peck at the glass. Leaving her dressing room, she hurried across to the window. Opening it, she retrieved the bird and carried her across the room to the bed.

Psalm lay on the coverlet, her wings outstretched her beak gaping. She needed to speak...needed to share her information, but for the moment breathing was her main priority.

Mira gently stroked her back. "Take your time little one." Seeing the spark of gratitude in the dove's eyes, she smiled. "Can I get you some refreshment?"

Psalm shook her head. She would have liked a drink, but at the moment swallowing was not an option. She could see the anxiety in Mira's eyes as she rose from the bed and hurried to the bathroom. A minute later she reappeared with a small ball of cotton wool. Curious, Psalm watched her approach.

Mira sat on the edge of the bed and gently supported Psalm's beak. "You need refreshment little friend." Placing the cotton wool close to Psalm's open beak she squeezed it; cool water flowed into the dove's mouth and trickled like a refreshing stream down her parched throat. Mira smiled, and asked. "Is that better?"

"Thank you," Psalm said her voice no more than a whisper. "I will be myself in a minute or two." She gratefully accepted the last drops of water Mira squeezed from the cotton wool.

Placing the cotton ball on the bedside dresser, Mira watched as Psalm slowly revived. "Thank God you're alright," she said. "I fear the task I gave you was too taxing, my apologies."

"No mistress, apology is not needed, I pushed myself. The news I bring is grave; I could not afford to delay." Pausing she stared anxiously around the room.

Following her gaze, Mira quickly reassured her. "It's alright Psalm, you can speak freely we are alone." Mira fingered her necklace as she waited for the dove to speak.

Gazing up at her mistress, Psalm lowered her voice. "When Irene and the guardsmen left the main path to follow the forest track, I decided to see if their caution was truly necessary. I flew above the main path keeping out of sight as much as possible." Her dark eyes clouded as she stared at Mira.

Mira placed a trembling hand over her heart. "What did you see?"

Psalm shuddered; her voice faltered as she spoke. "In a clearing a few miles from the village of Wedon, I saw six warriors...dark men, tall as trees... armed as though for war. Their horses were as black as night; at first I didn't see them as they were camouflaged in the shadows." She stared into Mira's troubled eyes. "My Lord the Prince was right; advising his guardsmen to leave the main path saved their lives."

Mira nodded, a deep frown etched her brow. "I must tell Zatao!" Wiping her hands on her skirt she rose to her feet. "Thank you my friend," she said. "The information you've brought is invaluable."

Psalm bowed her head. "It's a pleasure to be of assistance My Lady. Should you need me again I am at your service."

"Actually, there is something you could do." Mira moved across to the window. In the far distance she could see the mountain peak towering above the forest, thoughtfully she tapped her chin.

Psalm watched and waited. "Are you alright My Lady?" she eventually asked.

Mira's lips flickered in a smile as she turned and glided to the bed. "Do you live far from the mountain?" she asked.

"Not far My Lady. Why do you ask?" Tilting her head she gazed at Mira.

The dove's curiosity spurred Mira. Resting on her elbow she leaned closer. "Do you see much of Ezekiel? How is he?"

"I saw him a few months ago. He is old, and doesn't get around much. But on the whole he is well."

Mira sighed with relief. Sitting up she smoothed her skirt. "Do you think he would be fit enough to spy for us? I hate to ask, but—"

"I'm sure he would be delighted too, My Lady." Psalm lowered her head. "I apologise for interrupting you."

"Oh don't worry Psalm. I'm thrilled to hear he is well and still with us."

Psalm chuckled. "Indeed he is, My Lady. He remains as grumpy and impatient as ever."

Mira burst out laughing. "I love that old rodent."

Psalm's eye twinkled with amusement. "We all do. His oldest son, Prince Hood is a real chip off the old block…strong, brave and equally as annoying as his father. However, I believe both father and son; in fact the whole rodent clan would be honoured to assist you My Lady. As we know from past experience, not much gets past them. They are a mine of information." The little dove stared at her mistress. "Do you wish me to go to them?"

"Yes, if you would, Psalm. You have confirmed our worse fears. We were aware riders trespassed into our land, but we had no idea how often, and it would be helpful to know." She sighed and twisted a long coil of hair between her fingers.

Psalm moved closer. "Don't fret My Lady. Our enemy will not succeed."

Mira smiled as she gently scooped the little dove into the palm of her hand. "Thank you, Psalm, now come let me take you to the window. You need to get home before night falls."

156

Prince Aldrin reclined in a chair in front of the fire; his legs outstretched his hands behind his head. A discreet smile flickered at the corners of his mouth as he watched his brother pace the library floor. "Zatao, for goodness sake, you'll wear out the carpet."

Prince Zatao's eyes flashed with impatience as he swung round to face his brother. "As I've explained we are in dangerous times. My concern over my friend's safe arrival is justified."

Aldrin lowered his arms and straitened in the chair. "I understand, but working yourself into a frenzy of worry achieves nothing." He stared into his brother's troubled face. "You have done your best to keep her safe. You couldn't have chosen a better man than Sergeant Azar. If anyone can bring her here safely, he can."

Zatao lowered his tall frame into the chair opposite. With his elbows on his knees he rested his chin in his hands and stared into the fire. "I hope you're right," he said softly.

Both men turned at the sound of a gentle knock on the library door.

"Come!" Prince Zatao rose to his feet as Mira entered.

❧❧❧

Closing the door Mira paused before hurrying across the room to Zatao. She stared into his troubled face; the dark shadows under his eyes were evidence of lack of sleep. "You look tired my brother."

Ignoring the statement he took her hand. "What news?" he asked as he guided her to his chair by the fire. Moving behind Aldrin he rested his hands on the back of the chair, and studied her. The pallor of her skin and tense body language did little to ease his anxiety.

Mira tried to relax as she looked from one brother to the other. Prince Zatao stood behind Aldrin his handsome face clouded with worry; while Aldrin appeared curious and somehow vaguely amused.

Picking at a loose thread in her skirt, Mira stared at Zatao her eyes boring into his. She glanced quickly at Aldrin, then back at Zatao. *I wish I could speak with him alone.* Lowering her head she pulled at the thread.

Prince Zatao gripped the back of the chair. He could see her dilemma…knew what she was thinking. "Mira," he said gently.

Raising her head, Mira gazed into his dark eyes.

157

Prince Zatao took a calming breath and gave her a nod of encouragement. "You may speak freely, tell us what you know. Is Irene safe?"

Mira leaned forward; keeping her voice low she shared everything Psalm had told her. "Ordering them to leave the main path was wise Zatao. It saved their lives. It seems there were six warriors waiting in a clearing not far from Wedon."

Zatao's eyes widened, he gripped the back of the chair.

Seeing his concern, Mira raised her hands. "It's alright; Irene and everyone with her are safe. They are struggling to navigate the forest track, but Psalm thinks they will be here by late evening." Zatao's relieved expression brought a smile to her face. With a sigh she relaxed in the chair.

Prince Zatao glanced at the clock on the mantle. "They are making good time."

Mira nodded.

Leaving his chair, Aldrin grabbed the poker and stabbed at the burning logs on the fire. "What about those six strangers? Where did they go?" He asked. "They had no right to be here!"

Mira and Zatao exchanged a furtive glance. They could feel the tension radiating off him.

Gazing at him, Mira said calmly. "Psalm's not sure, but as she made her way here she heard the sound of distant hooves; so one must assume they've left. However, she is going to visit the rodent, Ezekiel. As you know his home is close to the border, so he will be able to let us know for sure."

Aldrin returned the poker and faced them. "I hope you're right and they have gone, for all our sakes." His brother and sisters scrutiny made him nervous. With clenched fists he strode from the room. "I'm going to bed."

Zatao eased into Aldrin's chair. Resting his elbows on the arms he steepled his long fingers, and stared into the distance...deep in thought.

Mira's heart sank as she watched him.

Zatao's eyes darkened as he returned her gaze. "We have a problem," he said softly.

Lowering her head, Mira brushed away a tear. "I know."

Rising from his chair, Zatao went to her; taking her hands he pulled her to her feet and embraced her. "Do not be concerned, sweet sister," he said softly in her ear. "Trust me."

Mira raised her head and stared into his eyes. The determination she saw in their depths filled her with confidence. Burying her face in his chest, she felt the coolness of his silk shirt against her cheek...heard the rhythmic thud of his heart. "I do trust you, Zatao," she whispered.

Putting a hand under her chin, Zatao raised her head. "I'm leaving now to meet Irene."

Mira pulled away and clutched at his shirt. "May I accompany you?"

"No Mira. I need you to stay here."

"But I so want to see her! Why can't I go with you?"

Zatao frowned as he eased his shirt from the clutch of her fingers, and strode to the door.

"Why can't I go?" Mira persisted. "You shouldn't go alone."

Zatao smiled. "I won't be alone. My trusted guard will accompany me." Taking his belt and sword from a hook by the door, he buckled it round his waist and put on his leather jerkin. Seeing Mira's crossed arms and tight-lipped expression, he chuckled.

Mira scowled at him and snapped. "It's not funny. You know how much I want to see Irene."

In two strides he reached her and took hold her hands. Staring into her eyes, his penetrating gaze silenced her. "I can't allow you to come, Mira; as I don't know what danger awaits us." He paused and stared thoughtfully over her head. "I dare not have all my eggs in one basket," he said softly.

"Please, stay here in the safety of the castle. Arrange food and liquid refreshment for when we return." He cocked his head to the side, his eyes pleading...a cheeky grin on his face.

Mira smiled, she knew the look from when he was a little boy. "Alright, I will do as you wish and stay here."

"Good, I am pleased." Zatao sighed inaudibly as he embraced her.

Mira wrapped her arms round his waist. "Be careful my brother. Return safely with Irene."

Zatao nodded. "God willing, we will return soon."

❧❧❧

Outside the closed door Aldrin paused and raked a shaky hand through his hair. He could hardly breathe. He listened to their muted voices but couldn't hear what they were saying. Putting a fist over his chest he tried to calm his racing heart. Glancing at the library door, his lips curled in anger. *I think they know, but I must allay any further suspicion.* With a scowl he hurried upstairs to his suite. Slamming the door he leaned against it. "They can prove nothing," he growled.

A sudden thought occurred to him. His jaw clenched. "I need to have a word with that little red head—if she betrays me!" In one fluid movement he swung round, pulled a dagger from his belt and threw it at the bedroom door. The dull thud of steel embedded in wood, and the gentle rock of the daggers handle satisfied his frustration and fear. *Betraying me will be the last thing she ever does!* His lips twisted in a cruel smile at the thought.

Chapter 23

Psalm soared over the forest canopy; her eyes fixed on the distant mountain. Behind her vibrant tones of red and gold bathed the evening sky, tinting the snow covered mountain peak in reflected hues.

Keen to reach her destination, Psalm weaved and soared pushing herself until every muscle ached. She could feel her heart pounding as she flew.

Skimming over the forest the trees gradually thinned; ahead she saw a vast clearing. A crystal clear lake mirroring the colours of the setting sun shimmered in the evening light. *Mercy falls; I wish I had time to stay and rest for a while.*

Setting her face she flew on. Below her the foaming waters of Mercy Falls cascaded into the lake below. The deafening roar assaulted her ears, as though urging her to stop and rest. She sighed. "I must keep going, I'm nearly there." Rising on a warm thermal she soared towards the mountain. The opportunity to help her mistress was all the impetus she needed.

She was breathing heavily by the time she reached the mountain. "Oh, thank the heavens, I've made it." Flying low she perched in a large oak tree and took a little time to catch her breath. Peering at the ground she spotted movement. Fluttering to a lower branch she waited until her eyes adjusted to the dim light of evening.

Rustling leaves and an occasional squeak told her the rats were up and about. "Hello," she called softly.

A young female scurried up the side of the trunk towards her. Seating herself on a large bough, she stared at Psalm. "Who are you? What do you want?"

"I am a friend of King Ezekiel. I would very much like to see him, it's important."

The sandy coloured doe tilted her head and studied Psalm. "How do I know we can trust you?" Her long whiskers twitched as she waited to be reassured.

Psalm's eyes twinkled as she returned the young doe's gaze. "Tell him Psalm the dove wishes to speak with him. He'll know who I am." She lowered her voice. "Tell him it's urgent!"

"Wait here." With a twitch of her long tail the young doe turned and scurried down the tree.

Psalm watched her race towards a burrow. A few minutes later she reappeared with a troop of rats in tow. Psalm flew down and perched on a branch a foot or so from the ground. Patiently, she waited as the rats cautiously approached her. "There's no need to be afraid," she called. "Have you not heard the expression, harmless as a dove?"

"And have you not heard the expression, don't trust everyone you meet."

Psalm chuckled. "Is that you Ezekiel? You old grump."

Below her, the troop separated allowing a huge elderly male to lumber through their midst. "Yes, Psalm it's me. Long-time no see."

"Oh Ezekiel, it's so good to see you. Sorry it's been so long."

Ezekiel lowered his heavy frame to the ground and stared at her. "I gather this is not a social call."

Psalm stared into his ruby eyes, still bright with life; unlike his fur...once so thick and snowy white...now wispy and in places bald. With a sigh she fluttered down beside him. "Princess Mira asked me to come to you. She wants to know if you've seen strangers cross this border into our land. If so, how often did they cross, and how many were there?"

Before Ezkial could answer, a big white rat with a black head pushed through the gathering throng. "Let me pass!" he ordered.

"My son," Ezekiel said, turning his head to welcome the young male.

Psalm bobbed her head as the large buck approached. "It is good to see you again young Prince."

"You too," Hood said. Settling beside his father he studied her. "How can we be of help?" he asked.

"She has come at the behest of Princess Mira." Ezekiel explained. "She wishes to know if we have seen strangers cross our border."

Hood's black eyes narrowed, his fur bristled. "Indeed we have! A few days ago two men dressed in black, riding mighty horses galloped across the border and disappeared into the forest towards the village of Wedon, they returned shortly after. Then again, early this morning we were disturbed by pounding hooves and the clatter of armour. Whoever they were disappeared into the forest before we could see them." Licking a paw, he wiped it over his face.

As Psalm waited for him to continue the same young doe she'd met earlier scurried forward. "They came back this way a few hours ago," she squeaked. "There were six of them."

Hood glared at her. "I'm telling her, not you."

Ezekiel cuffed him. "Do not speak to your sister that way." He turned to Psalm. "Fawn is right they galloped through here some time ago."

Psalm fluffed her feathers hoping it would hide her trembling. "Oh dear, but at least they've returned to their own land."

"Yes, but will they come back?" Hood asked.

"Probably," Psalm replied. "That's why we need your help."

"What can we do?" Ezekiel asked.

"Would you be willing to spy for us? Letting us know who enters our land uninvited. You can liaise with me through the birds of the forest, I will keep my mistress and Prince Zatao informed." She noticed Ezekiel's ruby eyes moisten at the mention of Prince Zatao.

"How is our Prince?" he asked. "I miss him."

"He is well; although understandably, the threat of war burden's him at the moment. Actually, I—"

Ezekiel studied her, huffing with impatience at her reticence. "What is it? Tell me."

He drew closer and stared into Psalm's face. "What are you not telling me?" he demanded. His ruby eyes flashed as he waited.

Averting her eyes, Psalm stared at the ground. *Oh dear, I'm not sure I should tell him about Irene?* Raising her head she returned his gaze. "I'm not sure if I should say anything."

"Say it!" Ezekiel demanded.

Psalm jumped at the tone of his voice. "Okay, keep your hair on. Irene has returned to us," she blurted out. "There, now I've told you."

Ezekiel stared open mouthed at her. "Irene is back?"

163

Psalm nodded. In a tremulous voice, she said. "As we speak, she is making her way to Castle Eternus. Prince Zatao sent his man servant and a company of guards to escort her."

Ezekiel raised his eyes to heaven and sighed deeply. "How wonderful, I can't wait to see her. Will she be here for long? Will she stay in the cottage or with Prince Zatao?"

Flapping her wings, Psalm cried. "Whoa! Too many questions, I can't answer them all at once." Ezekiel's sparkling eyes and excited posture warmed Psalm's heart. She realised she'd done the right thing telling him about Irene. "My dear old friend, as far as I know she's here for good and will be staying in the castle."

Ezekiel beamed at the rats congregating around him. "Do you hear that? My friend, Irene has returned to us. Some of you will remember her."

"Will she come here?" A rat shouted from the periphery of the group.

"I don't think she will," Ezekiel replied.

Fawn scuttled closer to him. "Won't we be able to meet her father? We've heard so much about her, and what she did for us."

"I don't know my little Princess." Ezekiel's excitement ebbed slightly as he turned to Psalm. "Do you think it would be possible? I would so love to see her again before it's too late."

Psalm stared into his ruby eyes. The longing she saw in their depths tugged at her heart. "I will speak to my mistress. I'm sure something can be arranged. I know Irene would wish to see you." Ezekiel's beaming smile and invigorated stance was all the thanks she needed.

"Thank you, Psalm. I know you will do your best." He stared up at the moonless sky and surrounding trees. Night had settled over the forest like a dark blanket. He turned to Psalm. "I know it's late, but can we offer you some refreshment before you leave?"

Psalm shook her head. "No thank you, I must go home. My family will be wondering where I am."

Ezekiel nodded. "Very well, I understand. Be assured we will keep a careful watch on our border. No one will cross that we don't know about."

Psalm fluttered to a high branch. "Thank you old friend, your assistance is much appreciated." Spreading her wings she launched into the night sky.

"Stay safe!" Ezekiel called. He heard her reply float back on the night air.

"And you too."

Ezekiel's eyes moistened as he stared after her. It was so good to see her again. Like old times.

Hood stood beside him, gazing into his face. "Are you alright father?" he asked.

Ezekiel could see the concern in his eyes and gave him a gentle nudge. "Yes, my son." Turning his head he stared at the rats grouped around him...waiting for him to speak. Ezekiel cleared his throat and swished his tail. "We have been given an important job." He said in a loud voice. "It is our responsibility to guard the border of our land." He studied the expectant faces staring at him. Some, particularly the does, looked at him with frightened eyes. The younger males including Hood fluffed their fur and swished their tails with excitement.

Ezekiel took a deep breath. He remembered the last time Irene visited their land. *We were victorious then, and we will be again.* His determination buoyed, he squared his shoulders and continued. "From now on when we forage at night, be even more alert and keep your eyes peeled."

"What about the daylight hours?" a couple of the rats asked.

Ezekiel frowned. "That's a good question."

A few of the younger does pushed forward. "We could do it," a large black doe said. "After all, hiding and keeping watch isn't dangerous, anyone can do that!" She stared round at the bucks and giggled. "We won't fall asleep," she said to the does nearest her."

Her last remark was greeted with irritated grunts.

Ezekiel huffed. "This is serious...not a game."

Fawn hurried to his side. "Please, father, let us do it."

Eager faces stared at him, willing him to say yes.

"Very well," Ezekiel said with a prolonged sigh. "You will be in two's, different pairs each day. And there will be no playing or noise!" He stared pointedly at Fawn, before focusing on the other does. "Do you understand me?"

Giggling with excitement, they nodded.

Ezekiel's ruby eyes flashed. "I am serious!"

Fawn gently rubbed against him. "Don't worry father, we won't let you down."

"It won't be me you let down, it will be Prince Zatao. We have been asked to assist our Lord at this perilous time, and assist we will." Rising to his feet he lumbered towards the den. "I'm going to rest. Stay alert, keep watch and let me know if you see or hear anything untoward."

Chapter 24

Sergeant Azar led his horse into the clearing. Squinting, he glanced around, before beckoning the others to follow him. Standing to the side he watched his men file past. "It looks safe enough," he said. "But we need to remain alert."

As Irene rode by he nodded respectfully. Seeing Merton he frowned. *He looks done in! But he'll recuperate, if we rest here a while.*

Handing his horse's reins to a guardsman, Azar patrolled the perimeter of the clearing. Finding the source of the stream brought a smile to his face. The water ran clear. Kneeling down he placed his hand in the cool water, cupping it he scooped a handful to his mouth. It tasted good.

Continuing his march around the clearing, he found the path that would take them out of the forest. It appeared wider and less overgrown than the path they had travelled for so long. Quietening himself amid the noise of men and horses he stared into the surrounding forest. Peering into the shadows, his eyes searched for any sign of danger. However, he could see nothing untoward...his senses tuned over many years of military service assured him they were alone. Nevertheless, he determined to remain alert, their lives depended upon it.

⩊⩊⩊

Sighing with relief, Irene urged Flame into the clearing and dismounted. As her feet touched the ground, her legs felt like jelly and threatened to give way. For a moment she leaned against Flame; clutching the pommel of the saddle she waited for the life to flow back into her legs.

She looked up as Merton came alongside. He looked tired and pale. Irene smiled at him. "Are you alright?"

"I'll tell you when I'm on terra firma," he said with a wry smile.

"Be careful how you get down," Irene warned. "I still feel legless."

Merton groaned as he disentangled his feet from the stirrups and struggled out of the saddle. His pained expression increased as he waited for his legs to support him. "Goodness, I see what you mean. My legs feel as though they don't belong to me."

Irene left Flame to graze and went to him. "You'll be okay in a minute," she said taking his arm. Supporting him she gazed around.

The troop and their horses filled the clearing. The small space rang to the sounds of clanking armour, snorting horses and the relieved laughter of guardsmen.

Irene patted Merton's arm. "Will you be alright?" She asked. "I want to see how Safi is."

Merton nodded. "I'm fine My Lady, you go."

Irene walked across the clearing to where Safi still sat on Guardsman Romure's horse. As she approached, Romure raised his arms and lifted Safi down.

Seeing Irene, Romure smiled. "She's still a bit sleepy," he said supporting Safi while she got her land legs.

Safi rubbed her bleary eyes and smiled at Irene.

Grinning at her, Irene asked. "Do you want to come with me and have a drink?"

Safi nodded and took Irene's hand.

As the two girls weaved their way between men and horses; Sergeant Azar's loud voice brought a hush over the clearing.

"Keep the noise down," he ordered. "We will stay here long enough to rest and water the horses."

⋙⋘⋙

Irene led Safi towards the stream. Sitting on a couple of boulders they watched the activity in the clearing. Guardsmen loosened their horse's girths and stood around chatting as the animals grazed.

Amid a chorus of complaint a young guardsman handed round pieces of dry bread.

Sergeant Azar growled as he moved among them. "If you don't like it, soak it in water. It's all there is till we get home."

Irene turned to Safi. "Do you want something to eat?"

Safi shook her head. "I'll have a drink."

Both girls knelt by the stream, and scooped the cold water into their mouths.

"It tastes good," Safi said. Cupping some in both hands she threw it over face. "Ooh, its cold."

Irene did the same and gasped as the cold water bathed her face. "It's certainly refreshing!" Using the sleeve of her jacket she wiped away the excess water and returned to her boulder. With a muted sigh she gazed unseeing at the surrounding forest. Remembering the time she'd sat with Stagman in a similar place brought tears to her eyes. *This is weird, like de ja vu.* Pulling a hanky from her pocket she blew her nose.

Safi tilted her head to one side as she watched her. "What's the matter? You look sad."

"I'm not sad. It's just sitting here like this brought back a memory."

"From your expression it looks like a sad one." Safi said.

Irene smiled and shook her head. "Not really, it's a memory that stirs various emotions."

Sensing Irene didn't wish to discuss it further, Safi refrained from asking more questions. Pulling her light weight jacket closer she fiddled nervously with a loose button.

Glancing at her, Irene wondered if she'd done the right thing bringing her along. *I suppose it was a bit presumptuous of me to assume there would be work for her in the castle.* She frowned; *I couldn't leave her in Wedon.* Resting her elbows on her knees she cradled her chin and sighed softly. *I'll talk to Mira about it, I'm sure something can be done to help her.* Thinking about Mira and Prince Zatao made her heart race.

Sitting there, she hadn't realised how insecure and vulnerable she'd felt. However, seeing Merton and the guardsmen allayed her fears. The Prince wanted her...making sure she arrived safely. The thought brought a warm flush to her cheeks. Placing the back of her hand on her face she could feel the heat. Safi's quiet voice broke in on her thoughts.

"How do you know they will allow me into the castle?" she asked.

Irene took her hand. "Because you're with me, they will." She stared into Safi's grey eyes. "Trust me, there's nothing for you to worry about."

"But I'm afraid, Irene." Her voice quivered. "Where will I live? What work will I do?" Pulling her hand out of Irene's she wiped away a tear.

Irene put a comforting arm round her. "There's no need to fear Safi. I'll take care of you, I promise."

As Irene reassured her, Merton hurried towards them. "The horses are rested, My Lady. We must move on. Sergeant Azar says if we ride without stopping we should reach the castle in a couple of hours."

Irene smiled and took Safi's hand. "Come on," she said. "It's time to go home." The word home settled in her like a familiar friend, bringing lightness to her step and joy to her heart. Her smile widened as she sat astride Flame and watched Romure help a giggling Safi onto his stallion.

With every one mounted, they left the clearing and followed Sergeant Azar into the forest.

Irene glanced back. Behind them the setting sun bathed the clearing in soft tints of gold. *So beautiful*, she thought. *Maybe it's a good omen*. The light bathing the clearing emphasized the deepening gloom of the forest, and for a moment a shadow smothered Irene's joy. *This is a different time, it's not like before*. Shifting in the saddle she chewed her lip. *So why do I feel anxious?* Realising she was gripping the reins she released her hold. Breathing deeply she rotated her shoulders in an effort to relax.

Riding behind, Merton could see her tension, he understood her anxiety. All around the strange light of dusk conjured weird shapes and shadows…flitting like spectres through the ever encroaching forest. Slumped in the saddle, Merton pulled his jerkin close against the evening chill. *This journey is bad enough. I'm glad Irene is unaware of the danger threatening our land*. His thoughts were interrupted, as his horse Sage stumbled throwing him forward. Righting himself he patted the horse's neck. "Nearly home boy," he said softly, praying his words were true.

❧❧❧

King Murkier sat on his throne, his back rigid with tension. With his right hand balled into a fist, he pounded the arm of the throne, glowering as he visualised his seers face pulped beneath his fist. His momentary enjoyment was halted as the massive throne room door swung open.

King Murkier watched his guard usher Muglwort and Zworn into the room. Stroking his black beard he watched them approach; his eyes narrowed in anger. "Failure is unacceptable!" he growled. "You have returned without completing your mission." Leaning forward he glared at them.

Visibly trembling, Muglwort and Zworn dropped to their knees, lowering their heads until their foreheads touched the ground.

Muglwort's stomach knotted, as he raised his eyes and glanced at the King. "A thousand apologies My King, the fault is mine." Without a pause he hurried on, desperate to explain. "While we waited in the clearing I had a dream. In this dream the palace seer told us to return, as those we sought had taken another path."

King Murkier stood and moved away from his throne. "Rise, follow me."

Scrambling to their feet they followed him across the vast throne room to a narrow door.

The king opened it and led them onto a balcony.

Muglwort and Zworn joined him and stared down into a small courtyard. Situated at the side of the castle this was not an area they were familiar with. The two warriors stared at each other, eyebrows raised in confusion…unaware of the king's secret smile. Silently they stood together holding onto the wrought iron balustrade, their eyes glued to the courtyard below.

A door on the far side opened and a troop of palace guard marched into the courtyard. The cobblestones rang to the sound of their pounding feet. Halting beneath the balcony they stood to attention.

Folding his arms across his chest, King Murkier turned and fixed cold eyes on Muglwort and Zworn. "Look below to your left."

They followed his gaze. Below out of sight, unless one leaned forward was a rough wooden block. Standing beside it was a giant of a man with an equally large axe.

Before they had time to register what they were seeing; high pitched cries and shuffling feet filled the air, as two guardsmen dragged the screaming seer towards the block.

Seeing the king, he cried out, his voice high pitched and pleading. "Forgive me My Liege, please, give me another chance. I won't let you down."

"No you won't," the king growled. Nodding his head towards the block he silently ordered the guards to drag the seer to his place of execution.

The terrified little man showed surprising strength as he fought against the guards. "Wait!" he screamed. In the momentary pause, he fixed defiant eyes on the king. "You will fail," he shouted. "She who comes brings love and with it power!"

"Execute him!" the king bellowed.

Silent now; the seer bowed his head to the will of the axe man. The dull thud and crunch of bone signalled his end.

Swallowing a nervous lump in his throat, Muglwort glanced at Zworn. Their eyes locked in acknowledgment of shared anxiety. Both men had spent the majority of their lives in the service of the King, fighting his wars and keeping the peace…they were unfazed by death and violence. So why did the death of an unknown seer disturb them? No one outside of the King's chosen guard was privy to executions. So what had they done to warrant the dubious honour of witnessing this event?

Muglwort frowned as the answer slowly dawned. Beads of sweat glistened on his top lip as he realised the King was sending them a message. *This is what to expect if you fail me!*

With a satisfied grunt the king swung round and led them back into the throne room.

Both men remained silent as they followed him.

Grinning like a Cheshire cat, King Murkier settled on his throne.

Muglwort and Zworn made to kneel, but the King indicated they should remain standing.

Reclined on his throne, Murkier said. "All this excitement has wearied me." Running a hand across his brow, his eyes narrowed as he studied the two men. When he spoke his voice was low and strangely breathy. "What you have witnessed is a warning. I will not tolerate failure. I want the woman who has come to Prince Zatao." Rising to his feet he placed his hands on his hips. His eyes flashed, his lip curled in a frustrated snarl. "I will have her!"

Retaking his seat King Murkier breathed deeply and slowly caressed his beard. "If you succeed in capturing her, your reward will be great." He stared at them, his eyes hard and threatening. "Fail me—" turning his head he indicated towards the tall door.

His message was clear. Muglwort and Zworn remained silent, their heads bowed.

Having their undivided attention brought a smile to the king's face. "The spy in Prince Zatao's castle is liaising with my advisors Grouchen and Ergon. They in turn will liaise with you." Thumping the arms of his throne, he leaned forward.

Startled, Muglwort and Zworn raised their heads, their eyes meeting the king's cold stare.

"Between you come up with a successful plan, or incur my wrath! Now go, and do not fail me." His long cloak swished as he left the dais and strode towards a concealed doorway behind the throne.

With gritted teeth, Muglwort hurried out of the throne room. The responsibility to succeed rested on him…he could feel his heart thudding in his chest.

Zworn followed, his thoughts consumed with the task ahead. Clenching his fists, he asked. "When do we see the King's advisors?"

Muglwort halted his headlong dash and faced him. "I will have them brought to my quarters."

Zworn could see beads of sweat glistening on his friend's forehead…it did little to ease his anxiety.

Seeing the fear in Zworn's eyes, Muglwort growled and swung round. "Come on, hurry up. We've work to do."

Squaring his shoulders, Zworn followed Muglwort along the dimly lit corridor. The stone floor resonated to their pounding feet. "The rhythm of doom," Zworn muttered, as he gripped the hilt of his sword and strode after Muglwort.

Chapter 25

Mira stood on the castle steps watching Zatao instruct his men. Nervously, she fingered the pendant at her neck. *Oh God, keep him safe.* A chill breeze blew across the courtyard; she shivered and pulled her fur wrap closer, snuggling her chin into its warmth.

Zatao leapt into the saddle, turning August, he smiled and waved at her. The sight of her huddled in the cold brought a lump to his throat. "We won't be long," he shouted, in a vain attempt to encourage her. "Go inside, it's cold."

Backing towards the door she called. "God go with you, and bring you safely home."

Nodding assent, Zatao tightened his reins and spurred August forward. "Come on boy, we have an important task to complete. Irene is coming home." He smiled at the thought.

The stallion's ears flicked; sensing his masters excitement his pace increased as he led the troop over the wooden bridge. The horse's hooves thundered as they followed him across the parkland towards the forest. High in the sky, the silver moon bathed the castle in an eerie glow.

Reaching the edge of the forest, Zatao raised a hand and slowed the pace. He knew the forests shadowy depths were unaffected by the moon's light, so must be traversed with caution. Slowing August to a walk he turned in the saddle. "Follow me men, and stay close together."

Zatao knew he could trust August to safely navigate the forest path. "Lead on boy," he said softly. Loosening the reins he gave the stallion his head.

Shrouded in darkness the narrow path was hardly visible. All around the trees encroached; like tall sentinels they towered over the small troop. Not a breath of wind penetrated, silence wrapped around them, ominous…threatening.

Zatao pulled his leather jerkin close and gripped the hilt of his sword. He listened for any sounds, human voices, or approaching horses...there was nothing.

҂҂҂

Reining his horse, Sergeant Azar stood in the stirrups and peered through the ever increasing darkness. *Is it my imagination or are the trees beginning to thin out.* Resting a hand on his horse's rump, he told the guardsman behind. "Tell the others to wait here. You come with me." Azar urged his horse forward, the guardsman followed. Pushing through shrubbery and ducking under low branches they noticed the path gradually widen and the forest appear to recede.

Azar pulled his horse up. His brow furrowed as he stared around. "This is strange," he muttered.

The guardsman came alongside. "Have we found the main path, sir?"

Azar grunted and wiped a sleeve across his brow. "I'm not sure, son. But it looks like it. Go and fetch the others."

As the young man rode away; Azar dismounted. Allowing his horse to graze he stared around. *I'm sure the Prince's map showed the track we are on, continues all the way to a large clearing.* Patting his horse's neck he watched as the others appeared out of the forest. Shortening his reins, he pulled his horse away from the grass, put a foot in the stirrup and swung into the saddle.

Irene heeled Flame close to Azar's horse. "Is there much further to go?" she asked. Even in the darkness, she noticed the concern in Azar's eyes.

Merton joined them. "Can we stop here and rest awhile, sergeant?"

Azar shook his head. "If we're on the right path, there should be a clearing a few miles that way." All eyes followed his pointing finger. Moonlight filtering through the tree tops illuminated the path ahead of them. "I know we're all tired...horses too. Nevertheless, we take this stretch of road at the gallop. Stay together and follow me." Without another word, he spurred his horse forward.

Irene, Merton and the guardsmen followed, pushing their horses to keep up with him. The forest echoed to the drum beat of hooves.

Blackwing flew ahead; even in the darkness his bright eyes missed nothing. Flying low, a hundred yards or so ahead of Azar, he noticed the path narrowing…the forest encroaching. *I must warn them!* Flexing his tail he did a quick U-turn and raced back. His strident calls were drowned by the thunder of hooves.

Slowing his flight he rose in the air, turned and flew alongside Azar.

Azar eased his horse back a-pace. "What is it?" he shouted.

"Up ahead, this path narrows and disappears into the forest again."

Azar frowned, "I can't hear you." Raising his arm, he signalled for everyone to slow down. "Stop for a moment," he shouted. Pulling his horse up, he waited as the others gathered round.

Steam rose from the horses bodies. The strong smell of sweat filled the air.

Azar turned to Blackwing…perched on a branch above his head. "Right, what were you trying to say?"

Blackwing rolled his eyes and fluffed his feathers. "I was trying to tell you that up ahead this path narrows considerably, and disappears in the forest."

The disappointed groans from those clustered around, irritated Azar. "Quiet!" he snapped. "From here on we walk the horses, they need to cool down."

"Can I get down and walk?" Irene asked.

"No, I'm sorry My Lady. We must remain mounted and alert at all times."

Irene sighed and glanced at Merton. He looked red faced and hot.

Merton half smiled at her and shrugged his shoulders. He too, would prefer to walk for a while. Nevertheless, he knew Sergeant Azar was right. If anything were to happen while they were on foot—well, it didn't bear thinking about. "Sergeant Azar is right, My Lady," he said.

Sergeant Azar's voice boomed in the silence. "Yes, I am! So, if you're ready, follow me."

Irene looked up as she passed under Blackwing's branch. "Thanks for the warning."

"You're welcome. Shall I fly ahead and see how close you are to the clearing?"

"Yes, that would be good." Raising a finger at him, she pleaded. "Blackwing, don't fly so low; something could easily catch you."

"Tck," he said. "We Blackbirds always fly low. I'm much too fast and nimble to be caught."

Irene sighed. "Have it your own way, but don't say I didn't warn you." She couldn't help smiling as she watched him skim over the ground and disappear among the trees.

✄✄✄

Irene rode alongside Merton, her reins loose, her hands resting on the pommel of the saddle. "Is it much further?" she asked.

Shaking his head, Merton said wearily. "No My Lady, once we reach the clearing, it's less than a mile or so to the castle."

Irene sighed and briefly closed her eyes. "Thank goodness for that; being in this saddle for so long, I'll be as stiff as a board tomorrow."

Safi chuckled, loosened her grip on Romure's jacket and turned round. "Me too; this horse is so wide my legs will be permanently bandy."

Romure's eyes crinkled in amusement. "You can always walk my dear, if you are worried about your legs." Reaching behind he made to take her arm as though to help her to the ground.

Squealing with laughter, Safi pulled back. "No! It's alright I can live with bandy legs."

"If you're sure," Romure teased.

Their interaction brought peals of laughter from everyone, and for a brief moment tiredness and anxiety vanished.

✄✄✄

Listening to them, Sergeant Azar couldn't help a brief smile as he guided his horse deeper into the forest and back onto the muddy track. *I pray we're on the right path.* The thought of being lost, plus responsibility for Irene's safety unnerved him. His stomach churned... he found it hard to distinguish between hunger and nerves.

177

Sighing, he rubbed the back of his neck and peered through the tree tops…grateful for the slivers of moonlight that managed to penetrate the forest canopy. Pressing his lips together, he squinted at the narrow track hardly visible in the dim light. He had hoped to reach the castle before darkness set in.

Aware of the danger, his body tingled with tension; his ears were tuned to every sound. His eyes searched the deepening shadows. Hearing a distant noise, he twisted in the saddle and raised a hand. Putting a finger over his lips he gestured to the leading guardsmen.

Two of them left the others and cautiously followed him. At a snail's pace they inched forward. The sound of muted hoof beats could be clearly heard coming towards them.

Reining his horse, Azar silently indicated they should dismount. Glancing nervously at each other they unsheathed their swords, and leading their horses, they crept forward.

⋘⋙⋘

Sighing with impatience, Irene asked. "Why do we have to wait here?"

Merton could understand her frustration. She was tired, they all were. "I don't know My Lady," he said with what he hoped was an encouraging smile.

Irene pursed her lips. "Well let's follow them." Urging Flame forward she tried to squeeze past Guardsman Romure's horse. However, the stallion's large frame blocked the narrow track.

Romure grunted as he steadied his horse. Raising his hand he glanced at Irene. "Stay back, My Lady. It's best we wait here. There could be danger up ahead."

Shivering, Irene pulled her jacket close and slumped in the saddle. Thoughts tumbled over each other in her mind. *Were they close to their destination? Would Zatao be pleased to see her?* Her stomach churned. Straightening in the saddle she eased the straps of her rucksack away from her aching shoulders. The brief movement helped to release her pent up tension. With pursed lips and jutting chin, she quashed her negative thinking, and allowed her mind to dwell on the exciting thought of reunion with the man she loved.

His presence filled her mind as though he were before her. His handsome face, framed by corn coloured hair, and eyes so dark and warm she felt she would need eternity to plumb their depths. Irene trembled at the thought of him …warmth suffused her body.

Safi's frightened squeals brought her back to reality with a start. In front of her Romure's stallion fidgeted and half reared, his skittish movements scaring Safi and disturbing the other horses.

Safi clutched Romure's jerkin. "What's the matter with him?" She cried.

Guardsman Romure took a tighter hold on the reins. "He's restless and feels the tension in the air. Just hold onto me and stay calm." Patting the horse's shoulder, he spoke softly.

The other guards were tense and alert, each man aware of the vulnerability of their situation. Standing single file on a narrow track, they could easily be picked off. Their anxiety was palpable.

Chapter 26

Prince Zatao reined August and signalled for the troop to halt. Tilting his head to the side he listened. His brow creased as he glanced at the captain of the guard beside him. "I don't hear anything. God willing they're safe, and on the right path."

"I hope so My Lord. The clearing can't be more than a mile or so away."

Zatao leaned forward and patted August's muscled neck. "Good boy, you've done well to get us this far." Urging the stallion forward they increased their pace. Zatao's mouth flickered in a smile as he gazed up at the forest canopy. *Thank God for a full moon.*

The path they travelled gradually widened as the forest receded, and a large clearing opened out before them. Bathed in moonlight the clearing looked strangely ethereal. Wisps of grey mist floated over the ground. Early frost coated the grass, glistening silver in the soft light. On the far side of the clearing a couple of grazing deer raised their heads...turned and melted silently into the surrounding forest.

Prince Zatao reined August to a halt under a massive oak tree. The troop gathered round him. Concealed at the edge of the clearing, they waited. Zatao whispered. "Stay mounted and don't make a sound." A slight breeze stirred the branches above their heads, leaves of red and gold floated slowly to the ground.

Pawing at the damp earth, August snorted and shook his head. His long, silky, mane shimmered in the moons glow.

Zatao's gentle pat calmed him. "Steady boy. It won't be long now." For a brief second his chest tightened as he focused on the far side of the clearing. *I hope it won't be long*! Removing a glove he blew on his chilled fingers, and silently prayed. The thought of Irene lost, and wandering around in the forest was too much to bear.

It seemed they stood there for ages, when suddenly a noise alerted Zatao. He noticed August's ears shoot forward...felt the stallion's body tense. Tightening the reins he held him steady. "Move back under cover!" he hissed. There was brief flurry of movement as his guard reined their horses back.

Peering through overhanging branches they watched as on the far side of the clearing, three men on foot cautiously left the safety of the forest...followed by their horses. The animals grazed the lush grass as the three men stared around the clearing, their swords held at the ready.

Zatao pulled an eye glass from his saddle bag and peered through it. His sharp intake of breath alerted his men.

The captain of the guard urged his horse closer. "Who is it, My Lord?"

Zatao smiled and handed him the eye glass. "See for yourself."

The captain whistled through his teeth. "If I'm not mistaken that's Sergeant Azar." With a relieved grin, he handed the eye glass to Zatao. "They've made it! Mind you, with Azar in charge I'm not surprised. He's a good man."

Zatao nodded. "Indeed, I felt he would be the best man for the job." Turning in the saddle, Zatao addressed the men. "We will stay under cover until Azar's party have entered the clearing, only then will we approach. Form a line behind me and stay back. There is no need for formality, we are safe."

The captain inched his horse closer. "My Lord, are you quite sure? You will be vulnerable away from us; I really think we—"

Zatao's raised hand cut him short. "Obey my order, captain! We are all perfectly safe." Zatao appreciated the concern he could see in his captain's eyes, but he knew they were in no danger.

Facing front he peered through the eye glass and watched Azar and the two guardsmen mount their horses. He saw Azar put two fingers to his lips, and give a soft whistle.

Zatao's hand trembled as he returned the eye glass to his saddle bag. Sitting tall in the saddle he took deep inaudible breaths. His heart raced...his mouth felt dry. *After all this time, she's here.* The thought of holding her in his arms brought a rush of colour to his cheeks.

Focusing on the far side of the clearing, he saw Azar and the guardsmen move their horses back as riders emerged from the forest. Zatao's heart pounded in his chest...his eyes widened. *There she is!* He swallowed, hoping to moisten his dry mouth...never before

181

had he felt so nervous. His emotions were in turmoil. Taking a deep breath he checked his attire, before urging August out of the trees into the clearing.

His guard followed at a discreet distance, forming a semi-circle behind him, they waited.

Smiling, Zatao watched Irene and the rest of her group emerge from the trees. Gazing heavenward, he stared at the star covered sky and whispered, "May God be praised, she is safe."

ॐॐॐ

Irene jumped at the sound of a whistle. It cut through the tension like a victorious trumpet blast.

The leading guardsman waved his arm and spurred his horse forward. "That's Sergeant Azar. Come on!"

Irene's heart leapt into her mouth as she gave Flame free rein to follow Guardsman Romure's horse.

"Wait for me," Merton shouted, as he kicked Sage, urging him to hurry up and follow the others.

Irene's mouth opened in surprise as they emerged from the trees. Mist wafted over the ground as high as the horse's knees. Shafts of moonlight reflected off its surface giving the large clearing a strangely magical quality...emphasised by the darkness of the surrounding forest. Irene had little time to dwell on the beauty of the scene, before Azar's voice called them to order.

"Stay together," he said. "I think it's safe, but once we leave the shelter of these trees we could be in danger."

Irene could hear him, but his voice seemed strangely distant. She was aware of the guardsmen surrounding Merton and herself, but somehow their presence didn't fully register.

Her attention was diverted, her eyes glued to the trees on the far side of the clearing. The hairs on the back of her neck prickled, her mouth felt dry. Hardly able to breath she placed a fisted hand to her chest. Cocooned in a bubble of silence, she stared wide eyed at the white horse slowly emerging from the darkness of the forest. In a voice breathy and faltering, she whispered. "Stagman." Tightening her reins, Irene kicked Flame, urging the mare to force her way through the guard surrounding them.

Sergeant Azar rode forward to stop her. "My Lady, stay—" His voice broke off as he caught sight of Prince Zatao. Flustered by

182

the unexpected sighting, he quickly raised a hand and called his men to order.

As the guard assembled in a line, Merton made to follow Irene.

Sergeant Azar blocked him. "Let her go. They will want a moment alone."

Merton glanced at him and nodded. "You are right of course. I find it hard to believe we have arrived safely and unharmed."

The sergeant smiled and clapped him on the back. "You've done well, Merton. Your task is complete, so relax."

Merton grinned and for a brief moment closed his eyes. His shoulders slumped with relief; it was a feeling no words could express. The trauma of disappointing his master, and nearly ruining his plan for Irene's rescue, vanished from his mind as he watched her ride across the clearing towards the Prince.

Guardsman Romure eased his stallion alongside Merton. He could feel Safi fidgeting behind him. "Keep still girl. You're making the horse nervous." Gripping the reins he steadied the jumpy stallion.

Safi ignored him; loosening her grip on his jerkin, she leaned towards Merton, and whispered. "Who is that, on the white horse?"

Looking up at her, Merton smiled. "It is My Lord, Prince Zatao."

Safi's hands trembled as she clutched at Romure. *Oh my. I've heard so much about him, and now I see him.* Resting her forehead on Romure's back, she sighed. *I should never have come!*

Sensing her fear, Romure reached back and patted her leg. "Don't be afraid little maid. Our Prince is a great and mighty man, but he is also kind. You have nothing to fear."

Safi chewed her lip as she held on to Romure. She wanted to believe him. But the sight of the Prince astride the big white horse left her breathless and afraid.

◈◈◈

Irene could feel her pulse racing. How she longed to urge Flame into a headlong gallop, but she knew the swirling fog could conceal uneven or dangerous ground, so she kept the mare at a steady walk, her eyes glued to the beautiful sight approaching her.

August appeared to glide through the fog. His luxurious mane floated extravagantly over his muscled neck, as soft and white as the mist beneath his feet. He snuffled a soft greeting as he drew closer.

Irene's eyes shifted from August, to his handsome rider; her Prince. Siting tall in the saddle, his dark eyes never left her face, his gaze welcoming…intense. His corn coloured hair hung loose around his shoulders, glistening gold in the moonlight.

Irene's eyes widened in awe as she gazed at him; under his gold edged cloak, he wore a frilled silk shirt open at the neck, black breeches, with knee length boots and a black jerkin. The sight of him took her breath away.

Glancing at her own clothing, her heart fell. She knew she looked a grubby mess. Her cheeks flushed with embarrassment. She had hoped for a chance to clean up before seeing him. Groaning softly she attempted to brush the dust and dirt from her jacket. The rucksack on her back suddenly felt cumbersome, weighing her down and adding to her sense of unease. *Oh God, I must look awful. What will he think of me?*

❦❦❦

Prince Zatao rode with a loose rein, keeping August at a steady walk. He needed the time to calm himself. He focused on Irene's face. The sight of her took his breath away. He watched her brush a hand through her tangled auburn curls. A soft smile touched the corners of his mouth.

Reaching her, the two horses stood head to tail. Dropping his reins, Zatao rested his hands on his thighs, lowering his head slightly he searched her face. "Irene, you've returned to me."

Irene's heart leapt. His voice sounded like a caress as he softly spoke her name. Glancing shyly at him, she whispered. "I couldn't stay away."

Reaching over, Zatao put his hand under her chin and raised her head. His eyes bored into hers. "You can't imagine my joy at hearing those words."

Irene clasped his hand in both of hers. "Really?" She said softly. "Do you mean it?" Her pounding heart all but took her breath away.

"Oh, my darling," Zatao said with a warm smile. "I have dreamed of this day…longed for it."

Irene stared into his face, tears of joy made tramlines through the dust on her cheeks.

Zatao reached across to wipe them away.

Pulling back, Irene rubbed at her face. "I must look an awful mess."

"No, you look as beautiful as you did the last time I saw you."

Irene's lips puckered. "Exactly, that's what bothers me; I looked a mess then, too!"

Zatao tossed his head back and laughed. "Oh, Irene, I've missed you so much. Come here." Before she could respond, he grabbed her, hauled her out of the saddle and sat her in front of him. "Let's get rid of this rucksack," he said pulling at the straps.

"But it has my things in it!"

"Don't worry one of my men will bring it."

Irene let the bag fall to the ground and wrapped her arms around his neck. Resting her head against his chest, she breathed deeply and sighed. The subtle, yet familiar scent of pine needles and bluebells caressed her senses. "Oh Stagman, I can't believe I'm here with you."

Zatao's heart lurched. Holding her in his arms, and hearing her use that name, brought back a flood of memories. "You belong with me my darling. Welcome home." Gently he lifted her chin and let his lips caress hers.

Warmth radiated through Irene's body as she returned his kiss.

Lost in the moment, they were both surprised by the sound of laughter and cheering.

Irene felt her cheeks flush pink as she reluctantly pulled away.

Zatao chuckled and raised a hand. "Home!" he shouted to the waiting guardsmen.

Chapter 27

Breathing hard, Grouchen hurried along the dimly lit passage.

Ergon followed, grunting with exertion. "Why do the warriors want to see us? We always liaise with the king."

"I don't know, but I guess we're about to find out."

"Well I don't like it, makes me feel uneasy," Ergon grumbled.

Without comment, Grouchen lowered his head and increased his pace. Ahead he could see the door to Muglwort's room.

The guard standing by the door watched them approach and stretched his pike across the doorway, forbidding entrance.

"Let us pass!" Grouchen ordered the man. "We have been summoned by My Lord, Muglwort."

The guard's piercing eyes studied the two elderly advisors.

Ergon stood close to Grouchen, his hands trembled as he gripped the collar of his cloak.

Taking a tentative step forward, Grouchen fixed the guard with as bold a stare as he could muster. "We are about the King's business. Let us pass!"

At the mention of the King, the guard raised his pike and banged on the heavy wooden door. Footsteps could be heard approaching on the other side. A deep voice, harsh with impatience growled. "Who is it?"

The guard gripped his pike and stood to attention. "It is the King's advisors, My Lord. They are here to speak with you."

The two advisors huddled together. Being summoned by the warriors, terrified them as much as standing before the King and Queen. Both men held their breath as a heavy bolt slid across and the door slowly opened.

Muglwort's massive frame filled the doorway. He couldn't help sneering as he stared at the two elderly men trembling before him. "Come on, hurry up, we don't have all night." Turning to the guard he snapped. "We do not wish to be disturbed."

"Yes, My Lord," the guard said with bowed head.

The two advisors jumped, as Muglwort closed the door and slid the bolt across. Trembling, they stared around. A couple of flickering candles, created shadows that danced macabrely around the room. Rain pounded against a small window set high in the wall. Under the window stood a large iron cot, on the dresser beside it…a bowl with a chipped water jug.

A massive tapestry adorned the far wall, depicting the gruesome aftermath of war. The subject matter appeared strangely animated in the gloomy candle light. The rush matting covering the stone floor, gave little protection against the cold rising through the flagstones. Apart from a couple of chairs in front of the fire and a round table in the centre of the room, there were no other furnishings.

Grouchen shivered; the cold seeped into his bones. *Typical soldiers living quarters*, he thought, as he placed his cold hands inside the wide sleeves of his cloak, he glanced at Ergon. His friend resembled a frightened rabbit. But before Grouchen could say anything, Muglwort's large hands clapped them both on the shoulder. "Come!" he ordered, pushing them towards the table in the centre of the room.

Zworn grunted as he hauled his heavy frame out of a chair by the fire, and joined them. His soulless eyes narrowed as he stared at the two older men. Focusing on Grouchen, he said. "So, when will you hear from the spy?" Pulling a chair out from under the table, he sat down. "It had better be soon, because I'm sick of hanging around waiting." A cruel smile flickered across his face. "The King's seer got it wrong, and he's paid the price. I advise you to get things moving and fast!"

Sitting beside him, Muglwort leaned back in his chair and placed his hands behind his head. Raising a bushy red eyebrow he waited for Grouchen to reply. The old man's fearful countenance made him smile. "Well," he prompted. "Have you heard anything from the spy, Traditor?"

Clasping his trembling hands, Grouchen replied. "No, My Lord, We've heard nothing. When he has a message, he sends it via pigeon." His voice faltered as he glanced at Muglwort and Zworn. "As yet, we have received no new message. But when we do—"

"We will be the first to hear about it," Muglwort growled. As if to emphasise the point, he rose from his chair, rested his huge hands on the table, and stared at the advisers through narrowed eyes. In a voice as rough as gravel, he said. "The moment you hear from the spy, you come straight to us, do you understand?" Glaring at them, he pointed to the door. "Go, and the next time we see you, you'd better have a message from the spy."

With frightened nods of assent, Grouchen and Ergon scrambled to their feet and hurried to the door. The minute they were safely inside Grouchen's room the two men stared anxiously at each other. "What shall we do?" Ergon asked.

A deep frown creased Grouchen's brow. "I will send a message to the spy. He must keep us informed."

Ergon nodded as he wearily slumped in a chair by the fire. "Do you think the King will appoint another seer? It is so much easier when we are informed of things ahead of time."

"I don't know." Grumbling to himself, Grouchen shuffled across the room to an old desk, and retrieved a small scrap of paper. Dipping his quill in the ink pot he scribbled a short note…rolled the paper tightly and stuffed it inside a small silver tube.

"What have you written?" Ergon asked.

"I've warned the spy to keep us informed, or pay the price." Going to the other side of the room he opened the door to a wooden cage and retrieved a plump pigeon. Fixing the tube to the bird's leg he opened a window and released it. "Right, that's done," he said wiping his hands together, as if touching the bird had contaminated him. "Now we wait." Lowering his heavy frame into the chair opposite Ergon, he offered him a nightcap.

Ergon shook his head. "No thank you. It has been a long night; if you don't mind I will retire to my room."

"Of course, I'll see you in the morning. Hopefully there will be news from the spy."

Ergon nodded as he pulled himself out of the chair. He could feel his insides quiver uncomfortably as he walked to the door. Reaching his own room, he reclined on his cot, but a strange heaviness denied him sleep. He lay there restless, listening to the dull drumming of his heart.

᪥᪥᪥

Prince Aldrin paced his room; making a fist, he pounded it into the palm of his left hand. For what seemed the hundredth time he went to the window, and stared into the darkness. "They must return soon," he growled.

In the moonlight a fluttering caught his attention, and his heart sank as a large pigeon landed on his windowsill. Opening the window he grabbed the bird and removed the small silver tube from its leg. "I'll take you to the pigeon loft later," he muttered, popping the bird into a small wooden crate.

Sitting at his desk, he carefully pulled the rolled note from the tube and smoothed it out. His jaw clenched...his dark eyes narrowed with frustration. "Don't threaten me," he growled. "When I know something, so will you." Leaving his desk, he scrunched the paper and threw it onto the fire. Wiping the sweat from his top lip he watched it burn.

Striding to the window he leaned against the frame and watched for his brother's return. Shafts of moonlight bathed his face, softening the hard set of his features. His tension eased as he peered into the darkness and spotted the white horse emerging from the forest, followed by the Prince's guard.

"At last, they're here!" Smoothing his shirt, he left his room and hurried down the stairs. "They're back," he shouted to Mira.

Closing the chapel door she glanced up at him. "I know."

Aldrin grabbed her hand and pulled her towards the door.

"Hang on!" She protested. "What's the hurry?" Glancing up at him, she chuckled as the realisation dawned. "You're not bothered about our brother. You just want to see, Irene." Her eyebrows rose in amusement at the flush on his face.

Aldrin scowled and dropped her hand. "Not true," he protested, wishing the guard would hurry and open the door. He could hear the clatter of hooves and the shouts of men as they galloped into the courtyard. Rolling his eyes, he was about to yell at the guard, when the mighty door swung open. Forcing the man aside, Aldrin growled. "Get out of my way!"

"Was that necessary?" Mira asked as she followed him.

"Probably not, but he was so slow," Aldrin said winking at her.

Mira ignored him, her eyes focused on Prince Zatao and the person sitting in front of him. "Irene," she whispered softly.

Chapter 28

Prince Zatao eased August back. The stallion walked out of the forest, into parkland shimmering in the moons glow. Taking Irene's hand Zatao kissed it. "Welcome home my darling."

Staring into his face, Irene smiled. "Thank you," she murmured.

Her first sight of castle Eternus took her breath away, she gasped with delight. Bathed in moonlight, the building's soft gold stone contrasted with the dark backdrop of night; giving the castle a magical, fairy-tale quality. Built in the shape of a square, huge turrets stood guard on either side of the wooden bridge spanning the moat.

Irene's eye's widened in awe as they clattered under the portcullis and into an immense quadrangle. Her mouth dropped open as she stared around. Surrounding them on all sides, the castle formed an impenetrable barrier. There was one way in, and one way out. Soft lights from innumerable windows highlighted a scene of joyous activity, fuelled by the Prince's safe return.

The air rang with the clatter of hooves, as guards dismounted, and their horses were led away by grooms who appeared as if from nowhere. The sounds and smells...the guard's loud laughter, and Sergeant Azar's booming voice, made Irene feel light headed. *It's like a scene from a medieval film*, she thought.

From her vantage point on August's back, Irene stared over the heads of the guardsmen in search of Merton and Safi. She spotted Merton handing the reins of his horse to a groom. Safi stood close by, her shoulders encompassed by Romure's protective arm.

Irene turned her attention to the main entrance of the castle. Deep steps led to a portico, supported by huge stone pillars. In the shadow of the portico two guards stood on either side of a massive wooden door. The door was open...light streamed out, illuminating two people standing at the top of the steps.

Placing a hand over her heart, Irene stared up at the Prince. "Is that Mira?"

Zatao nodded.

"Oh, I can't wait to see her. Who is the man beside her?"

"That's my brother, Aldrin."

Irene couldn't help noticing Zatao's frown, but made no comment. "Please can I get down?" she asked.

"In a moment, Irene, but first my guard wish to honour us."

Irene sighed inaudibly. *I must look a mess, the last thing I want are people staring at me.* Doing her best to remain patient, she watched the guard form a line; each commander took his stand on a step, with Sergeant Azar at the top, a few feet from Mira and Aldrin.

August whickered softly as a young lad approached and bowed low. "Welcome home My Lord. May I take the reins?"

"Thank you, Taris," Zatao said dropping the reins and placing both arms around Irene.

Leaning against him, she gazed into his face. The love in his eyes gave her confidence.

"You look lovely," he whispered.

"How did you know what I—" Seeing the twinkle in his eyes she tutted.

Chuckling, he squeezed her close. "You forget; I know what you are thinking."

Before she could reply, Merton approached and bowed low. "Can I be of service, My Lord?"

Prince Zatao smiled at him. "You may accompany us."

With a relieved smile, Merton bowed his head and stepped to the side.

The Prince turned to the groom. "Lead on, Taris," he instructed.

The young lad led August past the line of smiling guardsmen and up the steps. Reaching the top they halted, close to Aldrin and Mira.

Irene was amazed by Aldrin's likeness to Zatao. However, his unreadable and disturbing expression unnerved her. She shivered under his scrutiny. Looking away, she fixed her gaze on Mira, returning her friend's radiant smile of welcome. *Mira looks lovely, she hasn't changed a bit.*

Zatao dismounted and helped her to the ground. "I know you want to see Mira, but please, give me a moment." He held her close. "There is something important I need to do first."

Taking her hand he led her to the edge of the step. He gazed at her, his eyes filled with such intensity she could hardly breathe. Raising his voice, he declared to the watching guardsmen. "This is Lady Irene, my future queen." His voice echoed around the quadrangle.

His words left Irene speechless. She gazed up into his face, her eyes questioning.

Zatao lowered his head close to her ear and whispered. "I love you, Irene. Will you be my queen?" His eyes never left her face as he waited for an answer.

Irene could see the expectant hope in his eyes, it added to her confusion. *Is this real, or am I dreaming?* Briefly she stared around; things were different...not how she remembered. Stagman seemed different. She frowned. *Of course he is, this is his world, and he's a Prince!*

Tiredness washed over her, and for a moment she wondered if she'd done the right thing. Chewing her lip, she thought. *Maybe coming here was a mistake. But I do love him. I had to come.*

Zatao smiled, and said softly. "Don't be afraid, Irene. I know this is sudden, and you must feel overwhelmed. I can't explain now, but when I do, you will understand. Will you trust me?"

Irene's lips flickered in a smile, as she recalled the first time they'd met...the terrifying journey they'd taken together, and how often he'd asked her to trust him. It was a few years ago now, and yet it felt like yesterday. *Feels like de-ja-vu,* she thought. Staring up at him, she whispered. "Are you asking me to marry you?"

Prince Zatao's eyebrows arched slightly as he studied her expression. "I am," he replied. Reaching out, he took her hands in his. "Irene, will you marry me?"

Irene couldn't help smiling at his hopeful...pleading expression. Standing on tip toe, she pulled him towards her and whispered in his ear. "I will."

Zatao thumped a victorious fist to his chest. Drawing Irene close he declared to those watching. "Behold my betrothed, my queen."

The quadrangle echoed to shouts of, 'King Zatao! King Zatao!'

Gently, he placed a hand under her chin and raised her head. Placing his lips over hers; his kiss was soft and tender.

Irene's heart quickened. Lost in the power of his presence, she threw her arms round his neck, and returned his kiss; they were oblivious to the delighted shouts and foot stomping of those watching.

As their lips parted, Zatao wrapped his arms round her and held her close.

Irene's pulse raced as she rested her head on his chest. She could hear the thud of his pounding heart.

Closing his eyes, Zatao stroked her hair. When he spoke, his voice sounded warm…husky. "Your love has made me King," he said softly.

Irene peered up at him.

He nodded. "The day we marry, I shall become King, and you will be my queen." Lowering his head, he whispered in her ear. "On that day, I will reach the fulfilment of my power." Gazing round at the expectant faces, he smiled and took Irene's hand.

❧❧❧

Mira's eyes glowed with happiness as she watched Zatao lift Irene down from August. She longed to rush forward and greet her, but calmed her enthusiasm; aware there was something her brother needed to do first. She understood how important it was to him.

Mira smiled, as she watched her brother publicly declare his love for the young woman at his side. She knew, only too well, how quickly word would circulate throughout the land. Prince Zatao had claimed his queen, and would soon be King of Luminaire. Such news would bring rejoicing to the people, but fear to their enemies.

Glancing at Aldrin, Mira couldn't help noticing his tense stance…his hands were curled into fists, his eyes glued to Irene.

Mira placed a hand over her heart. She'd known something was amiss when she left the chapel, and met him hurrying down the stairs. He'd appeared anxious, agitated, but now as she watched him staring at Irene, his enigmatic expression made her nervous.

Oh Irene, what a time you've chosen to return to us; however watching her brother with the woman he loved, she realised the timing of Irene's arrival was perfect. Prince Zatao needed her here. Her presence would reinforce him, enable him to stand firm against their enemy.

Mira's heart leapt as Zatao turned from the steps and led Irene towards her.

"Come, Irene," she heard him say. "Let us greet Mira and Aldrin."

Mira opened her arms as Irene rushed towards her.

"Oh Mira," Irene cried wrapping her arms around her. "It is so good to see you again. I've missed you so much."

Mira eased her away and gently cupped her face. "I've missed you too, Irene. I can't tell you how wonderful it is to see you…knowing you are here to stay, gives me great joy."

Smiling, Prince Zatao watched their reunion. However, noting Aldrin's sidelong glance and the sneer on his lips, Zatao's smile faded, his expression darkened.

Aldrin, sensing his brother's hostility, realised he needed to be cautious. Raising his head he beamed at Zatao. "Won't you introduce us?" he asked. Turning to Irene, he gave her a welcoming smile.

Zatao moved towards his brother. The hair on the back of his neck prickled. There was something wrong, but as yet he couldn't put his finger on it. As he met Aldrin's gaze, he sensed danger.

Moving beside Irene, he placed a protective arm round her shoulders; his eyes never left Aldrin's face.

Irene smiled and stared up at Zatao, the visible tension on his face unnerved her. "Are you going to introduce us?" She asked.

Pulling himself together, Zatao smiled, but inside his stomach churned. "Irene, my love, this is my brother, Aldrin." He watched as Aldrin took Irene's outstretched hand and placed it to his lips.

"I am delighted to meet you," Aldrin said, in a voice as sweet as honey.

Irene found the likeness between Zatao and his brother fascinating. Both men were strikingly handsome, but something about Aldrin made her skin crawl. Not wishing to cause offence, she fought the desire to withdraw her hand. Her voice faltered slightly as she returned his greeting. "It's nice to meet you too."

As Aldrin raised his head, and looked at her; she stared into emotionless eyes. *Like a shark*, she thought. Stepping back she placed herself between Zatao and Mira. She could feel the colour drain from her face as exhaustion, compounded by anxiety overwhelmed her.

Mira noticed and took her hand. "I'm taking her inside," she said to Zatao. "She needs to rest and refresh herself."

Zatao nodded in agreement. "Indeed." Brushing a strand of hair away from Irene's face, he said softly. "I will see you later, my darling."

Irene smiled as he placed a tender kiss on her forehead. Numerous thoughts and questions buzzed around in her head as she followed Mira into the castle.

⊰⊰⊰

Prince Zatao stood close to Aldrin; his feet planted wide, his hand on the hilt of his sword. A few inches taller than his brother, Zatoa could always intimidate him. Aware the guard had not yet been dismissed, and Merton was standing close by, Zatao lowered his head and whispered in Aldrin's ear, his tone low and threatening. "As yet, I don't know what game you are playing, brother. But believe me I will find out, and when I do, your treachery will be punished." With an angry growl, Zatao turned on his heels and strode after Irene and Mira.

Scowling, Aldrin hooked his thumbs in his belt and watched him go. *Brother if you knew the seriousness of the game, you wouldn't be so confident.* Aldrin's nostril's flared with rage as he turned on Sergeant Azar. "Dismiss the men," he barked. Taking a few calming breaths, he stood on the top step watching the guard disperse, and planning his next move.

⊰⊰⊰

Relieved to have escaped the attention of Prince Aldrin; Merton wiped the sweat from his top lip, and hurried after Prince Zatao. Entering the great hall, he approached his master and dropped to his knees. "My Lord, is there anything I can do for you?"

Leaning down, Zatao took him by the shoulders and pulled him to his feet. "You have served me well, and have my deepest gratitude for bringing Lady Irene safely here to me."

"My Lord, it is an honour to serve you." Merton lowered his eyes and said softly, "I was pleased to have the opportunity to prove my loyalty."

Zatao smiled. "Indeed you have, and it will not be forgotten." Leaning against the mantelpiece, the Prince tapped a finger against pursed lips, as he stared into the flames.

Merton stepped closer and bowed his head. "My Lord, is there a problem?"

Without diverting his gaze from the fire, Zatao said. "Not so much a problem, as an inconvenience. For the moment, Princess Mira is assisting Lady Irene, but obviously such an arrangement is not acceptable in the long term. Lady Irene needs her own maid." Raising his head he noticed Merton's smile of triumph. "What is it?" Zatao asked.

"My Lord, I believe I may have the answer to your dilemma."

Moving away from the fireplace, Zatao said. "Speak man."

Wiping his hands on his jerkin, Merton's voice faltered as he said. "I hope I'm not speaking out of turn My Lord, but having found Lady Irene at the cottage, we made our way to the village of Wedon. We stayed there for an hour or two in order to rest the horses and refresh ourselves."

Prince Zatao shifted impatiently. "Get on with it man. What are you trying to tell me?"

Taking a deep breath, Merton continued to tell the Prince how Lady Irene had met, and wanted to help a young woman, who before the tragic death of her husband had run the local pub. "Lady Irene insisted we bring the young woman back with us."

"And what is this young lady's name?" the Prince asked.

"Her name is Safi, My Lord. At the moment I believe she is in the care of guardsman Romure. I only mention it, as I believe Lady Irene has grown fond of the girl, and I personally believe Safi would be the perfect maid for her ladyship." Taking a deep breath, he lowered his voice. "Her husband was murdered My Lord, by a warrior from beyond the mountain. She has nowhere to go, her plight is desperate."

On hearing about the warrior, Zatao's brows met in an angry frown. Taking a few calming breaths, he patted Merton on the shoulder. "You have put forth her case well. For now run my bath, and in the morning after breakfast bring the girl to my office."

Merton's heart leapt. "Thank you My Lord, I know Lady Irene will be pleased."

Zatao smiled. "Then it is pleasing to me."

With his head bowed, Merton backed away, turned and hurried up the stairs to his master's chambers. "I can't wait to tell Safi the good news," he said to himself, as he filled the bath with hot water. "I'm sure Prince Zatao will like her and I know Lady Irene will be thrilled." Placing his hand in the bath water to test the temperature, he murmured. "Everything has turned out better than I could have hoped."

Chapter 29

Having been dismissed, the castle guard milled around eager to discuss what they'd just witnessed and heard.

Romure looked around for Safi and spotted her hiding close to the stable block. Striding over he took her hand and smiled. "It's alright, no need to be afraid. I will take care of you." Seeing the fear in her upturned face he gave her trembling hand a reassuring squeeze.

Staring up at him, Safi asked. "What will happen to me?" Her voice faltered with anxiety. "Lady Irene will forget about me, I know she will." A lone tear trickled down her cheek.

Stooping, Romure stared into her face. "No, she won't. You need to give her time to settle in. This is as strange for her, as it is for you."

Safi dropped her head and wiped her eyes. "I suppose so." Raising her head, she stared at Romure. "Where will I stay?"

Gazing into her large grey eyes, Romure's heart melted. "Don't you fret little maid. I have a plan."

His wink brought a hopeful smile to Safi's face.

Romure gripped her hand and guided her towards a small door, half hidden by a clump of ivy. Lifting the door latch, he led her into a long passage, lit by a row of sconces.

Safi pulled back, squinting in the surprising brightness. "Please, Romure, what is this place?"

"Trust me, Safi. I'm taking you to Bella the housekeeper. She will find you a bed for the night, and look after you until Lady Irene sorts things out. So come on, stop worrying, all will be well." He felt her relax as she followed him.

Romure frowned slightly as they stopped outside the housekeeper's sitting room. *I see no light; I hope she hasn't gone to bed.* Sighing, he rubbed the back of his neck. The thought of the housekeeper half asleep and annoyed, was not pleasant.

Knocking on the sitting room door he called, "Bella." No response, so he knocked and called again, louder. Hearing a muffled sound on the other side of the door he stepped back.

Wiping her hands on her skirt, Safi moved closer to him...appreciative of the supportive arm he placed round her shoulders.

❧❧❧

Reclined in her armchair by the dying fire, Bella yawned. Her eyes felt gritty and her feet ached. *My, it's been an interesting night*, she mused. The Prince's return with a beautiful young lady had caused chaos and excitement in the kitchen. Trying to organise her staff to prepare food, and make sure the Prince's guest was comfortable in her chambers, was a major task.

With a sigh, Bella rose from her chair and dampened down the fire. *I best get myself to bed. I have a feeling tomorrow will be busy.* A loud knock on the door startled her, she froze. *Who could it be at this time of night?* However, hearing her name called, she relaxed. *If I'm not mistaken that's guardsman Romure.*

Opening the door she peered out; seeing Romure with a young lady, her brown eyes widened in surprise. "My goodness Romure what are you doing here at this hour?" She stared at Safi. "And who is this?" Even in the dim light of the passage she could see the girl looked pale and exhausted...her clothing rumpled and grubby. Bella's nose wrinkled. The distinct smell of horse filled the air.

Romure stepped forward and gave a slight bow. "I'm sorry for disturbing you at this late hour, Bella." He glanced at Safi. "This young lady was befriended by Lady Irene. Her name is Safi, and she needs a bed for the night."

Trembling with anxiety, Safi returned Bella's gaze and bobbed an unsteady curtsy. Seeing Bella's smile and the warm welcome in her eyes, Safi relaxed and crumpled in a heap on the floor.

"Oh my!" Bella cried. Placing a plump hand over her heart, she ordered Romure to pick Safi up.

Scooping Safi into his arms; Romure followed Bella to a small room at the rear of the kitchen.

Sparsely furnished; the room contained a sink, a chest of draws, and facing the door a small cot.

"Whose room is this?" Romure asked.

"This is a spare room," Bella replied. Tutting and fussing she watched as Romure laid Safi gently on the cot.

"You may go now," Bella said, waving a hand impatiently at him.

"Thank you, Bella," Romure said as she closed the door behind him.

Bella busied herself removing Safi's shoes. Placing them under the bed, she looked up to see Safi staring at her. She smiled reassuringly. "We need to take this dress off, looks to me like it could do with a wash," she said, undoing the small buttons on the bodice.

Safi placed a hand over Bella's. "Thank you, I can do it."

"Very well, strip to your underwear and get under the covers. If we can't clean the dress, I'm sure we can find something for you to wear."

Safi wriggled out of the dress and handed it to her. "You are kind, thank you."

"You're welcome my dear. Now, before I go do you want some refreshment?"

Safi shook her head as she curled up under the blanket. "I would like a drink of water, please."

By the time Bella took the dress to the laundry room, and returned with a glass of water; Safi was sound asleep. Placing the glass on the floor by the bed, Bella watched her for a moment. Tip toeing to the door, she paused. Concern shadowed her comely features. "I have a feeling you've suffered a lot, child. I pray God, in this place you will find peace," she whispered.

⋞⋞⋞

Irene's mouth hung open as she followed Mira through the great hall and up the magnificent staircase. Irene let her hand brush the ornately carved banister. Under her feet a plush red carpet cushioned any sound. Mother of pearl sconces in the shape of a shell illumined the artwork hanging on the walls. Family members, some stern, some smiling…dressed in their best attire, stared at her from huge canvases surrounded by gilded frames.

Taking Irene's hand, Mira led her down a long hallway. Halting outside a door, she pulled a key from her pocket. "Here we are she said." Turning the key in the lock, she pushed the door open. "I hope you like it. This suite affords wonderful views of the parkland."

Walking into the room, Irene gasped. A lush cream carpet covered the floor. Shimmering green drapes hung at the huge picture windows. Positioned in front of the roaring fire, were two small armchairs upholstered in mint green brocade. It was the largest, most beautiful room Irene had ever seen. Her eyes moistened as she stared at Mira. "Is this for me?"

Mira nodded. "Of course it is." Grinning, she grabbed Irene by the hand. "Come let me show you around. This—" she said gesturing with her hand, "is the sitting room. Next door is the bedroom and bathroom."

Irene could hardly breathe as she followed Mira into a cosy room, decorated in the softest blue with matching drapes. The coverlet over the large bed was decorated with tiny bluebells. On the cream dressing table, bluebells sat in a cut glass vase, their sweet scent filling the room.

Pausing, Irene put her hands to her face. "Oh, Mira, this is lovely. I don't know what to say."

Mira smiled and gave her a hug. "I'm glad it pleases you. We gave the room a few bluebell touches because we know how much you love them."

Struggling with emotion, Irene rubbed her eyes. "It's so beautiful." Gazing around, she cried with relief. "There's my rucksack!"

"Yes, we had a servant bring it up for you, and they have run you a bath...follow me." Mira led Irene into a room equally as large as the bedroom; she couldn't help smiling at Irene's wide eyed surprise.

A large roll topped bath with ornate clawed feet took centre stage. Irene stared at the steaming water, it smelt sweetly floral. *Oh, how wonderful, I can't wait to get in.* Looking at her grubby clothes, she frowned.

Noticing her embarrassment, Mira said. "Come on, let's get these clothes off. Leave them on the floor, and tomorrow a servant will take them to the laundry." She pointed to a towel rail. "There's a bath towel, and behind the door you will find a dressing gown, and on your bed a nightdress."

Irene smiled. "I'm so happy to be here, Mira."

Mira's emerald eyes sparkled in the soft light. "I can't tell you how much your return has blessed me." Pausing in the doorway of the bathroom, she noticed Irene's pursed lips. "Is there a problem?"

"Not a problem as such," Irene replied. "I met someone in Wedon and brought them here with me. She's been through a pretty awful time and needs to make a fresh start. I hoped she might find work here."

"I'm sure we can find a position for her. In a castle this size workers are always needed. What's her name?" Mira was pleased to see the tension fade from Irene's face.

"Her name is Safi. The trouble is I have no idea where she is. The last time I saw her she was in the quadrangle with guardsman Romure."

Mira smiled. "She couldn't be in better hands. Don't worry. Tomorrow I will speak to Zatao."

"Oh thank you. I appreciate it."

"Leave it with me," Mira said. "Now, before I go, would you like some refreshment?"

Irene shook her head. "All I need is this hot bath and some sleep."

"Very well; I will wake you for breakfast in the morning. Sleep well."

"I will, thanks, Mira." Sitting on a towel box, Irene removed her shoes, followed by the rest of her clothing. Leaving them on the floor she climbed into the bath. With a blissful sigh, she lowered herself into the hot water. Closing her eyes she allowed her tired body to relax in the sweet scented water. For a moment her thoughts turned to Safi and she silently prayed. *God, I don't know where she is, but please keep her safe.*

After some time reclined in the bath, Irene noticed she had wrinkly fingers. *I guess it's time to get out.* Grinning with satisfaction, she stood, grabbed a bath towel off the rail, and snuggled into its sumptuous warmth. With the towel wrapped around her she padded into the bedroom.

Dropping the towel to the floor, she slipped the lacy pink nightdress over her head. She would have liked to unpack her rucksack. Instead she succumbed to exhaustion. Taking a hairbrush from the dressing table, she dragged it through her unruly curls, before slipping under the covers and snuggling down. For a while she lay there, allowing her mind to mull over the events of the last forty eight hours. *It's almost too much to take in*, she thought. Yet the peace she felt indicated she'd made the right decision. Turning on her side, she yawned and slowly drifted into a deep sleep.

Irene woke to a soft tapping sound. It took a second for her brain to register. Momentarily confused, she gazed around the pretty bedroom. Sunlight filtered through the closed drapes, bathing the room in early morning light. Remembering where she was, she smiled, sat up and yawned.

Tap, tap, tap, she heard again. Clambering out of bed she went to the window and drew back the drapes. For a moment the sun blinded her. Covering her eyes with the back of a hand she waited for them to adjust. The tapping continued, growing louder!

Peering through her fingers, Irene saw Blackwing perched on the sill staring up at her, his eyes bright with impatience. Still half asleep, Irene searched for the window catch. "Wait a minute," she grumbled. Finding the catch she eased the window open.

"At last," Blackwing said, fluffing his feathers. "I've had quite a job finding you. This place is huge. My beak's sore from tapping on so many windows."

"Good morning to you, too," Irene said shoving her hair behind her ears. "I was wondering where you'd got to."

"I followed you here, and spent the night in the forest. There were a few Blackbirds roosting nearby, so I joined them."

Seeing the twinkle in his eyes, Irene smiled. "Is there by any chance a female among them?"

Embarrassed, Blackwing stretched a wing. "There might be," he said softly. "But the reason I've come, is to let you know; should you ever need me, just call."

Irene smiled and gently ran a finger down his inky black breast. "Thank you, I will."

Hearing a soft tap on the door, she swung round as Mira entered the room.

"Good morning, Irene. How did you sleep?"

"Very well, thank you."

Mira stood beside her and stared at Blackwing. "So who is this?"

"He's a bird I used to feed, when I lived in Zeal. Unfortunately for him, he followed me through the mirror. So now he's stuck here."

Blackwing shook his head. "It's not unfortunate; I'm perfectly happy, thank you."

Irene smiled. "You are now, and for that I'm relieved and pleased."

Mira chuckled as she stared at the perky little bird. "What's your name?" She asked.

"Blackwing," he replied.

"Well it's nice to meet you, Blackwing."

"Thank you." He turned to Irene. "Don't forget what I said. If you need me, call."

"I will, take care of yourself. And stop flying so low to the ground."

"Tck!" Blackwing replied, as he took to the air.

"He's a bit of a character," Mira said with a smile.

"He is. I just pray he stays safe. I feel guilty for getting him stuck here."

"He seems happy enough." Mira took Irene's hand and led her into the sitting room. A fire was burning in the grate and a tray of tea sat on the small table between the two armchairs.

Irene gasped. "Who did this? I didn't hear a thing."

Mira chuckled. "Our servants are trained to be unobtrusive." Pouring two cups of tea, she handed one to Irene. "Now, I have good news. I've found Safi. She's in the care of our housekeeper, Bella."

Irene breathed a sigh of relief. "That's great, I'm so pleased."

"It seems last night, Merton told Zatao about your friendship with Safi, and the circumstances relating to her presence here. My brother has thought about her situation, and decided she would suite you well as a maid, especially as we have no one else suitable for the task."

Irene's eyebrows arched in surprise. "I don't think I need a maid, Mira."

"Yes, Irene, you do. You have come to our world, and soon you will be queen. A personal maid is of paramount importance. She must be a person who is discreet and skilled in all aspects of beauty...above all, she must be loyal." Mira frowned slightly as she watched Irene sip her tea and stare thoughtfully into the fire. "What troubles you?" She asked.

"I don't think Safi possess the skills you speak of. She's a friend, someone who used to run a pub with her husband. I can't imagine she would want to be my maid." Noticing Mira's amused expression, she leaned forward. "What?"

Mira's eye's twinkled as she peered at Irene over the rim of her cup. "Safi had an audience with Prince Zatao early this morning. She told him she would be delighted to serve you."

Irene gasped with surprise.

Smiling, Mira placed her cup on the table and leaned back in her chair. "You're right with regard to Safi's lack of skill. However, the problem is not insurmountable. My maid Anya will teach her everything she needs to know; but in the interim I would ask you to be patient. It will not be easy for Safi to learn new skills. Not only that, she has the responsibility of looking after the future Queen of Luminaire."

Seeing the red flush on Irene's cheeks; Mira left her chair and knelt beside her. Gently she took one of Irene's hands. "There is no need to be afraid, Irene," Mira said patting her hand. "My brother loves you. He has always loved you."

"I love him, Mira; more than I can say."

"I know you do. And you will be a wonderful Queen! Now come." Pulling Irene to her feet, she wrapped her arms around her. "Don't be afraid, child. Your destiny is here with us; with the man you love. Trust him and be happy."

Resting her head on Mira's shoulder, Irene relaxed, gaining strength from the closeness of Mira's presence.

Easing her away, Mira gazed at her. "Are you ready to face this new day, in your new home?"

Irene smiled and nodded.

"Right then, you go and freshen up. I will send my maid Anya to assist you with your hair and dressing."

"But I don't—"

"Get used to it, Irene. I'm afraid it's the way it has to be. Anya will bring you a dress and do all that needs to be done. When you are ready she will bring you to the breakfast room." Mira gazed into Irene's eyes. "Your life is never going to be the same. You are marrying the future King; a man of great power and authority. Protocol, must be adhered too."

Irene nodded. "I understand."

"Good girl. I will send Anya."

ঙ্ঔঔ

Resting her hands on the sink, Irene stared at her reflection in the bathroom mirror. Her cheeks and neck were pink with anxiety. In the silence of the room her racing heart beat like a drum.

Deep in thought she filled the sink with warm water and splashed it over her face. *I understand what Mira was saying, but it's going to take me a while to get used to this new way of life.* Burying her face in a small towel she sighed. *Only God knows if I've made the right decision.* As she wiped her face, her thoughts turned to Zatao…she smiled. Deep in her heart she knew there was no way she could live without him. She'd made her choice, and there was no going back. Her heart felt strangely light as she resolved to embrace this new life with the man she loved.

Walking into the bedroom, Irene gasped with surprise. A young woman, with striking red hair was standing by the bed. In her arms she held a turquoise dress.

As Irene approached she bobbed a curtsy. "I'm sorry My Lady; I did not wish to startle you. I knocked, but—"

"It's alright," Irene smiled at the girl. "You must be Anya."

The girl nodded. "My mistress sent me to help you." Holding out the dress, her voice faltered slightly. "I hope this is to your liking. I felt it would suite your colouring." She blushed slightly as she draped the dress over the bed.

"It's lovely Anya, turquoise is my favourite colour."

"My mistress thought it might be." Smiling with relief, Anya approached Irene and reached for her nightdress. "Allow me to help you My Lady."

Irene could feel her face flush with embarrassment, as she backed away. "I can manage, Anya, thank you." Irene wished the floor would open up and swallow her. Not since she was a child had someone attempted to try and dress her.

Anya stood her ground. "Please, My Lady. There is no need to be embarrassed. This is my job. I have served Princess Mira for many years, and it is an honour to serve you, until Safi is trained."

206

Turning, she scooped the dress off the bed and held it up. "You see My Lady; the dress has small buttons all the way down the back. You need my help."

"Very well," Irene said with a resigned sigh. Removing her night attire, she slipped into the turquoise dress and waited patiently as Anya did up the buttons.

When the maid finished, she stepped away and stared at Irene.

Unnerved by Anya's silence, Irene anxiously ran a hand down the bodice of the dress. "What's wrong?" She asked.

Anya took her hand and led her to a free standing mirror.

Irene's brow's arched, her fingers rested on her lips as she stared at the image in the mirror. Shyly she glanced at Anya.

"You look beautiful, My Lady, the dress really suites you."

"Thank you, it feels wonderful," Irene murmured.

The dress was of a style Irene loved. The soft slinky material draped her body; extenuating her slim waist and the curve of her hips. She loved the softly scooped neckline, and the long sleeves buttoned at the wrist. Twisting round, she attempted to see the back of the dress. Small turquoise buttons followed the shape of her body ending at the small of her back. She could see her feet beneath the hem of the dress, and noticed it appeared slightly longer at the back, than the front.

Anya smiled. "Our Lord, Prince Zatao, will be delighted when he sees you." Noting the flush on Irene's cheeks, she apologised. "Forgive me, My Lady. I meant no offence."

Irene smiled. "It's alright, Anya."

The girl bobbed a nervous curtsy. "Thank you, My Lady. Pointing towards a small dressing table and matching stool, she asked. "May I dress your hair?"

Rather than cause upset by refusing, Irene followed her and sat patiently on the stool.

Anya brushed her hair, and with deft fingers pinned the sides…arranging the long auburn curls as a frame for Irene's face. "There, My Lady. You are ready. Now, if you will follow me, I'll take you to the breakfast room."

As Irene rose to her feet, she placed trembling hands over her churning stomach. *I'm not sure I can eat anything. I feel so nervous!* Her heart raced as she followed Anya to the stairs. Their descent was greeted by the sound of chatter, mingled with the clink of cutlery.

Recognising Zatao's voice, Irene felt a flush of excitement. Clutching the banister rail she paused and took a few deep breaths.

Anya glanced back. "Are you alright, My Lady?" She couldn't help noticing the rosy glow on Irene's cheeks.

Smoothing her skirt, Irene raised her head and nodded. "I'm fine, lead on."

Chapter 30

The breakfast room, with its informal decor and cosy atmosphere was a firm favourite with the family. Sunlight streamed through the large picture window, adding its warmth to the roaring logs on the fire. Landscape paintings and equine studies adorned the walls.

A long cupboard occupied the space of one wall. On its surface, were numerous hot serving dishes filled with scrambled eggs, devilled kidneys, bacon and mushrooms.

Standing by the door a young servant stood to attention his eyes cast down…his senses tuned to respond to the slightest request.

Prince Zatao sat at the head of the small table, a plate of scrambled eggs in front of him. Buttering a piece of toast, he glanced at Mira. "How did Irene seem this morning?" Noting her discomfort at the question, he frowned. "Is she alright?"

Mira placed her coffee cup in its saucer. Hearing the concern in her brother's voice she quickly reassured him. "Irene is fine. A little confused and overwhelmed, but that's to be expected. She was delighted to hear about Safi, although not so keen to have her as a maid, or anyone else for that matter. But after I explained, she appeared to understand. I left her in the capable hands of my maid Anya."

Zatao couldn't help chuckling as he bit into his toast. "I'm glad she hasn't changed. I love her sensitivity and touch of feistiness. It was that which kept her going when we rescued, August."

"That, and love for you," Mira reminded him.

Zatao nodded. "True, and now I am free to express my love for her."

Mira smiled at the faraway look in his eyes. Reaching across the table she placed a hand over his. "I'm so happy for you…for both of you. To find true love is a gift from God."

Zatao gently squeezed her hand, but before he could comment, Aldrin strode into the room.

"What's this about true love?" Aldrin asked a glint of amusement in his eyes. Pulling out a chair, he demanded his breakfast. While waiting to be served he studied Zatao, his brown eyes questioning. "So where is your lovely young friend this morning?"

Zatao saw the mockery in his eye, but made no comment.

"Will she be breakfasting with us?" Aldrin persisted.

Mira glared at him. "Yes, she will."

"Your news yesterday came as quite a surprise, brother." Forking a piece of bacon, he grinned at them before stuffing it in his mouth. "May I ask when the wedding will take place?"

"You will be informed at the same time as everyone else," Zatao said.

Noting the hard edge to Zatao's voice; Aldrin smiled at him. "I look forward to receiving the happy news."

Mira glanced at Zatao, her furrowed brow a warning not to respond to their brother's goading.

Zatao sipped his coffee and winked at her. He loved her gentleness; her attempts to keep the peace between himself and Aldrin. The corner of his mouth twitched in a smile, as he remembered their childhood…recalled the numerous fights and arguments he'd had with Aldrin. Even then, Mira played the role of peacemaker.

Zatao, being first born was destined to take the throne on the death of their father. This irked Aldrin, and he took every opportunity to compete with his brother and cause family strife.

Zatao's gentle nature and quiet strength endeared him to their father.

Aldrin on the other hand, was a wild and rebellious child. His behaviour declined further when he overheard his father tell Zatao. "My son, even if Aldrin were the eldest, I would not allow him to take my throne. His character is flawed. I could not safely place my kingdom in his hands. It is your destiny to rule Luminaire, and be the recipient of all that entails."

Hearing his father's words had devastated Aldrin…feeding his jealousy! Over time, as he watched his brother increase in strength and favour, his jealousy deepened…consumed him. Withdrawing from the family, he constantly looked for ways to undermine Zatao.

On the death of their father, he became more reclusive as he searched for ways to bring his brother down, and take the throne. The minute he'd heard someone was coming…someone important to his brother, he knew a situation was arising that could work in his favour.

Taking a piece of toast from the rack, Aldrin smiled. *This woman is Zatao's weakness. I will use her to break him.*

Zatao sat calmly in his chair, sipping his coffee, his dark eyes fixed on his brother.

Aldrin looked up from his toast and met his gaze. Feeling the hairs rise on the back of his neck, he lowered his head. *Damn it! He knows what I'm thinking.* Wiping a hand across his lips, he pushed his plate away.

Zatao raised an eyebrow. "Leaving so soon, Aldrin?"

As Aldrin rose to his feet; Irene appeared in the doorway.

All eyes turned as she entered the room.

Zatao hurried across to her. "Good morning, my darling." His eyes roved appreciatively over her. "You look wonderful."

Smiling shyly at him, Irene murmured. "Thank you."

Taking her hand, he gently kissed it, before leading her to the chair beside his. "How did you sleep?"

"Surprisingly well, really. When I woke I was a little confused and for a moment I couldn't think where I was."

Zatao smiled as he pulled the chair out for her. "It will be strange for a while, but we will do our best to make you feel at home."

"We certainly will," Mira said. "Would you like some breakfast?"

"Coffee and toast would be lovely, thank you."

As the servant poured her a cup of coffee and put fresh toast on the table, Irene glanced at Aldrin. Still on his feet, he stared at her open mouthed.

"Good morning," she said softly.

His voice faltered slightly as he reoccupied his seat, and acknowledged her greeting.

Zatao leaned protectively towards Irene. His eyes narrowed as he watched his brother. "I thought you were leaving?"

"I am, but first I'll have another cup of coffee." Smiling, he clicked his fingers at the servant.

Irene's stomach did a somersault. The tension in the room was palpable. She took a sip of her coffee hoping it would settle her.

Catching her eye, Mira asked. "After breakfast, would you like a walk in the garden?" Pivoting on her chair, she looked out of the large window.

Irene followed her gaze, and smiled. "That would be nice, it looks lovely out there."

"What a good idea," Zatao said. "I will leave you in Mira's capable hands."

Looking into his face, Irene's shoulders drooped. "Won't you come with us?"

"I'm sorry my darling, I can't. I have a meeting to attend." His eye's narrowed as he glanced across at Aldrin…already on his feet preparing to leave the room.

Zatao took Irene's hand and kissed it. "I will see you here later, for lunch." Rising from his chair, he stood beside her, his fingers twirling a curl of her hair. His eyes were glued to Aldrin retreating from the room. Glancing across at Mira, he frowned.

Irene stared up at him; concerned by the worry she saw in his eyes. Taking his hand, she asked softly. "Is everything alright?"

"We have a few problems, Irene, but nothing for you to worry about." Pulling her to her feet, he wrapped strong arms around her. Lowering his head he whispered in her ear. "This afternoon, you will have my undivided attention, I promise."

As Irene raised her head to smile up at him, he covered her lips with his own. Irene gasped, her breath quickened as she returned his kiss.

Gently, Zatao broke the moment, and eased her away. Holding her by the shoulders, he stooped and gazed into her face. "I will see you later. I have something I wish to show you."

Mira smiled as she joined them. "I will take care of her, Zatao. Go to your meeting."

"Very well, enjoy your morning." Rising to his full height, his smile encompassed them both as he swung round and strode from the room.

Noting the slump of his shoulders, Irene couldn't help a slight frown as she watched him leave.

Chewing her lip, she brushed a few crumbs from her skirt. *Something is wrong. I wish I knew what it was.*

Mira touched her shoulder. "Are you ready to go for a walk?"

Irene nodded; twisting the ring on her finger, she tried to dismiss a sense of foreboding as she followed Mira from the room.

Aldrin paced the great hall, his fists clenched tight. He relished the pain his nails inflicted on the palms of his hands. His eyes blazed with hatred and anger.

Hearing the door to the breakfast room open, he dashed across the great hall and flopped in a high backed chair in front of the fire. Concealed by the chair, he saw Zatao leave the breakfast room and hurry away to his office.

Peering around the wing of the chair, he watched Mira lead Irene towards the stairs. Their conversation floated towards him.

"I would like to unpack my rucksack, first," Irene said.

"That's fine," Mira replied. "I'll come up later with a warm cloak and some boots."

Aldrin watched Irene ascend the stairs. His eyes narrowed in a leer…he licked his lips. "I have a plan for you, my beauty," he muttered under his breath.

Concealed in the chair, he waited until Mira entered the chapel and closed the door, before rising to his feet. Resting an arm on the mantelpiece, he stared into the fire. He enjoyed watching the hot flames devour the logs.

Hearing a sound he turned. A servant appeared from the breakfast room, carrying a tray of leftover food. Clicking his fingers, Aldrin called him over.

The young man visibly trembled, crockery rattled on the tray.

"Find the maid Anya, and send her to my room," Aldrin commanded. "And make it quick."

"Yes, My Lord." With lowered eyes, the young man backed away.

Aldrin chuckled as he watched him hurry in the direction of the kitchen. Turning his attention to the portrait of his father above the fireplace, he grimaced. *I wish you were here, father…wish you were alive to see me instigate the demise of your kingdom.* Striding to the stairs he took them two at a time. Humming a tuneless melody he hurried along the corridor to his suite of rooms.

Closing the door, he settled at his desk and waited. His lips twitched in a smile as he pictured Anya's fear at being summoned. "Your work is not over after all, my pretty red head." Leaning back in his chair, he placed his hands behind his head and chuckled. His cheeks flushed with the thought of tormenting the young maid.

Deep in his deliberations, he was startled by a knock on the door. Straightening in his chair, he shouted. "Come!"

❧❧❧

In the kitchen, Anya hovered behind Safi, watching her iron the frills of a dress. "You're doing well. Carry on like this and in no time you'll be ready to serve, Lady Irene."

Safi glanced at her. "Do you really think so? I'm more used to pulling pints, than coping with all this finery." Placing the iron on the fire, she studied Anya. "How is Irene? Is she happy for me to be her maid? After all, I have no experience of such work."

Anya smiled, and indicated Safi should pick up the iron. "She has been concerned about you. And yes, she is delighted to have you as her maid."

Safi's face lit up in a slow smile. "I can't tell you how relieved I am to hear that."

Anya filled the big copper kettle and put it on to boil. "When you've finished that, I will show you how to make tea."

Safi laughed. "Anyone can make tea, surely?"

"Indeed they cannot!" A firm voice replied from the doorway.

Both girls swung round as Bella the housekeeper came into the room. "This is a royal household; and etiquette must be adhered to." Seeing the colour drain from Safi's face, she smiled. "Have no fear child. We will make sure you have the necessary skills to do the work required of you."

As Anya made the housekeeper a cup of tea, she told Safi where she would find the special trays, the bone china cups and saucers, tray cloths and everything necessary for serving tea to the members of a royal household. "Later, I'll show you what you need to do, for now come and have a cup of tea."

The three of them sat round the kitchen table chatting, when a male servant poked his head round the door. Seeing Anya, he came into the room. "Prince Aldrin has requested your presence in his suite." He saw the colour drain from her face, and gave her a sympathetic look as he backed out of the kitchen.

Seeing the fear in Anya's eyes; Safi stared first at the housekeeper, then at Anya. Her voice faltered as she asked. "What is it? Why are you both afraid?"

Bella rose to her feet. "It's alright, Safi. There's nothing to worry about." Turning to Anya, she smiled and patted her on the shoulder. "You'd best go, child. You don't want to keep the Prince waiting."

Anya felt a wave of dizziness as she stood to her feet. Taking a few deep breaths, she smoothed the front of her dress, and said softly. "I won't be long."

Rising to her feet, Safi stood beside the housekeeper. Gazing into Bella's kindly face, she asked. "Will Anya be alright?"

Bella put a plump arm round her shoulders. "She'll be fine. Now come, let me show you how to prepare a tea tray."

Chapter 31

Anya wiped her clammy hands together and sighed. *I had hoped never to come here again.* Her hand trembled as she tapped on the door. The authoritative, "Come!" from the other side sent a rush of fear through her body.

Feeling the colour drain from her face, Anya pinched her cheeks and took a deep breath. *I won't let him see I'm nervous.* Entering the room, she stood by the closed door, her eyes fixed on the Prince. His commanding presence shattered her resolve to be strong.

Aldrin sat forward in his chair, his arms casually resting on the desk top. Anya's attempt to project confidence vaguely impressed him.

Lowering her head Anya bobbed a curtsy. "You wished to see me, My Lord?"

"Come forward," Aldrin said gesturing with his hand. Leaning back in his chair he watched her approach. "I have a job for you." He found her look of surprise…mingled with fear, amusing. However, he refrained from smiling.

Anya's hands trembled as she clutched her skirt and lowered her eyes. "My Lord, I thought I would not have to—"

"Spy for me," he said quickly. "I am not asking you to spy, Anya. Just keep me abreast of Lady Irene and my sister's whereabouts." Rising from his desk he moved towards her. "You can do that for me, can't you?"

Holding her breath, Anya took a step back. The desire to flee the room was overwhelming. His towering presence weakened her resolve to be strong, to stand her ground.

"Have you lost your tongue, girl? Answer me."

Anya's mouth was dry, she could hardly swallow. Squeezing her hands together, she nodded.

Aldrin scowled and grabbed her by the arm. "Show respect, girl," he growled. "Answer me!"

The tightness of his grip made Anya wince. Knowing he wouldn't let her go until she agreed, Anya stared up at him. Her voice quivered slightly as she said. "I can do it, My Lord."

"Pardon, I didn't quite catch that."

Anya's face reddened with anger, her heart raced. Ignoring the mockery she saw in his eyes, she straightened her back, boldly raised her voice and said. "Yes, My Lord, I will keep you informed."

Releasing her, Aldrin stepped away. His eyes appraised her, noting the flush on her cheeks…the fire in her eyes. *You're appealing when angry, little red head.* Perching on the corner of his desk, he smiled at her. "That wasn't so difficult, was it?"

Lowering her head, Anya chewed her bottom lip. Bile rose in her throat at the thought of betraying her Mistress and Lady Irene.

Walking round his desk, Aldrin lowered his tall frame into the chair and studied some paperwork. Without looking up, he snapped. "You may go."

Anya stared at him, her eyes wide and questioning.

Glancing at her he growled. "Are you still here?"

"I'm sorry, My Lord, but people know I was summoned. What do I tell them?" Her voice quivered with anxiety.

Aldrin rolled his eyes and glared at her. "I have no interest in what you tell them. Now leave me!"

Anya fought to quench her tears. Bobbing a curtsy, she left the Prince and ran to her room. Sitting on the edge of the bed she wiped her eyes. Clenching the handkerchief in her hand, she groaned. *Oh God please help me! I must think of something. I dare not leave this room until I have.* Knowing Bella the housekeeper and Safi would be particularly curious, brought her out in a cold sweat. Her breathing accelerated as she perched on the edge of the bed, and struggled to find a feasible reason for the Prince's summons.

✎✎✎

Irene gazed around her room and smiled. She knew she'd taken a huge risk coming to Stagman's world, but it was a risk she'd been willing to take. She chuckled, *at least there's running water, and a few of the facilities I'm used to.*

Nevertheless, the realisation she'd stepped back in time came as a bit of a shock, to say the least! It was a situation she would need to come to terms with pretty quickly.

Walking across to the window, she leaned against the sill and looked out. Some distance away, magnificent cedars cast long shadows in the pale autumn sun. The splendour of the vast parkland took her breath away, she sighed with appreciation. *I think I'm going to love it here.*

She felt light headed with happiness as she unpacked her rucksack. *I'm not sure what people here will make of my clothes.* She couldn't help smiling as she put a pair of jeans, a couple of warm jumpers and some underwear in the small dresser.

Her unpacking finished, she sat on the bed with the small box containing the glass horse in her hand. Opening the lid, she lifted it out and placed it on the bedside table. Its crystal body glistened in the light from the window. "You've come home," she said softly.

Hearing a light tap on the door, she turned as Mira poked her head round. "May I come in?"

"Yes of course." Picking up the glass horse, Irene showed it to Mira. "Do you remember giving me this?"

Mira took it from her. "Indeed I do. I'm thrilled you still have it."

"Why wouldn't I. It's precious to me…a constant reminder of you and Zatao. In many ways it was the key to my return. Each time I looked at it, I became more restless, and unsettled."

Mira smiled, as she said, "Good, I'm glad." Putting the small horse back on the dressing table, she took Irene's hand. I have some boots and a warm cloak downstairs if you're ready to go for a walk."

"I would love to, lead on." Irene followed her downstairs to the hall, where a servant stood with their cloaks over his arm and boots at his feet. Irene sat on a small chair by the door, enjoying the new sensation of being waited on. The servant laced up her soft leather boots…they fitted perfectly.

While he attended to Mira, Irene posed in front of a large mirror on the wall. Twirling around, she admired the elegant way the cloak draped her body. The light brown material was heavy and warm. The luxurious fur colour complemented her skin. Lifting it up to her face she buried her chin it its soft warmth.

"Like it?" Mira asked.

"It's lovely, and so warm."

Mira took her hand, "Come let me show you the garden, even at this time of year we have roses in bloom."

Surrounded by tall hedgerows, the rose garden was sheltered and peaceful. A large ornate fountain took centre stage; surrounded on all sides by a variety of rose bushes, many of which were still in bloom. The wrought iron gate creaked, as Mira opened it and led Irene through.

For a brief moment, Irene stood in the entrance, her eyes wide with delight. "Mira, this is beautiful! Had you not shown me, I would never have guessed it was here."

Mira chuckled as she led her down the gravel path. "I knew you would like it."

"It's wonderful," Irene said, raising her head to sniff the air.

In certain places the scent was intoxicating. Taking a rest on a stone bench was one such place. Irene cupped a large rose growing close to the bench. Pulling back, she studied the beautiful flower head. The white petals were clear and delicate, almost translucent. Each petal tipped pink.

To Irene it looked as though an artist had taken his brush, dipped it in the softest pink, and gently edged each rose petal. "Oh, Mira this rose is the most exquisite I've ever seen. The scent is amazing. What's it called?"

Mira turned and caressed the rose nearest her. "Actually, it's named after me."

Irene gasped. "Wow, how lovely to have a rose like this named after you. So is it called Mira?"

"No," Mira said with a smile. "When I was a baby, the gardener found this rose, growing semi wild in another part of the garden. He cut a bud and took it to my mother. She was nursing me at the time, trying to get me to sleep. When she took the rose from him, and showed it to me, she said I reached for it, and as my hand touched a petal, I smiled and fell asleep." Pausing, she gazed into the distance.

Irene gently touched her arm. "Are you alright? I hope my asking has not upset you."

"I'm fine, Irene. I was thinking about my mother. As is the custom in our family, when I was born, I was given many names. My second name is Crystal.

The rose's calming influence, impressed mother, so she told the gardener to take a cutting...plant it in in the rose garden, and call it Crystal, in honour of her only daughter."

Irene stared open mouthed at Mira. Pulling herself together she said softly. "What a lovely story." Seeing tears in Mira's eyes she pulled her close, "You're shivering. Shall we go indoors?"

Mira nodded. "Yes, it will be lunch time soon." Leaving the garden, they walked hand in hand; a comfortable silence settled between them as they returned to the castle.

Chapter 32

Zatao sat alone in the breakfast room, awaiting Irene's arrival. He had requested some time alone with her.

Relaxing in an armchair by the fire, he mulled over the mornings meeting with his officers. Drumming his fingers on the arms of the chair, he gazed thoughtfully into the fire. *I would have preferred Irene to arrive in a time of peace. Nevertheless, she is here and it makes my heart glad.*

Leaning forward, he took the poker and pushed around the burning logs. Sparks flew as the flames rose higher; the soft scent of pine permeated the air. As he watched the flames devour the wood, his demeanour darkened. "I will not allow the enemy to take my land and destroy my people. We will have the victor—" His words petered out as Irene entered the room.

Zatao's countenance lightened as he left his chair and hurried to her. Taking her by the hand he led her to the armchair by the fire. As she made herself comfortable; he eased his tall frame into the chair opposite, and gazed at her.

Seeing the love in his eyes brought a flush to Irene's cheeks. Lowering her gaze, she stared into the fire.

"I'm sorry, my darling. Am I embarrassing you?"

Shaking her head, Irene murmured. "No, I love the way you look at me."

Zatao smiled, leaned forward and held her hands. "I have loved you from the first day we met." Raising her hands to his lips, he gently kissed them.

Irene's heart did a somersault; she was grateful to be sitting.

Gazing into her eyes, Zatao said softly. "I'm overjoyed you are here. At last we are together, and free to express our love."

A light tap on the door startled them. Zatao sat back in his chair, as a servant with a tray of food entered the room. "May I serve lunch, My Lord?"

"You may," Zatao said. Glancing at Irene, he winked.

Irene felt light headed…like some young thing hiding a secret dalliance. Her soft giggle threatened to erupt into laughter. Placing a hand over her mouth, she sat back in the chair attempting to hide from view.

Zatao grinned and raised an eyebrow.

"Stop it!" Irene hissed.

Leaning towards her, he whispered. "I'm not doing anything."

Irene scowled at him, but before she could answer, the servant informed them lunch was served.

Easing out of his chair, Zatao took her hand and led her to the table. "I hope you're hungry."

"It looks lovely. But where's Mira, and your brother?" Irene glanced towards the door. "Are they not eating with us?"

"No, I wished to spend some time alone with you. Mira is eating in her room. As for Aldrin, I have no idea where he is."

Irene looked up at him; she couldn't help noticing the fleeting darkness in his eyes at the mention of Aldrin. "If you don't mind me saying, I've noticed the relationship between you and Aldrin seems a little tense."

Zatao's jaw clenched. "We have a few issues. Our relationship has never been easy." Seeing the concern in Irene's eyes, he smiled. "Come," he said, changing the subject. "Let's eat."

Irene frowned. The obvious tension between the two brothers intrigued her. But it was obvious Zatao did not wish to discuss the matter. Settling in her chair, Irene relaxed in the warmth of the fire, and the peaceful ambience of the room.

Sitting beside her, Zatao reached for the carafe of wine, and poured them both a glass. Lifting his glass, he said softly. "I raise a toast to the woman I love; my future queen."

Irene rested the rim of her glass against Zatao's. The wine gently swirled, the crimson liquid harmonising with the warm flush on her cheeks. Overwhelmed by the emotion in Zatao's voice…his powerful presence; she broke eye contact and lowered her head.

Zatao took her glass and placed it on the table. Putting his hand under her chin he raised her head, and for a long moment gazed silently into her eyes.

Irene's pulse raced, heat flooded her body as she whispered. "I love you."

Leaning closer, he murmured. "I love you more." Tenderly his warm lips covered hers in a lingering kiss.

Irene wished it would last forever; never in all her life, had she felt this way. His presence consumed her; had he not pulled away...she dare not dwell on it!

Zatao held her face between his hands and gently kissed her on her forehead. "You have no need to fear, my darling. I would never take advantage of you. We will marry soon enough. I have waited for you...I can be patient a while longer."

Irene gazed into his beautiful face and pursed her lips. "You may be able to, but I'm not sure I can."

Zatao slapped the table, his loud laughter danced around the room.

Irene frowned at him. "What? I'm serious, it's not funny."

"It is funny, and you are adorable."

Irene's smile faded as she noticed his expression change.

Zatao took her hand and gently stroked it. "It would be wrong to do such a thing, prior to our wedding night. I apologise for my ardent kiss. I meant no disrespect."

Irene felt her heart would burst with love. She threw her arms around his neck and whispered in his ear. "I agree with you, we must wait."

With a warm chuckle, Zatao straightened in his chair and handed her a bread roll. "Let's eat, I'm starving."

Over a delicious lunch of various cheeses, homemade rolls, tomatoes, and fresh fruit, they chatted. Irene told him how she'd sold the painting, and then realised what a huge mistake she'd made. "My life was nothing without you. I couldn't get you out of my mind. I had to find the painting and buy it back if necessary."

"It was the same for me," Zatao told her. "I dreamt about you all the time." Pausing to spread butter on his roll, he smiled at her. "I was there when you found the painting in that old shop."

Irene gasped, her eyes widened. "So I was right! I knew I saw you."

Zatao nodded. "You did, and I can't tell you how happy I am to have you here."

Gazing at him, Irene felt an uncomfortable churning in her stomach, as she asked. "Do I sense a but?"

Zatao nodded. "I'm afraid so. Unfortunately, your arrival coincides with the possibility that we could soon be at war."

Irene's hand flew to her mouth. "Oh God, I don't believe it!" The sadness she saw in Zatao's eyes tugged at her heart.

"I'm afraid it's true. Sadly, for your own safety, your freedom to enjoy your new home is restricted. Obviously, you are free to move around the castle and grounds, but if you go further afield, you must be accompanied by the castle guard."

Zatao could see the tension on her face. "I'm sorry, Irene, but it's the way things are at the moment." Sighing, he gently brushed a long curl away from her forehead. "I need you to obey me in this. It's the same rule for Mira." He fixed her with his dark eyes. "You are both so precious to me."

Irene took his hand and nodded. She hated the fear she could see in his eyes. "Don't worry my darling. You have my word. And if there is any way I can help, you know I—"

"There is one way you can help me." Zatao wrapped his arms around her and gently rested his cheek on her head; he enjoyed the softness of her hair against his skin.

Pulling away, Irene stared up at him. "How?"

"By always doing what I tell you. I need to know where you are…to know you are safe." Seeing the disappointment in her eyes, he gently held her by the shoulders. "I'm serious, Irene."

His anxiety was palpable. Irene quickly reassured him. "Zatao, I will keep my word. Please believe me. I promise, if I should leave the castle grounds, I will make sure I am not alone." Raising a hand, she stroked his cheek. "I hate to see you looking so worried." His relieved smile reassured her. She chuckled as he stood and pulled her into a warm embrace.

"I have something I would like to show you," he said. "Let's go for a walk."

Irene looked down at her dress. "Do I need to change?"

"No, but you will need your cloak."

Warmly dressed, they left the castle and walked hand in hand through the grounds. Irene stared up at him. "Where are you taking me?"

"If I told you, it wouldn't be a surprise. Be patient, it will be worth it, I promise."

The gravel crunched under their feet as Zatao led her to the rear of the castle. Above their heads the autumn sun sparkled on the frost blanketing the grass. Away in the distance, soft pink hues tinged the skyline.

It will be a nice day tomorrow, Irene thought, as she hurried to keep pace with Zatao's long stride.

Passing a heavy wooden door, a guard stood to attention as they hurried past. Rounding a corner, Zatao guided her towards a narrow path. On either side tall Cedars, their trunks twisted and gnarled with age soared towards the sky. Underfoot, the ground felt soft and spongy due to the thick layer of needles. They moved silently along the path, their feet cushioned by nature's carpet.

Irene tightened her grip on Zatao's hand, and glanced back at the castle, hardly visible through the trees. *I wonder where we are going.*

"Not far now," Zatao said, answering her unspoken question. "I suggest you walk behind me, as up ahead the path narrows."

"I wish you wouldn't do that!"

"Do what?"

"You know jolly well, what I mean."

Zatao chuckled, "I have no idea what you're talking about."

"Reading my thoughts," Irene muttered under her breath.

Glancing round, he winked at her. "You sound like a little bird wittering in the treetops."

Irene frowned at him, but her frown softened into a smile, when she noticed the dwindling trees revealed a small brick wall, surrounding what looked like an orchard. However, it's what she saw in the orchard that caused her to gasp with delight.

As they approached the wall, two white horses, identical to August trotted over to them. The animals eyes shone with excitement...their lips made soft smacking noises as they stretched their necks towards Zatao.

"Hello my beauties," he said softly. Reaching into the pocket of his jerkin, he produced some small pieces of carrot.

The larger horse nipped the smaller, in her eagerness to reach the treat.

"Be nice," Zatao said sternly, as he divided the carrot between them. "Lovely, aren't they?" He said, glancing at Irene.

Irene could only nod. Apart from August, she had never seen more beautiful horses. Their fine heads resembled the Arabian. Dark intelligent eyes studied her, inviting her to come closer.

Reaching out a hand, Irene gently fondled the velvety nose of the larger horse. She grinned as the smaller horse whickered and stretched its neck towards her. "They are lovely, and so like August."

"They are mother and daughter. Allow me to introduce them to you. You are stroking Siren, the mother." He turned to the smaller horse and patted her neck. "This is Cloud, her father is August."

Irene gasped. "I'm not surprised, the resemblance is amazing. How old is she?"

"She will be three, next year. She still has a bit of growing to do, but from the look of her, I think she will be bigger than her mother."

Irene moved to Cloud and gently scratched her behind the ears. She chuckled as the filly leaned into her hand. Irene's eyes shone as she looked up at Zatao. "She likes this."

Zatao smiled. "She likes you; which is just as well."

"Why?" Irene asked.

"Because, my love, she is your horse…my gift to you."

Speechless, Irene gazed at him.

Grinning at her shocked expression, Zatao took her in his arms and kissed her.

Easing away, Irene stared into his face. "I don't know what to say, or how to thank you."

Returning her gaze, Zatao said. "No thanks are needed. I have waited eagerly for this day, and your delight is all the thanks I need. Obviously, Cloud is too young to be gentled, so until that time you will have to ride Flame."

Irene nodded. "I understand; Flame is a good horse." Wrapping her arms around him; Irene sighed and leaned her head against his chest, listening to the comforting beat of his heart. "I love you so much," she murmured.

Zatao stroked her hair. His heart felt heavy, his thoughts consumed with the threat of war. Watching the horses wander away to graze, and holding the woman he loved in his arms…war seemed unreal, a nightmare that would pass when waking. *But it isn't*, he thought. *And unless God intervenes, this woman I love, my family, my people are all under threat.* He gritted his teeth, as the tranquillity of the moment vanished.

Irene felt the subtle tension in his body, the quickening beat of his heart. Raising her head she peered up at him. "What is it? Are you alright?"

Stooping slightly, he kissed the top of her head. "I'm fine. It's getting late, we should return to the castle."

As they retraced their steps, the tall cedars cast long shadows over the path. Irene stared at Zatao's back, the uncharacteristic sag of his shoulders confirmed, he was lying to her...he was afraid! She shivered as an unpleasant sense of de-ja-vu settled over her, filling her with dread.

Chapter 33

In the days following Irene's arrival; she'd settled in well, and was surprised how natural she felt in this strange new world. It was as though she'd lived in Luminaire all her life. Her only concern was the tension she could feel in the castle. It affected everyone, from the kitchen staff to the castle guard. The rumour of war and border skirmishes, flourished in the tense atmosphere.

Irene spent most of her time with Mira, who did her best to appear at ease. Whereas, Zatao spent most of his time with the castle guard, and whenever Irene was with him, she couldn't help noticing, he appeared worried and preoccupied.

Safi's presence gave Irene comfort. They were both new to castle life, and found help and support in each other's company. Irene was pleased to see the sparkle had returned to Safi's eyes.

Under Anya and Bella's tutelage, Safi had learned quickly, and with little effort established herself as maid and companion to Irene. Her hairdressing skill came as a surprise to everyone, not least Safi.

Anya continued to keep an eye on her, to be sure the transition went smoothly. However, her concerns were quickly allayed. Safi fully embraced her role as maid to the future queen of Luminaire.

It had taken Irene a while to get used to someone being at her beck and call…no longer allowed to do anything for herself. Sitting at her dressing table, Irene couldn't help smiling as she watched Safi brush her hair.

Safi glanced at her in the mirror and cocked her head to the side. "What is it, My Lady?"

"I was just thinking, it's weird how quickly a person's life can change."

Safi nodded. "When my husband was killed, I felt as though my life had come to an end." Her eye's moistened with tears. "I loved him and miss him so much." Wiping her eyes, she glanced at Irene and smiled. "But now look at me. I never dreamed I would be a maid to the future queen of my country." She paused and looked away.

Irene could see her chin quiver. Swivelling on the stool, she took her hand. "Don't be upset."

"Oh, My Lady, believe me, I'm not upset. I can't thank you enough for what you've done for me. It is my desire to serve you for the rest of my life."

Irene patted her hand before facing the mirror. "You have nothing to thank me for, Safi. I liked you from the moment we met. And after all you'd been through, it was my pleasure to try and help."

"Well you have, My Lady. I love it here."

"I'm pleased. May I ask if some of your happiness is due to the presence of Guardsman Romure?" Seeing the embarrassed flush on Safi's cheeks, Irene smiled. "Sorry, I didn't mean to pry; but he is a good man and seems fond of you."

Safi smiled shyly as she tried to concentrate on Irene's hair.

Raising a quizzical brow, Irene studied her in the mirror.

Safi's cheeks reddened further as she met Irene's gaze. "Very well My Lady. Yes, we are seeing each other. I am growing fonder of him each day that passes." Her giggle was infectious and soon they were laughing uncontrollably.

They were still laughing when the door opened and Mira poked her head round. "Is it a joke anyone can share?"

Irene rose from the stool and smoothed the skirt of her dress. "It's nothing, Mira."

"In that case, are you ready for breakfast? Zatao will eat with us this morning." She smiled at the sparkle she saw in Irene's eyes. "It's been a while since he's joined us for breakfast."

"Oh, it has, Mira." Irene sighed. "It will be wonderful to spend some time with him."

Taking her hand, Mira hurried her towards the stairs. "Come he is waiting."

❧❧❧

Zatao sat at the breakfast table, his posture tense. Absentmindedly, he clicked his fingers, ordering a refill of the thick black coffee that helped keep him awake…helped his tired mind wrestle with the strategies of war.

Loosening the collar of his silk shirt, he sat back in his chair and sipped the hot brew, his thoughts focused on the day ahead. The sharp click of a servant's heels, followed by the announcement of Irene and Mira's arrival brought him out of his reverie.

Looking up, he felt the tension melt away as he watched the two young women enter the room. His eyes never left Irene's face as he rose from his chair to greet them.

In one fluid movement he crossed the room and took her in his arms. "Good morning my darling, you look wonderful. I've missed you."

Irene stared into his face, she could see the love...longing in his eyes. "I've missed you too," she murmured as his lips gently brushed her cheek. Her pulse raced at his closeness.

Dressed in black with his corn coloured hair tied with a strip of leather; his commanding presence took her breath away. All thoughts of breakfast fled her mind.

Mira stood with her hands on her hips, staring at them. Her emerald eyes filled with humour as she said. "Good morning Mira. Did you sleep well?"

Her sarcasm did not go unnoticed. Zatao and Irene glanced at her and burst out laughing.

Zatao chuckled as he gave her a bear hug. "Good morning sister; we apologise for ignoring you."

Mira smiled and slapped him on the shoulder. "I should think so. You forget I haven't seen you in ages myself."

Zatao's face clouded. "I know, and believe me I've missed you both." Taking their hands he led them to the table. "Now come, let's eat."

As they took their seats, Irene couldn't help noticing the effect his presence had on the servants. They scurried to serve, their eyes downcast.

Breakfast passed in a blur of happiness for Irene. So much so, she picked at her food, her focus consumed by Zatao. Pushing a piece of bacon round her plate, she discreetly watched him eat.

Zatao glanced at her. "Is the food not to your liking?"

"Oh, yes. I'm just not very hungry this morning."

With a slight tilt of his head and arched brow, Zatao gazed at her. "You should eat something," he said softly.

His knowing smile made Irene blush.

Reaching for her hand, he gently squeezed it. "You and I will take coffee together in my office."

Irene's empty stomach fluttered. She took a sip of her orange juice as Zatao turned to Mira.

"What are your plans for today?" He asked her.

Mira frowned. "I don't know. I would like to ride to the hamlet and check on Taris's mother. As you know, she's been unwell."

Irene perked up in her seat. "Can I ride with you? It would be good to get—"

Zatao's knife clattered on his plate. "No! I have told you both; you do not leave the castle grounds."

Mira huffed with annoyance. "But Zatao, she lives on the edge of our land; it's no distance."

Zatao rose from his chair, towering over them. "Enough! I have said no, so please obey me." Taking Irene's hand he led her to the door. On the way out he ordered coffee.

Irene glanced back at Mira and gave her a sympathetic smile.

❧❧❧

Irene snuggled beside Zatao, enjoying the warmth of the fire and some time alone with him. With his arm around her, holding her close, she felt safe.

Zatao put his coffee cup down and gently raised her chin. His dark eyes, warm with love bored into hers. "I apologise for my sharp tone earlier. But Irene, I must keep you safe, both you and Mira. War is imminent and I know spies have entered our land. As yet we are not sure how often, or how many, but I cannot afford to take any risks. You and Mira are the most precious people in my life."

Irene stared into his face, her eyes narrowed with concern. "Are you alright? You look tired." Pulling his face down, she kissed his cheek.

Zatao smiled and pulled her against his chest. "I am tired, but so are my men. We have very little time left to prepare."

Irene rested her head on his chest; the feel of his silk shirt against her cheek, the gentle throb of his heart held her captive. "I wish we could stay like this forever."

Zatao sighed. "So do I, my darling. I have no words to express my anger and frustration. Once again you are thrust into a dangerous

231

situation. However, I believe God brought us together, and by His grace no one will separate us."

Irene raised a hand and stroked his cheek. "I'm worried for you," she said softly.

Taking her hand, Zatao tenderly kissed it. "Do not be concerned. There is a scripture in our Holy book; it says, 'For you have armed me with strength for the battle. You have subdued under me, those who rose against me.' Zatao smiled. I believe God will protect me, Irene, and my people." Raising her chin he softly kissed her lips, before easing away from her and resting his head against the cushions. "When our enemy is defeated, I will make you my queen." The thought brought a smile to his face.

Irene's stomach fluttered with excitement. "I hope it will be soon."

Zatao nodded. "I pray it will." Rising from his seat he placed a fresh log on the fire and leaned his arm on the mantelpiece.

Irene gazed up at him. "What is it? You look thoughtful."

"Tomorrow afternoon, I ride with a large contingent to supplement one of my outposts. The majority of the guard will remain there with the arms and food we are taking."

"Is it far?"

"No, it's on the border of this estate, no more than ten miles away." Tapping his chin, he closed his eyes for a moment.

Irene tilted her head to the side as she stared at him. "What are thinking?"

"With so many to protect you, I'm wondering if it would be safe to allow you and Mira to accompany us."

Irene shot out of her seat and went to him. "Oh, yes please! I would love to spend more time with you." Taking his hand she begged to be allowed to go with him.

Zatao gazed into her pleading eyes. He could feel her hands tremble as he held them. His heart was torn. Was he wise to suggest this? Nevertheless, his pulse raced at the thought of spending some time together. Part of him embraced the joy of having her ride with him. However, a nagging doubt twisted in his gut. Stooping slightly, he stared into her expectant face. "I will pray about it, Irene, and let you know at breakfast tomorrow. For now I must go, as there is much to organize."

Holding her in his arms, he gently kissed her, before striding from the room.

As the door closed behind him, Irene clasped her hands. Resting them against her chin, she softly prayed. "Please, let us go with him."

Chapter 34

Anya stood in the laundry room watching Safi try to iron a strange looking garment. Her brow furrowed as she leaned over Safi's shoulder. "What is it?"

Safi shook her head. "My mistress calls it jeans."

"Jeans, what's it for?"

"It seems this garment is good for riding. I remember she wore something similar when we journeyed here." Safi placed the iron on the fire. "The material is so stiff; I have to get the iron really hot."

"Why would Lady Irene want to wear breeches like a man? I'm surprised My Lord the Prince allows it."

"It seems he has," Safi said placing the hot iron on the jeans; it had little effect on the creases in the heavy material. Safi frowned and glanced at Anya. "As you see, they are not like breeches, although they do fit my mistress rather tightly."

Anya raised an eyebrow. "Um, so why does Lady Irene want them ironed?"

"She and Princess Mira will be accompanying the Prince tomorrow after breakfast."

Anya's head jerked up. Catching her breath, she stepped out of Safi's line of vision and dabbed at the perspiration on her forehead. Struggling to keep her voice steady, she asked. "What sort of time will they leave?"

"As soon as they are ready, I believe; why?"

"Oh, no reason, I'm just concerned her Ladyship has something to eat."

"Don't worry Anya; you have trained me well. I will make sure she eats. Also I believe Bella will prepare food for the journey."

"Good." Anya turned and hurried from the room.

Safi placed the iron on the heat and watched her leave. *Strange, I wonder why she was so interested.* Shrugging her shoulders, she folded the jeans and hurried upstairs to her mistress.

❧❧❧

Anya's heart pounded as she stood outside Prince Aldrin's room. She felt exposed…afraid someone might come along and see her. Taking a few deep breaths, she wiped her sweaty palms on her dress. *I'm glad I've written a note. No way do I want to face him.* With a furtive glance down the hallway, she stooped and pushed the paper under the door. Tapping softly, she turned and fled to her own room.

Sitting on the side of the bed she rested her head in her hands and rocked. *Why does Prince Aldrin want to know what Lady Irene is doing? Oh Lord, I wish he would leave me alone. I don't want to spy for him.* Tears of frustration trickled down her cheeks. Wiping her eyes she banged a fist into the mattress. "I don't like him. He scares me."

❧❧❧

Hearing the soft tap on his door, Prince Aldrin looked up. Noting the small piece of paper on the floor, he hurried to retrieve it. "What a good girl you are, little red head."

Sitting at his desk he unfolded it and smirked with delight. "At last! This is perfect." Rolling the paper tightly, he pushed it into a small metal cylinder and sealed the end. Stuffing it safely in his jerkin pocket he hurried from the room.

Taking the stairs to the roof two at a time, he went to the pigeon loft and chose a bird. Attaching the cylinder to its leg, he set it free. Smiling with satisfaction, he leaned against the roof balustrade, and watched the bird fly towards the distant mountain.

Once it was out of sight, he brushed his hands on his breeches and sauntered down stairs to his suite of rooms. Deep in thought he was unaware of Mira walking towards him. Her soft greeting interrupted his reverie.

"There you are, Aldrin, I've been searching for you?"

"Well, you've found me," he said, curbing the sarcastic comment perched on the tip of his tongue. The affection he saw in her eyes, pricked at his conscience. His lips softened in a smile as she

235

linked her arm through his. He loved his baby sister; she was the only member of the family who showed him any affection.

"Where have you been?" Mira asked.

"The pigeons needed food and water." Gazing into her trusting eyes, he felt his throat tighten…felt the flush of heat on his cheeks; he looked away. "I like it up there. It's quiet, and I find the birds a pleasant distraction." That was true; as a boy it was his favourite place. If ever he was missing, the family knew where he would be.

"I know," Mira said squeezing his arm. "But tea has been served and I thought you might like to join us. It seems ages since I saw you."

Aldrin chuckled. "I don't think it has been that long. However, tea sounds nice."

Mira's animated chatter made him smile, as she led him to the small sitting room. The room had been their mother's favourite. With its chintzy curtains, warm décor and roaring log fire, it was one of the pleasantest rooms in the castle. Light streamed through a surprisingly large picture window. The stained glass at the top of the window depicted scenes of a large stage and a beautiful white horse.

As Mira and Aldrin entered the room, Zatao greeted them. "There you are, we were wondering where you'd got to."

"He was on the roof with the pigeons," Mira said taking a cup of tea from Irene.

"Come brother sit," Zatao said, indicating to a wing backed chair close to the fire. "You look tense, is everything alright?"

Aldrin reached for a sandwich. "Everything is fine. I'm a little tired that's all."

"You take those dogs for too many walks," Zatao said with a chuckle.

Aldrin shot him a sarcastic smile. "You're probably right." Biting into his sandwich, he discreetly studied Irene out of the corner of his eye. Her auburn curls sparkled like gold in the firelight, complementing her fair complexion. He watched her nibble on a sandwich, her eyes focused on Zatao. *She's lovely*. Aldrin's stomach hardened, the sandwich stuck in his throat. Clenching his teeth, he imagined what would happen to her when in the clutches of King Murkier. *Not my problem. All I have to do is deliver her to him.*

Nevertheless, watching her eat…seeing the sparkle of happiness in her eyes brought a flood of guilt. The tea cup rattled in its saucer, placing it on the table he smiled at their curious glances. Needing to deflect more questions he asked Zatao. "Are you riding with the guard tomorrow?"

Zatao nodded.

"I would like to accompany you, if it's alright? I could do with getting away from here for a while."

Staring at him, Zatao's eyebrows arched. "I'm not sure that's a good idea. Mira and Irene will travel part of the way with me, and if you accompany us—" Pausing, he lowered his voice. "You know I don't like having all my eggs in one basket." Resting his elbows on the arms of the chair, he stared at Aldrin. "Anyway, I didn't think you'd be interested in coming."

Averting his gaze, Aldrin stared at the fire and said firmly. "I told you, like everyone else, I'm sick of being cooped up in this place. I want to take a ride and get some fresh air." He faced Zatao. "Is that so hard to understand?"

Zatao's eyes hardened…tightness in his stomach made him uneasy. He knew his brother was lying. *There's more to this, than taking a ride.* Rising from his chair, he rested an arm on the mantelpiece. "I would prefer it if you remain here. With war looming, I feel it's important to have at least one family member in residence."

Zatoa's penetrating gaze and the hard edge to his voice made Aldrin nervous. Nevertheless, he had to find a way to join them; even if it meant following from a distance.

In the tense silence an idea dropped into Aldrin's head. His voice rose slightly as he said. "Have you considered if I accompany you, the ladies won't have to return so quickly, as I will be with them?" Glancing at Mira and Irene, he noticed his suggestion fuelled their excitement. A brief smile cloaked the glitter of triumph in his eyes.

Zatao, aware his brother was manipulating the situation, clenched a fist and frowned at him.

Aldrin held eye contact…smiled and raised his hands. "Surely my brother you can see the sense in my suggestion. The ladies can enjoy more of your company, and you can relax, knowing I will make sure they return home safely."

Zatao squeezed his fist tighter, pushing his nails into the palm of his hand. He knew Aldrin's game from of old, but would not give him the satisfaction of seeing his anger.

As boys, his brother often attempted to turn a situation to his advantage. Zatao clenched his teeth, but before he could comment Mira and Irene bombarded him with entreaties and pleading expressions.

Leaving her chair, Irene went to him. Linking her arm through his, she leaned her head against his upper arm. "Please, Zatao. If it means I can spend more time with you. Let Aldrin come with us."

Zatao took an inaudible breath; Irene's closeness, her scent…the warmth of her body against his and her soft pleading, undermined his ability to stand on his decision.

Mira's voice merged with Irene's. "Let him join us, Zatao. As Irene said, it would be good to spend more time together." She could see the tension on her brother's face, as he sought to uphold his authority, while accommodating the wishes of those he loved.

"I know if Aldrin is with us on the return journey, we will feel safer," Mira said brushing cake crumbs from her dress. She smiled up at Zatao, her emerald eyes pleading.

Irene nodded and stared into his face. "Please my darling," she whispered.

Aldrin sat stiffly in his chair; holding his breath, he glanced furtively at his brother.

Zatao's long sigh sounded more like a growl, as he gazed at them. His eyes dark with anger, fixed on Aldrin. "If any harm comes to either of them." The menace in his voice was clear. His arm tightened round Irene's waist. His voice rose as he glared at Aldrin. "You keep them safe, do you hear me?"

"I will guard them with my life. You need have no fear."

"I hope so, for your sake, brother."

Irene stared up at him. "Have you agreed? Is Aldrin to accompany us?"

Zatao nodded. "Aldrin's presence means you may ride further with me."

Throwing her arms round his waist, Irene rested her head against his chest and murmured. "Thank you."

Zatao's heart rate slowed as he stroked her hair.

Mira clapped her hands. "Yes indeed, thank you. It's been so long since we rode together as a family."

Zatao smiled as he cradled the back of Irene's head; however his smile faded as he glanced at Aldrin. His brother's encouraging nod did little to alleviate his sense of unease. *Something's wrong. I should have stuck to my first decision.* Tightening his hold on Irene, he pulled her closer.

Aldrin stared into the fire. He needed to concentrate if he was to block Zatao's attempt to sense his thoughts. *How come he got the gifting's, and I—* He knew why. Thoughts of his father brought an angry flush to his cheeks.

Unaware of the tension between the two brothers, Irene snuggled into Zatao's embrace. Raising her head she stared up at him and smiled.

The strength of her love empowered Zatao. Taking her by the shoulders, he eased her away and gently nudged her to sit beside Mira. The corner of his mouth twitched in a smile as he watched their excited interaction. *How can I shatter their happiness?* He thought. *I've agreed to their request, so I must keep my promise.*

Rubbing the back of his neck, he rose to his full height and moved to stand beside the fireplace. His eyes settled briefly on Aldrin. *I'm not sure what game you're playing. But you won't succeed!* Owning the thought, his chin jutted…his eyes darkened.

Irene stared at him, awed by his beauty and stature. Every nerve in her body tingled, as a vision of Stagman filled her thoughts.

Mira took her hand and gently squeezed it. Seated together on the couch they waited for Zatao to speak.

In a voice tinged with gravitas, he warned them of the possible danger they might face. "As yet war is not declared. But I'm aware enemy spies regularly enter the boundary of our land." Clearing his throat, he continued. "If I'm overly cautious, it's simply because I want to keep you safe." He looked at Aldrin, his eyes holding his brothers in a penetrating gaze.

Aldrin broke eye contact and fiddled with the ring on his finger. "I will look after them," he said, glancing up at Zatao. "You have no need to worry."

Zatao faced Mira and Irene. His heart welled with love as he stared into their expectant faces. "When you leave me to return home; stay close to Aldrin and the accompanying guard."

"We will," they said in unison.

Moving away from the fire, Zatao lowered himself into a chair beside Aldrin. Without looking at his brother, he said firmly. "When you bring the girls home; ride hard and fast. Stop for nothing and no one." Turning, he stared long and hard at Aldrin. "Do you understand me?"

Aldrin returned his brothers gaze and nodded.

"Very well," Zatao said drumming his fingers on the arms of the chair. "It's settled. We leave here tomorrow after breakfast."

"It will be so good to stretch our legs," Mira said.

Irene nudged her. "I think you mean the horse's legs." They broke out in giggles.

Aldrin shifted in his seat, and undid the top button of his shirt. *I need to get out of here.* Wiping a hand across his brow he eased out of his chair.

"Feeling the heat, brother?" Zatao asked.

Aldrin ignored the innuendo. "Yes, it's warm in here. I need some fresh air."

Mira stood and hugged him. "Thank you, Aldrin." She glanced at Irene. "We'll both feel safer knowing you're with us."

Irene joined her and held out a hand to Aldrin. "Yes, we will thank you."

Aldrin smiled and bowed his head as he took her hand. "It will be an honour to accompany you, My Lady." Glancing at Mira, he smiled. "I will take care of you," he said softly.

Mira tilted her head as she stared at his retreating form. *What a strange thing to say.* As the door closed behind him, Mira felt a strange heaviness in her stomach. Glancing at Zatao, his narrowed eyes and wrinkled brow mirrored her sudden sense of unease.

Chapter 35

Grouchen's heart lurched as he saw the pigeon settle on the windowsill. Opening the window he grabbed it. His gnarled hands shook as he retrieved the small tube from the bird's leg, before releasing it. Sitting at his table, he eased the small slip of paper out of the tube, spread it flat and eagerly read it.

The contents brought a smile to his face, although his smile faded, as he raised his head and stared out of the window. A frown emphasised the deep wrinkles on his brow. With the slip of paper clutched in his hand, he hurried from the room. "That wretched spy has given us little time; it will be dark in a couple of hours." He chuntered and grumbled all the way to Ergon's room.

Hammering on the heavy door, he shouted to Ergon.

"I hear you. Stop banging!" Ergon shouted from the other side.

Grouchen stepped back as the door creaked open. "It has come," he said, in a voice breathless with anxiety. "Quick, we need to alert, Muglwort."

Scowling, Ergon threw his cloak around his shoulders. "Why the big hurry?"

Grouchen rolled his eyes. "Because there is not much time; the warriors only have tomorrow in which to grab the girl."

"What! This is a disaster."

"Not if we hurry," Grouchen said pulling on Ergon's cloak. "They have time to get there, if we show them the note now. So hurry, follow me." He turned and headed down the corridor.

Slamming his door shut, Ergon hurried after him. With lowered heads and grim expressions, they shuffled along the dimly lit corridor. Dust rose as their feet disturbed the rush matting covering the cold stone floor.

❧❧❧

Muglwort hung onto the angry black stallion. With no saddle the beast's violent gyrations threatened to unseat him.

"Show him whose boss!" Zworn yelled from the side-lines.

"What do think I'm doing? If you can do—" his voice cut out as the irate stallion did a huge buck, throwing Muglwort forward. Clutching a handful of mane and gripping with his knees, he managed to stay on board.

Pulling on the reins, he yanked the vicious bit in the horse's mouth...his spurs raked the animal's sides, as he rode it round and round the small ménage, until all fight was gone and the horse stood trembling covered in sweat and bleeding.

Grinning, Muglwort jumped off and led the exhausted animal over to the fence. "I can find you another to break, if you think you're such a good horsemen."

Zworn shook his head. "No thanks. You break the horses; I'll stick to breaking women."

Laughing, Muglwort slapped him on the shoulder. "Break women! You don't have to break them; they fall at your feet."

Throwing his shoulders back, Zworn grinned. "True, and if not, they're a whole lot easier to deal with than this," he said, gesturing at the beaten down horse.

"You're right there," Muglwort said as he vaulted the fence, and strode towards the stables. "Go and fetch that horse!" He shouted to a group of nervous stable lads huddled in a doorway.

Zworn followed him across the courtyard. "Do you fancy a drink?"

"Good idea. Let me get cleaned up first."

Opening a side door into the castle they paused, allowing their eyes time to adjust in the dim light.

"We'll go to the tavern by the castle gates. I've done enough riding for today."

Zworn grinned. "That's fine by me. I quite fancy their serving wench."

Muglwort sniggered as he led the way down the long corridor. Turning a corner, they saw the King's advisors hurrying towards them.

Muglwort increased his pace. Standing outside the door to his room, he pounded a fist into the palm of his hand. He could feel his heart rate increase.

Zworn glared at the two men. "I hope your presence means you've heard from the spy."

Shoving his hands deeper into his sleeves, Ergon hurried to keep pace with Grouchen. He hated Zworn, and the thought of being in his presence forced him to breathe heavily, which in turn made his head spin.

Approaching the warriors, the two advisers bowed their heads. Their faces were flushed with haste; it took them a moment to catch their breath.

Ergon stood silent, his head bowed.

Grouchen raised his head and looked up at Muglwort. He stared into black malevolent eyes. His voice faltered as he said. "We have heard from the spy, My Lord." He gestured to the closed door. "May we speak in private?"

Muglwort ordered the lone guard aside and unlocked the heavy door. Leading the way into the room, he took a chair at the table. Rolling his eyes, he waited for Grouchen to give him the message.

Zworn hovered behind Muglwort's chair, a smirk on his face as he watched the two older men sit at the table. He found their terrified expressions amusing, especially Ergon.

"The message arrived a few moments ago, My Lord." Grouchen's hand shook as he handed the slip of paper to Muglwort. "I am afraid the spy hasn't given us much notice."

Muglwort scowled as he read the note. Handing it to Zworn, he glared at the two advisors. "How are we expected to get there in time?"

Zworn dropped the note on the table. "This means riding all night! It was bad enough in daylight, but now they have troops patrolling the forest. How are we supposed to get through in the dark?" His eyes blazed with anger.

Muglwort's chair scraped the floor as he stood and paced. "Getting there will be hard enough...returning with the captive will be nigh on impossible."

"I will deal with her," Zworn growled.

"That's not the point!" Muglwort slammed his fist on the table.

Grouchen and Ergon all but leapt out of their skins.

Muglwort rested his palms on the table and leaned across it...so close, Grouchen could smell his breath.

"You should have warned the spy to give us more notice," he growled.

"I'm sorry My Lord. This is the first time we've heard from him in quite a while."

Zworn tightened his belt. "Time is short. I'm going to my quarters to get my stuff."

Muglwort nodded and waved a dismissive hand at the advisors.

Grouchen and Ergon left the table and hurried to the door. Out in the corridor, they breathed a unified sigh of relief. For a brief moment they watched Zworn's huge form disappear down the corridor.

Ergon closed his eyes and exhaled.

Grouchen pulled on his sleeve. "Come, let's go."

Ergon needed no second bidding.

❧❧❧

In single file, Muglwort led Zworn and two powerful warriors, Freon and Putius away from the castle. They galloped through the village, and out onto the open plain. The silvery light of a full moon glistened on the snow covered landscape.

Easing their horses into a canter, they grouped together. The snow quickly thickened over the ground; dulling the thud of their horse's hooves.

"We need to keep a steady pace," Muglwort shouted to Zworn. "Once we reach the mountain and surrounding forest we'll be forced to slow down. This is our only chance to make up time." Raking his horse's flanks, he urged the animal into a gallop.

The snorting horses, the clank of steel, and the creak of leather, impinged on the snow induced silence.

❧❧❧

Deep in their den the rats clustered together. The trembling ground unleashed loose soil. A wave of panic moved through the colony, as dirt and stones peppered the rat's fur. Squealing with fright, they scurried about unsure what to do.

Huddled in their midst, Ezekiel raised his head. Rising on his haunches he listened. The ground shuddered beneath him. "They are close, somehow we must warn the Prince."

Clambering onto his favourite rock, Ezekiel demanded silence. The others seeing their Prince on his throne, so to speak, gave him their attention.

Ezekiel gazed around at the huddled rats. His long tail twitched. In the ensuing silence, the sound of approaching horses was unmistakable. Ezekiel hissed. "They are here, at the border of our land."

"What shall we do," a young rat cried from the rear of the troop.

"Panic, might be good idea," an old black rat replied.

"We stay calm," Ezekiel said firmly.

A large white rat with a black head approached him. "Father, should I take a small troop and go outside?"

"Yes, my son. But do not let yourselves be seen."

"Don't worry father." Moving through the troop, Hood chose a number of big strong males and led them out into the night. Scurrying under a large thorn bush, they crouched down and waited. No sooner were they settled, than four huge black horses thundered into the clearing, slipping and sliding on the snowy ground.

"Oh my!" One of the rats' whispered.

Hood glared at him. "Shush! Come on follow me." With pounding hearts they followed him back to the den, and stood trembling before Ezekiel.

"They are huge, father….huge and as black as night, even the riders."

Ezekiel's ruby eyes narrowed, his long white whiskers twitched. He refused to get caught up in the fear he smelt around him. "How many are there?" He asked calmly.

"Four, Sire." A young brown buck replied. "They sound like thunder."

Ezekiel scratched under his chin, he needed to think. *Psalm*, he thought. *I need to get in touch with Psalm.* Turning to Hood, he ordered him to take the brown buck and go to the burrow's entrance. "Let me know when the riders leave," he instructed.

Hood led the way, the young buck followed close on his heels. Hood's heart pounded, his limbs felt shaky. He needed to keep busy.

Together they crouched in the shadows. Out in the clearing the riders were re-forming. In single file they took the main path deep into the heart of the forest.

The young buck squinted at the white stuff gathering on his nose. Raising a paw he brushed it away. "It's snowing."

Shivering, Hood gazed up at the inky sky. Soft white flakes like a trillion stars filled his vision. "Come on, we need to tell father the riders have gone."

In the den, Ezekiel ordered a group of rats to dispose of the dirt and stone dislodged by the horses pounding hooves.

"It could have been worse," an old rat muttered, using his forepaws to brush the soil to the edge of the den.

"How much worse?" his companion asked.

"The whole den could have caved in." The old rat's eyes narrowed dramatically as he stared at the frightened youngster.

Pushing his way through the workers, Hood hurried to his father. In between gasping for breath, he shared his information. "The riders have gone father. They're headed deep into the forest."

"And it's snowing," the brown buck added in a solemn tone.

Ezekiel's body stiffened...his fur fluffed with anxiety. "We must get a message to Psalm, but we'll never get through if it's snowing. I need to think." Sitting on his haunches he closed his eyes.

The rats clustered together in silence watching him. They flinched when his eyes shot open.

Raising a paw, Ezekiel said. "I have an idea. Has anyone seen the old barn owl?"

A young female approached. "He was around earlier this evening. I saw him eyeing my little ones, so I called them in."

Hood stared at Ezekiel and frowned. "Why do you ask about the owl?"

Ezekiel stood and shook the dust from his coat. "Because my son; if we can convince him of the danger threatening our Prince, and this land, he may be willing to take a message to Psalm."

A big grey buck lumbered over. "That's if you can convince him not to eat us."

Ezekiel nodded. "True, that could be a problem, nevertheless I must try."

"No father!" Hood moved alongside Ezekiel and reached out a paw. "He will kill you. Please let me go."

Ezekiel smiled and rubbed his head against his son's neck. "It's alright, Hood, I am old. If I die, I die. But you are my heir...I cannot allow you to go. This is my responsibility. And anyway, I do not believe he will kill me."

Getting to his feet, he lumbered through the troop. Their heads bowed as he passed. Hood followed him. "How do you know he won't kill you?" He demanded.

Ezekiel paused and turned his head. His ruby eyes sparkled. "He won't kill me, because I am about the Prince's business; and loyalty to Prince Zatao comes before all else."

Fawn hurried to her father's side. "What if he doesn't believe you, father."

Ezekiel could smell her fear. "He will believe my daughter, trust me and have faith." Raising his head, he walked resolutely towards the entrance to the den. "Stay here," he said without looking back. "I do not wish to be followed."

Trembling, Fawn huddled at her brother's side. "Father, don't go!" She cried.

The poignant sound followed Ezekiel to the mouth of the den.

Chapter 36

The old owl flew over the tree tops; his wings beat a silent path through the falling snow. Below him lay a forest shrouded in white; snow crystals glistening in the moonlight.

Soaring above the trees, the owl searched the forest floor; his huge eyes missed nothing. His prey, clearly visible scurried over the blanket of snow. The owl's eyes narrowed. "I should be hunting," he grumbled. "Not flying on some half-baked mission. How do I know that old rat was telling the truth?" Thinking about the plump white rat made his juices flow. *He would have made a good meal.* Hungry and irritated he clicked his beak.

"Trouble is I dare not take the risk. If our Prince is truly in danger, then I must do all I can to help."

Veering right, he flew on towards the distant edge of the forest. Tiredness sapped his energy. *I hope the rat's directions are correct.* He could feel his heart racing. His body ached. *Maybe it won't hurt to stop and rest awhile.* Floating down, he perched on the snow covered branch of a tall pine. Dropping his wings, he opened his beak and gaped, breathing in some much needed air.

Gradually, his heart regulated, he could feel his strength return. Instinctively, he studied the forest floor. His eye's spotted a small rodent scurrying in search of food. His rumbling stomach was all the incentive he needed.

The wind ruffled his feathers as he glided silently to the forest floor. Nearing the prey he opened his talons and snatched the unsuspecting mouse. The rodent's surprised squeak echoed in the silence.

Rising through the branches he settled on a high bough and devoured his meal. He would have liked to stay a little longer, and continue hunting, but a distant sliver of light heralded the approach of dawn. *I'd best get moving.* Launching into the air he flew towards the rising sun, his eyes scanning the horizon. From what the rat told him, he guessed his destination was close. *I hope finding the dove won't be a problem. I need to give her the message, and go home.* With his eyes half closed against the swirling snow; the old owl flew on, his expression, determined. Having come this far, there was no way he would turn back. He would find the dove...give her the message, or die trying.

❖❖❖

Psalm flew low, skimming through the branches; she knew it was risky, but flying above the forest against the wind and swirling snow, quickly sapped what little strength she had. *I'm too old for this.* She could feel her heart beating in her chest; her wings felt heavy. They no longer possessed the fluid movement of youth.

The owl's arrival had taken her by surprise...the message he brought was disturbing. So after a quick farewell to her family, she departed on her journey. The owl accompanied her part of the way, before veering off to fly home. Psalm missed him, alone she felt strangely vulnerable.

She had no idea why the dark warriors had entered the land, or why they appeared to be heading for Prince Zatao's castle; nevertheless she knew she must pre-empt them. Her eyes narrowed as she thought of the evil King on the other side of the mountain. *Who are these warriors he sends against us? They are not spies; they are here for a purpose?* Even as she asked the question; anger heated her blood, her heart raced.

With a gaping beak she flew on, pushing herself until she could fly no further. *I must rest a while.* Perching on a branch, she peered up at the sky. It was no longer snowing. Early morning light filtered through the branches. Where it touched the forest floor, the snow sparkled like polished crystal.

Settling on the branch, she fluffed her feathers against the cold. "I'm half way there now, a short rest won't hurt." Her voice faded, her eyelids drooped as she fell into a deep sleep.

❖❖❖

Blackwing flitted over the ground, his bright eyes searching for anything remotely edible. Rising higher he perched on the branch of an old Oak. Gazing around, he noticed a small white bird huddled on a branch just below him.

Seeing the resting dove, reminded him of Psalm. *I wonder how she is. Its ages since I last saw her.* However, his thoughts quickly vanished in a wave of anxiety. His heart rate increased as he spotted movement close to the trunk of the tree. A large mink inched along the branch towards the sleeping dove.

The animal's dark glossy coat stood out against the snow coating the branch. But for the snow, Blackwing would have missed it. Flicking his tail, he hopped up and down; his raucous warning calls echoing in the silence.

The mink glanced up and glared at him. The creature's cruel beady eyes blazed with threat.

Desperate to help the dove, Blackwing continued to cry out. His gold eyes filled with panic. Flapping his wings, and flicking his tail, he did his best to wake the sleeping bird. "Tck! Tck! Tck!" He cried. "Wake up, wake up."

Too late, the dove opened its eyes, in time to see a black shape armed with razor sharp teeth bearing down on it. The dove's fearful cries filled the air, white feathers fell like snow.

Enraged, Blackwing flew at the mink, harassing the creature. But his attempt to rescue the dove was futile. The mink held the flapping bird in its jaws, its bright evil eyes mocking him.

The dove looked up at Blackwing, its eyes growing dim, as it went into shock.

Blackwing recoiled in horror! His heart all but stopped as he cried, "Psalm!"

With her last breath, she managed to whisper. "Go to Prince Zatao, warn him—"

The mink tittered as he carried Psalm's limp body down the trunk of the tree to the ground. Spots of pink stained the pristine snow as he carried his prize into the shrubbery and disappeared.

Blackwing followed, his voice faltering as he cried. "Psalm!" Settling on a low branch, he fluffed his feathers against the cold. Trembling with fear he stared wide eyed at the spots of blood, and listened to the scuffling and crunching sounds from deep inside the shrubbery.

Heavy hearted, he bowed his head. "I should have come sooner…should have made more noise. Maybe then I could have saved her." Sighing, he stared around, his eyes bright with anxiety. Alert for danger, he mulled over Psalm's last words. *Go to Prince Zatao and warn him.* Blackwing frowned. "Warn him about what?" Frustration added to his shock and sorrow.

Setting his face, he launched into the air and flew in the direction of the castle. "Maybe when I tell Irene, she will know what the message means." Skimming the ground as was his habit. He recalled Irene's warning him not to fly so low, and having just witnessed Psalm's demise, he rose higher.

His heart raced with a sense of urgency as he soared through the forest, twisting and turning to avoid branches. The sun was rising; Blackwing frowned. *Whatever the threat is, I hope I'm not too late.* His chest throbbed to the drumbeat of his heart. Driven by an overriding urgency, he pushed on, numb with sorrow and anxiety.

❦❦❦

Like black shadows, the four riders moved silently. The snow worked to their advantage, muffling sound. Muglwort's eyes narrowed as he gazed at the forest canopy, he wanted to be in the place of ambush before daylight.

However, his face relaxed in a smile, as ahead of them the forest path widened considerably, enabling them to move at a faster pace. Spurring his horse, Muglwort urged it into a canter. A layer of snow carpeted the ground, deadening the thud of hoof beats.

After a while the path narrowed, forcing them to slow down. Walking their horses, they pushed through shrubbery and found themselves on the perimeter of a large clearing.

Staying under cover, Muglwort raised a hand, indicating silence.

"What is it?" Zworn asked.

"I hear horses, they're coming this way," Muglwort hissed. Pulling on the reins they backed their horses under the trees, and pulled black hoods over their heads.

From the other side of the clearing, a group of guardsmen appeared out of the trees. Reining their horses they stared around, their eyes searching the shadows, before turning left and disappearing into the forest.

"That's the second patrol we've seen," Zworn said. "I've a feeling there's a camp near here."

Muglwort nodded. "I bet it's where Zatao is going later today."

Putius leaned forward in the saddle. "How can we be sure the girl will be with him?" he glanced down at the snow. "He may decide the weather is too bad."

Muglwort glared at him and growled. Nevertheless, he knew the man was right. It was a distinct possibility. But not something he wished to dwell on. "She will be with him," he insisted. "If not, the spy Traditor is a dead man."

Lowering his hood, Muglwort rubbed the back of his neck. Putius had given voice to his thoughts, and it filled him with anxiety. *She had better be there.* Gritting his teeth, he clutched the reins and slammed his spurs into his horse's flanks. The animal snorted and shot forward.

The others urged their horses after him. Tightly bunched they galloped across the clearing and melted into the forest on the other side.

Reining his horse, Muglwort turned in the saddle. "If we come across any patrols, hide in the undergrowth," he whispered. "From here on in, we go slowly and quietly." He fixed his eyes on Freon. "Our place of ambush is close, but this is where we could come up against trouble, so keep your bow at the ready. Death needs to be quick and silent."

Freon nodded. His lips twitched in a cruel smile as he stroked the bow at his back. "I will be ready," he said in a voice as deep as a black bear's growl.

"All right, let's go. Conceal yourselves," Muglwort said.

With a nod of understanding, they pulled their hoods over their heads, and in single file followed him. In the mounting tension, they rode with one hand resting on sword hilts. Cruel eyes...black as the night, narrowed to slits as they surveyed the surrounding forest. They were ready and eager for the battle.

Chapter 37

Irene's stomach churned. Pushing her food round the plate, she glanced anxiously at Zatao. *Will he allow us to ride with him in this weather?* Staring out of the window, her spirit lifted. It was no longer snowing.

Earlier that morning when she'd seen the falling snow; her instinctive response was, "Oh no!"

Safi had tried to reassure her. "It's only a light dusting, My Lady; I'm sure it won't settle for long."

However, until Zatao confirmed they were still going, she couldn't relax.

The Prince saw her fleeting glance and smiled. "You should eat some breakfast, Irene. You don't want to ride on an empty stomach." He grinned and gave her a cheeky wink.

Irene breathed a sigh of relief. "Really, we can come, even though the weather is a bit dodgy?" She noticed Mira staring at her from across the table...head tilted at an angle.

"What?" Irene asked.

"Dodgy," Mira repeated. "What sort of word is that?"

Aldrin stared at Irene, his brow furrowed.

Raising her hands, Irene laughed. "Alright, I mean snowy."

Taking her hand, Zatao's eyes shone with amusement. "It would seem we have new words to learn. However, on a serious note, it's been decided that due to the weather, you will only ride with me so far."

Irene put her arm through his and leaned against him. "I don't care, so long as I can spend a little time with you."

Zatao gently kissed her forehead. "You will, my darling." Raising his eyes, he stared over Irene's head at Aldrin. The fleeting jealousy he saw in his brother's eyes, made the hair prickle on the back of his neck.

Lowering his head, Aldrin nervously cleared his throat as he rose to his feet. His chair scraped the wooden floor as he pushed it back. Knowing his brother could occasionally sense a person's thoughts, brought a flush of heat to his cheeks. He needed to get out of the room. "I'll go to the stables and check on the horses."

Zatao nodded and said. "Make sure the wagon is loaded with enough supplies for the outpost. We don't know how long this situation could last." Zatao's eye's narrowed as he watched Aldrin hurry from the room.

Mira peered at him over her coffee cup. "Is there a problem?" She asked.

Irene shifted nervously in her chair. Her eye's darting between Mira and Zatao. The tension on their faces, made her uncomfortable. "Will someone please tell me what's going on? You can cut the atmosphere with a knife."

Zatao put his arm round her shoulders. "It's just a family thing, nothing for you to worry about."

"Really, so why are you both giving each other knowing looks?"

Smiling, Zatao suggested they go and change into riding clothes. "We will meet in the courtyard as soon as you are ready," he said.

Rising from her chair, Mira left the room. Irene made to follow her, but Zatao reached out and took her by the arm. "Stay a moment," he said softly. Dismissing the servants, he turned his chair and gently pulled her close. Wrapping his arms around her waist, he gazed at her, his eyes searching her face.

Troubled, Irene took his face between her hands and stared into his dark eyes. "What is it? What's worrying you?"

Holding her tighter, he rested his head on her breast. Comforted by the beating of her heart, he sighed.

Irene entwined her fingers in his hair. Her hand trembled as she brushed a strand away from his cheek. "Please, Zatao," she whispered. "Tell me."

Raising his head he looked at her, his eyes boring into hers.

Irene shuddered under the intensity of his gaze. The love she saw in his eyes…the smell of him and the muscular feel of his body close to hers, left her breathless. And yet there was something else she saw…something that made her draw back. It was as though his eyes were a camera, holding her image so as not to forget it.

Zatao felt her cringe. Shifting back in his chair, he took hold of her wrists.

Irene tried to pull free, but his grip was firm. She frowned at him. "Zatao, you're hurting me."

In an instant he loosened his hold. "I'm sorry, Irene. I just need you to listen to me."

"I will, but there's no need to hold me so tightly."

Releasing her hands, Zatao's lip twisted in an ironic smile. *Oh there is my love. If only you knew.* Pulling her chair out, he indicated for her to sit. "I need to speak to you before we leave. It's important."

"I can see that by the look on your face." Twisting the ring on her finger, Irene waited for him to continue. The sombre tone of his voice made the hairs rise on the back of her neck.

"My instinct is to forbid you and Mira to accompany me," Zatao said.

Irene's eyebrows shot up, her mouth fell open. "But you agreed, we could—"

"Yes I did," Zatao replied quickly. "And I will keep my word. However, there is one proviso."

Irene leaned forward in her chair, her eyes glued to his face. The nervous tick in his cheek troubled her; reaching out she gently touched his hand. "Whatever it is, I will do it."

Zatao smiled faintly and sat back. His long fingers tapped the wooden arms of his chair as he studied her. "I hope so, Irene. Your safety depends on it." Sucking in his breath he stared around the room, before leaning towards her. Resting his arms on his knees he gently held her hands. "I want you to stay close to Mira, and the three guardsmen who will accompany you back here."

"What about Aldrin? I thought he was coming to protect us as well."

Zatao lowered his voice. "Mira and I, have our doubts about Aldrin's loyalty. So watch him and be aware of your surroundings. If anything untoward happens, ride like the wind. My guard are loyal and will watch your backs."

Irene lowered her head and sighed. Her hands gripped Zatao's, as a combination of fear and anger, made her heart race.

Zatao pulled her onto his lap and hugged her close. He could feel the depth of her love; her desperate need to remain in the safety of his embrace.

Wrapping her arms around his neck, Irene nestled her head into his shoulder. Burying her face in the collar of his shirt, she breathed in the delicate scent of pine needles and bluebells. The sweet aroma filled her with a sense of peace. "Oh, Stagman," she whispered softly.

At the sound of his alter-ego's name Zatao's heart lurched, he could feel the power of the stag stir within him, hot blood pumped through his veins. He shivered as Irene's warm breath brushed his neck...stirring emotions...needs long buried. Unable to express his anguish, he raised his head and silently prayed. *Oh God, please keep her safe. Watch over her and Mira. Bring them safely home.*

Putting a hand under her chin, he raised her head and stared into her face. "I'm sorry my darling, for a second time you are plunged into danger. But do not fear; with God's help I will overcome. We will be together, and my land will be at peace." He placed a lingering kiss on her lips, her response urged him on. For a second they were lost in the moment. Aware of his racing heart, Zatao pulled away. Cupping Irene's face in trembling hands, he whispered. "Irene, when I have made you my queen. Then, I will show you my love."

Irene's body trembled. She longed to stay in his presence...feel his closeness, his love. With a slight nod, she smiled and lifted a hand to his face. Running her fingers through his golden hair, she whispered. "I understand."

Taking her hand, Zatao pressed it against his lips and gently kissed it. "Come my love; it's time to leave. Mira will be waiting and you need to change into your riding clothes."

Irene slipped from his lap. "I know, I promise I won't be long."

Easing his tall frame out of the chair, Zatao took her hand and led her from the room.

As they stood in the great hall, Irene gazed up at him. A warm smile bathed his handsome face. But the fleeting concern she saw in his eyes, felt like a clamp around her heart.

"I will meet you in the courtyard," he said, gently squeezing her hand.

Before she could answer, he turned and strode towards the door. Fingering the pendent at her neck, Irene's stomach tightened as she watched him leave. *It's like de-ja-vu. But I had no choice in the matter. I love him, I had to come.* Climbing the stairs she paused in her ascent and stared at the castle door. Placing a hand over her heart she softly prayed. "Please Lord, keep us all safe, and give Zatao victory over his enemies."

The word enemies brought Aldrin to mind, and her heart burned with anger against him. Squaring her shoulders, she strode to her suite. As she changed her clothes, she determined to enjoy her ride with Zatao. Nothing and no one, least of all Aldrin was going to spoil her time with the man she loved.

༄༅༅༄

Falling snow blanketed Aldrin's head and shoulders. Oblivious to the cold, he paced the stable yard his mind in turmoil. He knew Zatao, and possibly Mira where suspicious of him. Growling, he balled his hands into fists. He was in too deep now and there was no way out!

He felt the colour drain from his face. Who was he more afraid of; an evil King who manipulated his weakness, by offering riches and position? Or the brother he was betraying in the worst way possible?

The sound of hooves on cobbles interrupted his thoughts. Taking a deep breath he calmed himself, and marched towards the stable lad holding his horse. With a grunt, he took the reins and vaulted into the saddle. For a second he closed his eyes and lowered his head. *There's nothing I can do now, my path is set. Come what may, I must succeed.* With a grimace, he heeled his horse and cantered into the castle courtyard, where he joined hundreds of waiting guardsmen.

The men sat on their horses…eyes focused on the massive door of the castle, awaiting the arrival of their Prince.

As the huge door swung open, the vast courtyard echoed to the thunder of fists thudding against armoured chests. Aldrin's body trembled as he joined the salute.

Through narrowed eyes, he watched his brother, flanked by Mira and Irene walk to the top of the steps. Behind them he spotted Anya, and Irene's maid, Safi. Clenching a fist, he stared at Anya. "You best keep your mouth shut," he growled; knowing his words were lost in the tumultuous sound filling the courtyard.

His black stallion reared with excitement, pawing at the air. Calming the animal, he saw Anya glance in his direction...noticed the way she wiped her hands on her skirt. He grinned.

৶৶৶

Prince Zatao's voice echoed around the courtyard. His words of encouragement rallied the men, instilling courage and the desire to fight and win. Finishing his address, he took Irene and Mira by the hand, and led them down the steps to the waiting horses.

Three guardsmen dismounted...removing their helmets, they walked towards them and bowed.

Acknowledging them, Zatao turned to Irene and Mira. "These guardsmen will protect you on the homeward journey. They are three of my most trusted men." With a nod of his head, Zatao dismissed them.

Mira smiled as a groom brought Merry to her. Taking the reins she patted the filly's neck, before letting the groom assist her into the saddle.

Zatao indicated to another groom, who led Flame to Irene. "I thought you would prefer to ride a horse you know," he said with a smile.

Irene grinned with delight, as she took the reins. "Hello girl, it's good to see you again."

Whickering a soft greeting, Flame nudged her.

Zatao cupped his hands. "Let me help you mount." As Irene rested her foot in his hands, he whispered in her ear. "You look good in jeans."

Turning her head, Irene caught his cheeky wink. Giggling, she mouthed. "Behave!"

"I will, for the moment," Zatao replied hoisting her into the saddle. Having helped her adjust her stirrups, he rested a hand on her thigh and gazed into her face. "Stay safe my beautiful girl."

Seeing the love and concern in his eyes; Irene placed her hand over his and smiled. "Trust God, Zatao. We will be fine." Bending her head she kissed his upturned cheek. "I love you."

Swallowing the lump in his throat, Zatao could only nod as he turned away and took August's reins from his groom, Taris. Swinging into the saddle he perused his men, before leading them out of the courtyard, across the moat and away towards the forest.

Safi and Anya stood together, their cloaks pulled around them against the softly falling snow.

Anya's knuckle's whitened as she clutched the collar of her cloak. She shivered, not so much from the cold, as fear of Aldrin. As she watched Prince Zatao lead the guard out, she could see Aldrin a few rows behind. With his coat of arms emblazoned on the front of his armour, he was easily visible.

As Aldrin trotted past, he touched the side of his head in a mock salute.

Anya lowered her eyes and chewed her lip. Part of her had hoped; when his horse reared, it would have thrown him. She felt awful thinking such a thing, and kept her head down as he passed. Anyone who noticed would have assumed she was being respectful to the Prince.

Assuming Anya was concerned for her mistress, Safi touched her arm. "Don't worry; they will be home later this evening." She peered at Anya. "Are you alright? You look awfully pale."

"It's just the cold," Anya said. She tried to smile, but her lips were stretched too tight and wouldn't stop trembling.

Safi took her hand. "Come on; let's go in, it's freezing out here."

Anya's body shook as she followed Safi into the great hall. Removing their cloaks they huddled by the roaring fire.

Anya fingered the fur of her cloak as she glanced around. "We can't stay here, it's not allowed."

"Surely, it won't hurt for a moment, at least till you're a bit warmer."

"I'm fine thank you. I'm going to my room. I will see you later."

Safi nodded; pursing her lips, she watched Anya climb the stairs. *Something troubles her. I wish I knew what it was.* Clutching her cloak, she wandered downstairs to the kitchen. Her frown deepening with each step she took.

Lying across her bed, Anya took deep breaths in the hope of calming her racing heart. *Oh dear Lord. What have I done?* Her imagination ran riot, causing her to break out in a cold sweat. "I know he's planned something." Her trembling hands gripped the blanket. "I can't bear it," she groaned.

Rising, she sat on the side of the bed and dabbed at her eyes. "I need to think," she whispered into the silence of her room. "If I stay, it's certain he will turn me in, and blame me for whatever is to take place."

Rising to her feet, she paced the small room. *If I run away, they will find me and it will make matters worse.* She paused in her pacing, and for a second her eye's brightened. "Maybe I should tell someone?" She frowned and shook her head. "What's the point?" Her lip twisted in a cynical smile. *It's Prince Adrin's word against mine, and who would believe me, a lady's maid?*

She groaned as a nauseous cramp gripped her stomach. Doubling over, she slumped onto the bed...buried her face in hands, and sobbed.

❦❦❦

Riding beside Zatao, Irene felt a shiver of excitement. Realizing she would soon have to leave him tempered the feeling somewhat; nevertheless she would take what she could get; even if only a brief ride on a cold snowy day.

She glanced at Zatao, overawed by his beauty. He sat astride August, his armour glinting in the morning light filtering through the tree tops. Turning his head, his dark eyes twinkled as he smiled at her. Irene felt her cheeks flush as she returned his smile.

"Are you alright?" He asked softly.

"I'm wonderful, thank you."

"Indeed you are," Zatao said with a chuckle. Raising his hand, palm upwards, he watched soft snowflakes cover his glove. "Are you warm enough?"

Irene patted the thick fur coat Mira had given her. Looking behind, she grinned at Mira. "The coat is lovely and warm, thank you."

"You're welcome," Mira said, urging her horse forward to keep pace with Aldrin's stallion.

Irene stared at Aldrin; he bobbed his head politely, but she found his unremitting gaze disturbing and faced front. Nevertheless, she could still feel his eyes glued to her back. Determined to enjoy her short time with Zatao, she urged Flame to keep pace with August's long stride, and did her best to ignore him.

Her pulse raced, as she listened to the uniform thud of hundreds of hooves...the snorting and excited whinnies. The metallic clink of armour echoed in the stillness of the forest. The thrill of it sent a shiver down her spine.

Irene couldn't help smiling as she gazed around. Dressed in a thick blanket of snow and with more falling from the sky; the forest looked magical. *If I didn't know better, I would think I was in a fairy-tale world. It's certainly different from the world I've left behind*, but *I don't regret the move.*

With a contented sigh, she gazed up at the forest canopy, and jumped as a snow flake landed in her eye. Her sudden movement startled Flame; Irene gripped the reins as the mare shot forward.

"Best not to look up," Zatao said with a raised eyebrow and cheeky grin.

Irene felt a flush creep up her cheeks; she pouted but couldn't hide the smile in her eyes. They rode side by side, a comfortable silence between them.

The vast army followed. The only sound...horses and armour, not a human voice to be heard.

Irene shifted in the saddle. Realizing Zatao and his army were going to war, sent a cold shiver up her spine. She glanced at him, but even his reassuring smile did little to assuage her unease. And too soon, the wide path they travelled brought them to a crossroads.

Irene's heart sank as Zatao reined August, and lifted a hand to halt the army. She knew what he was going to say, and she didn't want to hear it. Fighting back tears, she straightened in the saddle and took a calming breath.

Zatao urged August alongside Flame, and took Irene's hand. The sadness he saw in her eye's tore at his heart. "I'm sorry, Irene, but this is—"

Irene's voice faltered as she said, "I know. This is where we must part."

Zatao nodded. "I'm afraid so." Raising her hand he tenderly kissed it.

A shiver went down Irene's spine as his warm breath caressed the back of her hand. Holding herself together she stared into his eyes, drawing strength from the love she saw in their dark depths.

"How will I know if you're alright?" Dropping her chin, she clutched the collar of her coat.

Placing his hand under her chin, Zatao raised her head and stared into her eyes. "Don't worry, I will find a way to keep in touch." He smiled and gave her hand a reassuring squeeze. "Please pray for us," he said softly.

"Of course I will," Irene said. Losing the battle with her emotions, she angrily brushed the tears away.

Zatao grabbed her hand and held it firmly in his. "Remember what I said. Be careful on the way home and stay safe."

Irene nodded. Leaning closer she whispered. "I love you."

Zatao smiled. "I love you more," he mouthed, before pulling August round and facing his waiting army.

Irene's heart weighed heavy, like lead in her chest.

Mira drew alongside and put a comforting arm round her shoulders. "Come, Irene. We need to go while it's still daylight." Reaching down, she took hold of a rein and led Flame away.

Irene twisted in the saddle her eyes glued to Zatao. His attention was focused on Aldrin, and the three guards who would accompany them to the castle. She couldn't hear his voice above the restless movement of men and horses. Nevertheless, his expression was plain to see, he was warning them. Irene sighed as she watched him turn August and ride to the front of the army.

Raising his hand, Zatao led them away at a canter. The thunder of hooves and clank of armour was deafening.

There was finality to the sound that made Irene cringe. They were riding to war, possibly death. Raising tear filled eyes heavenwards she prayed. "Oh God, watch over them." Lowering her head she tried to swallow the lump in her throat. *Please keep Zatao safe*, she pleaded silently.

As Aldrin rode towards them followed by the guard, a sense of doom overshadowed Irene, her stomach rolled uncomfortably. Glancing at Mira, she gave her a weak smile.

Mira reached and took her hand. "It's okay Irene. We'll be home soon."

Irene nodded, but still the feeling of dread weighed heavily upon her.

Aldrin smiled. "Right then, are we ready?" He turned to the three guardsmen. "I will lead the way. I want you two to ride either side of Princess Mira and Lady Irene." Indicating to the younger guardsman, he instructed him to bring up the rear.

Aldrin's brow wrinkled as he slapped his gloved hands together, and gazed up at the sky.

Storm clouds covered the sun. Falling snow swirled in a cold breeze, covering them all in a chilly white blanket. Had Irene not felt so nervous, she would have laughed at the incongruous sight. However, her only thought was Zatao's safety and their own.

Chapter 38

Aldrin led the way, pushing his horse into a canter. Squinting, he peered through the falling snow in search of the great oak; the landmark he had given as the best place to intercept them and take Irene. The long shadows of late afternoon, stood stark against the white backdrop. *I wonder if they're there.* His throat constricted, his body tensed, but he pushed his anxiety down, burying it in his desire for power and wealth.

They cantered on. Following a bend in the path he saw the tree, its thick boughs shrouded in snow. Aldrin's heart pounded, as his tension increased.

All of a sudden his horse slipped, the animal's hooves scrabbled for purchase on a patch of ice, nearly unseating him. "Whoa!" Aldrin's heart leapt into his mouth. Reining the horse to a walk, he settled back in the saddle.

"Are you alright?" Mira asked.

"I'm fine," Aldrin said raising a hand.

"Well let's keep going," Mira urged. "The weather is getting worse, I can hardly see."

"Don't worry, we are nearly home. With ice under the snow its best not to push the horses."

Irene shivered and banged her hands together, "I'm freezing. I can hardly feel my feet."

"It's not much further now." Aldrin lowered his head, for a brief moment he hated himself. But at the same time he wanted to scream. *Where are they?*

His tension was transferring to his flighty stallion. The animal shied at every shadow. Just as Aldrin was wishing he could give the stallion a thrashing, a movement in the bushes caught his attention. Holding the horse on a tight rein, he lifted a hand.

The others drew around him. The three guardsmen positioned their horses, so that Mira and Irene were protected. Unsheathing their swords, they scanned the surrounding trees.

Kor, the higher ranking guardsman, heeled his horse closer to Aldrin's. "What is it? What did you hear?"

Glancing at him, Aldrin said. "I don't know, but stay alert." Aldrin's heart hammered painfully in his chest.

Irene could feel the small hairs rise on the back of her neck. Urging Flame forward, she hissed. "Come on, let's go."

Aldrin shot her a look. "No, wait, do as I say."

"It might be a deer or something," Mira said softly. Her emerald eyes searched Aldrin's face, seeking assurance.

Aldrin averted his head, but not before Mira saw the regret in his eyes. Her heart sank. *Oh my brother what have you done?* Taking Irene's hand, she indicated with her eyes, *stay close to me.*

Irene's breath caught in her throat. She had no idea what Mira was trying to say. Nevertheless, she sensed they were in danger. Adrenalin coursed through her body, urging her to flee.

The horses, disturbed by their rider's tension, snorted and milled around in the snow, making it hard for the guard to shield Mira and Irene. Flame rose on her hind legs, her nervous whinny echoing in the silence.

"Keep her under control," Aldrin snapped. The wait was getting to him, testing what little patience he had. Heat rose up his neck onto his face, as he realised, once they had Irene, he could easily be disposed of along with the others. The thought brought him out in a cold sweat.

He could see the fear in Irene's eyes; hardening his heart, his gaze fastened on Mira. His affection for her brought a flood of fear for her safety.

Gripping her reins, Mira tried to steady her nervous horse. The wind caught tendrils of her blond hair, pulling it out from under her hood…whipping it against her face. She stared at Aldrin, her eyes moist with tears.

Breaking eye contact, Aldrin lowered his head; his heart thudded in his chest. Held in the grip of fear, he buried his guilt and unsheathed his sword. Prepared to rescue her…determined to keep her safe along with himself.

Turning his horse, he led them at a walk towards the tree. Each step his horse took felt like a nail in his coffin. He gripped his sword so tightly his knuckles hurt. Straightening in the saddle, he tried to breathe…remain calm, as he readied himself for the imminent attack.

Dismounting, Muglwort pushed aside the shrubbery. Forcing his way to the edge of the forest path, he listened. In the distance he could hear the faint sound of horse's hooves. Edging back to his horse he leapt into the saddle and indicated for Freon to come alongside him. His black eyes fastened on the archer's face. "They are close. Climb into this oak tree. Don't miss, I want no survivors."

Lowering his voice, Freon said. "Trust me My Lord, only one person will remain alive." Urging his horse close to the tree, he took his feet out of the stirrups and balanced on his saddle. Reaching for the nearest bough, he pulled himself up and climbed to a higher vantage point. Staring down, he whispered. "I have a clear view from here."

Raising a hand in acknowledgement, Muglwort led Zworn and Putius closer to the path. He hoped his idea of an aerial attack would work. *If they're busy looking up, they won't be ready for us.* He glanced up at Freon…a twisted smile on his face, as he imagined the suffering he would inflict on the man, if he failed in his task.

Peering through the shrubbery, Muglwort saw Aldrin's horse slip; he watched as the others bunched around him. Gripping the hilt of his sword, he growled. "What's he waiting for?"

He breathed an inaudible sigh of relief, as Aldrin turned his horse and rode slowly towards the tree. Muglwort's eyes glinted with pleasure as he watched them approach. "They're coming," he hissed to Zworn. "Get ready."

Zworn and Putius drew their swords in readiness. Zworn glanced up at Freon in the tree. "How many guard are there?" he whispered.

Freon raised three fingers.

Aldrin kept swallowing his throat was so dry. As they drew closer to the tree, his grip on his sword tightened. *Be ready*. As the thought entered his head he heard a swishing sound, followed by a cry of pain. Twisting in the saddle, he saw one of the guards on the ground, with an arrow in his chest; his life's blood colouring the snow crimson.

Aldrin's heart raced, as Muglwort and two huge warriors appeared out of the shrubbery. With swords raised, they rushed into the fray, fighting their way towards Irene.

In the ensuing chaos, Aldrin lifted his sword. Fighting back was not part of his agreement, but he must protect Mira. Her frightened cries mingled with Irene's, their voices drowned by the shouts of men and screaming horses.

A freezing wind whistled around them, blowing the fallen snow into drifts. Still it fell, stinging their faces, blinding their eyes, and hampering movement.

Kor and the young guardsmen formed a barrier in front of Irene and Mira.

Aldrin turned his horse and joined them. "Stay together," he shouted. "Don't let them separate us."

Mira and Irene fought with their horses. The terrified animals reared and swung around in tight circles; their only desire, to escape.

"These men are on foot," Irene shouted. "We can get away!" As the words left her mouth, she heard a dull thunk as metal pierced metal.

The young guardsman careered backwards over his horse's rump, crashing to the ground with an arrow through his heart.

Irene's hand shot to her mouth, muffling her terrified scream.

Mira's breath came in rasping gasps as she cried. "Quick! We must go."

Aldrin urged his frightened horse alongside Mira's. Reaching out he grabbed her reins. "Come with me," he yelled.

"Go My Lord!" Kor shouted as his sword crashed against Muglwort's. "I can hold them off."

"I won't leave without Irene," Mira cried.

As Aldrin struggled to keep hold of her reins; Putius reached up, grabbed his sword arm and attempted to pull him off his horse.

With an angry curse, Aldrin pulled his foot out of the stirrup and kicked him back. With his attacker unbalanced and his arm free, Aldrin raised his sword and brought it down across Putius's arm.

The big warrior cried out, but made another rush for him.

Aldrin's horse reared, causing the arrow destined for his heart to miss, and pierce his left shoulder. Aldrin's eyes widened with surprise. Clutching the arrow, he cried out as the searing pain tortured every nerve in his upper body.

"Aldrin!" Mira screamed, grabbing for him as he fell from his horse.

Putius made a grab for her, but Merry leapt forward mowing him down. The horse's hoof made contact with his head, killing him.

"Go, both of you!" Kor shouted. "I will foll—" His words petered out as an arrow speared his throat. Slumping forward in the saddle he toppled over his horse's shoulder and crashed to the ground.

❦❦❦

Irene heard a loud scream and realized it was her own voice. Her heart pounded painfully in her chest. Gasping for breath, she urged Flame closer to Mira's horse and reached for her arm. She could see the shock in Mira's eyes...the tears streaming down her face. Pulling at her cloak, she cried. "Come on Mira. If we ride fast we can escape."

Mira glanced at Irene and shook her head.

The sorrow Irene saw in her friend's eyes sapped her remaining strength. Her shoulders slumped as she twisted in the saddle and faced Muglwort and Zworn.

The two warriors stood a few feet away, staring at her. Stretching to their full height, their feet firmly planted; they grinned and fingered the hilts of their sheathed swords.

Irene tried to swallow the lump in her throat, as she glanced at the carnage around her. The bodies of Kor and the two guardsmen had all but vanished; buried under the swirling snow. Their blood soaked into the pristine whiteness, turning it crimson; a testament to their bravery.

Irene glared at Muglwort and Zworn. Their confidence enraged her. Heeling Flame closer to Mira's horse, she reached for the reins. *We're not beaten yet! We must escape, or their deaths were for nothing.* The thought stirred her into action; adrenalin coursed through her body, dampening her fear. "Come on, Mira!" She yelled. "We're going." Pulling on Merry's reins she turned the horse, urging it to follow Flame.

"Aldrin is dead." Mira said brushing a tear from her eye.

"I know, and I'm really sorry." Irene glanced back at Muglwort and Zworn. They were walking slowly towards them. *Why are they not hurrying to stop us?* A cold fear moved down her spine as her eyes darted around, searching the shrubbery for anyone else who might be hiding.

Her arms felt like led weights as she tried to hurry Mira's horse. The animal just stuck her head out, refusing to go beyond a walk. "Please Mira, we need to go. Now! If we ride fast we could catch up with, Zatao."

Hearing her brother's name motivated Mira. Snatching the reins from Irene, she kicked Merry in the flanks, the horse shot forward.

Irene breathed a sigh of relief as she followed. Staying low in the saddle she urged Flame into a canter. Both horse's slithered and slipped on the icy surface. Snow drifts made it hard to distinguish the path…falling snow fell like a curtain, drifting into their eyes, blanketing their faces in a cold mask.

Holding onto the pommel of her saddle, Irene glanced back. *Why are they just standing there?* She could hardly see the two men through the swirling snow; nevertheless she was pretty sure they weren't moving.

Irene could feel the hairs on the nape of her neck prickle. *Something's wrong. Why are they letting us escape?* Holding the reins in one hand and gripping the pommel of the saddle with the other, she hung on for dear life as Flame ploughed through the deepening snow.

Desperately, she pummelled the mare's flanks, urging her to keep up with Mira's horse. Despite the sour taste in her mouth…the unpleasant tightness in her shoulders. Irene prayed her overriding sense of doom was unfounded.

Chapter 39

Muglwort and Zworn glanced at each other and grinned.

Looking up at Freon, Zworn shouted. "Don't let them escape!"

With a confident nod, Freon drew an arrow and let fly. The missile of death was barely visible through the falling snow. Nevertheless, it found its mark, and a cry of pain echoed in the eerie silence.

Irene stared in disbelief, as she watched Mira tumble from her horse. "No! Mira," she screamed. Gasping for breath, she slapped the reins over Flame's neck, urging the mare to go faster...desperate to reach Mira.

Freon raised his bow and fired another arrow.

Irene cried out as it gouged her thigh, before burying itself in Flame's heart, killing the horse instantly. The animal crumpled to the ground, throwing Irene into the snow.

Winded, Irene lay there trying to catch her breath. Turning onto her side, she saw Mira a few feet away lying face down. The arrow rose through the blood stained snow like a ghastly marker.

Rising to her hands and knees, Irene crawled to Mira's side. Tears streamed down her face as she gently turned her over and cradled her in trembling arms.

"Mira," she whispered, running a hand gently down her cheek.

Opening her eyes, Mira's lips twitched in a faint smile.

Irene breathed a sigh of relief and held her close. "You'll be alright, Mira." Glancing round, her heart sank. Flame lay a few feet away, dead. Mira's horse had disappeared. *Oh God, how will I get her to Zatao?* Sinking back on her heels, she cradled Mira's head on her thighs.

Shivering with the cold she leaned over Mira, trying to protect her from the falling snow. As she stared into Mira's face, she noticed her lips moving. Lowering her face close to Mira's, she listened.

Mira lay face down in the snow, her mind numb…her body frozen with the cold. The realization, she had an arrow in her back, increased her trembling. She tried to raise her face clear of the snow, but every nerve screamed with pain…each tortured breath felt like a twisting knife. She could feel her life ebbing away with each laboured heartbeat.

As Mira embraced the numbing cold, she felt arms wrap around her, lifting her face out of the snow. Opening her eyes she stared into Irene's face. She tried to speak, but no sound escaped her lips.

She felt Irene's hand gently stroke her face. Closing her eyes, she blinked away the tears. With her head resting on Irene's legs, she felt warmth…a momentary strength. Staring into Irene's eyes, she moved her lips. As Irene lowered her head to listen, Mira drew on her remaining strength. Forcing sound through her dry, cracked lips, she whispered. "Trust in God, Irene. Stay strong." She felt Irene's arms wrap around her…felt hot tears fall onto her face.

Gazing up at Irene, she smiled before closing her eyes and sinking into the arms of eternal rest.

❧❧❧

Dazed, Irene stared into Mira's beautiful emerald eyes…watched them dim as life faded. Seeing the blood trickle from the corner of her mouth…hearing the gurgling from within her body. Irene sobbed and turned her head. Putting a hand to her chest, she managed to suppress the rising nausea.

Rocking back and forth, Irene held Mira close. "No, no," she moaned over and over. Throwing her head back, she screamed at the sky. "Why?" Her anguished cry echoed in the momentary silence. Tightening her hold on Mira's body, she closed her eyes and wept.

Too late, Irene heard the crunch of boots on snow. She cried out as a strong arm encircled her waist. She could hardly breathe, as she was lifted bodily and carried away. Looking up, she stared into Zworn's cruel face. His black eyes glittered with delight. "We've got you now, my beauty!"

"Let me go!" Irene cried. Struggling to free herself, she kicked his shins and pummelled his head with her fists.

271

With a growl of frustration, Muglwort strode towards them and pulled her away from Zworn. "Enough!" He bellowed.

Irene staggered as his hand struck her forcefully across the face. With ringing in her ears and blurred vision, she slumped to her knees in the snow.

"Be careful," Zworn yelled at him. "The king won't want the goods damaged."

Muglwort scowled and stared at the bloody carnage all around them. Grabbing Irene by her cloak, he yanked her to her feet and pulled her close. Lowering his head, he stared into her eyes. "They're all dead," he growled. "And unless you want to join them, I suggest you keep quiet and behave yourself."

Glaring at him, Irene struggled to pull away.

Muglwort released her and laughed as the momentum took her to the ground.

Laid on her back in the snow, Irene's cheeks flushed pink. "Prince Zatao will make you pay for this!" She shouted.

Zworn mimicked her, as he dragged her to her feet. "If it's any comfort, I'm sure he'll try." Lowering his voice, he smiled and said. "He won't succeed. Now we have you, the war is over." Holding her by her hair, he whispered in her ear. "We've won, pretty lady. It's all over."

Irene recoiled at his hot breath…the coarseness of his facial hair and the wetness of his lips on her cheek. Swallowing hard she turned her head away.

Laughing, Zworn grabbed her by the arm. Holding onto her, he waited for Muglwort to get the horses.

Looking up into the tree, Muglwort shouted. "Hurry up Freon, and check on Putius; we're ready to leave." Leading the horses onto the path they waited for Freon to join them.

Irene froze, when she saw they only had three horses. Lowering her head she took a deep inaudible breath. *Oh God, I'm going to have to ride with one of them.*

"Putius is dead," Freon said strolling nonchalantly out of the trees.

Seeing him, and the bow strapped to his back, Irene's heart drummed in her chest. Clenching her fists she glared at him.

Cocking his head, Freon grinned at her. "Well, well. So this is what the fuss was about." Turning his back on her, he went to his horse.

Irene felt heat rise up her neck…hot blood course through her body. With a scream of rage she tore free of Zworn, and went for Freon. Before he could turn round, she threw herself onto his back. With her arms round his neck under his chin, she squeezed as hard as she could. Her legs straddled him. It was like trying to ride an angry grizzly. She hung on as he twisted and turned. Reaching a hand back, he tried to grab her.

Muglwort slapped Zworn on the shoulder. "This is the best entertainment I've watched in a long time."

Doubled up with laughter Zworn couldn't reply.

Shaking with anger, Irene yelled in Freon's ear. "You killed my friend!" With an angry snarl she clamped her teeth onto his ear lobe and bit down hard; nearly vomiting as the coppery taste of blood covered her lips. She spat covering his cheek with spit and blood.

Freon's yell of pain alerted Muglwort and Zworn. In desperation, he reached back and managed to grab a fistful of Irene's hair. He pulled and twisted until she released her grip on his neck. Then with a forceful twist of his huge body, he dropped her to the ground.

"She's bitten my ear off!" He screamed at Muglwort and Zworn.

Irene sat on the ground holding her head and glaring up at him.

Muglwort tried not to laugh as he grabbed hold of her and dragged her towards the horses.

Freon followed, covering the ground in three huge strides, he pulled Irene away from Muglwort. "My honour is at stake here," he shouted. Rising to his full height he equalled Muglwort in stature. "She is going to pay for biting and humiliating me."

Irene's pounding heart drummed in her ears. Black spots flashed in front of her eyes as his huge hand closed around her throat. *I'm going to die, and I don't care.* The thought vanished as Zworn attempted to push between them.

"Let her go, Freon. Kill her and you're a dead man. The king wants her alive and unharmed." Zworn laid a hand on Freon's shoulder. He could feel the warrior's tension ease as he released Irene.

Stumbling back, Irene gasped for air.

Muglwort noticed the torn and blooded material on Irene's left thigh. Moving beside her, he nudged the area with his knee. Irene's loud cry...her hand quickly covering the wound, was all he needed to see.

Irene had forgotten being struck by the arrow. Losing Mira had overtaken her, to the exclusion of all else. She gasped as Muglwort took her by the arm and pulled her to Freon. Turning her sideways on, he pointed to the leg. "It seems your arrow inflicted this wound, before killing the horse. Will this be enough to satisfy your honour?"

Scowling, Freon moved closer to her.

Irene whimpered, and tried to pull away from Muglwort. She cringed as Freon's huge frame towered over her. She didn't see him raise a fisted hand, until it was too late. The excruciating pain, as his fist slammed into her thigh, took her breath away. Unable to make a sound, she slumped to the ground and fell into a welcome, all-embracing blackness.

Freon watched the colour drain from her face. He grinned, as her eyes rolled back in her head. "Now I'm satisfied," he said, as he watched her sink into the snow.

Taking his horse from Zworn, he vaulted into the saddle. "Right, I'm ready, let's go." Glancing at Irene's prone body, he raised an eyebrow and nodded at Zworn. "I suggest you pick her up before she freezes."

Zworn scowled at him, "Why should I take her? Where's Putius's horse?" He glanced at Muglwort for support.

"We're leaving it; we can't have her trying to escape."

"With all this snow, she'll hamper my progress," Zworn grumbled.

Mounting his horse, Muglwort smirked at him. "Yes, but she'll keep you warm."

Freon laughed, as he urged his horse alongside Muglworts. "Come on, man, hurry up."

"Yeh, for goodness sake get a move on," Muglwort snapped. "We need to go, it will be dark soon. If it makes you feel better, one of us will take her when we reach the border."

"You'd better keep your word," Zworn growled. Stooping down, he lifted Irene's inert body from the snow and eased her face down across his saddle. Mounting up, he shivered as her frozen body touched his legs. "Throw me a blanket," he growled at Muglwort. "I'm not going to get the blame if she dies."

Twisting in the saddle, Muglwort untied his blanket and threw it at him. "Here, catch."

Zworn caught the blanket and draped it over Irene.

Silent, and in single file, they skirted the carnage buried in the snow and rode away. Their progress was hampered by deep snow drifts, which at times reached above their horse's knees. A cold wind took the falling snow and swirled it around. The icy blast stung their faces.

Muglwort glanced at the sky. Clouds as black as ink, scudded across the heavens. "There's a storm brewing," he muttered. Aware the others couldn't hear him, he pulled his hood further over his head. Shivering, he slumped in the saddle. "Damn this weather," he grumbled. "We have to make it back before we're spotted."

They pushed on a bit further before stopping to rest the horses.

Freon urged his horse alongside Muglwort's. "When do you want to send the pigeon?"

Muglwort glanced up at the sky. "Now, give it to me. With any luck it should get there before the storm hits."

Reaching into his oversized saddlebag, Freon pulled the bird out and handed it to Muglwort.

Taking a tiny metal tube from his pocket, Muglwort attached it to the bird's leg and released it. "If it makes it, we will have reinforcements when we reach the border."

"And if it doesn't?" Zworn asked.

"Then, we're on our own," Muglwort replied. He glanced at Irene slumped over Zworn's saddle. "Is she alright?"

Zworn looked down at her. "She's warmed up; so I guess she's alive."

Freon's gaze darted around. "We should move on."

Seeing the anxiety on his face, Zworn and Muglwort nodded.

"We need to leave this path and go deeper into the forest," Muglwort said.

"Good idea," Freon replied. "The snow won't be so deep among the trees."

Zworn frowned, "Not only that. Our horses stand out in this snow."

Muglwort nodded, spurring his horse he led them off the main path and in among the trees. Blending with the shadows of early evening; they vanished.

⋞⋞⋞

Aldrin laid still, the left side of his face pressed into the freezing snow. His shoulder burned with pain from the arrow; the rest of his body was numb with cold.

Unable to raise his head, he managed to peer through the falling snow. His fingers curled, as he watched the men's rough treatment of Irene. *I should be on my feet helping her. But I don't care about Irene.*

Closing his eyes, Aldrin moaned softly. "I need to get to Mira." Recalling Irene's grief stricken scream, brought hot tears to his eyes. Clenching his fist, he winced with pain. Hearing footsteps close by, he prayed the men's focus would remain on Irene…diverting them away from him. Taking shallow breaths, he flattened his body into the snow.

He knew, if they noticed him and looked closely, they would see he merely had a shoulder wound, and finish him off.

Aldrin grimaced, as he watched Zworn throw Irene over his saddle, as though she were no more than a sack of coal…saw him throw a blanket over her, before urging his horse after the others.

Aldrin swallowed, the saliva stuck in his dry throat. "Oh God, I pray she's not dead." Closing his eyes, he tried to block out the vision of his brothers enraged face. The snow froze the cold sweat clinging to his body.

He waited a while; to be sure his enemy had gone, before raising his head and struggling to his knees. He crawled one handed to where Mira lay half hidden in the deep snow.

Sitting beside her, he cradled her head in his lap. Hot tears spilled down his cheeks, freezing on his skin as they fell. Staring up at the snow filled sky, he silently sobbed. "Mira, Mira." With trembling fingers, he gently closed her eyelids. His voice cracked as he whispered. "I love you, Mira."

276

Rocking back and forth, he brushed the snow from her face. Fresh tears fell as he gazed at the sister he'd always loved. Never again would her beautiful eyes smile lovingly at him. Never again, would her soft voice speak wisdom into his rebellious heart.

Rising to his knees, he gently lowered her head into the snow, and brushed it over her body. Using his good arm, he patted and pounded the snow until it was firm. Sitting back on his heels, his chin dropped to his chest. Cradling his injured arm, he stared at the mound of snow. Soon it would be dark. He could only pray he'd done enough, and no predators would disturb his sister's body.

Struggling to his feet, Aldrin seethed with rage as he gripped the shaft of the arrow buried in his shoulder. Gritting his teeth, he took a deep breath and pulled. As the arrow ripped from his flesh, the wound unleashed a stream of hot blood. Clamping a hand over his mouth he groaned with the pain...his body shook.

Grabbing a fistful of snow, he pushed it into the wound. Doubling over in agony, he slumped to his knees. For a moment, he could do nothing but gasp for breath. Eventually, as the pains severity diminished, he took a handkerchief from his pocket and plugged the wound as best he could.

Getting to his feet, he wrapped his heavy cloak tight around him, and pulled the hood over his head. Facing the way they had come; he ploughed through the thick snow in pursuit of his brother, Prince Zatao.

Chapter 40

Blackwing increased his pace, his heart racing with the effort. He could hear distant shouts and screams. Dropping low, he skimmed over the ground. With his eyes half closed against the falling snow, he just missed being hit by a galloping horse.

"Turn around," the horse squealed.

"What's happening?" Blackwing called. "Is Irene safe?" Breathing fast, he flew after her.

"Please, stop! Tell me what's going on."

The horse skidded to a halt. A broken rein dangled in the snow. Unable to keep still, she all but danced on the spot. Flecks of sweat mingled with the snowflakes falling on her.

Blackwing fluttered to a branch above her head; his heart slumped, as he stared into dark eyes wide with panic. "What's happened?" he asked as calmly as he could.

The horse snorted and shook her head. Hot breath billowed from her flared nostrils.

Blackwing ceased his questioning; giving her a chance to calm down and catch her breath.

Lowering her head, the horse pawed at the ground. "They're all dead," she whispered. Tears rolled down her face. "My mistress is dead." Her long chestnut mane floated in the air, as she angrily shook her head.

Hopping to a lower branch, Blackwing stared into her face. In a hesitant voice he asked, "Who is your mistress?"

"Princess Mira," the horse replied.

"I'm so sorry," Blackwing said softly. He stared at her, his eyelids blinking rapidly. "I need to know if—"

The horse raised her head. "As far as I know, Lady Irene is alive. But those brutal men took her away."

Blackwing breathed a sigh. *She is alive!* His bright eyes darted around. *But where have they taken her?*

Trembling, the horse turned her head and stared down the path. "They will take her to the land beyond the mountain," she said, as if reading Blackwing's thoughts.

Blackwing flapped his wings. "We must rescue her."

"What do you mean, we?" The horse said staring at him.

"I can't do it alone, and you know this forest." Blackwing stared into her sad eyes. "Help me," he pleaded.

The horse raised a foreleg and stamped at the snow. "Very well; for my mistress's sake I will help you."

Blackwing felt the tension ease from his body. "Do you think we will make it to the Prince's camp, in time?"

"No," the horse said, with a shake of her head. "The camp is on the other side of the forest in the Linguin hills. They will be miles away by now. We will never catch up to them in time."

Blackwing sighed. "So, what do you suggest we do?"

Seeing the frustration in his eyes, the horse shook her head and snorted. "I have an idea, but it could be dangerous."

"Dangerous, what do you mean?"

"Dangerous for me," she said.

"Why?"

"I'm going to make a lot of noise...pretend I am injured, which will attract the wolves."

"What!"

"It's the only way. We just need to pray that Grey Cloud is with the pack."

Blackwing stared at her, his eyes wide with alarm. "Who is Grey Cloud? And what will you do if he's not with them?"

"Panic!" The horse said.

Blackwing lowered his head, his loud "tck, tck," echoed in the silence.

"It's alright, don't worry," the horse said softly. "Most of the wolves know I am Princess Mira's horse. I'm sure they will give me a chance to explain about Irene."

Blackwing cocked his head to the side and stared at her.

Seeing the admiration...respect in his eyes, she lowered her head. "Hey, it's no big deal."

Blackwing couldn't miss her restless movement...the shadow of anxiety in her eyes. "Are you sure about this?"

She nodded. "Stay close to me, please."

"I'm going nowhere, so don't worry." He hopped along the bough closer to her. "What's your name?"

"Merry," she replied.

"Nice name," Blackwing said, hoping he wasn't about to lose a new friend.

⊷⊷⊷

The moon hung in the sky like a huge silver disk; bathing the plateau in a pale eerie light. Falling snow stirred by the stiff breeze, swirled at the entrance to a large cave. In the rear of the cave, the wolves yawned and stretched, slowly they emerged from the gloom. They were restless…ready to be on the move. Empty stomachs grumbled with hunger.

Grey Cloud yawned and stretched his front legs, followed by a careful stretch of his back legs; his spine rippled with the effort. Sitting down he leaned his head towards his back paw and enjoyed a good scratch behind the ear. As he stood and shook the dust from his coat, a twinge of joint pain made him yip.

Jet ambled up to him, her tail low, gently wagging. "Father, are you alright?"

Grey Cloud's lip lifted in a snarl of greeting. The pains of old age made him irritable. Each new day, he struggled with the challenge to hold his position as pack leader…ever watchful for any threat to his authority.

Glancing at Jet, he gruffly said, "Yes, I'm fine." Ambling to the cave entrance, he looked up at the night sky; his gold eyes sparkled. *This will be a good night for hunting.* He turned as Jet approached.

"I'm hungry father, when are we going hunting?" She asked.

Grey Cloud's eyes softened. "Fetch Remas and alert the pack." The glow of excitement in her eyes made him smile. Sitting down, he waited for Remas. He shivered as the wind ruffled his fur…not as thick as it used to be, he felt the cold. Snowflakes swirled around his face; squinting, he lowered his head.

"We should be able to catch larger prey tonight," Remas said sitting close beside him.

Grey Cloud nodded. "Indeed; when everyone is ready we will leave." Grey Cloud could feel the warmth from his young lieutenant's body; he resisted the urge to lean closer. Glancing at Remas, he saw loyalty in his friend's dark eyes. He relied on the big

280

brindle wolf to reinforce his orders, and keep the pack in order, which in the past had not been without its difficulties.

Grey Cloud remembered his battles to achieve the position of alpha-male. A position he had won and managed to hold on to, thanks to Remas' strength and loyalty.

The big wolf continued to instil Grey Cloud's authority. His scarred body and missing left ear was a testament to past battles, and occasional skirmishes. Undaunted, Remas was determined to show his gratitude...assist the one wolf, which had protected and fought alongside him against an angry she bear.

Remas knew when Grey Cloud was gone; he would rise to the position of Alpha-male. No one would challenge his ascension, not even Thor, Grey Cloud's son. Turning his head, he stared at Grey Cloud. "Are you ready?"

Grey Cloud snarled assent. Leaving the shelter of the cave's entrance, he walked into the snow, raised his head and howled at the moon.

In an instant the pack surrounded him, the air thick with anticipation. Long mournful howls filled the night sky, the primal song drifted over the forest, sending small animals scurrying to safety.

As if by an unseen signal, the howling ceased. In single file the pack followed Grey Cloud down the narrow path. Their descent into the forest could be dangerous at any time, but with the sheer drop on both sides, and a layer of deep snow, the path was particularly treacherous.

Reaching the forest floor they grouped together. Their ears twitched as they listened for any sounds...noses eagerly sniffed the air. In some ways the snow worked in their favour. Prey was more conspicuous, and had to travel further afield in search of food. However, it also worked against the wolves. The heavy fall of snow reduced sound and deadened scent.

Thor turned to Grey Cloud. "I smell something, father. It's faint, but it's this way." His excitement influenced the rest of the pack, they milled around keen to follow him.

"Wait! Remas growled. Raising his head he cocked his one ear. "I hear cries, something is injured."

The pack listened. "I hear it," Jet whimpered. Her body trembled with anticipation.

Grey Cloud tilted his head to the side. "So do I, it's this way. Follow me." With Remas at his side, he led the pack deep into the forest.

Motivated by the thought of an easy meal, Grey Cloud followed the cries. Racing through the snow, the pack fanned out behind him. Closing in on the injured prey; they silently approached it from all sides. There would be no escape.

Merry's ears twitched incessantly, her eyes widened in panic. "They're here," she whispered.

Blackwing fluffed his feathers; his bright eye's darted around. "I don't see anything."

Shaking her head up and down, Merry pawed at the ground. Her breath came in short gasps. *Oh dear, have I done the right thing?* Rising on her hind legs she pawed at the air.

Hidden in the undergrowth, the wolves watched and waited. Crouched by his father's side, Thor whispered. "It doesn't look injured to me."

"True," Remas said. "It looks like we'll have to fight to bring it down."

Grey Cloud snarled and crept forward. He had hoped for an easy kill, but this prey looked fit and full of fight.

"Maybe this isn't it," Remas whispered.

"It is," Grey Cloud said as he crawled on his belly to the edge of the path. Peering through the shrubbery, he studied the feisty chestnut horse. He could see no discernible injuries. *Why would it alert us to its presence?* His eyes narrowed in a frown.

"Are we going to attack it, father?" Thor held his tail between his legs, but the tip wagged with excitement.

Grey Cloud could feel Remas trembling beside him. "Call the pack out," Grey Cloud said to him. "Form a tight circle around it. Don't let it escape."

Remas snarled, exposing sharp fangs. "Don't worry, it won't."

Merry laid her ears back...her body trembled. Squealing and snorting she backed up, but there was nowhere to go. The wolf pack surrounded her.

"Tck, tck" Blackwing called, as he flew to a branch adjacent to Merry's head. He could see the whites of her eyes, the flecks of sweat on her neck and shoulders. In a loud voice he cried. "Stop panicking! Talk to them."

Realizing he was right. Merry stood her ground. Taking a few deep breaths she called out. "Where is Grey Cloud? I need to speak to him." Her heart raced as the wolves closed in. Slipping in the snow, she whirled around. Her eyes widened as she stared at each wolf. "Grey Cloud!" She squealed. "Where are you?"

Glancing at Blackwing, she whispered. "It's no good, he's not here." Lowering her head, she stood stiff legged and waited for the inevitable.

Seeing the hope fade from her eyes, Blackwing cried. "No, Merry, don't give up." His agitated, tck, tck's echoed in the menacing silence. Hopping and flapping on his branch, he did his best to distract the wolves.

Seeing a movement in the periphery of his vision, he ceased and turned his head. He watched a white wolf leave the pack, and plough through the snow towards Merry.

With a frightened snort, Merry raised her head.

The big white wolf halted in front of her. "I'm Grey Cloud. What do you want with me?" He growled.

Merry's heart raced as she stared at the wolf.

Grey Cloud's gold eyes darkened with impatience. "Well, what do you want?" He snarled.

Merry exhaled, her long breath forming a cloud around her head. Glancing at the waiting wolves, her heart raced; she knew she was still in danger. Nevertheless, she clutched at the brief respite. Staring into Grey Cloud's hungry eyes, she took a calming breath. In a voice choked with emotion, she said. "I belong to Princess Mira." Thinking of her mistress brought tears to her eyes. "My mistress is dead." Glancing back, she stamped her foot. "They're all dead!"

Grey Cloud studied her, his head cocked at an angle. "What do you mean they're all dead? Who's all dead?"

Realizing she had his attention, and seeing the rest of the pack settling in the snow, Merry's confidence rose; her words tumbled over each other as she told him what had happened. His reaction on hearing of Mira's death, and Irene's kidnap, took her by surprise. *He obviously cared a great deal for them.* She thought.

However, their conversation came to an abrupt halt, as a lone man appeared, shouting and waving his arm. The wolves scattered.

❦❦❦

Aldrin couldn't believe his luck, a few yards away was Mira's horse. But seeing the wolves surrounding her, his shoulders slumped…his lips pressed tight. *Can I get to her, before they attack?* Ploughing through the snow, he raised his sword and yelled at the top of his voice. Gasping with relief and grateful for the adrenalin rush, he forced himself to hurry; aware the horse, like the wolves, might flee into the forest and escape him.

Sheathing his sword, he approached, softly speaking her name. He could see a broken rein tangled round her leg; he prayed she would stay still. His heart raced…relief flooded his body as he reached her head and took hold of the bridle. "Good girl," he said softly patting her neck. Her skin felt cold, parts of her long mane were coated in ice. "We need to get you moving before you freeze," he said checking the girth of the saddle.

The unexpected release of tension, made his hands tremble. Cursing, he struggled to free the rein wrapped around her leg. The leather had frozen hard, but he managed to untangle it and lead her out of the deep snow. Gripping the pommel of the saddle, he hauled himself onto her back. His left shoulder throbbed with pain, nevertheless with a smile of triumph, he heeled her forward. He needed to reach his brother's camp, and tell him what had happened.

A stiff wind swirled the falling snow, whipping it into his face. Pulling the hood of his cloak further over his head, he hunkered in the saddle. He could feel the horse struggling beneath him. Her hooves fighting for purchase on the slippery ground.

Realizing he was riding his dead sister's horse brought a lump to his throat. Rubbing a gloved fist across his chapped lips, he swallowed hard. *I miss her, but she would be glad I'm safe.* Reaching forward he gave the horse's neck an encouraging pat.

He knew the journey would be slow and arduous, but he wasn't bothered. It would give him the time he needed to get his story right. *I'll be a hero.* He smiled with satisfaction at the thought.

Riding with a loose rein, he supported his left arm. His shoulder burned as though on fire, yet his body felt cold as if ice flowed in his veins. He shivered.

Chapter 41

Grey Cloud and the pack melted like ghosts into the forest. Crouched among the trees, they watched the man mount the horse and ride away.

Thor's stomach rumbled. "Now what do we do? I'm starving."

"We go hunting," Remas growled.

Grey Cloud stood to his feet and shook the snow from his coat. "Not yet," he said. "First we must do all we can to help Irene."

"How, father?" Jet's amber eyes searched his face. "We don't know who they are, or where they are taking her."

"I do," Grey Cloud snarled. "They are returning to the land of Feritas, beyond the mountain."

Tilting his head, Remas stared at him. "Do you have plan?" He asked.

Grey Cloud nodded. "I'm just not sure how to find him. It's been such a long time since I last saw him."

Remas frowned. "Who are you talking about?"

"I'm talking about Zenith, the great eagle."

Thor's eyes widened. "Father, how can we find him? He lives so far from here. And how can you be sure he will help us?"

"I know he will, because he loves Irene as I do." Lowering his head, he sighed. "The only trouble is we will never reach him in time." Snarling with frustration, he glared at the small blackbird flitting about on a branch above his head.

Jet growled and leapt into the air. "Clear off, this conversation is private."

Blackwing flew to a higher branch out of reach. "I was about to offer my assistance, but if you're going to be unpleasant, I won't bother." Nonchalantly, he preened a tail feather.

"How can you assist us?" Grey Cloud asked.

Blackwing fluttered his wings. "In case you hadn't noticed. I can fly."

The satisfaction in the bird's voice annoyed Grey Cloud, but he held his peace.

Blackwing flew to a lower branch and peered at the big wolf. "Irene is my friend. In our world she used to feed me. Unfortunately, when she came here, I accidently followed her." Lowering his head, his yellow eyes glistened with emotion. "She has done her best to help me, and I have grown fond of her. So, if there's a chance I can help. Please let me try."

"You don't know what you're asking," Grey Cloud said. "Zenith is a mighty eagle, and I can't guarantee his temper."

Blackwing cocked his head to one side. "Does he love Irene?"

Grey Cloud nodded.

"Then there is no problem. I will explain to him what has happened, and he will do what he will do." Flapping his wings, Blackwing asked. "Where does he live?"

Trying not to confuse them both, Grey Cloud did his best to explain.

"Don't worry," Blackwing said. "I'm sure if he's as big as you suggest. I should have no trouble finding him." Impatient to get going he flew into the air.

The wolves watched until he disappeared from sight.

"Will he make it?" Remas asked.

"He'll make it; but what Zenith will make of him is another matter!" Turning, he led the pack out of the trees and back onto the path. Lowering his head close to Remas, he growled softly. "Take them hunting. I must go to the mountain and find the rat Ezekiel."

Without waiting for a reply, Grey Cloud spun round and bounded into the forest. He quickly disappeared from view, his white coat camouflaged in the deep snow.

తత్తత్

Blackwing's bright eyes darted to and fro, searching for the landmarks the wolf had told him to look for. Tiredness crept over his body, he could feel his strength waning. His thoughts turned to the sheltered tree he now called home. How he wished he was perched in its boughs, safe and warm. Shrugging off the thought, he flew on, determined to do all he could to help Irene.

Rising higher, he fought against the wind and falling snow. The flakes hit him in the face, momentarily blinding him. The wind took

287

his breath away. *I can't go much further, I need to stop and rest.* Peering through the falling snow, he spotted the massive fir tree Grey Cloud had mentioned. With a sigh of relief, he perched in its highest branch. *I'll have a short rest, while I get my bearings.* Squinting through the snow, Blackwing's heart skipped a beat. In the distance, illuminated by the moon…towering crags soared into the night sky.

"Thank the heavens. I'm nearly there." For a brief second, anxiety at the thought of meeting Zenith caused his heart to race. Gripping the swaying branch, he puffed out his chest. "I will not fear him. I am doing this for Irene."

With his confidence buoyed, he spread his wings and soared into the sky. His only thought to tell Zenith that Irene was in trouble and needed his help.

⋘⋘⋘

With his massive wings outstretched, Zenith floated onto the wide ledge. Dropping the small deer held in his talons, he began the tedious job of de-furring it. He was so busy preparing his dinner, he didn't notice Blackwing approach.

"Tck, tck," Blackwing cried as he perched on a rocky outcrop, just above Zenith.

Zenith's head shot up, his golden eye's flashed with anger. "Who are you? How dare you enter my domain? Go, before it is too late." Rising to his full height, his massive curved beak, coated in the blood of his prey, was only a few inches from Blackwing's face. Staring at Blackwing, Zenith hissed with disdain. "You're too scrawny to be worth eating, but I will, if you are not gone right now!"

Blackwing blinked, as the eagle's hot breath hit him in the face. Instinctively, he moved back nearly missing his footing. Flapping his wings, he righted himself and stared defiantly at the mighty eagle. In a voice hardly more than a whisper, he said. "Irene is in trouble. She needs your help."

Zenith tilted his head to the side, his golden eyes studying Blackwing. "Irene has returned?" He took a deep breath. "She is here?"

Blackwing nodded. He was relieved to see recognition…a fondness for Irene in the great eagle's eyes. Plucking up his courage, he hopped closer. "I am Irene's friend; we arrived in this land together."

Shrugging his huge shoulders, Zenith stared at Blackwing. "I am delighted she has returned. However, you say she is trouble. What sort of trouble?"

Blackwing lowered his head and half closed his eyes. His heart raced...his voice faltered, as he said. "Irene has been kidnapped."

"What! Who has taken her?" Zenith's eyes blazed. "Tell me." He hissed.

Blackwing's head drooped. "Please, give me a moment and I will tell you everything." Taking a deep breath, he explained how Psalm had been killed by a mink. The sorrow he saw in Zenith's eyes touched his heart. He felt awful...hated to be the bearer of bad news. *I don't want to do this; I wish I could fly away.* But Zenith's powerful presence held him, willing him to continue.

Mustering his courage, Blackwing raised his head and told the great eagle. "Before Psalm died, she urged me to warn Irene, and Princess Mira, that warriors were waiting to ambush them."

Zenith's head shot up. "Are you telling me, Princess Mira was with them?"

"Yes, and Prince Aldrin and some guardsmen." Seeing the look of dismay on Zenith's face, Blackwing paused.

Zenith hissed the sound loud and agitated. "Where is the Prince, and Princess, now?"

Shaking his head, he frowned at Blackwing. "And where is Prince Zatao?"

Blackwing swallowed a lump in his throat, and instinctively stepped back. "Prince Zatao is at his outpost." He took a deep breath and stared into the distance. "He is unaware of what's happened."

"And!" Zenith said sternly. He knew the small bird was holding back...hesitant to continue.

Held in the eagle's intense gaze, Blackwing cringed. "The Prince and Princess are both dead," he blurted out. He felt a strange sense of relief, as the dreaded words left his mouth. However, the shock on Zenith's face, the eerie tap tapping of his massive claws as he paced, unnerved Blackwing. Hunching his shoulders he tried to appear invisible.

Zenith's golden eyes narrowed as he faced Blackwing. "Are you telling me, that Prince Zatao's brother and sister are dead?" His voice cracked with emotion.

Blackwing nodded. "I'm afraid they are, and Irene has been taken away." His wings drooped, as exhaustion and distress drained his remaining energy. "Please, will you help us rescue her?"

Zenith stood tall and stretched his huge wings. "You say us, who else is involved?"

"A big white wolf; he told me to come to you."

Zenith nodded. "That will be Grey Cloud."

Blackwing's head bobbed; his heart raced with impatience. "So, what shall we do?"

Zenith cocked a feathered eyebrow. "You will fly to Prince Zatao's camp and tell him what has happened. Tell him, Zenith the eagle will wait for him at the great mountain, on the border of our land." He studied Blackwing. "I know you are exhausted, but do not fail me," he said firmly.

Blackwing blinked and nodded. "What are you going to do?" He asked.

"I will summon my son Hunter. We will fly to the mountain, meet up with Grey Cloud, and wait for Prince Zatao to arrive." He frowned at Blackwing. "No pressure, but you need to fly as fast as you can."

"I will," Blackwing promised. "How do you know Grey Cloud will be there?"

"Grey Cloud will go there to speak with my old friend, Ezekiel the rat. He and his troop live inside the mountain. They always know what's going on."

"Thank you for helping us," Blackwing said softly.

Zenith's eyes flashed with grief and rage. "Of course I will help! Irene is my friend. I will rescue her." Pausing, he stared at the distant mountain, and in a voice deceptively soft, he said. "I will avenge the deaths of Princess Mira, and her brother."

Blackwing shivered at the menacing timbre of his voice.

Seeing the small bird's anxiety, Zenith softened his demeanour. "Now go," he said gently. "In the distance, you will see Prince Zatao's campfires." He indicated the direction with his head. "Follow the glow." Without another word, Zenith spread his mighty wings and soared heavenwards; his raucous call echoing over the forest.

Perched on his rock, Blackwing watched a large dark shape join Zenith. He watched until they were mere specks heading towards the mountain.

Chapter 42

Ergon wiped the sweat from his top lip. His eyes glistened as he leaned in close to Grouchen.

Grouchen held the exhausted pigeon close to his chest, and pulled the small tube off its leg, before releasing it out of the window.

Ergon followed him to the table, his heart raced as he watched him pull the scrap of paper from the tube and unroll it.

Scanning the note, they glanced at each other and grinned.

Ergon breathed a sigh of relief. "At last, our warriors have her."

Grouchen nodded. "Yes, good news indeed. Come, we must show this to the King."

⊰⊰⊰

King Murkier paced the throne room, the note crumpled in his hand. Halting in front of his two advisers, his lips softened in an uncharacteristic smile. "This is good news." He glanced at the note. "Going by this, they should cross the border in about an hours' time." Scrunching the note, he raised his fist. "At last, we have him! Prince Zatao will not escape this time." The King swung round; his long cloak brushed the stony ground, raising dust as he strode to his throne.

Huddled together on their knees, Ergon and Grouchen breathed inaudible sighs of relief.

Affected by the floating dust, Ergon tried not to sneeze. Lowering his head, he closed his eyes and thanked the gods for their deliverance.

King Murkier's black eyes blazed with fervour. "I will muster my troops and ride to meet them. I must see this woman, who has captured the heart of my enemy." Glancing at his advisors, he raised a dismissive hand. "You may go."

With their heads bowed the two men struggled to their feet and backed towards the door.

Pounding the arms of his throne, King Murkier laughed with delight.

Queen Ballista closed the small door behind the throne, and approached him. "Has everything worked according to plan, my love?"

Holding out his hand to her, he grinned. "Oh yes, and easier than expected."

Taking his hand, Ballista sat at his feet; her lips softened in a smile as she stared up at him. "Will we have his land, my love?"

Murkier raised his head and laughed. "We will have his land and much more. Power and riches beyond measure will be ours." Rising to his feet, he pulled her into a crushing embrace. Sweeping her long black hair off her shoulder, he nuzzled her neck. "When Zatao finds out we've captured his woman, he will capitulate." Releasing her, he paced, all the while thoughtfully tapping his chin.

Ballista reclined on her throne watching him. "You appear distracted my love, is there a problem?"

"No problem," the king said, raising a hand. "I have decisions to make. I need to think." Gathering his cloak over his arm, he swung to face her. "Go now, and wait for my return."

Slowly, Ballista rose to her feet, her eyes glinted. "You are going to war."

Murkier placed a hand on the hilt of his sword and shook his head. "Capturing Zatao's woman has removed the necessity for outright war. For the moment, I shall lead a small force to meet the warriors who have her, and escort them home in triumph."

Ballista clapped her hands with delight. "My love, is there no end to your brilliance?"

Murkier grinned. "Possibly not," he said, standing tall and puffing out his chest. "Now go, and wait for my triumphant return." His black eyes darkened with lust, as he watched her sashay from the room.

Turning to the guard at the door, he bellowed. "Muster my forces. Be ready to leave in ten minutes."

❧❧❧

Opening her eyes, Irene moaned, her frozen body screamed with pain. Feeling movement beneath her, and seeing her hands hanging down, she realized she was on a horse, face down over the saddle. For a moment she had no recollection as to what had happened. Gradually, as her foggy head cleared, she remembered.

She tried to move, but the pommel of the saddle bit further into her ribs. Groaning with pain, she cringed as a heavy hand grabbed her by the back of the neck.

"It sounds like she's awake." Muglwort said.

Zworn frowned. "She is, and it's time you took over."

Freon laughed. "I would have thought you'd enjoy having a woman so close."

Irene clenched her fists at the sound of his voice; but hearing Zworn's low growl she kept still.

With Zworn's hand on her neck, all she could see was the snow covered ground and the horse's flank. She had no idea where they were, or where they were taking her. Dizzy, and nauseous, from having her head down for so long, she tried to swallow the bile rising in her throat. "Let me up!" She cried.

Zworn tightened his grip on her neck. "Be quiet," he snarled.

All of a sudden, the horse stopped and she found herself sitting in deep snow. Ignoring the stiffness in her body and the throbbing pain in her thigh, she raised her head and looked around. Instantly, she knew where she was. It was the huge clearing at the base of the mountain. Her heart skipped a beat as a memory flooded back. *This is where Ezekiel lives. I'm sure it is.* Her eyes darted around...hopeful she might see him.

However, the base of the mountain was too far away, and blinded by the swirling snow, she could hardly see a thing. Struggling to her feet, she was quickly surrounded by the three warriors, and their horses.

She cried out as Muglwort's huge hand wrapped around her arm, and dragged her towards a massive black stallion. Lifting her up as though she weighed nothing, he seated her in the saddle and mounted up behind her. Rearranging the blanket round her shoulders, and holding her tight around the waist, Muglwort urged his horse forward. "Come on," he growled at the others. "We still have some way to go."

Clenching her teeth, Irene seethed with anger. Nevertheless, held tight against his body, at least she was warm. Lowering her head against the falling snow, she closed her eyes and, to her horror for a moment dozed off.

The silver fingers of dawn, rose above the horizon as they negotiated the clearing, and crossed the border into the land of Feritas.

A cold fear gripped Irene as she shot awake. No amount of swallowing soothed the dryness in her mouth and throat. She wanted to take some deep calming breaths, but knew it would betray her fear to the warrior holding on to her.

She gasped, as he lowered his head close to her ear, and whispered. "I can smell your fear, so there's no point hiding it." Feeling his hot breath on her neck, she cringed. Her face flushed with anger and embarrassment. Unable to stop herself, she kicked the horse's flanks as hard as she could.

With a squeal, the animal shot forward nearly unseating them both.

Cursing, Muglwort pulled on the reins, and quickly brought the stallion under control. Reining the horse, he grabbed a fistful of Irene's hair and yanked her head back, forcing her to look at him. Fixing her with a black stare, he growled. "There will be no escape, my dear. My King awaits your presence."

The ominous tone to his voice, made the hairs rise on the back of Irene's neck.

Seeing he'd made his point, Muglwort laughed and released her. "I advise you to sit still and behave yourself."

The three warriors were jubilant. Having succeeded in their quest, and safely crossed into their own land, they relaxed and bunched together. Around them, the vast flat landscape stretched for miles. Apart from the clink of the bits in their horse's mouths, and the soft creak of leather, an eerie silence surrounded them.

Underfoot, thick snow muffled the horse's hooves. It was no longer snowing, but a stiff wind blew loose snow into the air, adding to the chill factor.

Irene discreetly stared around; from the moment they crossed into this land, her heart felt heavy in her chest. The gloomy atmosphere was all pervasive. Glancing up at the sky, she frowned at the watery sun struggling to make an impression on the grey landscape.

Lowering her head, she closed her eyes. *Zatao will rescue me. I know he will.* His strong handsome face filled her thoughts, giving her the strength she needed to hold on.

❧ ❧ ❧

King Murkier heeled his horse, urging it into a canter. Followed by fifty of his bravest warriors, they clattered through the castle gates, along the main street of the village and out onto the snow covered plain.

The thick snow underfoot hindered their progress. The horses stumbled and slithered in their attempt to gain a footing. Tight lipped and grumbling, King Murkier reined his horse to a walk. Gazing up at the watery sun, he scowled. *Blasted weather!*

Even in the freezing cold, his hands sweated at the thought of seeing Zatao's woman. Licking his lips with anticipation, he removed a glove and wiped his sweaty palm on his cloak. *Once she is incarcerated, all power will be mine.* He chuckled at the thought.

Pursing his lips, he growled, and dug his spurs into the animal's flanks, forcing it to go faster.

Following behind, his warrior's horses slithered and slipped in their attempts to keep pace with him.

Riding behind King Murkier, the warrior holding the pennant urged his horse alongside the King's. "My Lord, would it be advisable to stop for a moment and rest the horses?" His voice faltered. "We have been riding hard for some time." His jaw clenched as he met the King's angry stare. Trembling with fear, he lowered his eyes.

Waving a gloved fist, the King snapped, "I say when we stop." Looking the young warrior up and down, Murkier's lips twisted in an angry snarl. "Your audacity will not go unrewarded," he growled. "Now get back in line!"

King Murkier's horse snorted it sides heaved with exertion, as it struggled through the deep snow. Gripping the pommel of his saddle, Murkier hung on and amused himself with thoughts of an appropriate punishment for the impertinent young warrior.

A loud shout from one of his warriors, brought him out of his reverie. "My Lord, Look!" The man shouted.

296

Raising a hand, Murkier shielded his eyes from the snows glare. Peering into the distance he could see a small group of horsemen approaching. His pulse raced at the sight. Making a fist he beat the air. "Victory is mine!"

❧❧❧

Muglwort reached across and slapped Zworn on the shoulder. "Look," he exclaimed. "The King is here."

Zworn's eyes followed Muglwort's pointing finger. Raising a fist, he grinned at Freon. "We've made it," he shouted.

Irene huddled in the saddle as the three warriors whooped and hollered.

With a shout of triumph, Muglwort urged his horse forward. The stallion's head dropped, every muscle strained, as he ploughed through the deep snow.

The others followed, their arms waving in triumph.

Grimacing, Irene clutched the pommel of the saddle with one hand, and a handful of the horse's mane with the other. Muglwort's hold on her had loosened, his attention focused on the advancing army. For a fleeting moment she contemplated escape.

As the thought entered Irene's head, Muglwort's hold on her tightened. Cringing, she felt the colour drain from her face as in a harsh voice, he warned. "Don't even think about it."

Irene slumped in the saddle, as the last vestige of energy drained from her body. Bitter bile rose in her throat, as she watched the King and his army approach. *Oh God, help me!* She pleaded silently.

Reining his horse, Muglwort breathed a sigh of relief. Zworn and Freon gathered round him, their faces wreathed in smiles.

As King Murkier drew near, they bowed their heads.

Muglwort couldn't help noticing the strange glow in the King's eyes as he drew alongside and stared at Irene. Grabbing a fistful of Irene's hair, Muglwort pulled her head up. "Honour the King," he growled. Looking at the King, he smiled. "My Lord, here is the woman belonging to your enemy."

King Murkier reached across and twirled a strand of Irene's hair. He liked its fiery sheen…the softness between his fingers. Grabbing her chin, he forced her to look at him. Feeling her flinch, and try to pull away, he smiled.

Letting her go, he grinned at Muglwort. "She's a feisty one."

Nodding, Muglwort opened his mouth to speak. But the King's darkening expression and raised hand silenced him.

"Why is her face bruised? She looks as though you've used her as a punch bag." His nostril flared as he looked from one to the other.

Freon's chin dropped to his chest, as the King's gaze settled on him. Swallowing hard, he slumped in the saddle.

Pointing at Irene, the King growled. "What is the meaning of this? If there was any beating to be done, I would do it. She is my leverage over Zatao. Her beauty in my possession would weaken him. But if he sees her in this state, it will enrage and strengthen him." The pitch of his voice heightened with anger. "You fool! For this you will pay dearly. Like for like," he growled.

"But My Lord, she attacked me…tried to kill me. I had to defend—"

"Be silent!" The King bellowed.

Freon lowered his head, shrivelling in the King's disdainful glare.

King Murkier swung his horse around and headed back to his waiting army. "Come," he shouted at them. "We must return to the castle before it is dark, and our enemy falls upon us."

❦❦❦

Irene's breath rasped in her throat. Shivering, she pulled the blanket tighter around her shoulders and tried to ignore the searing pain in her leg. In a way she was grateful for Muglworts tight grip around her waist…the warmth of his body against her back. She knew if he let her go, she would fall. Raising a trembling hand, she discreetly rubbed her sore chin. It was as though she could still feel the King's fingers digging into her flesh. She shuddered at the thought of him; the dead blackness of his eyes staring into hers, reminded her of a shark.

Her mind filled with the image of Mira's face, those lovely emerald eyes staring up at her. Sorrow like a knife twisted in her gut…hot tears spilled down her cheeks. The pain was too much to bear. Sniffing, she rubbed her nose with the back of her hand; no way would she give her enemy the satisfaction of seeing her grief. Irene knew she must stay strong, if not for herself, for Mira.

Staring at the army ahead of them, Irene trembled. Surrounded by the bleak, snow covered landscape, her sorrow and fear intensified. Her heart fluttered, as she thought of Zatao. *Where are you, my love? Will you be able to find me?* Trying to imagine how he would rescue her, pushed her faith to the limit.

Her throat constricted, as she tried to imagine how Zatao would cope, with the loss of Mira and his brother. The thought he might blame her, push her away…filled her with dread.

Glancing to her left, she caught sight of Freon. For a brief moment, anger like a burning fire coursed through her body. But remembering the King's threat to punish Freon brought a slight smile to her face. *If I could avenge you, Mira, I would. I pray he gets what's coming to him.* Catching Freon's eye, she glared at him.

Chapter 43

Blackwing's heart raced…not with exhaustion, but anticipation. He felt confident. Zenith's authority gave him the courage to believe. They would succeed in rescuing Irene.

The distant, orange glow of camp fires, drew him on. This would be his first time in the presence of Prince Zatao. He felt a little nervous, especially being the bearer of tragic news. Nevertheless, inspired by the thought of saving Irene, he pumped his wings, pushing himself to reach the camp as quickly as possible.

Drawing near, he could see the full extent of the camp, it was vast! His eyes widened in panic. *How will I find the Prince among so many?* Squinting through the falling snow, he searched for any indication as to the Prince's whereabouts.

During his second fly past, he noticed a log cabin. A long pennant fluttered on a pole close to the door. Four guardsmen stood to attention in front of the building. Tents of various shapes and sizes surrounded the cabin. Numerous camp fires cast a warm glow over the frozen landscape.

"Surely a Prince would be found in the cabin," he muttered to himself. Gliding towards a window, he perched on the snow covered ledge and peered in. Ice coated the glass. Inside, condensation dripped down the window impeding his view. All he could see was the glow from a lamp and a blazing fire. "I need to get in there." As the words left his mouth, the door opened.

Before the guardsman could close it, Blackwing left the ledge and fluttered into the cabin.

"Hey!" The guard shouted. "You don't belong in here."

Perched on the back of a chair, Blackwing shook his head and hopped from one foot to the other; his bright eyes darting around in search of the Prince. As the guard approached, he flitted onto the mantel shelf above the fire place. *Phew, it's a bit hot up here.* Before the guard reached him, Blackwing fluttered to the top of a half open door.

"Come here, you little pest. And don't you dare poop on the floor!" The guard's booted feet clumped on the floorboards as he strode towards the door.

"What's going on out there?" A loud voice exclaimed from the other side of the door.

"A bird has got into the cabin, My Lord. I'm trying to catch it."

Blackwing's yellow beak gaped as he exhaled. *It's the Prince, I've found him.* Flapping his wings, he hung onto his perch as the Prince pushed the door open.

"It's up there, My Lord," the guard said, pointing at Blackwing.

"Stop making so much noise, you're frightening it." Moving closer, Zatao's eyes narrowed as he stared up at the small bird. "What are you doing in here?" He asked softly.

"My Lord, I need to speak with you. My name is Blackwing. I came to this land with Irene."

Zatao raised a finger and smiled. "Ah yes, I remember. Mira said something about Irene having a pet black bird."

Indignant, Blackwing fluffed his chest feathers. "Excuse me, My Lord, but I am not Irene's pet!"

"My apologies," Zatao said with a slight smile. "So, what is it you wish to speak to me about?" The small bird's agitation quickly dispelled his amusement. The tension in the room was palpable. Dread as thick as treacle, crept over Zatao. He could feel the colour drain from his face. Clutching his shirt, he sucked in air. "The news you bring is not good," he said, in a voice no more than a whisper.

Blackwing nodded. "I'm sorry My Lord, perhaps it would be best if you sat down."

Squaring his shoulders, Zatao stood his ground. Planting his feet firmly, he insisted on being told everything. "Has something happened to Mira, or Irene," he demanded. The tremor in his voice belied the power of his stance.

Breathing hard, Zatao fought the icy fear creeping up his spine. The sadness in Blackwing's eyes did little to appease his anxiety. Tilting his head to the side, he stared at the frightened bird. "Tell me!" He demanded. "Spare me nothing."

Blackwing's heart ached. If he could have wept, he would. His voice faltered as he looked away and whispered. "My Lord, I am so sorry, but your brother and sister are dead. Lady Irene has been captured. As we speak, they ride with her across the border into your enemies land."

The Prince's anguished cry, though not unexpected, startled Blackwing.

The guard, his face creased with shock approached Zatao. "My Lord, maybe you should sit down."

Baring his teeth, Zatao raised his hands, halting the guards approach. "Leave me."

"But My Lord, please let—"

"I said, leave me!" Zatao swung round, his eyes blazing. "And tell no one what you have heard." He stared long and hard at the guard. "Do you understand me?"

The guard nodded and left the cabin.

Zatao waited until the door closed, before taking a seat by the fire and burying his head in his hands. *This is some kind of nightmare. It can't be real.* Hearing the flutter of wings, he looked up as Blackwing settled on the back of the chair opposite. The birds piercing gaze, momentarily wrenched Zatao out of his grief and shock. Rubbing his hands over his face, he took a deep breath and asked. "What happened? I need to know everything."

For the next few minutes, Blackwing described all he had seen and heard; culminating in his meeting with Zenith. Seeing the Prince's distress, spurred him to keep talking...let the horrifying words fly from his mouth, before his own grief silenced him. Pausing briefly to catch his breath, he stared at the troubled Prince. Lowering his head, he said softly. "Zenith the eagle is waiting for you in the clearing of the great mountain."

Zatao sniffed and wiped the tears from his face. Raking a hand through his hair, he stared at Blackwing. "Did Zenith say anything else?"

Blackwing hopped onto the arm of the chair. "He said he will have his son Hunter with him. He vowed, Irene will be rescued, and your sister, and brother, avenged."

Blackwing's spirit lifted, as he watched Zatao ease out of his chair and rest an arm on the mantelpiece. The Prince's jutting chin, and determined expression, gave Blackwing courage. "Is there anything I can do to help My Lord?"

Zatao rose to his full height and squared his shoulders. "Yes, fly to the mountain and tell Zenith I'm on my way. Tell him to do nothing until we arrive." Opening the cabin door, Zatao watched the small blackbird disappear into the night. "Fly safely, little friend."

The guardsman, who had heard the dreadful news, approached the Prince with bowed head. "My Lord, I am so—"

"Thank you," Zatao said cutting him off. The last thing he needed at the moment was to dwell on his grief. Scowling at the guardsman, he ordered. "Make haste and fetch sergeant Azar and guardsman Romure. We are going to war!"

Stretching his huge wings, Zenith rode the thermals. Rising high into the air, he escaped the buffeting wind below. Nevertheless, the snow fell thick and fast, hampering his ability to see clearly.

Squinting against the snow, his sharp eyes searched the tall crags below. *Where are you Hunter?* Flying in a wide arc, he dropped a little lower; unaware his son had heard his call and was approaching from the rear.

Hunter soared above Zenith, his eyes bright with mirth. Folding his wings back he dropped like a stone.

Out of the corner of his eye, Zenith glimpsed him. Rotating in the air Zenith touched talons with Hunter. For a brief moment they indulged in the obligatory aerial dance of greeting, before Zenith led Hunter onto a high wind swept ledge.

With lowered head, Hunter hopped to Zenith's side. "To what do I owe this visit, father?"

Zenith had not seen his son for some time. The young eagle had grown in stature. Standing eight foot tall and with a wingspan of fifteen feet, Hunter exceeded his father in height and power.

Feeling a little intimidated, Zenith folded his wings and stretched to his full height. "I need your help son. Prince Zatao's brother and sister are dead, murdered by warriors from the land beyond the mountain. These same warriors have snatched Irene, the Prince's betrothed."

Hunter studied his father, his feathered brows lowered over his eyes. "Is this the same Irene you told me about...the one who helped to rescue the Prince's stallion, August?"

Zenith nodded. He couldn't be sure how Hunter would respond, but he prayed he would be willing to help. Shifting from one foot to other, he tried to read his son's expression.

Hunter's eyes flashed. "Then we must rescue her."

Zenith exhaled silently and unfurled his wings. "I hoped you would agree to help us. We need to leave for the mountain, now. The Prince and his army will meet us there." Throwing himself from the ledge, Zenith soared into the sky.

Hunter followed, his racing heart drumming to the beat of his wings; his golden eyes gleamed at the thought of a battle.

In silence they flew, side by side; their massive wings scything a path through the falling snow. In no time they spotted the snow covered mountain, its tall peak rising into the stormy sky.

"There it is," Zenith shouted. "Be careful where you come down. Vicious thorn bushes grow in the middle of the clearing."

Hunter watched his father glide to the ground and move aside, giving him room to land. As they regrouped, a large white wolf loped towards them. Hunter stretched his neck and hissed. "Do I need to deal with this wolf, father?"

"No, leave him. This is Grey Cloud, a close friend of our Prince."

Grey Cloud raised his lips in a smile, the tip of his tail wagged in greeting. "It is good to see you again, Zenith. I'm saddened it should be under these circumstances." Lowering his head, he sighed.

Zenith nodded. "Indeed, my friend. Nevertheless, we are here to assist our Prince in his time of need."

"And assist Irene!" A squeaky voice shouted.

Zenith raised his head and peered over Grey Cloud. His eyes brightened in a smile as he greeted the big rodent lumbering towards him. "Of course we're here to save Irene, you big grouch." Glancing at Hunter and Grey Cloud, he chuckled. "He never changes." Lowering his head he gazed at the rat. "How are you, my dear old friend?"

Staring at Ezekiel, Zenith felt a twinge of sadness. Close up, his friend looked thinner. His white fur had yellowed, and lacked its usual lustre...his ruby eye's once so bright, had dimmed.

Sitting on his haunches, Ezekiel squinted in an effort to focus on his friends face. "It's so good to see you Zenith. How long has it been?"

Zenith shook his head and sighed. "Far too long I'm afraid." His eyes brightened in a smile. "But I'm relieved to see you are still—"

"Oh yes, I'm still here," Ezekiel quickly interjected. "The old bones ache and each winter takes its toll, but I struggle on."

"I know what you mean," Zennth said with a nod of understanding. Turning to Hunter, he indicated for him to come closer. "Grey Cloud, Ezekiel, allow me to introduce my son, Hunter."

"A fine young Prince," Ezekiel said softly.

Grey Cloud nodded in agreement.

Hunter stood beside his father, towering over the mighty old eagle. With a quick nod of his head, he acknowledged the wolf and the rodent. Studying the incongruous pair, his eyes narrowed. *The wolf with his pack could be of help*, he thought. *But of what use would an old rat be!*

Zenith guessed what his son was thinking and scowled. Turning his back on him, he addressed Ezekiel. "How long ago did they cross the border?"

Ezekiel raised a forepaw and scratched his cheek. "I believe it was just before Grey Cloud arrived, about half an hour ago." Lowering his body to the ground he trembled, his ruby eyes wet with tears. "Oh Zenith, I am so afraid for Irene. She looked dreadful; all beaten up and so afraid."

"Now, now, my old friend, you mustn't worry." Rising to his full height, Zenith glanced at Hunter. "We are going to rescue her. Even as we speak, my plan is coming to fruition."

"What plan?" Grey Cloud asked. Sitting on his haunches, he stared at Zenith.

Zenith met Grey Cloud's gaze; the expectancy in the wolf's eyes brought a smile to his face. Tilting his head on one side, he asked. "Do you remember the small blackbird?"

Grey Cloud nodded. "Of course, I sent him to you." His lips rose in a slight smile. "You didn't eat him, did you?"

"Hardly!" Zenith rocked with laughter. "Such a small bird would not be worth trying to catch. However, on a serious note, I sent him to Prince Zatao's camp, with a message to meet us here, as soon as possible."

Ezekiel fidgeted, his eyes darted around. "Who is this blackbird? Where's Psalm?"

Grey Cloud lowered his head, and gently touched Ezekiel on the shoulder with his nose.

The old rodent stared into his eyes and recoiled. "No!" He cried. "Are you telling me Psalm is dead?"

Grey Cloud nodded.

Zenith lowered his mighty body to the ground. Resting on his belly, he gazed sympathetically at the distraught rat. "I'm so sorry, Ezekiel. She was killed by a mink. The blackbird witnessed it. Before Psalm died, she asked him to help Irene. She knew he would, as he's Irene's friend." Zenith closed his eyes, allowing himself a moment to think of Psalm.

In the brief silence, Ezekiel took a few calming breaths. "I will miss her," he said softly.

"We all will," Zenith replied. "However, I have to say, this blackbird is proving to be as brave and as loyal as Psalm. I believe we can trust him." He winced at the pain he saw in Ezekiel's eyes. "Look, I'm not saying he's replaced Psalm, no one could do that. But she chose him, commissioned him if you like to carry on for her."

Ezekiel sniffed and brushed a paw over his long white whiskers. "I suppose you're right. We'll soon see if he turns up with the Prince."

Grey Cloud roamed restlessly, staring into the surrounding trees, his ears pricked at every sound. "Indeed," he growled. "And I hope it's soon. If we wait much longer, those warriors will be miles away, and we'll lose our chance to rescue Irene."

Rustling branches and the sound of flapping wings caught their attention.

Grey Cloud peered up, just as a clump of snow landed on his nose. Shaking his head, he growled. "Blasted pigeon's, they're such a pain!"

Ezekiel lumbered to his side and looked up.

The exhausted pigeon peered down at them, cooing softly.

"That's not any old pigeon," Ezekiel said. "It's a carrier pigeon, and if I'm not mistaken, it's the one that rested here briefly before flying across the border." He turned to Zenith. "You need to speak to it," he said softly. "I guarantee this bird has delivered a message to our enemy. It will have information helpful to us."

Zenith stretched his neck and studied the bird. "How can you be sure? Looks like any old pigeon to me."

"It's the same bird. I recognize the heart shaped ring around its neck."

The pigeon returned Zenith's gaze, fluttering nervously as the huge eagle moved closer.

"Stay where you are," Ezekiel urged him. "Speak softly, they are such skittish birds. We don't want it to fly away."

"It won't get far if it does," Hunter hissed.

"Be quiet son. Making threats is not helpful." In an attempt to appear less intimidating, Zenith lowered his huge body closer to the ground. Tilting his head sideways, he glanced at the bird. It appeared more relaxed. "Have you come a long way?" He asked softly.

The pigeon nodded. "I delivered a message for my master." Flapping its wings, it cried, "Bad! Bad!"

Zenith and the others froze…terrified the pigeon would take flight. Gradually the bird settled.

Zenith could see fear in the bird's eyes. Curious, he asked. "What is bad?"

The pigeon's head bobbed up and down. Focusing on Zenith, it whispered. "Evil is coming; must escape."

Zenith's heart raced as he saw the pigeon unfurl its wings. "No, don't leave!" He cried. "What do you mean evil is coming?"

The pigeon leaned over the branch and peered at him. "Soon you will hear the thunder."

Zenith turned to the others; he could see the confusion in their eyes. "I think he means the enemy is approaching."

"Yes!" the pigeon cried. "A mighty army is coming. We must leave; everyone leave, now." He pushed off the branch and fluttered into the air.

Grey Cloud watched the pigeon disappear into the forest. "We're too late," he groaned.

Ezekiel sat on his haunches and stared at the ground. "What are we going to do? We might be able to rescue Irene, but we can't fight an army."

Zenith raised his feathered brows and hissed with impatience. He was about to berate them for their lack of faith, when he heard a familiar tck, tck. With a huge sigh of relief, he cried. "It's the blackbird, he's here!"

᪂᪂᪂

Blackwing flew ahead of Prince Zatao and his vast army. The sight of hundreds of mounted men and foot soldiers, made his heart race. His emotions were torn between excitement, and concern for Irene's safety.

Up ahead he saw the mountain peak, towering above the forest. Its snow covered flanks glistened silver in the moonlight. Blackwing pumped his wings; tiredness vanished at the thought of telling Zenith the good news. The Prince was coming! *I just pray we're not too late.*

Blackwing flew into the clearing, and spotted Zenith and the small group with him. They looked dejected. Perching on a low branch, he alerted them to his presence. "Tck, tck," he called. Glancing back, he flapped his wings with excitement. "The Prince and his army are right behind me." He couldn't help smiling as four pairs of anxious eyes looked up at him.

Confused by their lack of enthusiasm, he frowned. "What's the matter? The Prince is here with his army…more than enough to rescue Irene."

Zenith sighed. "We are too late. The enemy is marching toward us as we speak."

"So is Prince Zatao with his army." Blackwing countered. "Enough, I'm sure to rout the enemy."

His positive attitude instilled a little confidence.

"How close are they?" Grey Cloud asked.

"Listen," Blackwing said.

Grey Cloud wagged his tail, his ears pricked as he listened.

Ezekiel stared at the ground and stepped back. "The earth is shaking," he squeaked.

Hunter turned to his father. "They are close."

Zenith listened. The sound of marching feet reverberated like thunder. He felt his body relax…felt the tension ease from his muscles. Turning to Hunter, he smiled. "You're right, they're here." His eyes narrowed slightly. "I just pray it's not too late."

Blackwing hopped on his branch, flapping his wings. "You'll see," he cried. "The Prince has a huge army."

308

Zenith smiled at his enthusiasm. "Numbers alone are not enough. We need a strategy."

"What's that?" Blackwing asked.

"A plan," Zenith said rolling his eyes.

"Don't worry about that," Blackwing said. "I believe Prince Zatao has a plan."

Zenith raised a feathered eyebrow. "I hope you're right. Our window of opportunity is diminishing as we speak."

Taking a deep breath, he moved closer to Hunter. Grey Cloud and Ezekiel crouched anxiously at their feet. Each one holding their breath, as they peered through the falling snow, listening to the sound of the approaching army.

Chapter 44

August's nostrils flared...hot breath billowed around his head. Ploughing through the thick snow, he struggled for purchase on the icy ground. Prince Zatao clutched the pommel of his saddle, concerned the stallion's frantic exertion would unseat him. Behind him, he could hear Guardsman Romure's loud voice, encouraging the soldiers.

Zatao turned to Azar riding beside him. "Are the foot solders coping?" he asked.

"The snow is hampering their progress, My Lord. But fortunately we will soon reach our destination." Azar urged his horse to keep pace with August. Looking discreetly at the Prince, he asked. "Are you alright My Lord?"

Zatao glanced at him. "What do you think?" He said, his voice thick with emotion. He could see the concern in his sergeant's eyes. Azar was more than an officer in the Prince's army. The man's loyalty and love for the royal family, Prince Zatao in particular, was irrefutable. On the death of Prince Zatao's father, Azar publicly pledged his allegiance to the Prince.

Zatao looked away. Thoughts of Mira and his brother lying dead in the snow, and the danger threatening Irene, was unendurable. The thick saliva in his throat, made swallowing difficult.

Azar could feel his Prince's grief. It weighed heavy. He wanted to extend a hand of comfort, but refrained. His voice cracked slightly as he said. "We will rescue Lady Irene, and avenge Princess Mira and your brother, My Lord."

Zatao straightened in the saddle. "Yes, we will," he said. "I have a plan, which if executed correctly will see the end of my enemy, King Murkier."

Azar tilted his head, his eyebrows arched. "You have a plan, My Lord?" Clearing his throat he stared at the Prince. "May I know what it—?"

"You will know when we reach the clearing," Zatao said abruptly. He glanced at Azar. "We are going to war, my friend."

Staring into the Prince's eyes, Azar cringed at the darkness he saw in their depths. *We have fought together in many campaigns, but I have never seen him this angry!* Azar lowered his head. *I pray his rage will not cloud his judgment.*

Both men rode in silence…deep in thought. Apart from the sound of snorting horses, clanking armour, and the thunder of marching feet…falling snow cloaked the forest in eerie silence. The virgin snow sparkled crystalline in the moonlight.

As they neared the clearing, the path widened. A wave of anticipation flowed through the ranks, as the men caught their first glimpse of the mountain.

Zatao could feel his chest tighten. Buried memories surfaced, his nostrils flared as he gulped air. He could feel August's body tense. The stallion shook his head; loud snorts carried hot breath into the cold air. Zatao reached down and patted the horse's neck. "Steady boy, it's alright." His voice calmed the agitated stallion. "You remember this place as well, eh. Don't worry, there's nothing to be afraid of." Gathering his reins, he heeled August into a canter.

Azar urged his big bay to follow. Soft snow swirled as the two horses cantered into the clearing, and halted in front of a small group of animals.

The four creatures stood with their heads bowed. Even the thunderous arrival of the army did not sway them from paying homage to the Prince.

Zatao leapt from the saddle and hurried towards them. Bending, he scooped Ezekiel into his arms. His brow creased as he felt the rodent's frailty beneath his hands. "How are you, my old friend?"

Ezekiel peered up at him, his ruby eyes shining with joy. "Seeing you My Lord, has filled this old rat with great happiness." Scrabbling onto Zatao's shoulder he huddled close to the warmth of his neck.

Zatao stooped and patted Grey Cloud. "Good to see you again, my friend." Turning to Zenith, he bowed. "There are no words to express my gratitude. Thank you for coming."

Zenith stepped forward; his height equalling that of the Prince. "My Lord, I am at your service, now and always." He turned to Hunter. "This is my son, Hunter. We are both ready to do your bidding."

"Your assistance will not go unrewarded," Zatao said. "You have my heartfelt thanks."

"We want no reward, My Lord." Zenith said firmly. "To serve you is a privilege. To help you rescue Irene is our pleasure."

Hunter came alongside his father and nodded.

Speechless, Zatao's throat tightened with emotion. Raising a hand, he stroked Ezekiel, before lifting the rat off his shoulder and placing him gently on the ground.

"I have a plan," Zatao said, making firm eye contact with each one. "And each of you has a part to play, if you are willing?" Their nods of affirmation brought a smile to his face. Encouraged, Zatao outlined the plan; their positive reaction increased his confidence. He could feel the tension ease from his shoulders. *This is going to work.* The thought of success made his pulse race.

Sergeant Azar sat on his horse, his eyes wide…fascinated by the scene before him.

Behind him the vast army marched into the clearing, positioning themselves in any available space. Many were forced to remain in the forest.

It was no longer snowing, the moon shone brightly in a clear sky. In its soft light, the spectacle in the huge clearing appeared dreamlike. The effect enhanced by the snow-capped mountain towering into the sky.

Azar glanced round as Guardsman Romure drew alongside him.

Romure's mouth dropped open, when he saw the Prince standing with a motley group of animals. "What's going on?" He asked Azar.

Azar smiled. "The Prince has a plan and I believe these creatures have a part to play in it."

Guardsman Romure's brow furrowed. "You're joking?"

Azar shook his head. "I'm not." He straightened in the saddle as Prince Zatao turned to face them. "It looks like we are about to hear the plan." Grabbing August's reins, he led the horse to Zatao. As the Prince mounted, Azar glanced at the creatures huddled together, watching them.

Shaking his head at the incongruous sight, he turned his horse and followed Zatao back to Romure, and the waiting army. "Is everything alright, My Lord?" He asked. The smile he saw in Zatao's eyes answered his question.

"I believe victory will be ours," Zatao said.

With Azar beside him, Prince Zatao sat on August and told his men the plan. "We leave now," he shouted. "Zenith and Hunter, the eagles will go ahead of us. Do not interfere with them, or hinder them." Holding his sword high, he stood in the stirrups and shouted. "Listen up, men! We are going to war. Fight bravely, hold your ground." Pausing, he stared at the sea of expectant faces…raising his voice, he cried. "May the God of heaven, protect and help us." The forest resounded to the thunder of fists on armour and shouts of victory.

Prince Zatao's eyes darkened as he sheathed his sword and beckoned to Guardsman Romure. Lowering his voice, he whispered. "Sergeant, I want you to send ten men to the main forest path. Somewhere in that area, they will find the bodies of my brother, my sister; and the soldiers that died defending them. I want the bodies returned to the castle. I will make funeral arrangements when we return." Pausing, he stared into the distance and took an inaudible breath, before continuing.

"When you have done that, rally the remainder of your forces, and follow us to the border. Wait there, until we are clear, then ride like the wind to King Murkier's castle and destroy it. Kill all who stand in your way. However, do not harm the Queen, or any of the villagers, unless they respond to you with hostility."

Romure straightened in the saddle, his heart drummed with excitement. Placing a fisted hand against his chest, he bowed his head to the Prince, before turning his horse and galloping towards the waiting soldiers.

Prince Zatao sat in the saddle, his shoulders hunched. His grip on the reins so tight; his hands throbbed with the pressure. His dark eyes studied the men before him. Each man was known to him, and his heart ached with the thought that many would lose their lives this night.

Lowering his head, he growled softly. "People must die, because of an evil tyrant's greed and hatred." Rubbing a gloved hand across his face, he sighed. *God forgive me. I have been forced into this war, it is not my desire to kill and destroy. Even so, your will oh God, be done this night.* With a nod to Azar, he turned August and led the army towards the border. His heart ached with love and concern for Irene. Raising his eyes heavenward, he prayed quietly. "God, keep her safe."

He could feel his blood boil, and took a few deep breaths. It would be so easy to hate and rage against, King Murkier. Nevertheless, Zatao knew he must remain dispassionate. If he allowed hatred for the King to take root in his heart, it would affect his actions…hamper his ability to lead his men, or worse, initiate the rise of the stag, which would play into the enemy's hands, bringing about destruction on them all.

ক্ষকক্ষ

Zenith and the others watched the Prince lead the army towards the border of their land. In the distance, a pale glow hovered on the edge of the horizon. Zenith stood tall and stretched his mighty wings. "Dawn is approaching; we must rout the enemy while it is still dark. The element of surprise is paramount, if the Prince's plan is to succeed." He stared at Grey Cloud and Ezekiel. "You know what to do?"

Their enthusiastic nods brought a fleeting smile to his face. "Ezekiel, I suggest you climb onto Grey Cloud's back. You need to reach Mercy Falls as soon as possible."

"Don't worry," Grey Cloud said squatting on his belly. "I'd already thought of that." His gold eyes twinkled as he glanced at Ezekiel. "If he were to travel on foot, we would never make it in time."

"No need to get personal," Ezekiel said swishing his long tail. Grasping Grey Cloud's fur in his paws, he clambered onto his back. His annoyance diminished as he nestled in the wolf's thick winter coat. His own white fur blended with Grey Clouds. However, the camouflage was negated by Ezekiel's ruby eyes.

Grey Cloud rose to his feet. "Are you ready?" He asked.

Huddled in the thick fur between the wolf's shoulders, Ezekiel mumbled, "Yes."

Grey Cloud's lip rose in a snarl. "Are you falling asleep?"

"No," Ezekiel squeaked and sat up.

"You'd better not," Grey Cloud warned. "I will be moving fast. So you need to hold on and stay alert."

"Stop worrying, I'll be fine."

Blackwing interrupted their argument, with a loud tck, tck. "What about me, what should I do?"

In the excitement, they had forgotten about the small blackbird.

"Um, let me think," Zenith said. Cocking his head to the side, he peered up at Blackwing. "I think it would be best, if you follow Grey Cloud to Mercy Falls and wait for us there. As you are Irene's friend, I feel your presence will be a comfort to her."

The suggestion appealed to Blackwing...he nodded enthusiastically.

Zenith and Hunter glanced at each other. Amusement flickered in their eyes. Clearing his throat, Zenith stared pointedly at Ezekiel. "Now remember, when you reach the falls, find as many healing leaves as you can, and wait for us to arrive. Do you understand?"

The rat glared at him. "Of course I do. I'm old, not stupid."

Zenith smiled and bowed his head. "Indeed; now go, and may the God of heaven be with you."

"And with you," Grey Cloud called as he raced into the forest, his tiny passenger clinging on for dear life.

"Tck, tck," Blackwing called as he skimmed over the snow covered ground in hot pursuit.

❧❧❧

Tilting his head to the side, Zenith raised a feathered brow and stared at Hunter. "Are you ready?"

Hunter could see the flicker of concern in his father's golden eyes. Standing tall, he nodded. "More ready than I've ever been," he hissed.

The fierce glint in his son's eyes encouraged Zenith. "Are you clear as to what you have to do?"

Hunter gazed into his father's face. "I fly high, and the moment I spot the King, I dive, and the rest is history as they say."

Zenith chuckled and nodded approval. "Indeed, and I will look for Irene." Returning his son's gaze, his eyes narrowed. "Understand this, my son. Once we spot our targets, we must attack simultaneously. If not, we lose the element of surprise." For a brief moment, he watched the remaining foot soldiers plough through the snow. Their heads down against the biting wind…their expressions grim.

Hunter unfurled his wings. "Don't worry father, I am well aware, Prince Zatao is relying on us to create panic among the enemy troops. Rest assured there will be panic!"

Zenith smiled at Hunter. *A chip off the old block*, he thought, noting the glint in his son's eyes.

Without another word, the mighty eagles soared into the sky. Rising on silent wings, they rode the thermals high in the clouds. Below them, Prince Zatao's army marched two abreast; they appeared as ants, dark against the snowy backdrop.

A few miles ahead, the eagles saw the enemy army and quickly spotted their targets. Irene and her captors were riding up front with the King. The army was moving fast, pushing their horses…intent on reaching the safety of the castle, before Prince Zatao could catch up to them.

The eagles' eyes glowed with anticipation. Folding their wings tight against their bodies, they plunged towards their individual targets. The wind whistled past them, as they dropped towards the ground, silent…deadly as an arrow fired from a marksman's bow.

Chapter 45

Crossing into the land of Feritas, Prince Zatao was relieved to find the snow was not as deep. Leaning forward in the saddle he touched August's flanks with his spurs, urging the stallion on.

Having paused in the clearing, the men and horses were rested, and keen to run down their enemy.

Sergeant Azar rode alongside Zatao, his eyes focused on the ground. "They are not too far ahead of us," he shouted. "From the hoof prints in the snow, I would estimate there are no more than fifty or so riders."

"I thought we would face the King's entire army," Zatao shouted.

"Not by the looks of these hoof prints," Azar replied.

Squinting in the surrounding whiteness, Zatao stared straight ahead. Uncertainty gripped him. *I pray God, I've not sent Romure and his small force to their deaths.* His pulse raced at the thought. However, it was too late now to do anything about it.

Azar's horse kept pace with August. The sergeant scanned the sky and distant horizon. *We must be close by now*, he thought. Falling snow swirled around them, hampering visibility. "That's all we need, a blasted snow storm," he grumbled. Glancing up at the sky, he caught sight of two large shapes plummeting towards the ground. "My Lord, Look!"

Zatao raised his head; a smile flickered on his lips. "It's the eagles. They've found them." Swivelling in the saddle, he yelled at the trumpeter. "Sound the charge." Pumping the air with his fist, he spurred August into a gallop.

The stirring notes of the trumpet rang out; mingling with the thunder of hooves and the clank of armour. The ground trembled, as Prince Zatao's army followed him into battle.

❧❧❧

King Murkier pulled back on the reins; holding up his hand he halted the army, the horses skidded to a stop around him. "Be quiet!" He shouted. Tilting his head to the side, he listened. The ground beneath their feet trembled. A low rumbling drifted towards them. Clenching his fist, Murkier frowned. "They've caught up with us," he growled. He was so intent on looking back; he didn't see the danger falling from the sky. None of them did, until it was too late.

King Murkier cried out, his face blanched as huge talons sank into his horse's neck and shoulders, the screaming animal struggled as it was lifted high in the air. Grabbing onto the pommel of his saddle, Murkier hung on, his legs swinging in the air as the horse's body dropped away beneath him. His heart hammered in his ears, his terrified screams drowned by the cries of his horse, and the men fighting for their lives on the ground below him.

Hunter's eyes gleamed with the joy of the kill. His heart raced as hot blood pumped through his veins. With a triumphant hiss, he sank his talons deeper into the horse's neck, puncturing an artery; the animal died in seconds.

Releasing the horse, Hunter grabbed the King before he plummeted to the ground, along with his horse. With one foot, Hunter held him by the shoulders, while the other encompassed the King's midriff. Holding his victim lightly, he flew higher, circling the frenzied scene below. "Take a look, your Highness. This will be the last thing you ever see."

King Murkier screamed and fought. Using his free hand he reached for his belt and pulled out a small dagger.

Hunter laughed. "Such a puny weapon; I'm offended your Highness." Bending his powerful neck, he stared into the King's face. Hate replacing the amusement in his eyes. Slowly he squeezed his talons into the King's body. Enjoying the surprise and terror he saw in the King's eyes.

Murkier dropped the dagger and clutched at Hunter's leg. "Please don't kill me," he cried. "I have the power to give you whatever you want." He gasped as a long talon punctured his lung.

"The only one with power is me," Hunter hissed. "Your death will come slowly." Flapping his mighty wings he flew higher.

Murkier's grip on Hunter's leg tightened. "Please," he gasped. His body tensed, as the eagle's massive talons punctured his armour...slicing through metal and flesh like a knife through butter.

As Hunter promised, death came slowly, one talon at a time…the last piercing the king's heart. Flying in a wide arch, Hunter dropped the King's body among the dead, and joined his father's unrelenting assault on the diminishing army.

Muglwort couldn't believe what he was seeing. His mouth opened in horror as he watched the King and his horse carried into the air…killed, then dropped unceremoniously to the ground. His stomach lurched. "The King is dead!" He shouted over and over.

Holding onto Irene, he attempted to gain control of his panicked horse. But as Zenith's shadow loomed over them, the horse bucked and fought…desperate to escape the ensuing carnage. The animals' terrified screams, drowned Irene's frightened cries as she clutched his mane.

Crouched in the saddle, Irene stared at the chaos around her. Men and horses struggled, screaming in fear as two gigantic eagles grabbed them, sometimes as many as three or four at a time…massive talons sinking and tearing into flesh. Soaring into the sky, they dropped the bodies from a great height and resumed their attack. The crushed bodies of men and horses littered the ground, their blood staining the snow crimson.

One or two brave archers crouched on the ground, their hands trembling as they fired at the attacking eagles. One or two arrows found their mark, but made little impression on the massive birds. In among the noise and carnage, Muglwort's loud cries rent the air. "The King is dead. The King is dead!"

Irene's heart pounded in her ears, adrenalin coursed through her veins. She could feel Muglwort struggling with the horse. Glancing at the ground, she determined to fall off. Loosening her grip of the mane, she prepared herself…aware that further injury could be the result of this desperate decision. Nevertheless, she had no other choice; this could be her chance to escape.

However, as she eased sideways in the saddle, she suddenly felt a violent pull from behind, accompanied by a ghastly scream. Glancing back, she saw Muglwort had vanished. Instinctively, she looked up, just as Muglwort's dead body fell out of the grip of huge talons. A voice she vaguely recognized shouted at her. "Ride Irene, go now!"

Holding onto the terrified horse, she shielded her eyes and looked up. "Zenith, is that you?"

"Yes, child, it is. Ride away from here. Prince Zatao is on his way, he will meet you."

Irene slumped in the saddle, her voice weak with pain and exhaustion. "I don't think I can ride, Zenith. This horse is too much for me." Tears trickled down her cheeks. "My leg hurts so much and my strength is gone." Wiping away her tears, she stared up at him.

"You can do it Irene." Zenith's eyes softened in a smile as he settled on the snowy ground in front of the horse and folded his wings. Stepping close to the terrified animal, he fixed it with a calm, authoritative stare. "Settle down. I'm not going to hurt you," he said softly. Staring into the horse's dark eyes, he watched the wild panic dissipate; he waited patiently for the animal to stop trembling. "I want you to take Irene, to Prince Zatao. Carry her gently and calmly, do you understand?"

The big black stallion nodded his head.

"Good, now go and let no harm come to her." Rising into the air, Zenith watched the horse turn and walk to meet Prince Zatao and the approaching army.

❧ ❧ ❧

Flicking his reins over August's neck, Prince Zatao urged the stallion on. "Faster, August," he shouted. Zatao was about to retrieve his sword, when he saw a horse and rider walking towards them. Behind the lone horse, he could see the eagles were still contending with the enemy.

Reining August to a walk, he lifted a hand and slowed his army. Shielding his eyes, he watched the lone horse and rider approach. Signalling the army to halt, he waited. The big black horse walked slowly, its head low. The rider slumped in the saddle... head bobbing with the movement of the horse.

Zatao tilted his head, his lips pursed. *Who is it? I don't recognize them.*

Sergeant Azar urged his horse alongside the Prince. "Do you know who it is, My Lord?"

Keeping his eyes on the lone rider, Zatao ran a hand through his hair. "I'm not sure," he said softly. "But somehow, they look familiar."

As if hearing his voice, the rider looked up and stared right at him. Zatao's stomach lurched. "Irene!" He gasped. Ordering Azar and the army to stay put, he spurred August forward.

The big black horse stopped, as August skidded to a halt beside him. The two horses fidgeted, pawing the ground and snorting threats.

"Steady August," Zatao said soothingly. Reaching for Irene, he gently eased her off the black horse and settled her in front of him.

Free of his burden, the black stallion swung round and galloped away towards the distant castle.

Groaning with pain, Irene nestled against Zatao, her head resting on his chest. "You came," she said softly. Feeling his strong arms around her, she slumped against him, closed her eyes and yielded to her desperate need of rest.

Seeing the congealed blood around the wound on her leg, Zatao's lips hardened. Putting a hand under her chin, he gently raised her head. Her pale face looked bruised, her lips were cracked. Zatao's body tensed with rage, clenching a fist he stared heavenward. "They will pay," he growled.

Taking some deep breaths, he kissed the top of her head and held her close. Her shallow breathing…the coldness of her body, stirred him to action. Pulling on the reins, he turned August and galloped back to the waiting army.

Sergeant Azar stared open mouthed at Irene. Urging his horse closer to Zatao, he asked. "My Lord, is she—?"

"She is alive," Zatao said quickly. "But only just." Struggling to keep his voice steady, he ordered Azar to ride and fetch Zenith. "Make haste my friend," he said, staring down at Irene.

Without a word, Azar spurred his horse into a gallop. Racing towards the eagles, he waved and shouted to get their attention.

Raising his head, Zenith left the horse carcass he was feeding on and rose into the air. "Wait here for me," he said to Hunter, before flying to meet Azar.

At the sight of the great eagle, Azar's horse skidded to a halt, and reared. Fighting with his frightened horse, Azar shouted to Zenith. "Please, follow me. The Prince needs you." Turning the panicked horse, he galloped back to Zatao.

Zenith followed, skimming low over the ground, he came to rest in front of August. His gold eyes focused on Zatao, and Irene's limp body cradled in his arms. "How may I serve you, My Lord?"

Zatao frowned as he stared down at Irene. "She is sick, Zenith. I need to get her back to the castle, but there isn't time." He glanced round at the army. "We must go to Murkier's castle and assist Guardsman Romure. It's possible he could be walking into a trap."

Zenith nodded. "I understand, My Lord. May I suggest taking her to Mercy Falls? It is closer than your castle." Zatao's penetrating gaze unnerved the eagle. Lowering his eyes he continued. "I assume My Lord, she needs medical help." He glanced under his feathered brows at the waiting army. "And before this day is out, there may be casualties from among your men."

Zatao made no comment, but nodded for Zenith to continue.

Raising his head, Zenith explained that Grey Cloud the wolf, and Ezekiel the rat were already at Mercy Falls. "They are searching for the healing leaves, and awaiting your arrival." Seeing the Prince's raised head and closed eyes, Zenith breathed an inaudible sigh of relief. "May I make a suggestion, My Lord?"

"Please do, we have little time to spare."

"Gather a few blankets and wrap Irene in them," Zenith said. "I will cradle her in my talons and fly her to Mercy Falls." He paused, noting Zatao's anxiety. "Do not be concerned, My Lord. The blankets will protect her from my talons, and also keep her warm. Once there, Ezekiel will apply the healing leaves. She is young and will recover quickly." Seeing the Prince's eyes brighten, he smiled. "We will stay at Mercy Falls and wait for you." Tilting his head to the side, he waited for the Prince's approval.

Zatao nodded and shouted for blankets.

Sergeant Azar dismounted, retrieved one from his saddle bag, and handed it to the Prince. Two guardsmen donated theirs.

Zatao lowered Irene's limp body into Azar's arms and dismounted. Between them they held her up and wrapped her in the blankets. Hearing her whimper with pain, Zatao groaned. Lifting her in his arms, he gently kissed her cold cheek. "It's alright my darling. Zenith is taking you to Mercy Falls; you will soon be well."

With a sympathetic nod, Zenith unfurled his wings, and rose a few feet off the ground. "Hold her out," he said.

Cold air swirled around Zatao, as Zenith gently flapped his wings.

Zatao's biceps bulged...his arms trembled as he struggled to hold Irene away from his body. A worried frown creased his brow, as he watched Zenith wrap his huge black talons around her. "Cradle her head, Zenith, don't let it flop."

"Don't worry My Lord. I will take good care of her." Without another word he rose into the air and flew away towards the mountain, and the forest of Luminaire.

Zatao put a fisted hand to his chest, it felt tight. Standing beside August, he stroked the stallion's powerful neck, his eyes glued to Zenith's disappearing form. He watched until the eagle vanished in the clouds. A strange sense of loss...loneliness, gripped him. "Keep her safe, Zenith," he whispered. Taking a deep breath, he sighed, and vaulted into the saddle.

He turned to Azar. "I want to check King Murkier is dead, before we ride to his castle and assist Guardsman Romure."

Sergeant Azar mustered the men. They were cold, restless, and eager for battle. "They are ready, My Lord."

Zatao nodded and raised a hand. At the sound of a trumpet blast, he led his men towards King Murkier's decimated army.

❧❧❧

Irene felt as though she were floating. She could feel something hard under her head. A cold wind whistled through her hair, blowing long auburn curls across her face. Her cheeks felt cold, and yet her body felt warm...warmer than it had for a while.

Opening her eyes, she tried to focus, but her head hurt. Groaning softly, she reached to brush the irritating hair off her face; her stomach lurched as she realised her body was tightly bound. Unable to move, her frightened cry alerted Zenith.

"It's alright, Irene. Don't be afraid. It's me, Zenith. I'm taking you to Mercy Falls where you'll be safe."

Irene squinted up at him through the cage that was his talons. "Why can't I move my arms?" She mumbled through cracked lips.

"You were so cold, we wrapped you in blankets," Zenith explained.

Irene tried to raise her head, but grimaced with pain.

"Stay still child. We're nearly there."

Turning her head, Irene tried to look down, all she could see was a forest of trees. Her stomach churned, nauseous, she stared up at the sky and closed her eyes. Her voice faltered as she asked. "Where's Zatao? I need him."

Glancing down at her, Zenith cleared his throat. "He has one last task to complete, before he joins us at Mercy Falls." Riding a thermal, Zenith looked up at the clouds. *God of heaven, keep him safe.*

Hot tears welled in Irene's closed eyes. She squeezed them tighter, but the tears escaped, trickling through her long lashes, they traced a line through the dirt on her cheeks.

Her body ached from her wounds, and Zenith's talons were not a comfortable resting place. She yearned to be in Zatao's strong arms, safe and well...the nightmare of the past few hours, nothing but a distant memory.

Her chest heaved with grief, as she thought of Mira lying dead in the snow. Fresh tears fell. Turning her head she stared up at Zenith's belly...watched as the wind ruffled his feathers. His bony foot dug into her cheek, but she didn't move. "I should suffer pain," she muttered to herself. "Everything that's happened is because of me." Beneath the blankets her fists clenched. *Oh God, please keep Zatao safe, I love him so much.* Her inaudible prayer brought a gut wrenching sob.

Glancing down, Zenith frowned. He knew she was worrying about the Prince's safety, and grieving for the loss of her friend, Princess Mira. Unsure what to say, Zenith said nothing, but fixed his gaze on the distant cliffs, an indication, they were approaching Mercy Falls.

Irene lay still in his talons, exhaustion taking its toll. She felt Zenith dropping lower, the cold wind eased as he circled the huge clearing. Relief washed over her, as she succumbed to the welcome oblivion of sleep.

Chapter 46

Hunter heard the thunder of approaching hooves; dropping the arrow he'd pulled from his leg, he watched Prince Zatao gallop towards him. With a brisk shake of his feathers, he stood to attention as Zatao dismounted.

Bowing his massive head, he asked. "My Lord, can I be of assistance." Seeing the Prince frown and stare at his chest, Hunter smiled. "There's no need for concern," he said grasping the arrow in his huge beak and pulling it out. "Some of them found their mark, but are no more serious than annoying porcupine quills." Chuckling, he lowered his head. "Would you help me, please? There's one here in my neck that I can't reach."

Prince Zatao's hands shook slightly, as he reached up and grasped the arrow.

"Don't break it," Hunter said. "Pull it out, you won't hurt me."

With the bloodied arrow removed and tossed in the snow, Hunter fixed the Prince with a hypnotic stare. "How can I help you?" He asked.

"I need to see the body of King Murkier," Zatao said wiping has hands on his breeches.

"He's over here," Hunter said stepping over the bodies of two mangled warriors. "He's definitely dead if that's what's worrying you." Seeing the spark of annoyance in the Prince's eyes, Hunter realised he sounded disrespectful. Bowing his head, he said softly. "Forgive my rudeness, My Lord. I meant no offence."

Zatao's expression softened. "No offence taken." His eyes settled on the broken body of his enemy. "Both you and your father, have honoured me with your loyalty. You rescued and avenged the woman I love. You will be richly rewarded."

Hunter bowed low. "We do not want a reward My Prince. To serve you is reward enough." Straightening to his full height, he stared in the direction of castle Feritas. "Is there anything else you would like my help with?"

Zatao pulled his leather gloves higher up his wrist and nodded. "I've sent a small troop to attack the castle and apprehend the Queen." He glared at the body of King Murkier. "I now realise, the King left the majority of his forces in the castle, and I fear—"

Hunter interjected. "You fear your men are riding into a trap."

"I do," Zatao said.

"Fear not My Lord. I will accompany you. Between us, we will destroy that castle and defeat its occupants." His gold eyes blazed as he stared into the distance.

Zatao quietly exhaled. "Thank you," he said.

"When do we leave?" Hunter asked.

Zatao's dark eyes narrowed. "Now," he replied. Squaring his shoulders, he stepped over the bodies and mounted August. "Follow us," he said. Spurring August into a gallop, he led his army towards Castle Feritas.

Hunter' heart raced as he rose into the sky. With massive wings outstretched, he flew high; his gold eyes fixed on the mighty army thundering across the snow covered plain beneath him.

◈◈◈

Guardsman Romure led his men at the gallop. Riding in a wide circle they avoided being seen by King Murkier. Raising a hand, Romure slowed the pace. Perched on its high hill, Castle Feritas loomed in the distance. In the darkness he could see blazing torches moving at the base of the hill. His lips pressed together. *I have a feeling this is not going to be as easy as we'd hoped. Seems they are ready for us.*

He knew with a backdrop of snow, and the bright moon overhead, they could easily be seen from the castle. Reining his horse, he gathered his men around him. "We could have a problem. They know we're coming."

A young guardsman heeled his horse closer. "I doubt there are many left in the castle, sir. There are over a hundred of us, so we should be able to deal with them."

"I hope you're right, Teran; but I have a nasty feeling about this." Staring at their expectant faces, he barked. "Follow me and keep your horses at a walk."

The snow underfoot muffled the horses' hooves. In the relative silence, they could hear the distant sound of fighting...the screams of dying men and horses floated on the air.

Sensing the men's agitation, Romure shouted, "Stay focused...stay alert."

The confidence in his voice...his powerful presence astride his big bay stallion, gave the youngest among them some assurance. In the soft light of a grey dawn, they slowly approached the village clustered at the base of the castle. Raising a hand, Romure halted his army and ordered them to dismount. The men gathered round him.

Romure could feel his skin prickle. In this flat landscape, they were visible to all. Pushing his cold fingers deeper into his leather gloves, he grimaced. "There's nowhere to hide the horses, so we'll have to leave them here." Beckoning to Teran, he ordered the young guardsman to take half the men and go through the village. "Search every building...every room. Kill only those who resist you. I will take the castle. If you finish before we do, join us."

"Yes sir," Teran said with a quick nod of his head.

Romure stood to his full height; pulling his sword from its sheath, he raised it high and shouted. "To war men; may God go with us."

In an instant the air resounded to shouts and pounding boots, as Teran and his men took to the village streets.

Romure led the remaining guard to a rocky outcrop leading to the side of the castle. The building towered above them as they scrambled over the rocks. Below, they could hear the peoples' frightened cries, as Teran and his men searched the village.

For a moment, Romure paused in his climb and glanced up at the castle. He could feel the familiar knot in his stomach; a sure indication, danger was close at hand. Shading his eyes, he saw the castle guard leaning over the battlements, their bows at the ready. Before he had time to warn his men, arrows rained down like steel tipped rain. Cries rent the air as they found their mark. "Damn! I should have gone through the village," he growled.

Glancing round, he could see his men hunkered behind every available rock. From where he crouched, he could see at least three were dead. Another sat with an arrow in his arm. Romure's throat tightened. *I've put them in unnecessary danger.* Crouching down, he waved a hand ordering them to stay put. The next wave of arrows mercifully hit the rocks. Nevertheless, Romure knew they could not afford to stay there; but they were pinned down.

Romure gingerly raised his head, but quickly ducked down. The castle guards were preparing to let loose more arrows. Embarrassed by his failure, he cursed under his breath. *All I can hope is that Teran succeeds and gets through. We need a distraction.*

As the thought entered his head, he heard shouts and screams coming from the castle. Frowning, he tilted his head to the side; but before he had a chance to take a look, one of his men stood to his feet.

"Look!" The man shouted. "It's the eagle."

Romure and the rest of his army left the protection of the rocks to see what was going on. A massive eagle had the castle guard running scared. It grabbed two and three at a time, and dropped them over the castle ramparts to die on the rocks below.

This is our chance, Romure thought as he scrambled over the rocks. "Come on men," He shouted. "Follow me."

With whoops of triumph they scaled the cliff and crouched close to the castle wall. Romure grinned; the way the castle had been built, the use of huge uneven stones would make scaling it reasonably easy. He picked two fit young men and ordered them over the top. "Open the gates as quickly as you can," he ordered. "And keep your eyes peeled."

With nods of enthusiasm, they climbed; scaling the wall with ease.

The remaining men followed Romure to the castle entrance. Huddled against the wall they waited. Romure breathed a sigh of relief, when he saw Teran running up the road towards him, followed by his men and a large number of villagers...armed with pitchforks, shovels and anything else they could get their hands on. As they approached, a loud creaking indicated the two men had made it. Slowly, the portcullis rose enough to allow Romure and the army entrance.

"If you find the Queen," Romure shouted. "Do not kill her."

Hollering and whooping, the men raised their swords and rushed en masse towards the waiting guard. The castle rang to the sound of clashing metal, and the screams of the injured and dying.

Up on the ramparts, Hunter made short work of those who were not quick enough to escape.

Clutching his sword, Romure found a small side door and slipped into the castle. Inside it was cold and strangely quiet. Shivering, he took a tighter grip of his sword. *This place is huge. I should have brought some men with me.*

At that moment, the massive doors of the castle flew open, and Prince Zatao, accompanied by at least a hundred men burst in. Seeing Romure, his lips flickered in a smile. "Well done, sergeant. Join me." Turning to the army surrounding him, he separated them into smaller groups and sent them to investigate the various parts of the castle. "Remember what I said," he shouted. "Leave no one alive. But bring the Queen to me."

Clapping Romure on the shoulder, he led him, along with a dozen trusted men towards the throne room. "How do you know where it is, My Lord? Will she be there?" He had to trot to keep up with Zatao's long stride.

"I don't know, is the answer to both your questions. Either way, we will tear this castle apart until we find her." He glanced at Romure. "No doubt you've heard the old cliché, behind every great man there is a woman."

Romure nodded.

"Well in this instance it's true. The woman we seek is the power behind the throne. She is more dangerous than you can imagine." Pausing, he stopped and stared at Romure. "She must be found and dealt with. However, she is of royal blood, so I must be the one to do it." Swinging round he broke into a trot. Romure and the others followed, their feet pounding the long dark corridor.

Rounding a corner, they hurried towards a pair of massive doors, their shadows lengthened, dancing macabrely in the light from the sconces attached to the walls. Two huge guards in front of the doors lowered their pikes. With growls of disdain they approached the Prince and his men.

Romure stepped forward. "Stay back My Prince, We will deal with this."

Zatao made to argue, but seeing the determined look in Romure's eyes, he acquiesced. With a grin, he waved Romure and the men forward. "Be my guest," He said, with a mock bow to the approaching guard.

Insulted, the two guards raised their pikes and charged forward. Uncoordinated in their anger, they were easily dealt with, as the Prince intended. Stepping over their bodies and the blood pooling on the ground, Prince Zatao pushed the throne room doors wide and strode in. Romure and the men clustered around him.

A red carpet stretched from the door to a large raised dais. A woman reclined on one of the thrones. "Welcome, Prince Zatao. You are indeed more handsome than I imagined." she said in a voice rich and husky. "If you are here, it must mean my husband the King, is dead."

Romure and the Prince's guard, stared open mouthed at the Queen.

Hearing their awed gasps, Zatao hissed. "Stay here. Guard the door and watch her."

"Oh we are," one of the guards whispered a distinct hint of lechery in his tone.

Zatao swung round. His blazing eyes fixed on the man's face.

Terrified, the guard fell to his knees. "My Lord, please forgive me," he pleaded.

Zatao's eyes narrowed. "Your disrespect must be punished. However, due to the circumstances, I will temper it with mercy." Indicating to two of his men, he ordered them to escort the offending guardsman to Sergeant Azar.

Reclined on her throne, Queen Ballista smiled. "You are indeed gracious and merciful Prince Zatao," she said in a voice as sweet as honey. Twirling a strand of her long lustrous hair; she rose to her feet. Her rich turquoise gown rustled as she walked towards them. To the men watching her, she appeared to float. The gold crown upon her head glistened in the light from one of the windows.

Nearing the Prince, she dropped to her knees. Lowering her head she stared at the floor. None of them saw the smirk on her face, the glint in her grey eyes. Raising her head, her expression dignified and tranquil, she stared up at Zatao. "My Lord," she said softly. "May I be a recipient of your renowned mercy?"

Zatao took an inaudible breath. She was beautiful. Her large grey eyes stared into his; they reflected the colour of her dress...bluer than the sky on a summer's day. Her waist length hair, shone as black as a ravens wing. Zatao's pulse raced, he wanted to brush the beads of sweat from his top lip, but his arms refused to move.

The silence in the room hung as heavy as a wet blanket. Queen Ballista knew she had them in her power. The desire to laugh was overwhelming, but she maintained an expression of sweet serenity. "Will you show me mercy, My Lord?" she asked again.

To Prince Zatao and the men with him, her voice sounded as soft as a kitten's purr.

Smiling sweetly, she raised a hand.

"Imprisonment is the only mercy I can show you," Prince Zatao said, as he raised her to her feet.

Queen Ballista held onto his hand and moved in close, so close, Zatao could feel her warm breath brush his neck. "Such punishment is too severe," she whispered. "Let me stay here and I will serve you."

"You are fortunate, I do not have you executed," Zatao growled. Aware she had a hidden dagger; he stepped back and grabbed her arms. Tightening his hold, he gestured to Guardsman Romure.

Ballista's eyes flashed with rage, as rough hands pulled her away from the Prince. Her screams of protest echoed round the vast throne room. "You will pay for this!"

"I don't think so," Zatao said with a smile. "Search her Romure; but be careful," he warned. "She has a knife."

Ballista's nostrils flared with rage as she fought against the grip of the guardsman holding her. "Let go of me, you oaf!"

"Hold her still." Guardsman Romure ordered the man. Deftly he searched her dress and found the knife in a side pocket of her voluminous skirt. "Here it is My Lord." His face creased in a satisfied smile as he ran a finger along the blade.

Too late, he heard Prince Zatao's warning shout! But before he could react, Ballista threw herself at him. He felt the knife enter her body...felt her warm blood trickle through his fingers.

Romure's breath caught in his throat, his eyes widened as he watched her slide to floor. Seeing his blood covered hands, he stared at Zatao. "My Lord, I am so sorry." His voice faltered. "I did not mean for this to—"

"Don't worry sergeant. In many ways her death is preferable. But I did not wish for it to be by my hand."

The guardsman charged with holding the Queen, slumped to his knees. "It was my fault, My Lord. Please forgive me."

331

"Stand up," Zatao ordered the man. Stooping, he pulled the crown from Ballista's head, and handed it to Romure. "Have her buried with her husband out on the plain. Bury them deep…bury them where no one will ever find them."

"Yes, My Lord. What do you want us to do about this castle and the village?"

Zatao ran a weary hand through his hair. "Sack the castle, keep everything of value, then burn it to the ground. As for the village, leave it for the time being. It is not my wish to uproot the villagers, unless they desire it." Glancing round the throne room, he sighed. "I trust you to fulfil my wishes, Romure."

Romure bowed his head, "It is my privilege to serve you My Lord."

Zatao placed his hand on Romure's shoulder. "I am riding to Mercy Falls, with Sergeant Azar and a few men." He stared into Romure's face. "I'm leaving you in charge. Don't let me down. When everything is done here, return home and wait for us."

Romure nodded. "Everything will be done according to your orders, My Lord."

As Zatao strode towards the door, the corridor echoed to the sound of struggling and complaints. Two guardsmen appeared in the doorway, dragging a couple of elderly men. Forcing the prisoners to their knees, the guards bowed before the Prince.

Zatao studied the prisoners. "Who are they?"

The two old men peered up at him, their faces white with fear.

One of the guards stepped forward. "We don't know who they are, My Lord. We found them hiding in a large cupboard."

Grouchen raised a trembling hand. "May I speak, My Lord?"

Prince Zatao nodded.

"We are King Murkier's advisors," Grouchen's voice faltered as his eyes rested on the dead Queen. "It would be an honour to serve you, My Lord." Lowering his head, he glanced sideways at Ergon. "My name is—"

"I don't care what your names are!" Resting his hands on his hips, Zatao scowled at them. "It's enough you were in the employ of my enemy. You most certainly will not be in mine." Glancing at Romure, he growled. "Let them gather their possessions, give them a horse and let them go."

Crawling on their hands and knees, Grouchen and Ergon clutched at Prince Zatao's legs. Tears trickled into their beards as they cried. "Thank you My Lord."

"Unhand me!" Zatao ordered.

Two guardsmen quickly grabbed the men and hauled them to their feet.

Glaring at the two advisors, Zatao said. "You have fifteen minutes to gather your belongings and leave."

Bowing their heads, the two advisors thanked the Prince before being escorted away by the guard.

Prince Zatao's shoulders slumped as he made his way to the main entrance. Standing on the castle steps, he surveyed the carnage. "So much death," he groaned. Hearing the clatter of hooves, he swung round as Sergeant Azar rode into the courtyard, leading August.

Azar's brow wrinkled, as he watched the Prince descend. *He looks exhausted.* He forced a smile as he held out August's reins. "Here's your horse, My Lord." He glanced around as Zatao mounted. "I've ordered a number of guardsmen to clean up here, and bury the bodies."

Zatao shook his head. "Are all King Murkier's men dead?"

Azar nodded.

"Very well, I want the bodies put in the castle. The building is to be burned to the ground." Glancing up at the sun, he frowned. "Gather two or three of your best men. We are riding to Mercy Falls. I am leaving Guardsman Romure in charge here. He knows what I want."

"As is your wish, My Lord." Pulling his horse round, Azar cantered across the courtyard. His voice echoed as he mustered a group of guardsmen. "Mount up; we are to escort the Prince."

While he waited, Zatao stared up at the battlements. He could see Hunter's head bobbing up and down; Zatao guessed what he was doing. His stomach knotted in disgust. Swallowing hard, he called the great eagle.

With a hiss of annoyance, Hunter raised his head and peered at the Prince.

Zatao cringed at the sight of human flesh hanging from the eagle's beak. "Come with me," he shouted. I'm going to Mercy Falls."

Flapping his huge wings, Hunter flew onto the edge of the parapet. "Lead on, My Lord, I will follow you."

Prince Zatao urged August into a trot, Azar and the guard followed in single file. The horse's hooves clattered on the cobbles as they followed the narrow road through the village.

Overhead, Hunter stretched his wings and glided on the warm thermals.

Zatao sighed. *What a joy it must be...flying high and free.* In the distance he could see the mountain peak and surrounding forest. He felt a fluttering in his belly. "Irene my love," he whispered. "I'll be with you soon. I pray God you are healed and well." Closing his eyes, he rubbed the back of his neck. "Are you ready sergeant?" He said to Azar.

"We are My Lord."

"Good, then let us make haste to Mercy Falls." Breathless, with anticipation, Zatao spurred August into a gallop. He knew the snow covered ground was treacherous, but still he urged the stallion to go as fast as he could; his need to reach Irene outweighed any sense of caution.

Chapter 47

Mercy Falls enjoyed a temperate climate. Sheltered by a natural fortress of rocky crags and surrounded by forest, it remained a tad warmer than the surrounding countryside. Nevertheless, a light dusting of snow glistened in the sunlight.

The waters of the lake lapped gently at the shoreline, its clear surface reflecting the blue of the sky. At the far end of the lake, the falls cascaded over a sheer rock face, foaming in the waters below.

Zenith breathed a sigh of relief. Glancing down at Irene, he smiled. "We've arrived at Mercy Falls," he said.

Irene gave him a weak smile. "Thank God," she said softly. *No way could I have gone much further.* Even with the blankets, her body felt cold and stiff. She knew Zenith did his best to fly as smoothly as possible; nevertheless the slightest jarring, or movement from his talons, caused her to moan with pain.

Zenith spotted Grey Cloud waiting by a rocky outcrop, close to the falls. Holding his huge wings forward, he flapped gently in an effort to slow his descent. "This could be a little uncomfortable, Irene," he warned.

Closing her eyes, Irene clenched her fists. Tensing her aching muscles, she waited for the inevitable crash landing. It didn't come.

Zenith got as close to the ground as he could before releasing her. As his talons uncurled, Irene's body gently rolled towards Grey Cloud.

"Irene, how good it is to see you again." His long tongue licked her cheek.

Staring into his gold eyes, Irene smiled. "It's wonderful to see you Grey Cloud." She longed to wrap her arms around his neck, but not possible while she was trussed up like a turkey. She struggled to sit up, but was too weak.

"For goodness sake help her!" A squeaky voice chided.

Irene's heart leapt. Craning her head she tried to see him. "Is that you Ezekiel?"

"Indeed it is, child. You are safe now, and we'll soon have you well."

Unable to stop herself, Irene wept; her tears a mixture of joy and exhaustion.

Zenith leaned over her. "Don't fret, Irene. We will soon have you free."

"I'm not fretting Zenith. I'm just grateful to you, and thrilled to see Ezekiel and Grey Cloud."

"Tck! Tck! And me," Blackwing said fluttering to the ground. "I'm so glad you are safe."

Turning her head, Irene smiled at him. "It's good to see you, Blackwing. Thank you for all you've done."

"It was a pleasure, glad to be of help." Noting the impatient glances from the others, he hopped closer to Irene. "I'd better go. I only came to make sure you were alright." Cocking his head to the side he stared at her. "You are alright?"

Irene gave him a weak smile. "I'll be fine. I'll see you soon."

With a nod of his head, he rose into the air. "Safe journey home," he called.

Hissing with impatience, Zenith glanced at Grey Cloud and Ezekiel. "Right, Come on; let's get these blankets off her."

After a lot of pulling, tugging, and chewing, Irene was free. She shivered as the cool air hit her.

Grey Cloud pulled on her sleeve. "Can you make it over to that rock?"

Irene knew she couldn't walk. Her injured leg had swollen, and she felt as weak as a kitten. "I think I can crawl. I'll try." On her hands and knees, with her bad leg dragging, she managed to reach the rocks, where Grey Cloud and Ezekiel had made a bed out of leaves and bracken. Gasping for breath she collapsed onto it.

"We need to apply the healing leaves, Irene," Ezekiel said.

Irene could hear the urgency in his voice. "I know, just give me a minute." Sitting with her back against the rock, she closed her eyes and waited for the dizziness to pass.

Ezekiel's long tail twitched with impatience. "Are you ready now?" He asked.

Irene opened her eyes and stared at him, the corners of her mouth lifted in a smile of amusement. "As impatient as ever, I see."

Ezekiel's ruby eyes narrowed. "I need to put the leaves on your leg," he insisted.

"Alright, hang on a moment." Turning her leg over, Irene stared at the wound and cringed. Blood and pus oozed from it. The torn material around it was soaked in blood.

Ezekiel shuffled towards her, holding the leaves by their stems. "Don't touch the actual leaves," he said reaching towards her outstretched hand.

"Don't worry, I remember." Taking the leaves from his mouth, she realised, to get the leaves over the wound; she would have to tear the surrounding material. Resting her head against the rock; she groaned. "I need to make room for the leaves to fit over the wound. But I'm not sure I can."

Sitting on his haunches, Ezekiel rested his forepaws on her foot. "Remove the trousers or tear them, either way, you can do it. Take some deep breaths," he advised.

"Stop pushing her, Ezekiel," Grey Cloud said.

Ezekiel swished his tail. "I'm not, but she needs to get the leaves on that wound."

"Leave her alone both of you!" Lowering his head, Zenith stared into Irene's face; he could see the fear in her eyes. "Take your time child. If it will cause you less pain to remove the trousers then do so."

Irene shook her head. "No it's alright, I can tear it." Buoyed by Zenith's encouragement, she gritted her teeth…held her breath, and ripped the blood soaked material away from the wound. The noise of the falls drowned her cry of pain. Panting, and with tears streaming down her face, she covered the bleeding wound with the leaves.

The three animals glanced at each other, as they watched her slump onto her side and pass out.

"Leave her to rest," Zenith said softly. "How long will it take the leaves to do their work?" He asked Ezekiel.

"The healing will only take a few minutes, but she needs to eat to gain her strength."

"Well, leave her for the moment and let her sleep."

Grey Cloud lay beside her, snuggled against her back.

Zenith nodded with approval. "Good idea my friend; she's in shock and needs to be kept warm." Using his beak, he pulled the blankets over them both. "Do we have any food to offer her?" He asked Ezekiel.

"I've collected some special berries," Ezekiel replied. "They will renew her strength and give her energy."

"Good, when she wakes, offer them to her. For now, rest is the best healing." His eyes creased in a smile as he watched Ezekiel crawl under the blanket and join Irene and Grey Cloud.

Unfurling his wings, he flew to a craggy rock. From this vantage point, he could see Irene, and watch for Prince Zatao's arrival. *I hope he will be here soon. His presence will cheer Irene and speed her recovery.*

❧❧❧❧

Wincing with pain, Aldrin dismounted and led Merry to a large wooden cabin surrounded by empty tents. Securing the horse to a flag pole, he climbed the wooden steps and gazed around the vast camp. The silence was deafening. "Looks like they've already gone," he grumbled.

Swinging round, he entered the cabin and slammed the door shut. Removing his gloves, he cursed and banged them on the table. However, glancing at the fireplace, the burning embers brought a smile to his face. "They can't be too far ahead. Maybe I can catch up to them."

Perching on the edge of a chair, he managed to throw a couple of logs on the fire, but reaching for the poker sent a searing pain down his arm. Grimacing, he unbuttoned his shirt, and gingerly eased the bloody material away from the wound. Unable to see it, he went to the bathroom and peered at in the mirror. His heart sank, the skin around the wound was angry and red, a yellow discharge mingled with the oozing blood.

Cursing, he searched a wooden cabinet for something to bind the wound. He found a jar of antiseptic ointment and a roll of bandage. *This will have to do. At least it will keep it clean.* Clenching his teeth, he managed to smear the ointment over the wound; but trying to bandage it was not so easy. Covering it as best he could, he went into his brother's room and found a clean shirt.

338

Right, that's the best I can do; now for something to eat. Striding into the kitchen, he rooted in the cupboards until he found a small loaf of bread, and a piece of cheese. Taking the food into the sitting room, he sat by the fire and devoured it. He hadn't realised how hungry he was.

Resting his head on the chair back, he closed his eyes. The relative warmth of the room, and the fever induced by his wound, caused him to drift into a deep sleep...a sleep plagued by unsettling dreams. Mira's sightless eyes peered up at him, beseeching him to help her, but as he reached to take her in his arms, her body disintegrated, melting into the snow.

His tortured scream, was drowned by Irene's desperate cries for help. He watched as a huge dark figure scooped her up, and carried her into a howling snowstorm. Aldrin gasped and shot awake. His hair slick with sweat clung to his neck and face.

Trembling uncontrollably, he scrambled to his feet and stumbled into the kitchen. Finding a bucket of cold water, he splashed it over his face and slaked his thirst. *I need to go, if I'm to catch up with Zatao.* Holding onto the sink, he waited for his legs to stop shaking; he knew he was in the grip of a fever. His head pounded, everything in the room seemed distant...unreal.

Retrieving his cloak, he staggered outside. He shuddered as the cold air hit him; it felt like he'd walked into a sheet of ice. Pulling his cloak around him, he struggled through the snow to the horse. His lips twisted in a grimace, "Damn it, I should have put her in the barn." The animal stood with head bowed, her body covered in snow, her mane and tail festooned with icicles.

Untying her, Aldrin brushed the snow off the saddle and led her towards the forest. "We need to get the circulation back in those legs," he said glancing at her. Grumbling at his thoughtless stupidity, Aldrin ploughed through the snow, each step making him wince. Nauseous, he struggled on, aware the horse must warm up, before he could ride her.

Leading her into the forest, he breathed a sigh of relief. Surrounded by trees, they were shielded from the biting wind, and the air was a little warmer. He could see the snow melting off her skin, and her head was raised. Throwing the reins over her head, he patted her neck and struggled into the saddle. For a moment the world swirled around him, closing his eyes he gripped the pommel, and waited for the dizziness to pass.

Merry walked slowly, she could feel her rider sway in the saddle...hear his groans of pain. She knew where the others had gone; all she had to do was follow. Above them, the canopy of trees shielded the forest floor from the worst of the snow fall, making progress a lot easier.

Shaking the snow from her neck, she snorted, her warm breath vaporized in the cold air. Lowering her head she plodded on, grateful the feeling had returned to her legs...grateful that movement brought warmth to her body.

Moving silently through the forest, an owl's hoot startled her. She heard her rider groan as he gripped the reins. Glancing up, she saw the ghostly owl glide ahead of her and perch on a low bow.

"You scared me," she whispered.

"Sorry, but I thought you should know. Prince Zatao has destroyed King Murkier. And even now, as I speak, his castle burns."

"That is good news," Merry said nodding her head. "So where should I go? How will I find them?"

The owl glided to another branch. "The main army is returning to castle Eternus. Prince Zatao and a small company of guard are on their way to Mercy Falls, where Lady Irene is waiting." The owl smiled at the hope he saw in Merry's eyes.

"So Irene is safe."

The owl nodded. "She is safe, and by now she is well."

Merry increased her pace. "How do I get to Mercy Falls?"

"Follow me," the owl said.

"Don't fly to far ahead, as I dare not alert my rider, or he may stop me."

The owl chuckled. "Don't worry about him; he's well out of it. I'm surprised he is still in the saddle. Who is he, by the way?"

Merry snorted. "Prince Aldrin, the brother of my mistress." She lowered her voice. "I believe him to be a traitor."

The owl's huge eyes widened, his neck all but turned full circle. "Traitor you say. That's a strong accusation!"

Merry's eyes darkened. "It is true." She swung her head round towards Aldrin's leg. "Because of him, my mistress is dead, and Irene was kidnapped."

"Wit-woo," the owl hooted. "I'm surprised you've not thrown him into the snow."

"Believe me, I am tempted."

"Best to let him face his brother, the Prince." The owl tilted his head and studied Aldrin. "That's if he lives that long!" Taking to the wing he flew ahead of Merry. "Follow me," he called. "It's not too far."

Chapter 48

Irene stirred in her sleep and stretched. In an instant she was awake, her eye's shot open. *My leg doesn't hurt, nothing hurts!* Sitting up, she pushed the blankets away and stared at her torn blood stained jeans. Where the wound should have been, there was nothing; she was healed. "My injury is gone," she cried. She felt her face, and gently prodded her ribs, no pain.

Grey Cloud stirred and stared up at her.

Ezekiel yawned and stretched out a paw. "What's all the fuss?" he asked. He squeaked as Irene scooped him into her arms, and nuzzled her nose into his warm neck. "Thank you," she said holding him close.

Grinding his teeth with pleasure, Ezekiel scrambled out of her arms, and climbed onto her shoulder. "You are most welcome, child. Now I suggest you have something to eat."

"Like what? I don't see any food."

"Here," Grey Cloud said indicating with his nose.

Irene stared at the fruit. "They're berries; big berries I grant you, but still berries."

"There is more goodness in one of those than a piece of chicken," Ezekiel said. "I suggest you eat them, you need to gain strength."

Irene shrugged. "Okay, if you say so."

"I do."

Irene reached for the fruit. They tasted good, sweet and juicy, like a ripe plum. Out of the corner of her eye, she could see Ezekiel watching her. "I suppose you want some?"

He nodded and reached with a paw.

When they finished eating, Irene rose to stretch her legs. She followed Grey Cloud down to the lake. As he drank, she gazed into the distance. *Where are you Zatao?*

Snuggled against her neck, Ezekiel said softly. "He'll be here soon."

"How did you know what I was thinking?"

"I felt it," he murmured.

Behind them, Zenith flapped his wings and hissed with excitement. He could see a large shape soaring over the forest. "Hunter is here," he cried. Launching into the air, he flew to meet him. Escorting Hunter to the ground, he asked. "Where is Prince Zatao?"

"Right behind me," Hunter replied.

Stepping forward, Zenith introduced him to Irene. "This is my son, Hunter," he said proudly.

Facing Irene, Hunter bowed his head. "My Lady, I am happy to see you are well."

Still not used to being called My Lady, Irene smiled. "Thank you and I am pleased to meet you."

As they chatted, Irene felt a sense of anticipation...a strange fluttering in her heart. Breathless, she put a hand to her chest and instinctively gazed across the lake. Her eyes widened when she saw Zatao, making his way down the steep slope towards them. "He's here," she shouted.

"Go to him," Ezekiel said.

Placing the big rodent on the ground, she ran to Zatao.

The animals watched her, their faces wreathed in smiles.

Irene felt weightless as she raced to meet him. Tears of joy streamed down her face. Throwing her arms around his neck, she cried. "Zatao, my darling, thank God you are safe." Feeling his strong arms pull her close, crush her to him, she melted into his embrace. Held in his arms, their tears melded as they kissed.

❧❧❧

Prince Zatao pushed August, spurring him ever faster. The big stallion complied, his nostrils flared as he gulped air. His hooves pounded the ground, eating up the miles; but once they reached the mountain, and crossed the great clearing, the dense forest forced a slower pace.

Zatao knew there was only one way into Mercy Falls, and a horse would not safely negotiate it, so they would have to leave them with the guard in the forest.

Reaching a break in the trees, Zatao reined August and dismounted. "This is it, the entrance to Mercy Falls. From this point I go on alone."

"But My Lord, it could be dangerous!" Azar protested.

"Nothing can harm you, in Mercy Falls. I will be quite safe. Stay here with the men and horses. I won't be long."

"As you wish, My Lord," Azar said with a shake of his head.

Zatao smiled and clapped him on the shoulder. "I'll be fine, stop worrying."

Handing the sergeant, August's reins, Zatao pushed aside the shrubbery and followed a narrow track. Reaching the top of a steep descent, he paused for a moment. Scanning the beautiful clearing below, his heart thudded in his chest as he spotted Irene. With his eyes fixed on her, he slithered and slipped down the steep slope, his feet scrabbling for purchase on the snowy surface.

Reaching the bottom, Zatao's pulse raced as Irene ran to him, and fell into his waiting arms. She clung to him, her arms entwined around his neck. Zatao scooped her up and held her close. Feeling her warm breath on his neck, he shuddered. Their kiss was long and tender. In the privacy of their moment together, he allowed tears of relief to fall.

"My darling, you are well?"

Irene gazed into his dark eyes glistening with tears. "Yes, I am healed," she said softly. Stroking his cheek, her brow furrowed. Mud splatters clung to the beginnings of a beard shadowing his face. "You look tired, Zatao," she said, placing a gentle kiss on his cheek.

"I am," he said with a slight smile. Placing her on the ground, he took her hand and led her to where Zenith and the others were waiting.

"My Lord," they said in unison. Raising their heads they looked into his smiling face.

"I don't know how to thank you," Zatao said looking from one to the other. "I never will." Putting his arm round Irene, he pulled her close, and gazed into her upturned face. "This young woman means the world to me." Raising a hand he indicated to each one of them. "She is safe and well, because of you...all of you."

With a glance at the others, Zenith stepped forward. "It is an honour to serve you, My Lord," He bowed to Irene. "My Lady, we are relieved you are fully recovered."

Irene smiled. "There are no adequate words to express my gratitude." She glanced at Hunter. "Thank you both," she said softly.

"You are welcome, My Lady." Zenith said. Facing the Prince, he asked. "May Hunter and I request permission to leave, My Lord?"

Zatao smiled. "You have my permission, Zenith. The God of heaven go with you both."

The mighty eagles took to the air. Circling over the clearing they bid a final farewell, before disappearing in the clouds.

Irene squatted, and put her arms round Grey Clouds neck. Nuzzling her head into his coarse white fur, she whispered her thanks. Pulling away, she cradled his head in her hands. Staring into his warm gold eyes, she giggled as his long wet tongue snaked out and caressed her face.

Prince Zatao laughed as he patted the big wolf's head.

Taking Zatao's hand, Irene asked. "Where's Ezekiel?"

"I'm here," Ezekiel said scrabbling at her leg. Scooping him into her arms, Irene held him close. His body felt cold and fragile in her hands. "Are you alright?" She asked.

The old rodent snuggled under her chin. "I am now."

Zatao wrapped his arm round Irene's shoulder and led her to a large flat rock by the lake. Sitting close together, Irene leaned against him enjoying the warmth of his body, the intimacy of his presence. A comfortable silence rested between them.

Ezekiel snuggled inside her jacket. Grey Cloud lay at their feet, his chin on his paws, his ears twitching.

A soft wind rustled through the surrounding forest; the waters of the lake lapped gently at the shoreline. In the distance, they could hear the roar of the falls as it cascaded into the water below. Above them, the sun slowly set, in its dying light their shadows lengthened.

Irene wrapped an arm round Zatao's waist. Staring up into his face, she whispered. "It's lovely here, so peaceful."

Zatao gazed down at her and smiled. "Mercy Falls is special," he straightened and stared up at the sky. "Sadly, we need to make a move. It will be dark soon."

Gazing at his profile, Irene could feel his weariness...couldn't help but notice the anguish in his eyes when he'd looked at her. They shared grief over the loss of Mira. But what she saw in his eyes was something else, something painful, whatever had happened over the past few hours, had clouded his joy...darkened his soul.

Irene shuddered. She wanted to ask him…help him. However, wisdom dictated she remain quiet. She knew, at some point he would share with her. But until then, she would support him. Give him the time he needed to heal. She felt his hand gently rub her arm and glanced up. Her breath quickened, as his lips covered hers in a warm lingering kiss.

Easing away, Zatao held her gently by the shoulders and kissed her on the forehead. Rising to his feet, he smiled and reached for her hand. "Come my love, it is time to go home."

Pleasant warmth radiated through Irene's body, as he said the word, home. Feeling strangely light, she took his outstretched hand and followed him.

They paused at the bottom of the ascent, long enough for Irene to remove Ezekiel from inside her jacket. She felt mean, disturbing the sleepy rodent, and he was quick to make his feelings felt.

"Give him to me," Zatao said. "He'll be safe inside my jerkin."

Ezekiel huffed. "Why can't I stay with Irene? I was comfortable."

"Because we have a steep climb to make, and my jerkin will hold you more securely." Holding the big rat in front of his face, Zatao stared into his ruby eyes. "If you're going to be awkward, I'll put you on Grey Cloud's back."

"Oh no, My Lord, best not," Grey Cloud said, raising a lip. "This is a steep climb and he will definitely fall off."

"There you are, Ezekiel; so what's it to be, me or Grey Cloud?"

Ezekiel's ruby eyes narrowed. "I suppose it will have to be you, My Lord."

Zatao smiled as he put the disgruntled rat inside his jerkin and took Irene's hand. "This won't be easy," he warned as they started to climb.

Grey Cloud bounded ahead, his paws scrabbling for purchase on the loose, snow covered surface.

Halfway up Zatao and Irene paused to catch their breath. As they prepared to continue the upward struggle, a length of rope fell at their feet.

"Take a hold of the rope My Lord," Azar shouted. "We will pull you up."

Grabbing the rope, Zatao wound it round his hand. "Pull!" He shouted.

Held in the grip of his other hand, Irene breathed a sigh of relief, as he hauled her up. Reaching the top she crumpled in an exhausted heap at his feet.

Sergeant Azar rushed forward.

Prince Zatao raised a hand. "It's alright, sergeant. Take the rope, and thank you for your timely assistance." Stooping down, Zatao lifted Irene in his arms and carried her to August. "Mount up," he ordered the guard. "We're going home." But before he could lift Irene onto August, a loud rustling in the shrubs alerted them to danger.

Ezekiel's head poked out of Zatao's jerkin. "What's going on?"

"Nothing for you to worry about," Zatao said handing him to Irene. He could see the concern in Irene's eyes as she stared up at him. "Just in case," he said.

"What am I, some sort of parcel?" Ezekiel grumbled.

"Shush!" Irene said, putting him inside her jacket. She stared up at Zatao. "What do you mean, just in case?"

"If there's a clash of swords, I don't want him to get hurt."

Irene frowned at him. "I don't want you to get hurt, either."

Holding her face gently between his hands, Zatao kissed her. Staring into her eyes he whispered. "I'll be fine."

With swords drawn, Sergeant Azar and his men formed a tight line in front of Zatao and Irene. Their eye's searching the surrounding shrubbery.

Zatao drew his sword and joined them.

Irene stayed close to August. She could feel the colour drain from her face. Chewing her lip, she watched Zatao and his small guard hold their ground against presumed danger.

"Come out," Zatao yelled. "We know you're there. Face us now and I may spare your life."

Taking his cue from the Prince, Grey Cloud stalked forward; his lips raised, a low threatening growl rumbled in his throat. Crouching close to the shrubbery, he waited, poised to attack.

The rustling in the shrubs grew louder, branches snapped and swayed, as whom, or whatever it was, forced them aside.

The horses, agitated by the men's apprehension, fidgeted and pulled at their reins. Their loud snorts adding to the tension.

Zatao and his men gasped, and stepped back a pace, as a bedraggled figure clutching a sword stumble into view.

Grey Cloud attacked, hackles raised, teeth barred.

Zatao rushed forward. "No Grey Cloud! Leave him." Running his hands through his hair, he stared open mouthed at the man. "It's my brother Aldrin."

❧❧❧

Clutching the pommel of the saddle, Aldrin swayed precariously. He had no idea how long he'd slept, or where they were. Lifting the water bottle he took a long drink, but it did nothing to slake his unquenchable thirst. Sweat clung to him, like a freezing blanket. He shivered and wrapped his arms round himself. The movement brought a searing pain in his shoulder and down his arm. Closing his eyes, he groaned.

The horse's ears flicked at the sound. Nevertheless, she appeared oblivious of him as she plodded on, her head down, exhaustion apparent in every step she took. *Does she know where she's going?* He wondered.

Aldrin flinched as an owl skimmed past him, and perched on a branch close by. He noticed the mare seemed interested in the bird, which surprised him. *I know I'm sick, but it seems to me they're communicating.* Brushing a trembling hand across his hot forehead, a faint smile flickered on his lips. *Don't be stupid man, you're losing the plot.*

The owl fixed his huge eyes on Merry, "They're up ahead," he said. "Prince Zatao and Irene have joined the waiting men."

"I hear them," Merry replied.

The owl glanced at Aldrin. "I think he does too."

Tilting his head, Aldrin listened; he could hear voices. Recognizing Zatao's, he pulled on the reins and struggled awkwardly out of the saddle. Grabbing a handful of the mare's mane, he leaned against her for a moment, until his legs stopped shaking.

I must get to them before they leave. If Irene lives, I must silence her. The thought gave him the impetus he needed. Drawing his sword, he pushed through the shrubbery and saw them. At the sight of Irene, he felt his muscles tense. "She lives," he growled through gritted teeth.

Invigorated by adrenaline, he forced branches aside and stumbled into the open, to be met by a large snarling wolf. Raising

348

his sword, he stood his ground. His heart pounded painfully in his chest. His throbbing left arm hung useless at his side. Nevertheless, he prepared to face the charging wolf. But Zatao's loud shout halted the animal's attack. Realising his brother recognized him; Aldrin breathed an inaudible sigh of relief.

Wiping the sweat from his brow, he rubbed at his eyes. It was as though he looked through lace curtains. Shaking his head he approached Zatao, his sword clutched in his hand and pointing towards Irene. "This is your fault," he yelled. "If you had not come here, none of this would have happened."

Irene attempted to face him, but Zatao put out his arm and held her back. Irene felt her cheeks flush with anger. Her hands trembled as she pushed against Zatao's arm. "You betrayed Mira, and caused her death!" she shouted. "You betrayed us all." Sobbing, she rested her head on Zatao's outstretched arm.

With the anguished cry of a wounded animal, Aldrin slumped to his knees. The sword fell at his side.

Zatao's chest tightened, as Irene's words rolled painfully around in his head. Turning, he held her by the shoulders, and stared into her tear stained face. "What are you saying?"

Irene glared at Aldrin. "Ask him."

Zatao ordered Azar to watch over Irene, as he hurried to Aldrin's side. Kneeling in the snow, he stared at his brother. The bleeding, festering wound in his left shoulder was clear to see, as was his waxen skin, and glazed eyes now fixed on Zatao.

Grabbing Aldrin's shirt, Zatao shook his brother. "What is she saying?" he demanded, glancing at Irene.

Aldrin groaned with pain and held onto Zatao's wrist. Through cracked lips he whispered, "Forgive me, brother."

Throwing his head back, Zatao cried. "No!" Clenching his fists, he allowed Aldrin to slump against him. Zatao felt the last vestige of energy drain from his body. He shivered as coldness chilled him to the marrow. His voice faltered as he lowered his head close to Aldrins face and asked. "Why?"

Wearily, Aldrin glanced up at him and slowly shook his head. Pulling Zatao closer, he mumbled. "I am guilty, but so is another." A tear trickled down his cheek as he stared at Zatao.

"Who is it?" Zatao swallowed hard as he gently shook him. "Tell me," he pleaded.

Lowering his head closer to Aldrins mouth, he listened.

Aldrin trembled as the coldness of death crept up his legs. The tightness in his chest restricted his breathing. Talking took every ounce of his remaining strength. In a voice no more than a whisper, he said. "Any—"

Pinching his lips together, Zatao growled and shook him. "Aldrin, I don't understand, who's Any? Tell me who it is!" He yelled. Feeling a hand on his shoulder, he shrugged it off.

"My Lord, Prince Aldrin is dead," Azar said softly.

"I know," Zatao said rising to his feet. Seeing Merry approach from the trees, Zatao lowered his head and rubbed at his eyes. His chest ached as he remembered his morning rides with Mira. "Fetch that horse and put Aldrin's body on her." he said to Azar. "He will be buried with our sister."

Irene's heart slumped as she watched him walk towards her. She had no idea what Aldrin had said. *Maybe he lied*, she thought. *If Zatao believes him, where does that leave me?* Taking a deep breath, she stared into his eyes. She saw no reproach, but a desperate sadness.

Zatao saw her concern…her insecurity. Reaching out, he pulled her into his arms, cradling her head on his chest. "Don't ever doubt my love, Irene," he said. "Aldrin was—" he paused and closed his eyes. "Never mind; it doesn't matter now." Gazing into her upturned face, he said softly. "Come, let's go home."

Putting her arms round his waist, Irene hugged him, her loving gesture eliciting a loud squeak from inside her jacket. "Oops, sorry Ezekiel, I forgot about you."

"So it would seem," Ezekiel grumbled, as he struggled out of her jacket, and climbed onto Zatao's shoulder. His long white whiskers tickled Zatao's ear, as he whispered. "I'm so sorry for the loss of Princess Mira, My Lord."

Raising a hand, Zatao gently scratched the old rat's neck. "Thank you my friend. Now, how are you going to get home?"

Grey Cloud padded up to Zatao and sat at his feet. "I will take him, My Lord. He will be safe on my back."

With a nod of approval, Zatao handed Ezekiel to Irene for one last hug.

Holding him close, Irene stroked his coarse thinning fur. Knowing how old he was, she knew she might never see him again. She sniffed, as tears pricked at the back of her eyes.

Ezekiel peered up at her. "You're not getting all emotional on me, are you?"

"Maybe I am." Staring into his ruby eyes, Irene saw love in their depths. "You did it again," she whispered.

"Did what?"

Irene smiled and tweaked his tail. Turning her head, she let the tears fall. In a faltering voice, she said. "You saved my life, Ezekiel. Thank you."

"Child, I merely put healing leaves on your wound, and fed you berries. Not exactly lifesaving." He stared into her eyes. "As long as I live, it is my pleasure to serve you. Now, where's my ride," he said, wriggling with embarrassment. "It's time to go home."

"You've got a cheek," Grey Cloud complained. "I should make you walk, or maybe the word is waddle."

"Enough," Zatao said with a smile. "Take him home, Grey Cloud. And thank you both for all you've done. It will not be forgotten."

Grey Cloud bowed his head. "It has been an honour to serve."

Nestled in between his shoulder blades, Ezekiel nodded in agreement.

Watching them leave, Irene sighed. "I will miss them."

"We will see them again, I'm sure," Zatao said as he helped her into the saddle.

Placing her arms round his waist, Irene rested her head on his broad back.

"Hold on tight Irene, we must make haste to reach the castle before dark."

"I'm more than happy to hold on to you," she whispered.

Zatao laughed and patted her hand.

Irene smiled; it was a sound she'd not heard in a while. She knew there were problems waiting, but prayed, they would be resolved quickly, and laughter would again fill castle Eternus.

Chapter 49

Anya rubbed the misted window with her sleeve. Even in her room, high in the castle, she could hear the thunder of horse's hooves. Leaving the room, she lifted her skirt and ran along the passage.

Doors opened and others joined her, their voices raised with excitement.

"The army has returned," a young man shouted.

"Is Prince Zatao with them?" Merton asked.

The head butler joined him. "It appears not," he said. Glancing at the staff hurrying past, he shouted. "Now, you all know the rules. There is to be no running in the hallways."

Bella the housekeeper joined him. "Quiet everyone," she said clapping her hands. "It would seem Prince Zatao will be here shortly." She nodded politely at Merton and the butler.

Merton smiled at her. "That is good news. I was getting worried."

"Indeed it is," the butler said. Marshalling the staff, he ordered everyone to make their way to the great hall. "I want the men on one side of the main doors, and ladies on the other," he instructed. "I expect this to be accomplished with decorum and silence," he said, staring pointedly at the younger members of staff.

Safi found Anya and stood beside her. Wringing her hands, she asked. "What's going on?"

"Nothing to worry about," Anya said. Her pounding heart belied her confidence. "The Prince and men of war are returning. The enemy is defeated."

Safi glanced at her and smiled. The thought of seeing Guardsman Romure, brought a warm flush to her cheeks. Staring into Anya's eyes, she saw a flicker of fear. "That's good, isn't it? Will Lady Irene be with them?"

"I imagine so."

Taking Anya's hand, Safi patted it. "I'm sure there is no need for you to look so worried. I know there have been tragedies, but war has been averted. We should be celebrating."

Anya eased her hand out of Safi's, and placed them in her pockets.

Staring at her, Safi's hand shot to her mouth. "Oh, Anya, I am sorry." She glanced at the chapel. "I had forgotten the sad loss of your mistress. You must be concerned for your future."

Anya looked away and swallowed hard. Hot tears pricked in the back of her eyes. If her situation had not been so dire, she might have laughed. Concern didn't come close to expressing how she felt. Thoughts of a traitor's death sent a chill up her spine.

Safi put an arm round her. "Don't worry, Anya. I'm sure the Prince will reward you, for your service to his sister."

Putting a hand to her mouth, Anya covered her ironic smile. *The Prince's reward is what bothers me*, she thought. A cold draft whispered across the back of her neck, she shivered.

❧❧❧

August's hooves clattered on the cobbled courtyard. Zatao reined him to a halt and patted his neck. "Good boy, time for you to rest." Dismissing the accompanying guard, he eased Irene's tight grip off his waist, lifted his leg over the stallion's neck and slid to the ground.

"Come on Irene. We're home." he said holding up his arms.

Yawning with exhaustion, Irene slid into his waiting arms. Her legs felt like jelly as he placed her on the ground.

"Are you alright?"

She nodded. "I'm just tired."

Zatao put a supportive arm round her shoulders. "I'm sure you are, my darling."

Turning to the young groom, waiting at a discreet distance; he handed the lad August's reins. "Feed him well, Taris. He deserves it."

"Yes My Lord," the boy said with a quick bow.

Zatao patted August affectionately on the rump, as the horse followed the groom to the stables.

"Now, my darling, let's get you indoors."

Putting her arm round his waist, Irene leaned against him as they climbed the steep steps. The main doors of the castle swung open, and they were greeted by lines of happy smiling faces.

Later that night, as Irene luxuriated in a hot, sweet scented bath, her thoughts drifted, replaying the terrifying events of the past few days. Envisioning Mira's body lying downstairs in the chapel; grief like a knife twisted in her heart. Resting her head against the bath, she let the tears fall. *I miss her so much. It won't be the same without her.* She flinched at the gentle knock on the door.

"May I enter My Lady?"

Irene sniffed and splashed water over her face. "Yes Safi, I'm ready."

"Are you alright?" Safi asked as she wrapped her in a thick fluffy towel. "You look as though you've been crying."

"I was thinking about Princess Mira. I can't believe she is no longer with us. She was beautiful, like a warm bright light."

"I didn't know her well, but it seems everyone loved her."

"We did," Irene said following her into the bedroom. As Safi helped her dress, Irene chewed her lip.

"What is it, My Lady?"

"I feel awful. Anya was Mira's maid, for many years. I believe they had a close relationship." Irene sighed. "I can't imagine how she feels. I must talk to her." Staring in the mirror, Irene noticed Safi's perplexed expression. "What?" She asked.

Safi returned Irene's gaze. "She does seem terribly upset. None of us can comfort her, not even Bella the housekeeper. Most of the time she hides in her room; we are worried about her."

"That does seem a little excessive; she was after all Mira's maid, not family, or a trusted friend."

Safi nodded. "That's what the housekeeper says."

Irene's brow wrinkled as a disturbing thought took root in her head. She felt her face flush as an uncomfortable knot formed in her belly. Rising to her feet she brushed at her skirt and hurried to the door. "I'm having supper with the Prince." She said glancing at Safi. "There is no need to wait up for me."

Safi bowed her head. "Yes, My Lady." Staring at the closed door, she rubbed her clammy hands on her skirt. *Something is wrong.* She shivered as chills went up her spine, confirming her troubled thoughts.

Irene sat beside Zatao and sipped her coffee. A fire roared in the grate, the sweet smell of pine permeating the air. Of all the rooms in the castle, the library was one of her favourites. Putting her cup down, she stared at the hundreds of books lining the walls. The anticipation of browsing the shelves brought a smile to her face.

"Come in here whenever you like, Irene," Zatao said, his gaze fixed on the fire.

Irene knew he was reading her thoughts, but made no comment. Discreetly, she studied his strong handsome profile. Clean shaven, and dressed in black, he reclined next to her on the couch, his long legs stretched out in front of the fire. The collar of his white silk shirt, open enough to reveal the gold hairs on his chest. His corn coloured hair glistened in the light of the fire. Irene fought the desire to reach out and touch it. Resting against his arm, she reflected on their supper together.

Neither of them had much appetite, and the need for food vanished completely when she informed him about her conversation with Safi. Irene's stomach had churned as she watched him push his plate aside. Resting his elbows on the table, he'd leaned his chin on his linked fingers and studied her. His eyes darkened as he spoke, the dread in his voice was unmistakable.

"Before my brother died, he tried to tell me the name of someone in this castle. I believe this person was his co-conspirator, but all he managed to give me before he died was Any."

Irene stared at him. "Any?" As she said the word an unpleasant heat rose up her neck and suffused her face.

Zatao sat back in his chair. "You're thinking the same as me?"

Irene nodded. "Yes, especially after what Safi told me." Moving her chair closer to Zatao, she gazed into his face.

Zatao brushed a strand of hair off her shoulder. He knew what she was thinking. "I'm sorry Irene; but there's no one in this castle whose name begins Any; other than my sister's maid, Anya." Pausing he picked up a fork and stabbed at the table cloth.

Gently taking his hand, Irene removed the fork. Her voice faltered as she asked. "What will you do?"

"This woman was Mira's maid; because of her complicity, my sister lies dead in the chapel. My brother though guilty, died in the snow in my arms. His body stored in an empty stable awaiting the coffin."

Irene could see his face reddening with anger and grief.

Banging the table with his fist, Zatao got to his feet, his chair crashed to the floor. Sweat glistened on his top lip as he paced back and forth. "She's a traitor, she must be punished!" Standing with his back to her, he fought the rising stag within him. His body screamed with rage and pain. Fists clenched, he doubled over, his loud "NO!" thundering in the room.

Trembling, Irene prayed as she left her chair and went to him. "Zatao," she pleaded softly.

Swinging round, he pulled her into his arms. His hold so tight, she could hardly breathe.

Irene could hear his heart…feel it thudding in his chest as he held her. Frightened by his anger and passion, she struggled to pull away. With her palms on his chest, she pushed, but it was useless, he was too strong. Staring up at him, she cried. "Please Zatao, you're scaring me."

Gradually, she felt his hold on her loosen. His breathing slowed. "I'm sorry Irene, are you alright?"

She nodded. "You're upset, I understand. But I have never seen you like that."

Holding her gently, he kissed the top of her head. "I pray you never will again. For a moment my loss of control and rage, threatened to unleash the stag within me. However, holding you in my arms diffused its strength. I am sorry if I hurt you. I wouldn't hurt you for the world."

Staring up at him, Irene saw the love and pain in his eyes. "I know you wouldn't. It's been a horrendous few days…a nightmare, and you have suffered great loss. Zatao, if I can, I want to help and support you. Resting her head on his chest, she looked up at him. "Please my darling, don't make a decision while you're upset and angry. You know Mira wouldn't want that. Let God guide you."

Gazing into her eyes and seeing her earnest expression, Zatao smiled. "Don't worry I won't, I shall sleep on it." Lowering his head he kissed her tenderly, before whispering in her ear. "You my child are indeed wise."

Pulling away, Irene glowered at him. "Wise I maybe. Child I am not!"

Taking her by the shoulders, Zatao held her at arm's length. His eyes unashamedly perused her body. "No, I have to agree, you are definitely not a child." Raising an eyebrow, he smiled with amusement at the pink flush on her cheeks. "Come," he said taking her hand. "Merton has left coffee for us in the library."

In the peace of the library, Zatao reclined on the couch, watching the remaining logs, spark and splutter, as the fire slowly died. He knew Irene was watching him. He prayed she would forget his earlier lack of control. Raising his arm he put it round her shoulder and pulled her close. He could see her eyelids drooping. "You need rest, my darling. You have been through a dreadful ordeal. I suggest you go to bed."

"What about you? You must be exhausted."

"I am, but as the ruler of this land, I have decisions to make." Lifting her hand to his lips, he kissed it. "I will get some rest I promise. Now go my sweet, I will see you in the morning."

Irene's shoulders drooped as she got to her feet.

Zatao reached out and took her hand. "Thank you," he whispered.

"What for?" Irene asked.

"For being here with me…giving up your own life, to share mine."

"There's no other place I want to be, than by your side. It's where I belong. I know that now."

Zatao smiled and nodded. "Sleep well, my darling."

Breathless, Irene felt as though her heart danced in her chest. Climbing the stairs to her suite of rooms, she wanted to sing; yet beneath her joy, there brooded a niggling worry. Try as she might, she couldn't shake it off.

Chapter 50

Zatao slumped forward in his seat; resting his elbows on his knees, he propped his chin in his hands and closed his eyes. *Going to war...fighting man to man is one thing, but putting a woman on trial is something else entirely.* Running his hands through his hair, he groaned.

Before I make any decision, I must hear her side of the story. Raising his eyes heavenwards, he whispered. "I need your wisdom and guidance."

Easing out of his chair, he stretched and yawned. "I'll talk to her in the morning."

Leaving the relative warmth of the library, he shivered in the chill of the great hall. Above the fireplace, his father's portrait stared down at him. Zatao frowned. *I could do with your help. You would know what to do.* Staring at his father's strong face, he sighed. *Across this land, and beyond, you were known as a just and merciful King.* Lowering his head, his shoulders drooped, as he prayed for the power to follow in his father's footsteps. *God forbid that grief and a desire for vengeance should cloud my judgment.*

Climbing the stairs, he paused and looked back at the portrait. The tension in his shoulders eased as a sense of peace wrapped around him. Drowsy, his eyes half closed he entered his suite, crashed fully clothed onto his bed and fell into a deep sleep.

Waking to a knock on his door, Zatao groaned as Merton's cheery voice greeted him.

"Good morning, My Lord. I hope you slept well." Merton's eyebrows rose at the sight of his masters crumpled clothing.

Zatao made no comment as he took the cup of coffee handed to him. "I slept well, thank you Merton."

"It's a lovely bright day," Merton said eager to change the subject. "Shall I run your bath?" He asked as he pulled the heavy drapes back.

Zatao propped himself against the headboard and nodded. Lifting the cup, he sipped the strong black coffee, grateful for the hot brews stimulating properties. Hearing Merton's tuneless humming from the bathroom brought a smile to his face.

"Your bath is ready My Lord," Merton said handing the Prince his robe. "What clothing do you wish me to lay out for you?"

Groaning, Zatao lowered his long legs over the side of the bed. This morning after breakfast, he planned to question Anya. His heart sank at the thought.

Standing to attention, Merton cleared his throat. "Your attire My Lord, what would you like me to lay out for you?" He asked again.

Zatao glanced at him. "I won't be riding this morning. So whatever you select will be fine." Slapping his thighs he rose to his feet. "When you go downstairs, Merton, ask the housekeeper to send Anya to the library." The servant's look of surprise didn't go unnoticed.

"What time My Lord?"

Downing the remains of his coffee, Zatao strode to the bathroom. "I will expect her at ten," he said closing the bathroom door.

For Zatao, breakfast passed in a blur of grief, he had no real appetite. The two vacant places at the table were a painful reminder of his loss. The thought of dealing with Anya, added to his stress. Staring at his sister's empty chair, his heart ached. Lowering his head, he quenched the hot tears pricking at the back of his eyes. *Oh Mira, I miss you so much.*

Sensing his grief, Irene gently touched his arm. "Are you alright?" she asked.

Zatao's head jerked up. Putting his knife down, he took her hand. "I'm sorry, I was miles away. I was thinking about Mira."

Irene nodded with understanding.

Pushing his plate aside, Zatao leaned wearily back in his chair. "This morning I am questioning Anya about her possible collusion with Aldrin." Glancing at the clock on the mantel, he frowned. "In a few minutes I need to go. Pray for me," he said kissing her hand.

"Of course I will." Irene stared into his troubled face. "Please don't take offence, Zatao. But I hope you will give her a chance to explain. In my short dealings with her; I found her a pleasant and open girl. I'm sure there is more to this than we realise." Tilting her head slightly Irene smiled at him. "You are a powerful man. Being in your presence is bound to intimidate her. Please be gentle."

Without a word, Zatao pushed his chair back and rose to his feet.

Irene gazed up at his tall frame towering over her. Shifting nervously in her chair, she chewed her lip. Her voice faltered as she said. "I'm sorry, I didn't mean to—"

"Offend me," he said.

Irene nodded. Looking into his dark eyes, she saw the flicker of a smile, as he pulled her to her feet and held her in a tight embrace. His kiss was soft, his lips warm against hers.

Reaching up, Irene put her arms round his neck.

"You could never offend me, Irene," he whispered softly in her ear. "Your words were wise, and I shall give Anya every opportunity to explain her actions." Holding her gently by the shoulders, he eased her away. "Finish your breakfast," he said lowering her into the chair.

"Will I see you later?" She asked.

Nodding, he gently stroked her cheek.

Basking in the warmth of his smile; Irene watched him stride from the room.

❀❀❀

Bella tutted, as she placed a steaming mug of tea in front of Anya. Lowering her ample frame onto the chair opposite, she stared at the terrified girl. Anya's nostrils flared; as she gulped air…her eyes bulged. Bella felt sure if she didn't calm down, they would likely bulge out of their sockets.

Reaching across the table, she gently patted Anya's hand. It felt cold and clammy. "Look, my dear. I'm sure there is no need for such fear."

A tear trickled down Anya's cheek. "You don't know what I've done," she mumbled.

"Maybe not; but I do know the Prince we serve. He is not a cruel man, he is merciful and just."

Sat at the far end of the table, Merton nodded. "Indeed he is. I can vouch for that." Gazing at Bella, he raised a finger. "Do you remember what happened before I went with the guard to find Lady Irene, and bring her here?"

Bella smiled. "Indeed I do, you were so scared."

"My fear was justified, for he was enraged." Merton gazed at Anya. "However, look." Raising his hands, he smiled. "I'm still here, and in his service." Lowering his head, he stared at Anya. "Whatever you do, young lady, I advise you to tell the truth, because if you don't, he will know, and it will not go well for you."

Bella nodded, "Yes, whatever you have done, tell him everything, hold nothing back." Bella gave her a reassuring smile. "Now drink your tea, the guard will be here soon to fetch you."

Anya's hands trembled as she raised the mug to her lips. "I just want to get it over with; to know my fate."

"Soon enough, child, soon enough," Merton said gently.

As he finished speaking, the door opened and a burly guard entered the kitchen. He smiled. "Hello Bella, Merton, how are you both?"

"We're alright, Thomas, and yourself?" Merton asked.

"I'm fine. Are you Anya?" He asked glancing at her.

Anya nodded and rose to her feet. Her legs wobbled as she made to follow him. Her mouth was so dry, she could hardly swallow.

"You'll be alright, love," Bella called after her.

I hope you're right, Anya thought. Wiping her sweaty hands on her dress she hurried after the guard. Passing the great doors to the throne room, she frowned. "Where are you taking me?"

"The Prince wishes to see you in his library."

Anya gasped, she felt her muscles relax. "Maybe they're right…maybe I'm not going to die." For a moment the sense of relief made her feel light headed. Taking some deep breaths, she calmed her racing heart.

Standing behind the guard, she waited as he knocked on the door. Hearing the loud authoritive, "Come!" from the other side, her stomach lurched. Her hand clutched at the bodice of her dress. *It's not Prince Aldrin*, she told herself. *It sounds like him, but it's not him.*

"In you go, miss," the guard said holding the door open and standing back. Seeing the fear in her eyes, he nodded encouragement.

Taking a deep breath, Anya walked slowly into the room. Right away her eyes went to a large desk by the window. Sunlight streamed in, bathing the Prince in a golden glow. Anya stood for a moment allowing her eyes to adjust to the light.

"Sit down," Prince Zatao said indicating to the chair on the other side of his expansive desk.

Anya's legs trembled, as she curtsied and walked to the chair. Folding her hands in her lap she kept her head down.

"Look at me," Zatao said.

Anya's body quivered, his voice sounded like Prince Aldrin's. Raising her head, she met his gaze. His dark eyes bored into hers, she felt as though he could read her thoughts. Lowering her eyes, she stared at him under her lashes. Bathed in the light from the window, he looked like an angel. She prayed an angel of mercy.

❧❧❧

Leaning his elbows on the desk, Prince Zatao studied the girl. Thick red hair framed a pale complexion; hazel eyes, wide with fear stared back at him. His natural reaction was to reassure her, but he fought it. Narrowing his eyes, he stared at her. *Is she guilty? Somehow I think not.*

Leaning back in his chair, he rested his hands on the arms. He could feel her tension radiating across the desk. He didn't feel exactly comfortable himself. Digging his nails into the leather arms of the chair, he sighed inaudibly. *I guess, now that my kingdom has increased; executing judgment is a task I'll have to get used to.* For a brief second, he closed his eyes. *I pray my judgments will be as wise and merciful as my father's.*

Staring at Anya, he said calmly. "I've chosen to question you here, as I do not wish to jump to conclusions regarding your guilt in this matter. However, take no comfort from these informal surroundings. If I find you guilty of treason, you will be judged in my throne room. Do you understand me?"

Anya nodded and mumbled. "Yes My Lord."

Zatao frowned. "Kindly speak up when you answer my questions. I wish to know your full name, and how long you were in service to my sister Princess Mira?" Mentioning Mira's name, Zatao's throat constricted painfully. Clenching his fists under the desk, he battled the emotions threatening to surface. Scowling at Anya, he asked. "What was your relationship to my brother Prince Aldrin?" His eyes narrowed, as he watched her ponder the question.

Aware the penalty for treason was death. Anya nevertheless determined to tell the whole truth. She knew her testimony would destroy the reputation of Prince Aldrin, she also knew there was every chance Prince Zatao would choose not to believe her. *Why would he?* She thought. *I'm merely a servant, Prince Aldrin was royalty.*

Taking a deep breath, she straightened in her chair, looked Prince Zatao squarely in the eyes and calmly answered his questions. Holding nothing back, she told him how Prince Aldrin had all but blackmailed her into obeying his wishes. "He told me there was a spy in the castle, and I was to let him know if anything strange or new took place. He said the information I gave him, would protect you, My Lord, and my Mistress."

Lowering her head, her voice faltered as she told him how she'd overheard Merton telling Bella the housekeeper about his journey to fetch someone…someone who was special to his master. Raising her head, Anya paused and brushed the tears from her cheeks. Staring at the Prince, she saw his nostrils flare…saw the pain and anger in his eyes.

Zatao's heart thudded painfully in his chest. His eyes narrowed as he returned her gaze, and ordered her to continue.

Wiping her clammy hands on her skirt, Anya twisted her fingers as she explained how she'd written a note, telling Prince Aldrin what she'd heard. "I pushed it under his door. I was so afraid, My Lord. I know I should have come to you, but I didn't think you would believe me. It was my word against your brother, a Prince!" Her tears fell freely. "I was so afraid of him." She stared at Zatao through tear filled eyes.

As he looked at her, Zatao's heart softened. He knew she was telling the truth. And knowing Aldrin as he did, he could understand her fear of him.

Seeing the belief in his eyes, Anya buried her face in her hands and sobbed. "I'm so sorry, My Lord. Please forgive me."

Not sure how to respond, Zatao left his chair and went to the door. "Call Lady Irene," he instructed the guard. "And tell Bella to send up tea for three." As the guard hurried away, Zatao returned to the library, and tentatively stood beside Anya. Placing a hand on her shoulder, he attempted to comfort the trembling girl.

Zatao sighed with relief as Irene hurried into the room. "She has told me everything," Zatao said. "I believe she is innocent...merely a pawn in my brother's evil plan." he growled.

Irene gave his arm a quick squeeze, before hurrying over to Anya. The distraught girl threw herself into Irene's arms. "My mistress is dead and it's my fault," she sobbed.

Glancing at Zatao, Irene saw him shake his head. Holding Anya close, she stroked her hair. Gradually, the girl's crying ceased. Irene gently lowered her into the chair and handed her a handkerchief. "Here," she said. "Wipe your eyes."

A light tap on the door heralded Bella's arrival, with a tray of tea. Curtseying to Prince Zatao, she put the tray on the desk. "Do you require anything else, My Lord?" She asked.

"Nothing, thank you," he said gesturing for her to leave.

As Bella left, she gave Anya a sympathetic nod.

Irene poured the tea and handed Anya a cup.

Anya's hand shook as she took it. Sipping the hot liquid, she glanced across the desk at Zatao...unsure what was to happen next.

Irene stooped, and whispered in Zatao's ear. "Would you rather I leave?"

Zatao shook his head, and pointed to a chair by the fire. "Stay, this won't take long," he said softly.

Choosing a chair with its back to the desk, Irene stoked the fire and sat down. She could hear Anya whimpering and snuffling. *Poor Zatao*, she thought. *I don't envy him this situation.* Sipping her tea she prayed silently. Behind her, Zatao was speaking to Anya. She couldn't hear what he was saying. But the authoritive edge to his voice was unmistakable.

Zatao stared into Anya's face. Her red rimmed eyes stared back at him. "For every decision we make," he said sternly. "There are choices that must be faced."

Anya nodded, "I know My Lord. Were it not for me, Princess Mira would still be alive. I can't live with what I have done."

Zatao's voice rose sharply. "Well, you're going to have too. As I have to live with the loss of my sister. However, I'm tempering your punishment; because I believe what you've told me is true." Pausing, he gazed out of the window. When he looked back at Anya, his face creased in a frown. "I can't believe, after all these years of service to my family, you didn't trust me enough, to tell me what my brother was planning."

Anya cringed and buried her head in her hands.

Leaving his chair, Zatao walked round the desk and stood beside her.

Trembling, Anya raised her head and stared up at him. "May my punishment be severe My Lord. Death would be too merciful." Lowering her eyes, she didn't see Zatao's lips flicker in a smile.

"I think working in the kitchen with Bella, is severe enough, don't you?"

Anya gasped; her hands shot to her mouth. Falling to the floor, she knelt at his feet. "My Lord, I don't deserve your mercy. Thank you," she cried.

Reaching down, Zatao took her by the arms, and pulled her to her feet. "I merely show you the mercy, God shows to me. Now, go to the kitchen and report to Bella. For three years, you will work as her kitchen maid. However, after that time, you are free to leave, if you wish."

Speechless, Anya took his hand in both of hers and kissed it.

Zatao smiled, at the relief and gratitude he saw in her eyes. "You may go," he said.

"Thank you, My Lord." Anya's face creased in a grateful smile as she curtsied and hurried from the room.

Chapter 51

Irene rose from her chair as Zatao walked towards her. She could see the relief on his face. "Are you alright?"

Zatao nodded. "I'll never be comfortable with this particular Princely duty. Nevertheless, it has to be done, so I suppose I'd better get used to it. My birthright gives me the authority to govern. God gives me the discernment needed to govern wisely." He smiled. "With my growing kingdom, He will need to increase it."

Taking his hand, Irene rested her head against his arm. "I'm sure He will."

Zatao gazed down at her. "My father would have loved you," he said softly. "He was a great King, endued with vast power and authority; yet a man known for his wisdom and mercy."

Irene squeezed his hand. "You are your father's son, Zatao. You will be a wonderful King."

Taking her by the shoulders, Zatao pulled her in front of him. Stooping, he gazed into her eyes. "Talking of Kings, my darling; I have a request."

Tilting her head to the side, Irene returned his gaze. "Is it a request or an order?" She asked.

Zatao winked at her. "Let me see," he said pulling her closer. "Maybe I should make it an order."

Standing on tip toes, Irene wrapped her arms around his neck. "I love it when your authoritive," she whispered in his ear.

"Really," he said his voice low and husky. "You'd best come closer then." Cupping her upturned face in his hands, his warm lips covered hers in a long, passionate kiss.

Irene clung to him, melting into his embrace. Breathless, she could feel her heart racing, its quickening beat in rhythm with Zatao's. As they slowly eased apart, she rested her head against his chest.

"Irene, be my Queen," Zatao said softly. "Marry me."

The depth of his voice vibrated in Irene's ear, his thudding heartbeat all but drowning his words. Lifting her head, she stared up at him.

Zatao raised a brow, his eyes widening as he waited for her answer.

Irene felt a wonderful lightness in her chest...excitement tingled up her spine. "Yes, oh yes! I'll marry you," She said.

Wrapping his arms round her, Zatao hugged her tight. "Thank you my darling. You've made me the happiest man in the world." However, a tinge of sadness marred Zatao's joy. He knew before anything else could take place, arrangements had to be made for a state funeral. *Oh God, how I wish Mira could be here to witness my coronation and marriage to Irene. Mira loved her as I do.* Zatao sniffed and rubbed at his eyes. His chest ached, the pain of loss tore at his heart.

Seeing his grief, Irene took his arm and guided him to the couch by the fire. "What is it, my darling? Is it Mira?" She asked softly.

Staring into the flames, Zatao nodded. "I miss her so much."

Reaching up, Irene turned his face to look at her. Her stomach knotted at the pain she saw in his eyes. "I miss Mira too. I never met anyone like her....so beautiful and strong."

A slight smile flickered on Zatao's lips. "She was my rock. I could always rely on her judgment." Lowering his head, he stared at his clenched hands. "Mira was the only one in the family who could bring the best out in Aldrin, but now they are both gone." Rubbing at his face, he groaned softly.

Resting her head on his shoulder, Irene wrapped her arms around him. In the silence of the room, they embraced the sadness, acknowledging the grief they both shared. Closing her eyes, Irene listened to Zatao's steady heartbeat...felt the tightness melt from his muscles as he relaxed. A log on the fire thudded gently as it burned and fell lower in the grate. On the mantle, the old clock ticked softly, keeping time it seemed with the rhythm of Irene's heart.

Opening her eyes, Irene glanced at Zatao, he appeared to be sleeping. *That's a good thing,* she thought. Resting back on the couch, she gazed around the room. A warm tingling sensation, radiated through her body. Looking up she smiled. *This is my home now, it's where I belong.* Gazing at Zatao's relaxed profile...the beauty of his countenance as he slept, Irene felt her heart would burst.

Tears of joy filled her eyes. *Why did it take me so long to realise, there could never be another? This is the man I love.* Silently, she thanked God for bringing them back together, and for keeping them both safe through the nightmare of the past few days.

Zatao stirred and opened his eyes. Sighing deeply, he took Irene's hand and gently squeezed it. "God's timing is always perfect, my darling," he said softly.

Irene stared at him. "I didn't say anything." She frowned at him. "I wish you wouldn't do that."

He smiled. "Do what?"

"Read my mind."

"I don't read minds, Irene. Your thoughts are your own. As I rested, I sensed your happiness and the regrets that accompanied it."

"But you seem to do it a lot, especially to me," Irene said.

"I've told you, I am able to discern, it's a gift my father had; so did Mira to a certain extent. It empowered my father's rule. I pray it will increase in me, enabling me to emulate him."

"Is that why you were so sure, Anya was telling you the truth?"

Zatao nodded.

Irene snuggled against him. "You will be a great King."

Taking her hand, Zatao placed it on his chest and covered it with his own. "And you my darling will be my wise and beautiful Queen." Tilting his head, he grinned at her. "I promise, where you're concerned. I will keep my discernment to myself."

Irene playfully thumped him on the chest. "I hope you do." Wrapping her arms around his neck, she kissed his cheek. She could feel her pulse racing… warmth rising up her neck. "Make me your Queen soon," she pleaded.

Zatao stared into her sparkling eyes, caressing her forehead with his lips, he whispered. "Be patient a while longer, my love. In a few days, you will know how much I love you."

Irene sighed. "It's hard, but I can wait. I love you so much." Staring up at Zatao, the intensity in his dark eyes left her breathless. She could feel the tension in his body as he held her close. She shivered as his hot breath brushed her neck. Her heart soared as he said softly.

"I love you more."

Twelve Months Later

"She is beautiful," Zatao whispered. "Like her mother." Putting his arm round Irene's waist, he held her close.

Staring up at him, Irene smiled and said. "Have I told you recently how happy I am?"

Zatao winked at her. "Does this morning at breakfast count?"

Chuckling, Irene gazed around the cosy nursery. "I love this room. Thank you for allowing me to decorate it."

"You've done a wonderful job. It didn't look like this when I was a child." Zatao gazed at the pale pink walls, bedecked with images of dancing white horses, resplendent waterfalls, and colourful swirling rainbows. Soft drapes decorated with bluebells, hung at the ceiling to floor window. The drapes shifted gently in the soft breeze wafting into the room.

"Should I close the window?" Irene asked.

"No," Zatao said. "People are gathering below, waiting to see the baby. We cannot disappoint them."

Resting her head against him, Irene sighed.

"I'm sorry my darling, but it's the custom."

"Oh, no, Zatao; I sighed because I'm happy." Glancing up at him, she smiled. "So much has happened in the past year, I can hardly take it in. Being able to get married on the day you were crowned King was awesome...like a dream," she said softly. Closing her eyes, she let her mind play the memory like a cinematic film.

The excitement, the nervous somersaults her stomach had insisted on doing, as Safi dressed her in the most beautiful white gown she had ever seen.

The crowning ceremony passed in a blur of colour and pageantry. Zatao's beauty took her breath away; she couldn't take her eyes off him. Dressed in black and gold, with an ornate cape draped over one shoulder...the diamond encrusted crown on his head. He was every inch a King.

The wedding ceremony in contrast was simple and intimate, with a handful of guests and witnesses.

Protocol dictated a royal wedding should take place in the throne room. However, Zatao and Irene chose to break with custom and honour Mira by marrying in the small chapel, the room she loved best.

The baby's gurgling brought Irene out of her reverie. Smiling at the chubby baby, Irene's voice choked with tears "And now we have our beautiful daughter."

"She's the icing on the cake," Zatao said. "Have you thought of a name for her yet? We can't keep calling her, little bundle."

Irene laughed. "I suppose not. I have thought of a name, but I'm not sure you would like it—"

Her hesitation unnerved Zatao. "Come, Irene, you can tell me. What is our daughter's name to be?"

"I would like to call her Crystal" Irene she said softly.

Hearing Zatao's sharp breath, she looked up. She could see tears glistening in his eyes. Taking his hands she faced him. "I'm sorry, my darling, I didn't mean to upset you."

Shaking his head, Zatao smiled. "I'm not upset, Irene. You could not have chosen a more beautiful name for our child. I pray she will grow to be as wise and gentle as Mira." Pulling Irene to him, he wrapped his arms around her. "I know she would be as thrilled and honoured, as I am."

Cocooned in Zatao's arms, Irene listened to the myriad voices rising from the courtyard below. Fingering her necklace, she glanced up at him.

His warm smile encouraged her. "It's time for the people to meet their new Princess," he said gently.

Lifting the baby out of the crib, Irene handed her to Zatao. She watched him trace a gentle finger down the baby's face…grinning with amusement as the baby gurgled and kicked her legs.

"Her skin is so soft," he murmured. Smiling, he took Irene's hand and kissed it. "Come my darling, our people are waiting." Guiding her onto the balcony, they were greeted by joyous shouts.

Peering down, Irene could see Safi standing beside Romure, the sergeant's arm draped over her shoulder. Irene smiled. *They will be married soon*, she thought.

Just behind them, Anya stood with Bella and Merton, their upturned faces wreathed in smiles.

Holding the baby in his hands, Zatao raised her high. In the hush that followed, he shouted. "My people, here is Crystal, your Princess."

The sound that followed rose to meet them like the roaring waves of the sea. The melodious peal of chapel bells joined the celebration.

Holding the baby close to his heart, Zatao wrapped his arm around Irene. "Look up," he said.

Following his gaze, Irene saw Zenith and Hunter fly past dipping their wings in salute. Tilting her head, she thought she heard the distant howl of a wolf, accompanied by the raucous call of a blackbird. "I wish Ezekiel was still with us. I miss him."

"I know, but if he was, he would want to be organizing everything."

Tears trickled down Irene's cheeks, but she couldn't help laughing.

Placing the baby in her arms, Zatao cupped her chin and gazed into her tear filled eyes. "I love you Irene."

Holding his hand, Irene closed her eyes and breathed, "I love you too."

Below, the happy shouts of the people, merged with the joyous sound of church bells ringing out across the land.

Hugging Crystal, Irene gazed into the baby's wide eyes. In the sunlight, the unmistakable glint of emerald stared up at her. Breathless with joy, Irene kissed the baby's head.

Gazing down at them Zatao's heart raced. Resting his arm over Irene's shoulder, he sighed.

"What is it?" Irene asked, tilting her head.

Waving farewell to the people below, Zatao led Irene off the balcony. "There are no words to express the way I feel."

Settling the baby in her crib, Irene faced him. Wrapping her arms around him, she rested her head on his chest and murmured, "I know what you mean."

Stroking Irene's hair, Zatao said softly. "I thank the God of heaven, for all His goodness to us."

Hearing the emotion in his voice, Irene hugged him tight, and whispered, "Amen."

The End

About The Author

Y I Lee was born in Swindon Wiltshire, the eldest of three children.

From a young age, her greatest joy was to curl up with a good book. And over time she naturally progressed into writing.

At the age of ten she ambitiously attempted her first novel, but quickly gave up. However, the seed was planted. And in the coming years in between a successful singing career, she continued to put pen to paper, writing poetry and short stories.

In due course, Y I Lee found herself in the enviable position of being able to write full time, and her love of fantasy found its full expression.

Y I Lee and her husband Keith live in the UK, in the beautiful county of Warwickshire.

All her books are available in paperback and ebook, from Amazon and other online stores.

THE SHADOWED VALLEY
A RAT AND A RANSOM
THROUGH A GLASS
GATHERING STORM, the thrilling sequel to THROUGH A GLASS.

Acknowledgements

First and foremost, I thank God, who is the inspiration and encouragement for every book I write.

My grateful thanks go to David and Ruth Rhodes. I appreciate you both. Your editing skills and input are invaluable.

I would also like to thank Jo Harrison for her brilliant formatting. I couldn't be published without her.

And last, but not least, I thank my husband Keith for his patience, and for always believing in me.

Made in the USA
Charleston, SC
24 January 2015